THE CROSS-LEGGED KNIGHT

CANDACE ROBB

ARROW

Published by Arrow Books in 2002

1 3 5 7 9 10 8 6 4 2

First published in the United Kingdom in 2002 by William Heinemann

Arrow Books
The Random House Group Limited
20 Vauxhall Bridge Road, London SW1V 2SA

Random House Australia (Pty) Limited
20 Alfred Street, Milsons Point, Sydney,
New South Wales 2061, Australia

Random House New Zealand Limited
18 Poland Road, Glenfield
Auckland 10, New Zealand

Random House South Africa (Pty) Limited
Endulini, 5a Jubilee Road, Parktown 2193, South Africa

The Random House Group Limited Reg. No. 954009
www.randomhouse.co.uk

A CIP catalogue record for this book is available from the British Library

Papers used by Random House are natural, recyclable products made
from wood grown in sustainable forests. The manufacturing processes
conform to the environmental regulations of the country of origin

ISBN 0 09 927830 8

Typeset by SX Composing DTP, Rayleigh, Essex
Printed and bound in Germany by Elsnerdruck, Berlin

TABLE OF CONTENTS

ÐEÐICATION

In memory of two dear men lost to me this year, Dad (Benjamin Chestochowski, 9 March 1920–12 August 2001) and Uncle John (John Wojak, 7 August 1925–3 January 2001).

acknowledgements

I am indebted to Ed Robb for bringing to bear his 35 years of expertise in research at Shriners Children's Hospital, a pediatric hospital for burns, in answering my many questions about burns and the healing methods available to Magda Digby; to Charlie Robb for all his support, particularly in mapping the city of York, describing the archbishop's palace, and brainstorming on the plot; to Lynne Drew, Sara Ann Freed, Evan Marshall, and Patrick Walsh for patience and sympathetic support during a difficult year; to Joyce Gibb, Laura Hodges, and my generous colleagues on Chaucernet, Medfem, and Mediev-1 for advice and comraderie throughout this project; and to Jacqui, Mark, Nathaniel and Emily Weberding for their boundless love and compassion.

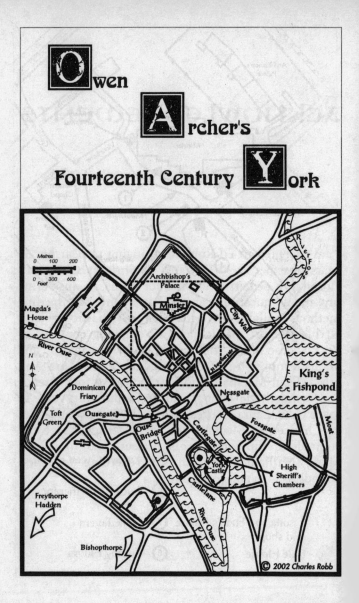

Owen Archer's Fourteenth Century York

Metres
0   100   200
0   300   600
Feet

Magda's House

River Ouse

Archbishop's Palace

Minster

City Wall

St Leonards

King's Fishpond

Dominican Friary

Nessgate

Toft Green

Ousegate

Ouse Bridge

Castlegate

Fossgate

Moat

Freythorpe Hadden

York Castle

Castle Lane

High Sheriff's Chambers

River Ouse

Bishopthorpe

© 2002 Charles Robb

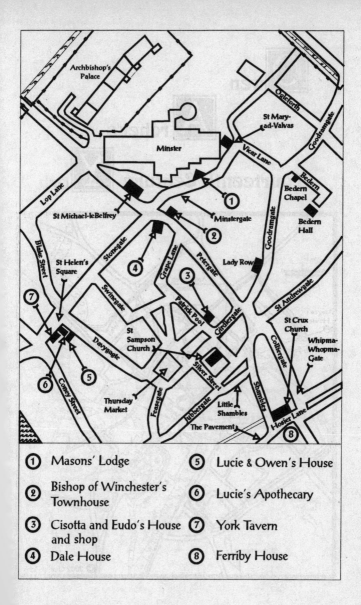

① Masons' Lodge

② Bishop of Winchester's Townhouse

③ Cisotta and Eudo's House and shop

④ Dale House

⑤ Lucie & Owen's House

⑥ Lucie's Apothecary

⑦ York Tavern

⑧ Ferriby House

PROLOGUE

October 1371

William of Wykeham, Bishop of Winchester and late Lord Chancellor of England, sat in the mottled shade of Archbishop Thoresby's rose arbour wiping his irritated eyes and cursing all that had brought him riding to York four days ago. The horses' hooves had stirred up summer's dust and the mould from the autumn leaves. He and his entourage had ridden with cloths covering their faces from their chins to the bridges of their noses. Wykeham might have pampered himself within the curtains of a litter, but he had not wished anyone to misconstrue such a nicety, spread word that he had hidden from the curious along the way, or, worse yet, that he was ill, weak. So he had ridden north on the King's Highway with his men, regretting that the rains of autumn had held off for his journey to York.

They had stopped frequently and broken their journey early in the evenings. Wykeham would have preferred a brisker pace, but now that the chain of lord chancellor no longer weighed down his neck, he did not push his men, for they, too, as his household, had lost

1

stature this past year. It was not as fine to be the household officers of the Bishop of Winchester as it had been to be the officers of the lord chancellor of the realm. Wykeham wanted them content. His enemies would be only too happy to make alliances with his staff.

He had used the time to pick at his wounded dignity. God knew he could have found better occupation for his hours in the saddle, but he was weak, too proud, he knew that of himself.

Their small wagon had creaked and groaned over the ruts in the road, its cargo the heart of a York knight who had gone in his dotage to France as a spy and had been caught and imprisoned, dying there while Wykeham was negotiating his ransom. The Pagnell family were making much of what they considered Wykeham's failure, though he was of the opinion that Sir Ranulf Pagnell had simply been a foolish old man. However, as the family was influential in Lancastrian circles Wykeham had tried to appease them by escorting Sir Ranulf's remains to York, the heart that he had coaxed from the French king with his own money. The Pagnells did not think even this sufficient retribution. For all his efforts, Wykeham was not to preside at the knight's requiem. Indeed, he had not even been invited to attend.

As Wykeham sat in the archbishop's garden, miserable in his self-pity, a shadow fell across him and the scent of lavender drew him from his thoughts. He squinted up, his eyes watering in the light. Brother Michaelo, the archbishop's elegant secretary, stood before him.

Wykeham assumed the monk had come to deliver a message. 'What news from Lady Pagnell?'

Michaelo bowed his head slightly. 'The lady sends

her apologies, but she cannot meet with you until her departed husband's month's mind.'

Wykeham bristled. 'How can there be a one-month mass for Sir Ranulf when we know not the date of his death?'

'She means a month from his burial, My Lord Bishop, a month from tomorrow.'

Lady Pagnell and her son and heir, Stephen, were being guided in this shunning of him by their Lancastrian friends, Wykeham was sure of it. But to press her would merely inspire accusations of cruelty to the widow in her mourning. He could ill afford to make himself more unpopular in the city than he already was.

Brother Michaelo held up to him a glass vial. 'If I might suggest, My Lord Bishop, a soothing wash for your eyes? This is from Captain Archer's wife. She is as skilled as any apothecary you might have in Winchester.'

Wykeham grunted. 'I am in your debt. Take it to my servant. I shall try it later.'

'I could assist you in applying a few drops now, My Lord Bishop.'

And make him look a fool, with the liquid staining his face, his silk clothing. 'To my servant, Brother Michaelo.'

The monk bowed and withdrew.

Wykeham fell back into his dudgeon. Ungrateful family, the Pagnells. But they would see, he would not idle away the rest of his life waiting on the likes of Lady Pagnell. The king would have him back.

He shaded his eyes and gazed upon the great minster across the garden. A building project would be to his liking right now. As he rode north he had thought about the ruined church of All Saints in Laughton-en-le-Morthen. Though it was no longer his prebend, he meant to rebuild it. He rose with a thought to observe the work on the minster lady chapel, a better occupation than wallowing in self-pity.

Wishing to be truly free for a little while, Wykeham watched the household guards for a chance to depart unescorted. He felt like a truant schoolboy as he hurried through the gate and towards the minster. Winded and silently laughing at his foolishness, he almost forgot the grit in his eyes, but soon the burning began anew. He caught his breath and dabbed at his eyes, determined to enjoy this moment alone.

To his left the south side of the minster nave soared above him, to his right St Michael-le-Belfrey cast a late-afternoon shadow. As he rounded the south transept his view of the construction was blocked by a huge mound of stones and tiles butted up against what had been the far south-east corner of the minster before work on the lady chapel began. The church of St Mary ad Valvas had been dismantled to create room for the construction, and the stones and tiles were being reused, though much of them merely for rubble within the walls. Skirting the mound Wykeham saw two men chiselling stones in the mason's lodge. As he considered whether to interrupt their work a shout startled him.

'My Lord, drop down and cover your head!'

He did as he was told, and just in time. A heavy clay tile thudded on to the path a hand's breadth short of him, cracking on impact. He curled into himself so tightly he had difficulty breathing. But he would not lift his head; he dared not. He did not mean to play Saint Thomas Becket to the Duke of Lancaster's Henry II. He would not be so easily murdered.

One

ΤΟΕ BISHOP'S
ΟREAD

O wen Archer feared the worst as he crouched beside the unmoving figure. 'My Lord, are you injured?'

As he was searching for a pulse the bishop stirred beneath him. Slowly Wykeham raised his head. 'Archer, I do not think I am injured.' He was very pale and his breathing shallow.

By now masons and soldiers crowded round the kneeling pair, and Alain, one of the bishop's clerks, assisted Owen in helping Wykeham to stand.

'My Lord –' Alain shook debris from his master's robes.

Once on his feet Wykeham held himself erect. 'I must remove myself from the danger,' he said, stumbling.

The clerk caught his arm. Excellent reflexes for a man who looked to Owen a pampered noble. The crowd parted for Wykeham and Alain. Owen followed close behind.

Halfway through the palace garden the bishop's other clerk accosted Owen. 'Your men were to guard Bishop

William,' Guy said, shielding his eyes and squinting at Owen. He had the ruined sight and stained fingers of a scholar.

'Your master has much experience on building sites,' Owen said. 'He knows they are unsafe, that he must have a care.'

'Are you calling him careless?' Guy demanded.

One of Thoresby's servants saved Owen, summoning him to the archbishop's parlour.

'I shall see to Bishop William,' Brother Michaelo assured him.

As Owen entered Thoresby's parlour the ageing archbishop reached down to a fist-sized clump of something on the table before him and poked idly at it, making it flake and finally crumble.

'Your Grace,' Owen said.

Thoresby did not look up. 'Crushed stone,' he said. 'Better than a crushed skull, that is what you are thinking.' Now the archbishop raised his head, fixed his deep-set eyes on Owen. 'But you must do much better than that, Archer. Wykeham's enemies must not find him easy prey while he is a guest in my household.' Aged he might be, but when Thoresby spoke in such a quiet voice it raised the hackles on Owen's neck as it always had.

'It might have been an accident, Your Grace.'

'He must not have accidents while here.'

'He would have been safe had he not slipped away.'

'It is your duty to ensure his safety with or without his co-operation.'

A curse rose in Owen's throat, but he swallowed it back.

'How did this happen, Archer?'

'He chafes at such close guard, Your Grace.'

'Chafes,' Thoresby growled, turning away. 'Has there

ever lived a being more dangerous to himself than this obstinate and contradictory bishop? He swallows his pride to appease friends of Lancaster, but rides openly across the country to prove he is not afraid of the duke, belatedly worries about his safety and demands a constant guard, then escapes his guard to prove – what? Damn him.' The archbishop turned back, his bony face twisted in temper. 'He won't be caught here in York, Archer, I won't have it!' He pounded the table, flattening the pile of crushed stone.

Owen knew his best defence was silence.

Thoresby pressed his temples and muttered a prayer, composing himself. 'Perhaps he realizes he has overestimated his importance to Lancaster.'

Owen judged it safe to speak. 'I do wonder about this issue with the duke. He is sailing home with his new wife, aye, and will be closer to Wykeham than he has been in a long while. But he comes to plot his acquisition of the crown of Castile and León, does he not?' Lancaster had recently wed Constance, the daughter of the late King Pedro of Castile. 'He has far more important things to consider than his irritation with the bishop.'

'Lancaster's net is wide, his coffers deep, and the number of his retainers greater than that of any man in the realm save his father the king. Wykeham is right to fear him. But I do not understand this chafing you speak of. He asked for my protection. Indeed, he asked for you by name. Have you offended him, Archer?'

'If I have, I know not how.' Owen did not like the way Thoresby was studying him.

'He has asked many questions about your time in Wales. You were working for Lancaster – I'd forgotten that.'

'On your orders, Your Grace.' Owen did not believe

Thoresby had forgotten that. He had recommended Owen to the duke. Owen had not gone willingly. The inducement had been the opportunity to accompany his father-in-law Sir Robert on a pilgrimage to the holy city of St David's, fulfilling a dream that Owen could not deny the elderly man. Owen's assistance had been Thoresby's gift to Lancaster to ensure his continuing favour now that Thoresby and the king were at odds.

'You returned long after the work for which Lancaster said he needed you had been completed.' Thoresby's expression grew cold. 'Perhaps Wykeham knows something I do not, is that it? I did not ask enough questions about that time? Did Lancaster give you any instructions to which I was not privy?'

This was a twist Owen had not anticipated, that Wykeham mistrusted his Lancastrian connections. He prayed Thoresby could not see the twitching of his blind eye beneath the patch. 'He did not speak of the Bishop of Winchester.'

'Anything.'

'He spoke only of the missions you know of.' It was ludicrous for Thoresby to question Owen so. 'I chose to serve you rather than the Duke of Lancaster.'

'That was many years ago. A man can change his mind. What did you do in St David's?'

'Your Grace, you know that I remained on the orders of the Archdeacon of St David's.'

'I know some of the tale, but I do not believe I know all.'

And Owen did not wish him to know more. For in Wales Owen had been indiscreet – to the point of treason. But it had to do with the desire of his Welsh countrymen to thrust off the yoke of England, not with Lancaster's machinations. It was quite possible that

Wykeham knew of Owen's flirtation with treason, having been Lord Chancellor at the time. Owen had thought himself safe. It was over a year ago that he had returned and in that time no one had confronted him about it. Perhaps there had simply been no need to use the information until now.

'I should perhaps question Brother Michaelo,' Thoresby said. His secretary had accompanied Owen to Wales, though he had returned to York before Owen was delayed in St David's.

It was plain Owen must humble himself, not give Thoresby cause to probe. 'I'll speak to my men, Your Grace, impress upon them the importance of the bishop's safety.'

Thoresby lowered himself down into his cushioned chair. 'Good.' He pushed the crumbled stone aside. 'How is your wife?'

'She has regained much of her strength, Your Grace.'

'I keep her and all your family in my prayers,' Thoresby said in a quiet voice that held no threats.

Crouching atop the masons' scaffolding, Owen Archer looked down on the pile of stones and tiles stacked in the south yard of York Minster, more than thrice a man's height. He was looking for signs that someone had climbed the mound and waited for the Bishop of Winchester to walk past two days earlier. But it was no good – Owen needed to get closer. Holding on to the scaffolding with one hand, he stepped down on to the pile and balanced there, testing its stability. A few tiles moved, but he was able to find a reasonably firm footing. Slowly shifting his weight, he lowered himself into a crouch on the stones and tiles.

'I cannot see you now, Captain,' shouted Luke, a mason who stood below.

So someone could have hidden up here, out of sight of the bishop as he walked by.

'Now back up towards the south transept,' Owen shouted.

Shortly, Luke came into view. 'I see you now.'

On hands and knees, Owen pressed lower.

'Gone now.' The mason laughed self-consciously.

Grabbing a tile, Owen crawled forward with an uneven motion. 'Now walk towards the chapel again,' he called.

The mason soon reappeared, and Owen rose a little and tossed the tile, then flattened again. He felt the pile shift beneath him, but kept his head down.

'Just missed, Captain, and I do not think I would have seen you if I had not known to look.'

Owen sniffed, rolled over onto his side, eased up on his knees. Unless his sense of smell had weakened with his easy life, it was human urine he smelled. A long watch challenged a man's bladder. Someone might have lain in wait here, though they would have risked being seen. As Owen crawled back towards the scaffolding he was visible to several of the masons at work on the chapel. Surely they would have noted an intruder in such an unusual place. They claimed they had been working on a different wall that day, further down, but the supposed attacker could not have foreseen that. Most baffling was the question of how the person had hoped to predict precisely when Wykeham would wander towards the masons. With his well-known passion for building it was inevitable the bishop would frequent the site while he was staying at the archbishop's palace next door, but someone would have needed to lurk on the stack indefinitely. Owen thought it unlikely.

'I am coming down,' he called.

Once more on the scaffolding he had a view of the city, the Ouse Valley, the Forest of Galtres. He looked away and climbed down. In his youth such heights had not bothered Owen, but since losing the sight in his left eye he did not trust his judgement of just where the edge lay, doubting what he thought he saw.

Some placed the blame for the accident at the feet of Sir Ranulf's family. Owen could not believe they were involved. Proud they were, and angry about what had befallen Sir Ranulf, but surely they would not stoop to such depths to seek vengeance. Wykeham himself suspected John of Gaunt, the Duke of Lancaster. With the king in his dotage and Prince Edward an invalid, the king's second living son was eager to establish his power, and weaning the king from Wykeham was rumoured to be a high priority. But Owen could not imagine the duke behind such an act, either. In fact, he thought the incident had probably been an accident, with no one but a careless worker to blame for it.

Luke was waiting at the foot of the scaffolding. 'I heard you moving around up there. But I do not suppose the bishop would have made note of such noises. He would have thought it was one of us.'

'You stand by your statement that you saw no one lurking about?'

Luke stiffened. 'Why should I lie, Captain?'

'Why indeed.' Owen silently noted that the mason had answered a question with a question.

Luke reached up – Owen was taller than most men – and touched the beard that followed Owen's jaw line. 'Your hair's so dark, the stone dust shows. It's on your curly pate as well.'

Brushing dust from his hair, Owen thanked the mason for his assistance and headed for the minster gate. He suspected the mason was holding something back, perhaps the clumsiness of a fellow worker, but Owen had wasted enough of this fine day. There was much to do in the apothecary garden before the first frost, and he did not want Lucie to grow impatient and see to it herself. She was still weak. Bending still sometimes made her dizzy.

Just before Lammas day Lucie had fallen from a stool while replacing a large jar on a shelf in her apothecary. The jar had badly bruised her left hand and cut her arm as it shattered. But far worse, she had lost the child who would have been born a few months hence. She had bled much during and after the accident, particularly when she lost the child, and her strength had been slow in returning despite Magda Digby's tisanes of watercress, nettle and beetroot, and her Aunt Phillippa's additional concoctions of eggs and cabbage. The physicks could not restore her spirit.

For days Lucie lay in bed whispering prayers of contrition. Cisotta, the young midwife who had attended Lucie in those first days, had assured Owen that women often behaved so after losing a child, some even after having a healthy baby. But when Magda Digby had returned from a birthing in the country and took over Lucie's care, Owen could see her concern.

Long after they had closed the account books, Lucie and Owen lingered at the table in the hall in the pool of lamplight. Jasper, Lucie's apprentice and their adopted son, had gone to see a friend, and Phillippa and the children were in bed. Such a quiet moment seemed rare to Owen these days. Lucie did not seem to welcome idleness, but sought activity until she dropped on to the bed, exhausted. He knew she did not wish to think of the child they had lost. Even now her hands were not idle, she was tying mint sprigs together, her long, slender fingers moving quickly. The ghost of a smile touched her lips, in fact, her pretty face was alight with a calm contentment. She loved her garden almost as much as her first husband had, found in working with the plants a peace much as Owen's mother had so long ago in Wales. He wished Lucie might have known his mother – they had much in common, a gift for healing, for knowing the right combination of herbs and roots for a person's ailments. His mother would have liked the level regard with which Lucie viewed the world – though of late there was a darkness in her gaze.

Tonight Owen noted deep blue shadows beneath her eyes. 'You should have left the mint harvest to me,' he said.

'I took joy in it.' She lifted one of the sprigs, held it close so he could smell it. 'A few more days and it would be too late. Perhaps if Wykeham forgets about his mishap the other day you can help me with some of the other autumn chores.'

'I am afraid he means to keep me occupied.'

'I am sorry for that.' As Lucie reached for another clump of mint she winced, withdrew her hand and pressed the other to her shoulder.

'It is painful?'

'It aches, yes, but lying abed will not mend it.' She shook her head at him. 'And your worry weakens me.' She had made this argument before. 'You think – she fell once, she shall fall again. You think the accident has changed me for ever.'

He did not know how to answer this. It was true and not true. He knew now that it could happen. 'I meant nothing but that I had promised to harvest the mint. Guarding the Bishop of Winchester put it out of my mind. He wishes to ride to his former parish of Laughton. He means to rebuild the church.'

'Where is that?'

'At the south end of the shire. Near Sheffield.' Several days' ride, he guessed.

'He wishes to go soon?'

'Aye. He had thought to leave it until his business with the Pagnells was concluded. But Lady Pagnell refuses to see him yet. The journey would fill the time.'

'Poor Emma. Her mother's presence is making everyone in her household ill at ease.'

'She is a difficult woman?' He had met Lady Pagnell only at formal events.

'Yes, both she and her steward are intrusive guests. Emma came today, asking for a sleep potion for herself. I shall make up something to soothe her – Jasper!'

Their fourteen-year-old adopted son had come rushing in, panting and flushed from a good run, skidding to a halt by the table. Lucie steadied the pile of books as he dropped his hands on to the table, leaning, catching his breath. He raked his pale hair back from his face with an impatient gesture. 'There is a fire in Petergate. The house of the Bishop of Winchester.'

'God have mercy.' Owen got to his feet. So did Lucie. He leaned across the table, took her hand. 'Stay within, eh? One of us heading into danger is enough.'

She shook her head. 'I can help those who breathe too much smoke. Passing round a soothing drink is not dangerous.'

He did not like it, but he saw she was determined. 'Aye, you are right.' He grabbed a cloth from a basket of laundry by the door to the kitchen, thinking he might need something to protect his nose and mouth from smoke, then headed for the door.

Jasper was right behind him with a bucket.

Two

A FIRE IN
PETERGATE

Smoke already masked the October smells when Owen stepped out into St Helen's Square. Shouts drifted down from the scene. Owen looked up, expecting to see the glow of fire in the sky above Petergate. But the sky was a deep blue, the stars silvery white. Perhaps God was with them and the fire had been caught early. People ran past him. By the time Owen reached the top of Stonegate several chains of folk stretched along Petergate passing buckets of water from the nearest wells. A boy clutching an empty bucket emerged from the smoke near the burning house and headed down one of the lines. Another followed close behind.

Owen stopped him. 'Where is the fire? I see no flames.'

'The fire is down below, in the undercroft, Captain. They pulled out a servant – his clothes ablaze. They doused him with water and rolled him in the dirt. The other is dead, they say. A maidservant.'

Owen let him go, hurried on. The street was already slippery with spilled water. As he moved closer, the vision in his one good eye blurred with the smoke that belched from the undercroft doorway. The walls of the undercroft were stone and the roof tile, but the support posts and the storey above were of timber. Near the door stood Godwin Fitzbaldric, the bishop's new tenant, here in York only a few months. He was calling out orders, hurrying the bucket wielders along. His face was streaked with soot, his shirt torn. He was a tall man, leaning towards fleshiness, almost bald but for a dusting of dull red hair running from temple to temple across the back of his head.

'Is everyone out of the house?' Owen asked him.

Fitzbaldric drew an arm across his broad brow. His wide sleeve was heavy with water and torn, the tight sleeve of the shift beneath soiled. 'They pulled two of my servants from the undercroft. They were alone in the house.'

'You were not at home when it began?'

'No. We dined at a neighbour's.'

'Did you ask the injured servant whether any others were in the house?'

'He is past speaking.'

'Not dead?'

'Not yet, but how he can survive with such burns –'

'Has anyone searched the upper storey?'

Fitzbaldric shook his head. 'They were . . .'

Owen did not wait to hear the man's repeated assurance. Anyone in a crowded city knew to search a house on fire. Servants had friends, neighbours might be visiting. Having moved from a village near Hull a few months ago, perhaps Fitzbaldric did not understand that – fires were a regular occurrence here. Owen pushed past the human chain passing buckets, dipping the cloth he carried into one of the pails of water. Tying the wet cloth over his nose and mouth, he mounted the stairs, which were shielded so far from the flames by the stone wall of the undercroft, pushed open the door and shouted, 'Is anyone here?' Stepping within, he found the crackle of fire and the shouts of the people muted. His voice echoed loud in the hall as he called again. Smoke seeped up through the floorboards, a flame licked over in the front corner. Two lamps were alight on the trestle table, and a lantern on a wall sconce. Already their flames were blurred behind the smoke in the air.

Something clattered up in the solar at the far end of the hall. As he rushed towards the steps his eye watered from the smoke coming up from below. 'Come down! The undercroft is ablaze!'

A foot appeared on the steps, then a second. So much for Fitzbaldric's stubborn certainty. It was a woman, her skirts hitched up to descend. She moved slowly, looking about her as if confused. Her cap was askew, her dark hair tumbling down her back.

'Poins?' The woman's voice trembled.

'Hurry. This is too much smoke for anyone to breathe.'

Seeming only now to focus on him, she crouched down on the steps and reached towards his outstretched arms as if she thought to take his hand, but she was now so unbalanced that she lost her footing and slipped down the last few steps, landing in Owen's arms. She had fainted.

He pulled her away from the steps, crouched, lifted her up and hoisted her over his shoulder as he rose. His back would wreak vengeance for that on the morrow. Pray God he lived to suffer it. He blinked against the smoke, took a step forward, checked himself. The smoke was obscuring his vision. He cursed the French-woman who had cost him the sight in his left eye.

Trying to establish the angle at which he had approached the steps to the solar, he prayed he was headed in the right direction. The cloth over his mouth and nose had dried in the heat. The smoke burned deep in his chest. He felt from the vibration of the floorboards someone striding towards him.

Alfred, his second in command, materialized. 'This way, Captain.'

Out on the porch Owen crouched down and slid the woman from his shoulder. He did not trust himself to bear his own weight and hers down the stairs, not with his lungs on fire. He ripped the cloth from his face and gasped the cool air.

Alfred took up the woman. 'Mistress Wilton awaits you below, Captain. She has been passing round a syrup for our raw throats.'

Fitzbaldric met them halfway up the steps. He lifted the woman's head. 'But this is May, my maidservant. I thought . . . What was she doing up there?'

Owen wiped his face. 'Sleeping, from the look of her. Turn round, the steps will catch any time.' Alfred had already continued down, keeping well to the outside edge. Nearer the house, the steps were catching sparks from the upper storey.

Fitzbaldric turned, shouted, 'Wet the steps!'

One of the human chains shifted direction.

Lucie awaited Owen on the ground, standing still in the roiling sea of people, too close to the fire for his liking. When he reached her, she embraced him, hugging him tightly, then stepped back, plucked off his cap, ran her fingers through his hair, took up his hands and examined them. 'Thank God you are unharmed.'

'I did nothing foolhardy.' He gladly accepted the flask she offered. 'Did you see where Godwin Fitzbaldric headed?'

'Across the way. Come.' Lucie guided him through the crowd passing buckets, shouting, away from the house, the smoke, the sound of cracking timbers.

The Fitzbaldrics stood beneath the overhang across the way, watching Alfred. With the maid in his arms, he was following Robert Dale and his wife Julia to their house at the corner of Stonegate and Petergate.

Lucie had paused in a pool of torchlight set in the wall of one of the houses opposite the bishop's, far enough from the Fitzbaldrics that they would not be able to hear her. 'The Dales hosted a banquet to introduce the Fitzbaldrics to some of their acquaintances this evening,' she said. 'Now they have offered the couple a bed for as long as they need, as well as the maid and cook.'

'You have spoken to them?'

'A little.'

'What of the injured manservant?'

Lucie did not answer at once. She watched not Owen but the mass of people working on the fire.

Owen touched her arm. 'Lucie?' He had come to dread her silences.

She pressed his hand, a gesture she had made seldom of late. 'They might yet save the upper floors. Listen. It is quieter now.'

It was difficult for him to block out the sound of the people, but gradually he was able to hear what she did – the fire hissed rather than roared. Yet he remembered the burning corner in the hall. 'I do not think we can hope for that.'

Still facing the burning house, she said, 'I told them to take the manservant to our home.'

He had forgotten his question and did not at first grasp what she was saying.

Lucie turned to him. 'Owen?'

Her meaning dawned on him. 'We cannot care for him. You are yet weak –'

'It is done. He is on his way and Magda Digby with him.'

In the torchlight Owen could see the set of Lucie's jaw, the challenge in her eyes, and against all reason he was glad of it, for he had not seen that spirit in her for a month. 'So be it.'

She pressed his arm. 'Come home?'

'Not yet. I want to see the dead woman.' He shook his head at her. 'Why would you do this? You do not know these people.'

'Why did you go in search of the maid?'

The Fitzbaldrics were looking their way. It was not the time for an argument.

'We have been noted,' Owen said. 'I would talk to them. Your flask is empty now.' He handed it back to her. 'Go home. I'll follow when I can.'

'We are most grateful to you, Captain,' said Fitzbaldric as they drew near. 'God help me, but I was certain the house was empty.' He did not look Owen in the eye.

'We could not know she was up there,' said his wife.

Owen was not interested in their excuses. 'Have you seen the woman found in the undercroft?'

'I did,' said Fitzbaldric, 'when they carried her out.'

'You had identified her as your maid. Does she look like her?'

'Have you seen the body, Captain? I could tell little else than that it was a woman. I assumed it was May.'

'And you?' Owen asked of Mistress Fitzbaldric.

'I saw no cause to upset Adeline,' Fitzbaldric said.

Owen ignored him, wanting his wife to answer for herself. 'You cannot account for her?'

Adeline Fitzbaldric shook her head. 'Our cook

assisted at the Dales' dinner. But May and Poins stayed at home. I do not allow my servants to entertain while they are in charge of the house.'

A crash drew all eyes back to the fire across the way. Flames shot from the doorway at the top of the steps.

'We are ruined,' moaned Adeline Fitzbaldric. 'All the goods you had stored in the undercroft lost.'

Fitzbaldric put an arm round her. 'We have the warehouse in Hull, Adeline. And the support of the guild.'

Thinking the couple caught up in one another, Owen began to cross over to find where the corpse lay. But he discovered Fitzbaldric hurrying after him.

The merchant stopped him in the middle of the street. 'Is it true you are seeing to Poins?'

'My wife so ruled.'

'God bless you and all your household, Captain. He was in terrible pain.'

And might not live to tell the tale, or face punishment.

'Who is that woman, Captain? We had no other women in the house.'

'I have yet to see her. Where have they taken her?'

'The neighbour's shed, on the far side of the house. They put her there awaiting the coroner.'

'See to your throat, your wounds, Master Fitzbaldric. You have been through much this night.'

As Thoresby sat over wine with Wykeham, listening to his complaints, his fears, the seriousness of the rift between Wykeham and Lancaster became clear to him. On the surface, Lancaster and Wykeham were alike in their lack of those pleasing graces that bind people to great men out of love, though where Lancaster was flint-eyed and cold, Wykeham was pinch-lipped and stubborn. The dangerous difference – dangerous to the bishop and all who crossed the duke – was Lancaster's passionate nature. And in alienating Lancaster by the rumours of his lowly birth – or the failure to contradict the rumours in a sufficiently public arena – and then giving voice to the criticism of the duke's ability as a general, Wykeham had insulted the man to the very heart. Which put much weight behind Wykeham's fears.

Thoresby was considering how to express his thoughts diplomatically when he was distracted by voices from the hall entrance. What had been a murmur grew louder.

Wykeham shifted in his chair, glancing towards the carved screen that shielded them from the doorway.

From behind it came Brother Michaelo, his elegant face flushed, his bow and apology curt. 'There is terrible news. The bishop's house in Petergate is ablaze. A woman is dead, a man badly injured.'

'God rest their souls,' Thoresby said as he crossed himself.

Wykeham did the same, then demanded, 'Who? The Fitzbaldrics?'

His clerk Alain hastened in after Michaelo. His pale hair clung damply to his head, his gown was spotted with water, his shoes created puddles. 'Their servants,' said Alain.

'You were there?'

'I was eating in a tavern when news of the fire drew all my fellows out to help – I followed, helping pass buckets until enough folk had arrived that I could slip away. I thought you should hear.'

Wykeham groaned. 'God save us.' He moved towards the screen passage, checked himself, raised a hand to his brow. 'How bad is it?' he asked Alain. 'Is the house lost?'

'Most of the house is gone. It began in the under-croft,' said Alain.

'What devil has been loosed against me?' said Wykeham in a choked whisper.

'Fires are common in a city such as York,' Thoresby said, but Wykeham was not listening.

'You said the undercroft – did it begin in the records room?' Wykeham asked his clerk.

'I do not know, My Lord Bishop.'

'You had documents stored in the undercroft?' Thoresby asked, belatedly understanding the implications of Wykeham's questions.

'Yes. Property records, accounts.'

'Can anything be saved?' Wykeham asked Alain.

'If so it will be thanks to the folk of this city. They streamed from their houses with pots and buckets in hand, shouting directions to the nearest wells.'

'They are saving their own properties,' Thoresby noted.

'Were any others injured?' Wykeham asked his clerk.

'I heard of no others. My Lord, I fear for your safety in York.'

Wykeham turned to Thoresby. 'Captain Archer – he has investigated such things for you before.'

Seeing the fear in the eyes of the bishop and his clerk, Thoresby did not argue. 'Michaelo, send for Archer.'

'According to Alain the captain is at the fire, Your Grace.'

'He rescued a maidservant from the solar,' Alain said. 'He is a courageous man.'

'We have no need for heroics, just answers,' Thoresby snapped. 'Send for him.'

Crossing back towards the fire, Owen found Alfred. As they searched for a lantern and then headed for the shed, Owen asked what Alfred knew of the woman taken from the burning undercroft.

'She was lying on her stomach just beyond the outstretched hand of the manservant.'

'What else?'

'If she had been lying any farther inside, they would not have seen her. Though that matters little to her.'

'Someone will miss her, Alfred. At least they will know what happened. Has the coroner been here?'

'He is helping with the fire. I do not think he has viewed the corpse.'

Owen could not fault him. The fire threatened the city. The unfortunate victim could wait. 'What of a priest?'

'Father Linus from St Michael-le-Belfrey gave her the last rites, in case her soul had not yet departed.' Alfred nodded towards a man who had stepped away from the chain of water carriers and was drinking from a tankard being passed along. 'One of the rescuers. Folk are making much of the two men who threw water over each other and went in to bring her out.'

'They deserve the praise,' said Owen, 'to walk through fire for a woman they do not know.'

'Who can say whether they know her? She is charred far worse than the man, as if she had lain in the heart of the fire. But the earth floor protected her face, and the front of her body.'

'Then someone should be able to name her.'

'She is not a pretty sight, Captain. Her face swelled in the heat and her hair is burned away. Her body is several times its size like someone pulled from the flood.'

They stood now before the shed.

'Do you need me in there?' Alfred asked in a voice that made it plain he prayed Owen would not.

'Stay without, let no one disturb me.'

'Gladly.'

The air in the shed was heavy with the odour of burned flesh. Owen left the door slightly ajar. The body had been laid out on a wattle panel, face up. Owen crouched down and slowly moved the lantern the length of the body. Alfred had been right, she was a piteous sight, half her face blackened, misshapen, the unburned side bloated, distorting her features. Her torso was swollen, and charred but for a hand's span down the length of it, where it had been protected by the earth floor. Owen shuttered the lantern and stepped outside for air.

Alfred was talking to one of his fellow palace guards.

'I thought you were on duty at the palace,' Owen said.

'I am, Captain, but His Grace the Archbishop sent me to fetch you. He wants to hear what you have observed here.'

Brandywine, fragrant air free of smoke, far away from the stench of burned flesh – Owen minded the summons far less than was his habit. The prospect provided the spur he needed to return to the corpse within the shed, a respite at the end of the dread task of examining her. But he should also have a look at Poins. 'Tell His Grace that I shall come soon, after I have been home to see how the injured servant is faring.'

The guard shook his head. 'His Grace said he would accept no excuses, no delays.'

So Thoresby would get half the story. 'Why is he so insistent, I wonder?'

'He has asked for extra guards on the palace, also.'

Thoresby must believe the fire was a threat to Wykeham.

'I shall follow soon.'

'But . . .'

'If I do not examine the corpse, I shall have little to tell His Grace.'

'Aye, Captain.'

Owen withdrew to the shed and once again shone the lantern along the length of the woman's body. He saw no remnants of a veil or cap, which might have protected some of her hair. One side of her head was caked with mud where it had been pressed to the earth. He found a length of sacking hanging on a hook on the wall of the shack and used it to wipe away some of the grime. He could see that her eyebrow was a light brown, a shade too common to set her apart. He tried to imagine her skin slack, her features more defined, but it was beyond his powers to do so. She was someone's daughter, perhaps wife and mother. Someone would come forward to claim her. He thanked God he knew that all the women in his family had been safe when the fire began.

Something around the woman's neck caught the lantern light, but her flesh had swelled around it. A piece of jewellery, perhaps. That might be useful in identifying her if the Fitzbaldrics did not come up with a name. Owen tilted her chin back gently. With the sacking protecting his hand, he reached for the item. It was polished metal, large for a lady's neck, almost four fingers long, cutting into the swollen flesh above and below. A leather strap hung from it, the end so charred it crumbled in his fingers. He realized it was a buckle and a belt, or strap. The rest of the belt was deeply imbedded in the swollen flesh of her neck, secured by the brass buckle. Easing the leather through the buckle, he worked it out, trying not to tear the flesh. He was sweating and nauseated by the time he held the charred belt in his hands. The buckle had been positioned over her throat and had probably crushed it.

Owen's discovery changed the temper of his examination. The woman was no accidental victim, a neighbour coming to talk with Poins while he fetched something from the undercroft, caught in a sudden blaze caused by an overturned candle. She had been murdered, her executioner, no doubt, hoping the fire would mask the deed, not counting on the quick response of the neighbours.

But they had not come in time to save her. *May she rest in the light of Thy grace, dear Lord.*

Gently Owen arranged the woman's head so that the band of unburned flesh at the side of her neck, where the leather had protected it, was not noticeable. Whoever wrapped her in a shroud for burial might make note of it, but there were other abrasions and raw areas on her flesh where fragments of charred, brittle clothing had been pulled away, perhaps when she was moved. He hoped that only the murderer would know how she had died. With care, Owen coiled what was left of the belt around the buckle, wrapped it in the cloth, and tucked it into his scrip. He would show it to Thoresby and Wykeham, but no one here, not even the coroner – his job was but to record that she had died and how. For now he would be satisfied with death by burning.

Owen shuttered the lantern and stepped out of the shed. Alfred awaited him.

'Get me some water to wash my hands. Then I want to talk to the men who carried her out.'

Owen leaned back against the wall while he waited, hands hanging at his sides, eye closed, breathing. Even the smoky air was better than the air in the shed.

Alfred returned with the man he had pointed out earlier. Owen recognized him as a blacksmith's apprentice – someone unafraid of fire. He had little to add to what Owen had already heard.

Another man came forward, holding out a leather strap decorated with glass beads. 'This dropped from the woman, I think,' he said, placing it in Owen's hand.

It was a pretty bauble, or had been before the fire had ruined it, perhaps the woman's girdle. Owen added it to the other piece of leather in his scrip. It was something by which she might be identified.

'Tell me about the other, the injured man.'

'He lay beneath a burning barrel. His arm broken.'

'Why did he not free himself?'

'His head was bleeding. Perhaps he was in a faint.'

'The barrel was atop him?'

'Aye.'

Owen drew Alfred away from the others. 'I want a guard on my house, where the injured man lies.'

'Protecting a witness?'

'Aye.' *Or the murderer.* 'And my family.'

'Colin is in this crowd. I shall find him and take him with me.'

'Good man.'

Three

PAINFUL REMEDIES

S oaking a cloth in a bowl of water, Lucie knelt to the injured man. Poins, the Fitzbaldric couple had called him. He had patches of dark hair between the burned areas, trimmed close to his head, prominent bones, a broad forehead underscored by dark, straight brows – though all the hair might be burned and not naturally dark at all. On the right side of his face he had blisters high on his cheek and forehead, and his right ear looked as if it had been even more severely burned. There were perhaps bruises on his left cheek – it was difficult to tell with his face streaked with soot. She dabbed at the dirt. He winced. She guessed by the condition of his clothes that he had burns on all his limbs, though his principal injuries were the gash on his head and his shattered and burned right arm. He lay with it thrust out from him as if he would shake it off if he could. The colour of the arm was unnatural. Every now and then he gave a violent shiver. Though it was warm here by the fire, she knew that after such an injury one often needed extra warmth.

Lucie's elderly aunt sat on a stool nearby, clutching

her elbows as if protecting herself from the man's agony. Phillippa had been confused when Poins was brought into the house, thinking she was back on the manor of Freythorpe Hadden the night the gatehouse had been ablaze. It had taken the maid Kate a long while to convince her that this had been a different fire, involving none of her family, none of her property. But it was clear that Phillippa was still ill at ease. Lucie thought some occupation might calm her.

'Aunt, would you fetch some cushions and blankets from the chest at the top of the stairs?'

Phillippa responded slowly, moving her fingers as if rediscovering them. Then she rubbed her cheeks, her eyes. 'What did you say, child?'

Lucie repeated the request.

Phillippa rose and came over, holding her hands close to the fire while she gazed down on Poins. 'He cannot be cold – it is so warm here.'

'Yet he shivers, Aunt.'

Phillippa watched until she saw the tremor move through Poins. 'I see. I shall bring what I can carry.'

Lucie bent to him again and gently pressed the cloth to his soot-streaked forehead, his cheeks, his chin. Except for the blisters on his cheek and forehead his face was untouched. She set the cloth aside, picked up the brandywine and a spoon. Before she tried removing the rest of his clothing she would numb him, if she could. Wheezing and occasionally moaning, Poins did not respond to Lucie's efforts to get him to drink the brandywine. She kept up a soft patter, using his name, telling him that the brandywine would ease the pain, that he would soon be warm, that the Riverwoman was on her way. Phillippa returned with the blankets and they tucked them around him, lifted his head and gently placed a cushion beneath it. After a while his shivering ceased and at last he began to suck at the spoon. He seemed quieter by the time Magda Digby arrived.

Even so, Lucie thanked God for the Riverwoman's presence. With little ado, Magda set her pack down on the small table Lucie had placed nearby, then crouched beside her.

For a long while Magda considered Poins, holding his right hand, touching the elbow, the shoulder. At last she said, 'Magda will need thy help.'

'Of course. I thought first we should undress him.'

'Aye, see what else he suffers.'

Phillippa handed Lucie a pair of scissors. 'It is no use saving the cloth, the fire has ruined it.'

The poor man whimpered when they pulled the cloth from his left calf, which was already blistering. His right thigh looked worse, but he did not flinch when they pulled the cloth from it.

'All feeling has been burned from it,' said Magda. 'That is not a good sign.'

Elsewhere, he had abrasions and some small blisters, but Lucie was relieved to see no additional life-threatening injuries. The arm was bad enough.

Magda stopped her when she drew near that arm with the scissors. 'No need.' She withdrew to the table. From her large leather pack Magda drew out bottles, jars and pouches, arranging them on the table. 'Fetch Magda wine.'

To Lucie's surprise, Phillippa rose to respond, taking the ruined clothing with her. From where she knelt Lucie watched as the Riverwoman set a small pot over the fire. Magda noticed her interest and named the ingredients as she slowly mixed them in. 'Three spoonfuls each of the gall of a barrow swine, hemlock juice, briony, lettuce, poppy, henbane and vinegar.'

Recognizing the ingredients of dwale, a potent mixture Magda used for surgery, Lucie realized that the arm was to be removed. She had been afraid of that – she had never witnessed an amputation, much less helped with one.

Magda told Phillippa to have vinegar and salt ready for afterwards, when they must rub Poins's temples with the mixture until he woke, for it was important that he not remain long in the deep slumber the dwale would induce, or he might never wake. As Magda brought the mixture to a boil, she asked for a butchering knife or an axe, and a block of wood. Lucie did not want Phillippa handling blades. Asking her aunt to take her place dribbling the brandywine over Poins's lips, Lucie fetched the butchering knife from the rack on the wall, placed it by Magda, then went out to the garden shed for a block. She wished Owen were here. During his last months as captain of archers, when he was recovering from the terrible wound that cost him the sight in his left eye and the shoulder wound that made it difficult to handle a bow, Owen had helped the old duke's camp surgeons in Normandy. Surely he had assisted with many amputations. And he was strong. He would have been of more use to Magda. But God had not seen fit to arrange that.

When Lucie returned to the kitchen, Magda was mixing the wine into the dwale. She glanced up at Lucie. 'Canst thou hold him once he has drunk his fill?' she asked. When Lucie hesitated, Magda said, 'Thou shouldst not be ashamed to admit thou canst not bear his pain.'

'It is not that. I have never assisted with such a surgery. But I believe God will give me the strength.'

Magda grunted. 'The strength comes from thee, not

thy god. Stand at his head. Dame Phillippa, Magda will call thee when she needs thee.'

Phillippa rose and retired to the hall without argument.

'She was frightened at first,' said Lucie, 'thinking we were back at Freythorpe, at the fire.' It was more than a year since a group of thieves had attacked the manor, set fire to the gatehouse, but Phillippa often wandered in time.

'Magda has oft seen an alarm sharpen the wits of such as Phillippa.' She poured some of the mixture into a cup, crouched down by Poins. 'Thou art ready?'

Lucie nodded.

'Lift his head now.'

Slipping one hand beneath the back of the man's head and the other beneath his shoulders, Lucie lifted him. Magda brought the cup to Poins's lips, helped him drink a goodly amount, and then again. As he began to swoon, she took the hide she had brought and covered him, slipped the block beneath the burned arm. Poins jerked at her touch, then moaned, a more heart-rending moan than what had gone before, and was still. Lucie remembered her pain after the fall. Her bruised hand had ached, her torn arm had burned and could not support her, but worst of all had been the deep, twisting pain in her womb and groin, for she had known it meant an irreparable loss. Was Poins aware he was about to lose his arm, she wondered.

Magda had taken three lengths of rope from her pack. With one she was tying Poins's legs together below the knees. Lucie marvelled at the strength in the small, elderly woman, the calm silence in which she prepared for a terrible surgery. She moved up to Poins's waist with the second length of rope, lifted his lower back and drew the rope through, tied his good arm down

33

against his side. His eyelids fluttered, he muttered something unintelligible, rocking his head from side to side, then lay still again. Donning a leather apron, Magda took the knife in both hands, nodded to Lucie. 'Hold his head still.'

'Will I be enough against his strength?'

'Thou seest how little he moves. Magda has given him much of the drink.'

Her heart pounding against her ribs, Lucie took a deep breath and placed her hands on either side of Poins's head. Magda knelt down beside the pallet, felt about the upper part of the burned arm, prodding so much that Lucie expected Poins to jerk and cry out, but he merely moaned softly once as he moved the arm. Magda bent close, whispering calming words to him, and smoothing his brow. The muscles in his face relaxed beneath the Riverwoman's touch. Gently, Magda arranged the arm over the block and tied off his upper arm with the last length of rope, tugging it tight. Lucie shivered and realized she was sweating with fear. *Holy Mary, Mother of God, give me strength to help this suffering man.*

Magda moved back to the table, brought another cup of the dwale, set it beside Lucie. 'If he cries out, get him to drink more.'

And now she brought the knife. It was large, with a wide, heavy blade suitable for the preparation of meat. Lucie watched Magda's face as she weighed the knife in one hand, moved it to the other, trying its heft, experimenting with how she might wield it. She saw no emotion, only deep concentration. Suddenly Magda met Lucie's eyes. 'Ready.' She held the knife blade just over the upper arm for a moment, then lifted it with a deep intake of breath and brought it down with great force. Lucie gasped at the sound, and the shudder that went through Poins. He barely stirred. But sharp though the knife was, and powerful as Magda's cut had seemed, the arm was not severed. She took aim again, struck once more.

The sickening sound of the bone splintering caused Lucie to cry out, 'Holy Mother!'

Magda set the knife beside the arm, took a flask of wine from the table, passed it to Lucie. 'Drink, just a little, so that thou mayest still hold him while Magda seals the wound with the hot metal.'

Magda took up the knife and went to the fire.

Lucie took a cloth, wrapped the severed arm in it, put it aside on the blood-spattered rushes. With another cloth she dabbed at the blood that had splashed on Poins, the bed, the cup and spoon. She set the bloody rag on the wrapped arm and took her place again as Magda returned with the red-hot blade. As the heat touched Poins's stump he shuddered and cried out.

'Go out now,' Magda told her. 'He will be still. Magda will fetch Dame Phillippa, then join thee in the garden.'

'I should take the arm.'

'Magda will see to it. Go without, thou hast need of air.' She nodded at Lucie. 'Wipe thy chin.'

Lucie did so, her hand coming away with blood. She did feel faint. Crossing the rush floor seemed a long journey. The house felt as if it was tilting, righting itself, then tilting the other way. When she reached the door she fumbled with the latch, her hands trembling, her vision still uncertain. At last she felt it slide up. Pushing the door wide, she stumbled out into the night, doubled over and retched.

Someone guided her to a bench under the stars. A moment later, Magda placed a cup in Lucie's hands.

She sipped, and though the first taste of the brandywine made her cough, she sipped yet again. As Lucie set the cup down, she noticed a man standing beside Magda, pale of hair and wearing the archbishop's livery. She remembered the strong hands guiding her. 'What are you doing here, Alfred?'

'The captain sent me. Colin watches on Davygate.'

'Why? What does Owen fear?'

'That Poins might be a witness someone might wish to silence.'

'For a fire?' Magda said.

'The Bishop of Winchester has many enemies.' Alfred bowed to Lucie. 'With your leave, Mistress Wilton.'

'Keep your watch, Alfred. The captain must have his reasons.'

Magda joined Lucie on the bench and helped herself to some of the brandywine. When she moved, her gown seemed to glimmer in the darkness and when she faced Lucie her eyes reflected what little light there was. 'Thou art made of strong stock, Lucie Wilton. Thou hast some of thy warrior father in thee.'

'I could not do what you have just done.'

'Magda thought of the healing she was making possible, not the horror of the act. Thou couldst do the same, in time.'

'I count myself fortunate to be an apothecary, not a healer.'

'Thou art taking on the work of a healer with Poins.'

'The most difficult part is done.'

Magda shook her head. 'He may die, he may heal slowly, his master may say a one-armed servant is of no use to him. There is much ahead and thou hast taken him in at a difficult time for thee.'

'I am much recovered.'

'Art thou?'

'You know that I am.'

'In body, mayhap, but thou art battling a darkness. Magda sees it. It draws thee down.'

Lucie glanced over at Alfred, who stood beneath the eaves at the corner of the house with head cocked, one leg before the other, as if ready to pounce.

'He is not listening to women's talk,' Magda said. 'He hath his ears pricked for trouble. Thy husband inspires fast loyalty in his men.'

Lucie did not wish to be reminded of all she had to be thankful for. It made her troubled state harder to forgive in herself, which pulled her down yet further. This was her terrible sin – that she knew she had no cause to feel this way, that God had showered blessings on her. When she had sought guidance from Archdeacon Jehannes, he had offered comfort, saying that it was much like a crisis of faith, which most priests experienced at least once in their lives, and that prayer was the best cure. But prayer had not helped Lucie. 'I have not spoken of this with Owen.'

'Thou thinkst he cannot see?'

'Is it so plain?'

'To thy husband it must be. Why hast thou not spoken to him of this?'

'He watches me as it is, has Jasper staying close by me. If he knew the thoughts I have he would not leave my side. I thought work would help. Archdeacon Jehannes suggested it. And prayer.'

Magda sniffed. 'A priest? What does a priest know of a mother's mourning?'

'Such despair is sinful. I was afraid for my soul.'

Magda handed Lucie the cup. 'If thou didst not mourn, they would call thee unnatural.'

'What if I cannot bear another child?'

Magda grunted in understanding. 'Eventually thou shalt cease to bear, aye, and whether it be after two or twenty babes, thou shalt mourn the passing of that part of thy life. But that time has not yet come for thee.' She bent to reach a twig of rosemary, broke off a piece, pressed it between her hands, slowly rubbed. 'Thou shouldst do likewise. Thy patient should not smell his blood on thee.'

Lucie took another sprig from the bush of rosemary.

'Hast thou brought Poins into thy house as a penance for thy despair?'

Lucie disliked the question, feeling naked to Magda's probing mind. 'I thought it was charity, but I do not know myself these days.' Lucie thought of the man's suffering and how much worse it would be when he woke to discover the loss of the arm. 'I should go in to him.'

'Phillippa is there.'

'What of the arm?'

'It is in the shed out here. Someone should bury it on the morrow, before a pig or a dog sniffs it out.'

Lucie thought of her own partly formed child, baptized by Cisotta and buried so recently. 'The arm was part of him.'

'Aye, that it was. As thy child was part of thee.'

'Are all my thoughts so plain to you?'

'In this time, mayhap. Magda lost children as well.'

'I mourned Martin when he died of the pestilence, but not like this, not with such hopelessness, as if now all I love are marked for death.' Martin had been her first-born, her child with her first husband, Nicholas Wilton.

'Each loss is as if the first, and yet ever different.'

'Tell me about your sorrows.'

Magda tossed the rosemary into the darkness. 'Those

are tales for another day. Let us see whether Phillippa has drawn Poins out of his swoon.'

While Owen waited to be shown into Thoresby's parlour, Wykeham's two clerks descended upon him.

'Why were no guards posted at the townhouse when we know the bishop has enemies?' Alain demanded, though his attack was diminished by a fit of coughing. The clerk was suffering the result of being near the fire – or in it. And his dark robe was stained with wet ash near the hem, one sleeve hanging damply.

'That omission was at your master's request,' said Owen.

'You remember,' said Guy, who showed no sign of having been near the fire. 'The bishop did not wish his new tenants to be inconvenienced or unnecessarily concerned.'

'You have breathed too much smoke this evening,' Owen said to Alain. 'Word came quickly to the palace, did it?'

'I was about in the city when the alarm was rung.'

Owen noticed the singular. 'Where in the city?'

'You have no right to question me.'

'His Grace will wish to know.'

'He is right, Alain,' Guy told his fellow.

Alain cleared his throat. 'I dined at the York Tavern.'

'And what of you?' Owen asked Guy. 'Where were you?'

Guy dropped his gaze. 'I have spent the evening in prayer,' he said in a quiet voice.

Owen leaned back, looked at the two men, considering them. Both seemed devoted to the bishop and protective of him. But at the moment Alain seemed concerned about his own status and Guy anxious to ensure peace. Before Owen could speak again one of

Thoresby's servants announced that His Grace and the bishop were ready to see him.

Owen bowed to the clerks. 'I shall want to talk with you later.'

In the parlour, Wykeham stood clutching the back of a chair. He was not dressed in his clerical robes, but in an embroidered silk houppelande. Thoresby sat near the fire in a deep-blue velvet gown. Their ruddy faces suggested they had drunk and dined well this evening.

It irritated Owen. 'You sent for me, Your Grace?'

'I did, Archer.'

'You must find the arsonist, Captain,' Wykeham said in a tight voice. 'We must know the enemy.'

'My Lord, a fire such as this –' Owen stopped as Thoresby shook his head in warning.

'The bishop is understandably concerned,' Thoresby said, emphasizing the last two words. 'What do you think? Was the fire set?'

'It seems likely.' Owen wondered what Thoresby knew.

Wykeham pressed his hands together as if in prayer and bowed his head, but as Owen described what he had discovered, drawing the belt from his scrip, and the piece of girdle, the bishop leaned forward, muttering something to himself.

'God have mercy,' Thoresby murmured.

Owen noticed the stench of death on the pieces of leather. He wondered whether Wykeham and Thoresby smelled it, too.

'Who has seen these?' Wykeham asked, not touching them.

'The girdle was handed to me by one of the men who carried the woman from the fire. The other, only me.'

'Then it is not widely known she was murdered?' said Thoresby.

'I may be the only one who knows, besides the murderer. And possibly the servant Poins, if he is not the guilty one.'

'Where is this servant?'

'At my house.'

Thoresby nodded. 'If he talks, it will be to a member of your household. You can trust your servants?'

'Aye, Your Grace.' Owen was more uneasy than ever about taking Poins in.

'Where have the Fitzbaldrics gone?' Wykeham asked, as if only now remembering that his townhouse had been occupied.

'To the home of a goldsmith on Stonegate, Robert Dale and his wife Julia.'

'Such charity might not be long extended once the gossips spread fear in the city,' Thoresby said.

'It was aimed at me, it is plain,' Wykeham said with a catch in his throat.

Thoresby's expression was cold as he glanced at the bishop. 'You must work quickly, Archer,' he said. 'The good bishop's name must not be dragged through the mire.'

It is too late to prevent that, Owen thought as he departed. And the bishop's reputation should suffer if that was the extent of his concerns. What of the dead? What of the family now homeless?

Owen fought to put the two clerics out of his mind as he walked through the now quiet city to his home. In the dim kitchen he found Magda nodding in a chair beside Poins. Seeing the stump where the injured arm had been, Owen felt sick at the thought of Lucie assisting in the amputation. He would have spared her if he could. He took a flagon and two cups up to their chamber.

She had fallen asleep waiting for him, lying atop the covers, still in her clothes though she had removed her cap and her long hair fanned out on the pillows. A lamp burned brightly beside the bed. As Owen began to undress, Lucie turned, asked sleepily, 'Is the fire out?'

'Aye.' He bent to her, kissed her cheek. 'I saw your night's work below. You held him down?'

Lucie sat up, blinking. 'It took little effort. Magda's dwale mixture is potent.'

What a beautiful woman, this wife of his, Owen thought, despite a softening to her jaw, silver strands in her warm brown hair. Carrying a child took a toll on a woman and with each child a little more, it seemed. It was a brave thing, to bear a child, and to bear the loss. He tried to remember whether those signs of ageing had appeared before her fall.

'Help me with my sleeves?'

He sat down on the bed, untied her sleeves from the bodice of her gown, kissed her neck.

She reached back and held his head there a moment. 'Your hair smells of smoke.'

Thank God that was all she smelled. Though he had stripped down to his leggings Owen still smelled death on himself.

Lucie stood to step out of her gown. He noticed how she held on to the corner of the bed to steady herself. She had not done that before the accident. 'Did His Grace send for you?' she asked.

'He did.'

She looked so weary and so thin – he had not realized how much weight she had lost this past month. Or was it the loss of the child, the bloom of carrying the baby shattered? He would save the worst news for the morrow. 'I brought wine.'

She had crawled beneath the covers. 'Why did you post a guard on our house?'

'You saw them?'

'Magda and I saw Alfred in the garden. He said that Colin watched, too, out in Davygate. Why?'

'I thought it best to protect Poins, in case he is a witness. Has he said anything?'

'Nothing. Was the bishop of help?'

'He fears that the fire was set because the house belongs to him. He glances over his shoulder at the slightest sound.'

'Do you think he's right?'

Owen could not answer that. To murder a woman and set fire to the house in which she lay was a terrible act, but to have done it to teach a lesson or threaten the absent bishop would be even worse. 'My mind is a muddle.'

Lucie drew his hand to her mouth and kissed it.

He thought to coax the conversation into less dangerous territory. 'You are a good woman, to bring Poins here. But it means more work in the household.'

'I cannot deny that. I should not have put off finding a new nurse for the children. It is too much for Kate, with Aunt Phillippa underfoot.'

Owen knew why Lucie had put it off – first she had hoped Phillippa might recover enough to return to Freythorpe, then they had hoped being with the children might balance her. And once Lucie knew she was with child, no one had seemed quite right to take care of the older children and the baby to come.

'Magda suggested I have someone help while Poins is here,' said Lucie. 'She suggested Cisotta.' Cisotta was a young midwife who had helped Lucie in the first days.

Owen poured a cup of wine, handed it to Lucie. She shook her head.

He slipped into bed beside her, sitting up to drink his wine. 'You truly want none?'

'I need no wine to coax me to sleep.' She turned to face him, though she did not sit up and barely opened her eyes. It was not like her to be so drowsy when so much had happened. 'It is passing strange, that of all the houses in York, it is Wykeham's that catches fire, and less than a week after he arrives,' she murmured.

'It is a dry autumn.'

'Still.'

'I pray you do not dream of the surgery you just witnessed.'

Lucie did not respond. Her breathing was deep and slow.

Four

RUMINATION

Thoresby paced his parlour long after Wykeham had retired for the night. Never had Thoresby disappointed the Church when he might help her and he would not fail her now. He would protect the Bishop of Winchester even against his ally the Duke of Lancaster, putting aside his disapproval of the man himself.

But how? He must try to reconstruct the events since the mishap with the tile a few days earlier. The Pagnell steward had come but a few hours after the incident at the lady chapel with a note from Lady Pagnell angrily denying a rumour that her family was behind it and requesting that under the circumstances Wykeham absent himself from Sir Ranulf's funeral – as if the bishop had intended to play the uninvited guest. It was the first Thoresby had heard of the rumour. But by the following day even Sir Ranulf's level-headed daughter Emma Ferriby was caught up in the atmosphere of ill will.

*

After presiding over his old friend's requiem mass, Thoresby had been restless, unable to apply himself to any task. He had returned to York Minster seeking a quiet moment in the Pagnell chapel to make peace with Ranulf. But he found Emma Ferriby still kneeling before her father's tomb, her veiled head bowed, her gloved hands pressed in prayer. A wisp of incense hung in the air over the marble effigy, not yet dispelled by the drafts that criss-crossed the great minster.

Thoresby had imagined the family and mourners long dispersed. Not wishing to interrupt Mistress Ferriby's grief, he began to back away, but a pebble betrayed him.

Emma raised her head, turned towards him abruptly, her back tensed. 'Who is it?' As the veil swung away from her face Thoresby saw the marks of her weeping and was even sorrier for having disturbed her.

But the damage had been done. 'Forgive my trespass. I did not think to find you here still.'

'You are welcome here, Your Grace.' Emma had a low voice for such a small woman, a calming voice, even when ragged with emotion, as now.

Thoresby knelt beside her and bowed his head in the prayer that had been his purpose in returning to the minster. His old friend's death had been difficult to bear, dying in a French prison of a wasting disease while his ransom was being negotiated. Wykeham was sadly right, Sir Ranulf had been too old to return to France and resume the persona he had created thirty years before as a spy for King Edward – his failing memory had betrayed him. Thoresby had warned Ranulf, but the knight had insisted that God called him on the mission. Despite his frailty the old knight had been honourable to the end, refusing to divulge any other names to his captors. For that he had been tortured, Thoresby was sure of it, though diplomatic channels denied it, claiming that it was the heat of summer that had led them to bury Sir Ranulf in haste, saving only his heart, now buried here.

Thoresby had grieved to hear of that last indignity. Ever since he had witnessed the removal of a heart from a corpse, seen how the flesh was torn open, the ribs cracked, he had agreed with Pope Boniface that severing or removing any part of the body was a desecration. It seemed impossible after such mutilation that the body would arise whole on the day of resurrection. Sir Ranulf had not deserved that.

Thoresby's aged knees began to ache. Emma Ferriby had lifted her head and now studied her father's tomb. She had taken charge of the stonemason for the work, knowing her brothers would settle for something less than Sir Ranulf deserved, that they had thought him foolish to return to the king's service in France. Emma honoured his loyalty and courage. As it had been her father's dream to go on crusade against the infidel, she had ordered his effigy carved as a cross-legged knight, which was the style of many crusaders' tombs, with heart in hand, which now gave it a terrible poignancy. The face was very like Sir Ranulf's, even down to the way he squinted his left eye. Emma must have stood by the carver as he worked on the face. Thoresby found it disturbing.

He wondered whether she regretted the accuracy. He glanced at her. 'Your father was fortunate in his daughter.'

The silk of her veil whispered against the fur trim on her collar as she turned to him. The clothing was too festive for the face. 'He would not be proud of his family. There has been so much rancour, even at the

47

minster doors. There was little love among us as we knelt for your blessing.'

Thoresby had noticed. Only in blaming William of Wykeham for abandoning Sir Ranulf were the family united.

Emma leaned forward and stretched out a hand to the tomb. 'I no longer know what to feel about the king. How can I honour a man who so abandoned one of his most faithful servants?'

'The king did not abandon Sir Ranulf. The Bishop of Winchester was in negotiations –'

'Do not speak to me of his laggard negotiations!' Her voice rang out in the church. 'I would have done better had I gone myself to France,' she said in a quieter tone. 'No wonder Wykeham is no longer chancellor.'

This would not do. 'You must be chilled and exhausted, my child. Even mourning should be done in moderation. Your family will suffer if you sicken. Come to the palace and rest yourself.' Thoresby rose.

Emma did not move.

Several chantry priests and a handful of lay worshippers now stood outside the openwork wooden screen. Word of Emma's outburst would spread through the city, tongues would be wagging in the market, in the taverns, in the communal dining halls of the Bedern. She was usually more sensible than this.

'You say you are fighting for your father's honour,' Thoresby said in a quiet voice that he hoped only she would hear. 'But look at the crowd you have drawn.'

She glanced over at the doorway. '*Deus juva me.*' She rose, genuflected, crossed herself.

Thoresby led the way past the growing crowd, responding to their bows and curtsies with a slight nod of his head. In the sunlight he realized how pale Emma was and offered his hand. Hers was cold as she rested it in his.

'I thank you, Your Grace.'

Together they walked through the palace gardens at a measured pace. Thoresby thought he felt her hand warming, either from the sun or his own warmth, it did not matter. He was glad of it.

Thoresby's recollection was interrupted by the creaking of the parlour door.

Brother Michaelo poked his head round it. 'Forgive me, Your Grace. I feared you had fallen asleep.'

'Are all the others abed?'

'Yes, at long last.'

'Bring me some brandywine.'

Michaelo bowed and departed.

In his mind, Thoresby returned to the day of the funeral, he and Emma Ferriby crossing the garden. When they entered the palace she had withdrawn her hand as Wykeham came forth to greet them, his elegant robes flowing, the jewels on his fingers winking in the shafts of sunlight coming from the high windows.

'My Lord Bishop.' Emma did not bow, but held herself straight. Her head trembled, her colour rose.

'May God be with you on this day of mourning, my child,' Wykeham said.

'You must excuse us,' said Thoresby. 'Mistress Ferriby was overcome just now in the minster. I have brought her here for comfort.' He swept her through the door of his parlour that was held open by a servant, ordered wine. Only when the door was safely shut did he look again at Emma. 'I did not expect him to be in the hall.'

'I had forgotten he was your guest. I had imagined him at his own home in Petergate. I should not have come here. I cannot think how you can welcome the bishop into your house.'

'My dear Emma, sit down, calm yourself.'

She chose to pace, her silk skirts rustling as she turned and turned again. She had dressed in her finest for the funeral. Her husband was a prosperous merchant, but not so wealthy that his wife commonly dressed in silk. Even her hair beneath the thin veil had been elaborately coiffed for the occasion, held in place by jewelled combs. Today she had gathered all her wealth and will around her to give her strength.

'I imagine he did not wish to disturb his new tenant,' said Emma. 'A member of parliament for the shire – the bishop has cause to stay in the good graces of such a man. Our opinion, on the other hand, is of little consequence to him.'

'Godwin Fitzbaldric was a member for Kingston-upon-Hull, Emma. He will not enjoy such prominence in York until he rises through the ranks. The bishop knows that.'

She was shaking her head. 'Two years,' she cried. 'Two years the Bishop of Winchester was in negotiations while my father wasted away in prison. And he could not even reclaim Father's body.' Tears slipped down her flushed cheeks.

Oh, sweet child, I heed well your frustration. I feel the same. Sir Ranulf was my dear friend. But the Bishop of Winchester must not be brought down by this. 'Your father understood the risk in what he did.'

'His king abandoned him.'

The king is inconstant in his affections, yes, I know. 'If the king admitted to having such men as your father established in French court circles, many more would die. The king needs to move with caution.'

She had been walking away from him, but turned, looking at him with an expression of disbelief.

'I know they sound like empty words,' he said. 'They do to me as well. But it is true, the king must move cautiously in France.'

'My father was your friend.'

'He was. And I mourn his passing. But he would agree with me. He did not wish the king to risk the safety of others to save him. That is why he refused to name any other spies.' Thoresby nodded towards the wine the servant had left. 'Sit down and warm yourself with some brandywine.' As Archbishop of York he must support the Church, particularly now. 'Wykeham has of late suffered for the king's cause, also.'

'There are many say parliament was right in their judgement of Wykeham,' said Emma, 'that he does not have the talent of diplomacy, much needed in a chancellor. Father suffered for no fault of his own.'

The opinion of a fond daughter. Thoresby did not share it. But it was not his purpose to disillusion Emma.

His silence, however, caught her attention. She had stopped her pacing and, after studying his face for a long moment, sank down on a chair and bowed her head. 'I have nightmares of Judgement Day.' Her voice was now but a whisper. 'Father lies in a pit, watching all the bones round him gather and rise, becoming whole. But he cannot lift his head, nor his arms, his legs will not move. He tries to cry out, but he has no voice.'

Thoresby crossed himself. 'It cannot be so, Emma. All the saints would suffer likewise.' It was what he used to comfort himself.

'The bishop is a coward! He could not even keep track of my father's ransom money.'

It was true. Someone had altered the documents passed between the family and Wykeham to record a lesser amount offered by the Pagnells. Wykeham had not discovered it until he returned the ransom to the family and they declared it short a considerable sum. 'Wykeham has made recompense, has he not?'

'If you mean did he return the entire amount after being convinced of his error, you know that he did. But he can never make recompense for my father's life.' Emma pressed a gloved hand to her mouth and with the other hand pressed her heart. 'And now he insults us with charges of trying to harm him.'

'Did he behave as if he believed that when he greeted you? It is his retainers, made uneasy by the climate at court, who suspect ill of anyone who crosses him of late.'

And his fear of John of Gaunt, Duke of Lancaster. Wykeham had insulted the second most powerful man in the kingdom and quaked now at the thought of what form the duke's vengeance might take.

Michaelo set the brandywine on the table. 'Your Grace, shall I send your page to bed?'

'I'd forgotten him. Yes, do that.'

Tonight Wykeham's two clerics – Thoresby had come to think of them as the bishop's shadows – had been told to take their dinner where they might, their lord and Thoresby would dine alone. It had been Thoresby's hope that good wine and a leisurely dinner would warm up the bishop, encourage him to speak more of the court, of the king. Not long ago Thoresby had also been lord chancellor and close to the king. But his feud with the king's mistress, Alice Perrers, had not sat well with Edward and Thoresby had resigned as chancellor.

Although his duties as Archbishop of York called him south often, he felt distanced from the court now, out of touch.

The evening had not gone quite as Thoresby had hoped. Wykeham sat across from him, swirling the wine in his cup, picking at the fish course and staring silently at the fire in the hearth. The strain of court life told on him. He had aged and broadened in the years since they had last sat companionably before a fire, just the two of them. That had been before his promotion to bishop and then lord chancellor. Wykeham had been the king's privy counsellor and one of the wealthiest clerics in the English Church, thanks to King Edward's favour. As such he had been much at court, but he had not had the cares of the chancellor's office. Since then a habit of pursing his lips had etched lines around his mouth and the frown mark between his brows looked as if it penetrated to the bone. Beneath his cap his forehead was broader, his temples silver.

'Tell me the gossip of the court,' Thoresby said. 'How goes the king?'

Wykeham did not answer at once. He took a bite of fish, sipped some wine, as if considering what to say. 'He is not the man he was.'

'He is ailing?'

'God forgive my saying it, but his age is telling. He grows forgetful, loses his temper with no provocation. And the vultures are moving in. The household is ruled by Mistress Alice, who guards the king night and day. It is difficult to get past her.' Thoresby flinched at the mention of his nemesis. 'She has grown too powerful since the death of the queen,' Wykeham concluded.

'The king should marry,' Thoresby said.

'He is too old.'

'Mistress Perrers does not think so.'

Wykeham grunted.

'Yet you would return as his chancellor?' *Is the man mad?*

'Once I thought all I wished for was to be Bishop of Winchester. But my king raised me higher, and I saw how I might serve him and all the kingdom. I cannot now forget that vision.' Wykeham lifted his hand as if to feel the chain of office about his neck and, finding none, dropped it. 'But you know my situation.'

'I know that you agreed to be parliament's scapegoat for the losses in France.'

A slow blush gave Wykeham some much-needed colour. He attempted a chuckle, but it sounded more like a cough. 'You are kind to put it so.'

In spring, parliament had refused to consider King Edward's request for a new tax for the war with France until the clerical ministers were replaced with lay ministers, particularly Wykeham, who was unpopular among the nobles. They blamed the clergy in high office for prolonging the war with France because as Churchmen they did not answer to secular authorities, so they pursued their own interests. The delays counselled by the ministers had allowed France time better to fortify its army and defences. Although the king believed the clergy were merely convenient scapegoats, he had bowed to the will of parliament and asked Wykeham to step down, hoping to replenish his war chest with a new tax. In the end, the king had gained little. He was still in debt to his Italian bankers and the crown of France was ever farther from his grasp.

'I know my lord king,' said Thoresby. 'He heard the demands, looked at you with expectation and you could not deny him.'

Wykeham reached for the wine, took a long drink,

set the cup down with a clatter. 'It is as you say. I could not do less for him.'

'I warned you – I expect you remember.'

'You warned me of the court, not parliament.' Wykeham cut a chunk of bread, dipped it in the fish sauce.

'I did not expect your problems to come from the people. The king's war has given them an unfortunate power over him.'

'It is ever unwise to be ruled by one's purse.' Wykeham lifted the dripping bread to his mouth, holding a linen cloth close beneath his chin. 'I counselled caution, the parliament judged that caution cost too dear.' As he chewed, he wiped his fingers, then the edges of his mouth. 'The members of parliament are fools, but the king needs their money.'

The long war with France had depleted the royal coffers and taxed the people to the point where all grew stubborn about further taxes.

'I understand that the new tenant in your townhouse has been a member for Kingston-upon-Hull. Wealthy?'

Wykeham had been lifting his cup of wine. He took the time to drink before answering. 'Not wealthy enough to buy a townhouse in York, or to build one.' He placed the cup on the table and sat back, folding his hands. 'Are you wondering whether he might be a donor for your lady chapel?'

Thoresby deserved that. It had been a clumsy question. 'As you have seen, there is still much to do.'

'It will be a worthy monument to you and your predecessors,' Wykeham said.

'But I am also curious about Godwin Fitzbaldric,' Thoresby said. 'I know he must earn his standing in York, become bailiff and mayor at least before he has another chance at parliament.'

'Why do I woo him, is that your question? Who are his friends? How influential is he? Can he help me regain the chancellorship?'

Wykeham's touchiness answered most of Thoresby's questions. 'I grow transparent in my old age.'

'I needed a tenant, he and his wife found the space pleasing. That is all there is to know about Godwin Fitzbaldric.'

Thoresby was relieved when the servants entered with the meat course and another flagon of wine. While they fussed with serving, Wykeham resumed his study of the fire, though now with cup in hand, sipping frequently. Thoresby let the meal continue quietly, his thoughts on Wykeham's strained relations with Sir Ranulf's family, how impatiently he awaited Lady Pagnell's summons.

As if reading his mind, Wykeham's first words when the servants withdrew were, 'I would be far wiser to befriend the Pagnells than the Fitzbaldrics. This property exchange – let us pray it softens the lady.'

'You have gone forth with it?'

'Alain delivered several deeds this morning. I trust one of them will be to her liking.'

'I am glad you have done this.'

Sir Ranulf, in keeping with his conceit of crusader, had borrowed money from a neighbour for some of the fittings he needed on his venture, signing a contract that if he died in France the land was forfeit, as a crusader would have agreed had he died in the Holy Land. The neighbour had legally, albeit greedily, exercised his right in seizing the land. Unfortunately, it was the piece of property on which Lady Pagnell had intended to build a small house in which to live as a widow. She did not care for her son Stephen's wife and children, and wished to establish her own household.

Thoresby had suggested that Wykeham offer Lady Pagnell a comparable piece of property that she might trade the neighbour for the land she desired.

'You think much of the Pagnells,' said Wykeham. 'But tell me, did Sir Ranulf not bring much of this on himself, ignoring his age, pretending he was going off on crusade? The deeded property was unnecessary, that is evident from the quality of his tomb, the family's chantry chapel – they are not lacking wealth. I have said it all along, his wits were blunted by time.'

Thoresby was sensitive about this issue, having of late wondered whether his own mind grew dull. 'The king chose Ranulf to spy on the French.'

Wykeham shook his head. 'I saw the correspondence. Sir Ranulf opened the discussion. He offered his services.'

'To fight, not spy.' Thoresby wondered whether the knight's family had been aware of that. Emma had spoken as if her father had answered King Edward's call and Thoresby had chosen not to correct her – it was true, in a sense.

Wykeham watched Thoresby with lips pursed and a just perceptible nod. 'Sir Ranulf had not mentioned spying in his offer, I grant you that. I think by your expression you had doubts about the wisdom of his undertaking the mission.'

Thoresby had indeed been blunted by time if he was so easily read by Wykeham. 'I thought it ill-advised.'

'So, too, did his lady, if the gossip is true that she did not approve of the cross-legged knight carving for his tomb.'

'Yes. But his daughter Emma understood. He was a pious man who wished, towards the end of his life, to devote himself to God. Lady Pagnell would not have him withdraw to a monastery, so he conceived of another way to dedicate his life, serving his king.'

'Sir Ranulf chose a peculiar form of piety,' Wykeham said.

Coals shifted in the brazier, startling Thoresby from his reflection. It must be very late – he wondered whether Wykeham's townhouse still smouldered.

Owen sat for a while in bed beside Lucie, sipping his wine, but he was restless and worried that he would wake her. Slipping away to the kitchen, he found the patient alone, the door to the garden open. Poins lay still, breathing, but Owen knew from other such surgeries that for a few more days the man would balance between this world and the next. It would be a difficult time for the household. He had meant it when he said it was good of Lucie to take in the injured man, but he wondered what had possessed her to do such a thing when she was still weak, when the family was still worried for her. Surely she saw how frightened Hugh and Gwenllian had been by her illness, and now they must be kept from the kitchen or face a mutilated man with burns on his face, a gash in his head. And when in the morning he told Lucie the man might be a murderer, what might her reaction be? Two months ago he would have had no qualms, he would have known she would accept the news as God's wish, that they shelter this man and not condemn him. But she was so changed.

He wished Magda had waited to work on the arm until he had come home. Without the dwale, Poins might have been coherent enough to talk, if not tonight, surely in the morning. As it was, Owen must wait.

Magda's pack was on a pallet on the other side of the fire, but the covers had not been disturbed. She had set a pot to cool on a small table near Poins. Owen sniffed it – recoiled. It smelled like the tanners' yard. Another bowl, covered with a cloth, smelled of rotten meat. Owen went out into the garden in search of Magda.

Alfred whispered a greeting from his post beneath the eaves. Magda sat beyond him, on a bench that was being crowded out by rosemary, her head lifted to the starlit sky. How quiet the city was now, where just hours ago folk fought a conflagration that might have taken many homes as well as the bishop's. Even the Fitzbaldrics were probably in bed by now. Owen wondered about the loved ones of the woman who lay in the shed on Petergate. Had they gone to bed knowing she was lost?

'Thou art wakeful?' Magda said, breaking the silence.

Owen joined her, stretching out his legs, bending forward to ease his back. 'I'm worried about Lucie, about Poins being here.'

'Thy priests would say charity is ever right.'

'You think not?'

'Dost thou think Magda is a healer for her own amusement?' The moonlight seemed to move along her multicoloured scarf and gown as she turned to him. 'Dost thou mourn the loss of the babe?'

'Why–?' he stopped himself. Long ago he had learned not to answer Magda's questions with questions, or she withdrew. And tonight he needed her wisdom. 'I do mourn.'

'Dost thou blame thyself?'

'I was not in the shop when Lucie fell.'

'Magda did not ask thee where thou wast.'

He felt a tingling in the scar beneath his eyepatch.

Without being aware of forming the thought, he said, 'I should have been there.'

Magda grunted. 'Why? Dost thou no longer trust Lucie to go about her work?'

'I should have arranged the shelves. She was with child, awkward . . .'

Magda was shaking her head slowly. 'Heal thyself and Lucie will heal.' She shifted on the seat, looking down at her hands. 'She is strong, thy Lucie.'

'Every bow has a breaking point. This loss – it took her back to Martin's death.'

'But the bow did not break, eh?'

They sat quietly listening to the wind sighing through the trees, dancing through the leaves already fallen.

'Quiet thy mind and leave the women's work to the women. Thou hast much trouble ahead of thee.'

'What do you know?'

'Know? Less than thou dost, but Magda senses an ill wind. Is she right?'

'Aye.' He told her how the woman had been killed.

'Is this why thou art questioning thy wife's charity?'

'How will I tell her?'

'Open thy mouth and speak. Thou canst not hide this from her. Describe to Magda how this poor creature looks.'

Owen did so, surprised by how painful it was to recall his time in the shed.

Magda let the night sounds settle about them before commenting, but Owen sensed her energy, knew she was thinking, not dozing.

'Her burns sound far worse than his,' she said at last. 'So he came later.'

'Do you think so?'

Magda stood stiffly. 'Come, Poins must be cared for

so that he might tell the true tale.' She headed towards the kitchen, her gown flowing behind her.

Owen rose to follow. 'I'll sit with Poins for a while.'

Magda did not respond, but moved on through the kitchen door.

'A canny crone,' Alfred said as Owen reached the door. 'Only a fool would attack a house when she was within.'

'Then let us hope there are no fools in the city tonight.'

'Aye.'

Five

ThE RUINED GIRDLE

In the kitchen, Magda bent over the sleeping man, her ear close to his mouth, then straightened, shaking her head. 'The rhythm of his breath is not right.' She handed Owen a cloth, gestured towards a bowl sitting near Poins. 'Rub salt and vinegar on his temples while Magda attends to his burns.' She took the bowl with the noxious concoction over to the fire to warm it.

Owen eased down on the stool beside the injured man's pallet, found it too low, sat instead on the edge of the straw-stuffed mattress, reached for the bowl. As he leaned close to the patient the smell of singed flesh conjured flashes of battlefields slippery with blood, men groaning, begging him to help them die. He crossed himself at the memories and then pushed them back before they sickened him. He wet the man's temples, glad of the clean odour of vinegar. In a short while the man's belly rumbled. The purge that was incorporated in the dwale was at last working, the poison leaving his body. When the sounds ceased, Owen lifted Poins's legs and pulled the waiting cloth from beneath him.

'It is good that he fouled himself,' said Magda.

Owen took the cloth out to the midden at the end of the garden, noting as he passed the corner of the house that Alfred was not at his post. Owen held his breath, listening. Gravel crunched near the roses, against the back wall of the garden. The night was still clear, with enough moonlight to outline shapes. The fruit trees shivered in the light wind, something skittered beneath the hellebore leaves, but other than that all was still, and he picked out no unexpected silhouettes.

With a sudden rush of noisy movement, a shape emerged from his left, blocking the path.

'Who goes there?' Alfred demanded in a loud, resonant voice.

'Your captain,' said Owen, stepping into the light. 'What were you doing back there?'

'I thought I saw someone. Creeping along, staying low, as you were just now. But I can find no trace. If someone was here, he escaped over the wall.'

At four feet high, that would not be difficult for an agile person.

'I fear you were right that we should watch,' said Alfred.

He deserved to know just how dangerous this was. 'Someone murdered that woman in the undercroft tonight. If the man in my kitchen is not the murderer, it might be the intruder you just frightened off.' Or there might have been nothing in the garden but Alfred's imagination. Owen must remember that.

'I guessed her death was no accident when you set us up to guard, Captain. You are not an idle worrier.'

'I intend to move him on the morrow' – as soon as Owen told Lucie what they were dealing with. He hoped she would agree with him. 'I commend you for your quick response.'

63

'Get some rest, Captain. I'll be watching.'

When Owen returned to the kitchen, Magda had removed the cap that had held her grizzled braids from her neck and was pinning them high on her head.

'Trouble?' she asked.

'Alfred fears we had an uninvited guest.'

'It is good thou hadst the foresight to set a watch. Help Magda shift Poins on to his stomach.' She tucked the light cover around the injured man, took her position at his feet.

Her lack of concern regarding a possible intruder calmed Owen. He bent to slip his hands beneath the man's chest, smelling the noxious lotion Magda had spread on the right side of his face. Poins shuddered with pain, cried out at the movement beneath his shoulders and the rasp of the rough cloth against his burns as they lifted and rolled him on to his stomach, the cover now beneath him. Here were the worst of the burns, on his upper back, the back of his head, his buttocks. Some of the flesh was blistered, some of it burned more severely.

Magda began tucking folded cloths and cushions beneath Poins to ease the strain on his neck and allow him to breathe freely. Though her skin was a web of wrinkles, she was yet a strong woman, manipulating the man as if he were but a child.

'Bring Magda the ointment she was stirring.'

'It smells as if you mean to tan him.'

'Magda must cleanse the wounds, prepare the flesh for healing. Adderwort, oak bark, lady's mantle . . .'

'. . . and urine.'

'Dost thou suddenly have a weak stomach?'

'No. We used it in the camps. But it is not a pleasant odour in the kitchen.'

'Thou shouldst move him above the shop, keep him

and the guards from thy children.'

'I mean to move him at least that far.'

The oil lamp was flickering, about to go out, when Poins groaned and blinked rapidly.

Owen spoke his name.

Poins struck out with his remaining arm, knocking aside the bowl Owen had left beside him.

Owen caught his arm, held it down. 'You are safe, Poins.'

The injured man opened his eyes, staring wildly. He opened his mouth, but had little voice. Twisting away from Owen, he arched, trying to roll on to his back.

'You do not want to do that,' Owen said, holding fast.

Magda appeared at Owen's side. 'There is sometimes this wildness after the dwale leaves the body. Magda is grateful thou wert wakeful.'

Poins began to breathe shallowly. 'I am burning,' he moaned. His face contorted. 'My arm.'

'Thou art saved,' Magda said. 'Sleep now. Thou hast much healing to do.'

His breathing slowed.

Magda turned to Owen. 'Take thee up to thy bed. Thou hast returned him to the living. For now.'

Lucie lay in the darkness just before dawn. Owen had come to bed only moments ago and had fallen asleep at once. She listened to his deep, steady breathing, such a counterpoint to her own pounding heart. She fought against rising and going to see the children. Too often of late she had done so, only to wake them and spread her fear. They sensed a tension in her, that she was not the same, and she could see it frightened them. Even if they had been old enough for her to explain to them that she had lost a child, a half-formed soul, and now she woke each night terrified that God had taken

65

another, she had no right to give them such a dark gift, rob them of all joy. They were too young to learn that life did not go on for ever. There was time enough for them to learn of death.

She would go down to the hall and watch the dawn in the garden, but Magda was in the kitchen. She felt she had told Magda too much already.

A cock crowed, a sound that both heartened and saddened Lucie, the end of the long night, another day in which her steps faltered, her attention wandered. People noticed her strangeness. Her friend Emma Ferriby had yesterday come for a draught to induce a dreamless sleep. Lucie had noted at Sir Ranulf's requiem how her friend had stood with her gloved hands clasped tightly against her middle, her lips pinched, her back too stiff, fighting the anger and grief that warred in her.

'You are unwell?' Lucie had asked.

'I cannot sleep – no, that is not true. I fear sleep. I am plagued by bad dreams.'

Lucie had searched her friend's eyes for a desperation mirroring her own, but had seen only sorrow and exhaustion. 'I can give you something to help you sleep, but I cannot promise it will be dreamless.' She had taken Emma's hands. 'You must swear to me you will take only as much as I tell you.'

How strange she must have sounded. Emma had tried to laugh, but it came out an uneasy sound. 'Sweet heaven, of course. I fear the night, I fear the dreams and it is all the worse for knowing nothing can be done, nothing. But I would not harm myself.' She had withdrawn her hands from Lucie's. 'I swear it.'

'I did not think you would,' Lucie said. 'I shall mix something for you. But it is a potent sleep draft. Too much will make you senseless.'

'You are looking pale. Should you be in the shop?'

Lucie turned over in bed, dispelling the memory. The shop was precisely where she needed to be, mixing what she had promised Emma. The accounts and then the fire had distracted her from the task. But first she would check on the injured servant. She would tell Magda that is what had wakened her at dawn, concern for the man who lay so near death in her kitchen.

Owen reached out for her in his sleep. Lucie kissed his forehead. Strange how she could distinguish the smell of the smoke in his hair as something foreign, not from their own hearth fire. She reached out to trace the lines that had lately deepened on his forehead, but stopped herself, not wanting to wake him. She wished she had been able to stay awake last night, alert enough to ask what he was keeping from her. He had learned something troubling, she could see that in his eyes, in the way he held himself. Now she might need to wait until the end of the day to learn what it was, when they were alone again. But he must sleep. Gently she slipped out of his grasp, rose to dress herself.

She opened a shutter wide enough to see the dawn. A soft rain had begun to fall, but to the east the sky was bright. She used the light to examine the clothing Owen had worn the previous night. Sometimes it helped to do ordinary things. He had worn his own clothes, not the livery of the archbishop. The simple russet tunic was singed and grimy with water and ash, the leggings past saving, she feared. His boots had been soaked, but they could be worked back into good condition. She lifted them to the chest, catching his belt with them. The scrip that hung from the belt slipped along the leather and she caught it as it was about to fall. She wondered at its heft as she set it down beside his boots and turned to leave. But curiosity pulled her back. She drew the leather flap out of the long loop that held it and gently shook the scrip to free the contents, not too far, just a glimpse. A leather band set with large glass beads slipped out. Lucie caught her breath.

It was Cisotta's new girdle, but only part of it, the edges charred, crumbling as Lucie touched them. She sank to her knees, running her fingertips over the glass beads.

Cisotta had been wearing it yesterday. Lucie could see it clearly, on the young midwife's blue dress.

Lucie had come through the beaded curtain from the back workshop to find Jasper ducking his head and laughing in the self-conscious manner he had of late when a pretty woman was around. But there seemed to be no one in the shop. 'Jasper?'

'Lucie?' Cisotta's voice had risen from somewhere in front of the counter.

Jasper had blushed. 'She is fetching a jar for this.' He had pennyroyal measured out on a piece of parchment. 'Her basket is on the floor.'

A brightly veiled head rose then, blue eyes, blonde hair in braided rolls on either side of a lovely face. Cisotta's gown matched her eyes and the beaded girdle called attention to her narrow waist, how the gown was cut to cling at her hips. The effect had not been lost on Jasper. Lucie had mixed feelings about her presence. Though thankful for the care Cisotta had given her, seeing her touched wounds still raw. She had felt ungrateful – after all, the midwife had baptized her stillborn child.

Cisotta stood with jars in hand, studying Lucie. 'You still lack some spark. Is the Riverwoman satisfied with your improvement?'

'She does not say.'

'Then she is not. Jasper might help you more. And Dame Phillippa.' She set the jars on the counter.

'You have been a stranger,' Lucie had said. 'I thought you might have deserted us for another apothecary.'

Cisotta's face had dimpled in a brief smile. 'I should be a fool to do so, my friend.' She glanced behind, checked that they were indeed alone. 'I have been busy trying to feed my family, spreading the word among women about the births I have attended, particularly among merchant's wives – they pay the best.'

Lucie had heard why Cisotta needed work. The cordwainers were angry with her husband, Eudo, for making shoes of tawyed leather for a neighbour. He had been reprimanded by his guild and had lost the business of most of the guilds in the city, a loss he could not afford, for he offended so many who came into the shop with his silence, rarely sparing a moment for a civil word, that many left without buying. Cisotta complained of it often.

It was not Magda's custom to gossip, but she distrusted Cisotta, saying she did not have the soul of a healer. Though she had been relieved to see Cisotta at Lucie's bedside when she returned from the country-side and heard of the fall, the miscarriage, she had lost no time in sending the younger woman on her way. 'She depends too much on charms,' Magda had said.

But Cisotta had been good to Lucie, so she had tried to comfort her. 'Eudo is skilled with hides. The glovers will return to him when the tawyed leather they buy elsewhere stretches and tears as they work it.'

'You are kind to say so.' Cisotta crouched to place the filled jars in her basket.

'I could carry that for you,' Jasper had said.

'Stay here to help your mistress. My daughter is sitting without, we shall share the handle.'

Lucie had wondered about that. Eight-year-old Anna was a wraithlike child who had been racked by illnesses from birth.

'Eudo is so harsh with her,' Cisotta had said as she lifted the basket, leaning back a little to cope with the weight. 'He calls her lazy, expects her to fetch and carry. He needs another apprentice, but he has no one to back him in the guild. I look forward to the day when my boys are big enough to help him. God forgive me for complaining, he is as good a husband as most, all in all. God go with you, Lucie, Jasper.' She had headed for the door, her beaded leather girdle jingling as she walked unevenly with the load.

Lucie pressed the scrap of girdle to her heart. Owen's scrip dropped to the floor, spilling the rest of the contents.

The bed creaked. 'Lucie?'

'You said you did not know her.'

Owen sat up. 'Who?'

'The beaded girdle. It was in the fire. Was it on the woman they took from the undercroft?'

'One of the men found it on the ground. He thought it had fallen from her when they carried her from the fire. Do you recognize it?'

'You do not?'

'No. Tell me.'

'You saw this every day after my accident.'

Owen was shaking his head. He had the look on his face she had come to know all too well of late. He would speak softly to her now, trying not to anger her, attempting to reason with her.

'It is Cisotta's girdle,' she said, speaking before he had the chance, 'the one Eudo made for her.'

'Cisotta?'

She watched him take it in, realize what it meant to

70

her. He threw aside the bedding and hurried to her, kneeling as she knelt. He reached to pull her into his arms.

She resisted. She did not want comfort. 'Did you see her?'

'Lucie, I am so sorry. But I did not know. I could not –' he stopped himself.

He need not have. She heard the rest of it – it echoed in the room as loudly as if he had shouted it. 'She is that badly burned?'

'Aye,' he whispered, looking down at his hands. 'But it is worse than that.'

'Did you not recognize the bright blue of her dress?'

'What was not burned was smeared with mud and ashes. I swear I have never seen the beaded girdle.'

Lucie looked down at the belt that had fallen from the scrip. It, too, had been in the fire, but it was not familiar. She reached down.

'Do not touch that.' Owen did not use the gentle voice meant to soothe her. He sounded edgy and hoarse from the fire and lack of sleep.

'What did you mean, worse than that?' She joined him on the bed, shook her head at the wine he proffered. 'What did you keep from me last night? What happened to Cisotta?'

'I have told only Thoresby, Wykeham, and Magda. You must speak of this to no one else, not Jasper, not Phillippa –'

'You have never hesitated to tell me anything before.'

He said nothing.

'I swear I shall tell no one.'

'She was murdered, Lucie. The belt on the floor – it had been tightened round her neck, the buckle pressed into her throat.'

Lucie touched her own neck as she looked down at the belt that had fallen from the scrip. She took the wine now, let it course down her throat. It burned. She shivered. 'Then she did not die in the fire.'

'I do not think she could have yet been breathing.'

She did not know which would be the more terrifying way to die, to have such a thing cut off the air, to feel the belt tightening, or to choke on smoke, feel the searing pain of the heat on the skin. The wine soured in her stomach. Holding her hand to her mouth, she rushed to the window, pushed open the shutters and leaned out, breathing in the damp, chilly air.

Owen followed, put his arms round her, drawing her from the window.

Meddling man, could he not see she needed air? She turned in his arms. 'That man in our kitchen, the man I nursed last night – do you think he did that to Cisotta?'

'I do not know.'

'You describe her burns as much worse than his.'

'He lay by the door.'

'Who, then?'

'That is what we must discover. Come back to bed. It is cold here by the window.'

He was shivering, standing there naked, his hair tousled. There was a time when they would not have stood there long, but would have tumbled back into bed for lovemaking.

'Go back to bed, then.'

'It is early yet. You fall asleep so quickly at night, but every morning you are up long before me. What wakes you? Are you still in pain?'

'No.' For a little while she had forgotten her petty anguish. What was her sorrow compared with what Eudo would feel, and his young family. He was left with four children, Anna, the eldest, only eight years old, and three boys, one not long from his mother's breast.

Owen sat down on the chest and reached for her hand.

'Do you mean to keep this a secret?' she asked. 'How can you? What of Eudo? You cannot keep it from him.'

'Even from him, for now.'

'But he is her husband.'

'No, Lucie.'

'Do you suspect him?'

'Is it impossible? You have told me there was much discord in that house.'

'Eudo loved her too much to harm her.' Lucie knelt to pick up the girdle. 'Who will tell him of her death?'

'I shall send a priest.'

'I could go –'

'No!'

'I shall attend the funeral.'

'That is a different matter.'

They both looked up as someone banged on the door down below.

Six

INTRUSIONS

Lucie dropped Cisotta's ruined girdle on the bed and hurried out of the room. Owen grabbed his clothes, fumbled through dressing and followed her downstairs. The trestle table was set up in the hall and Kate was feeding the children there rather than in the kitchen. Gwenllian sat, straight-backed and solemn, watching the door that led out to the kitchen as she chewed a piece of bread. Hugh sat in Kate's lap.

'I thought to keep them out of the way,' the maid said.

'You will have your kitchen back soon, Kate. It was a mistake to bring Poins here.' Owen kissed both of the children.

Gwenllian wrapped her arms round his neck and whispered, 'Aunt Phillippa says you walked into the burning house and saved a woman. Is it true, Papa?'

'Aye, my little love. But the fire was down below. I was in no danger.' It was one of Phillippa's most annoying intrusions into their lives, to tell the children about incidents that Owen and Lucie chose to keep from them. 'Where is your mother?'

'She took that man to the kitchen.'

He looked up at Kate.

'Master Fitzbaldric, Captain.'

Here was another reason to find some other place for Poins – the house would have no peace while he was here.

'You will not go back into his house?' Gwenllian asked, touching Owen's cheek with the back of her hand, so gently, just as her mother would do.

'Not until carpenters shore it up. Now you must not frighten Hugh with tales of fires.'

Gwenllian nodded and let him go.

The warmth of the kitchen intensified the odours of blood, sweat and Magda's remedies. Owen was grateful Kate had the sense to keep the children out of the room. Lucie stood beside Magda, holding the bowl of foul-smelling lotion Magda had made during the night. Poins still lay naked on his stomach, his eyelids trembling as Magda anointed his blisters, smoothing in the ointment with her knobby fingers.

Fitzbaldric held back from the trio, eyeing them uneasily. 'Good-day to you, Captain,' he said in a quiet voice, as if unwilling to call attention to himself. He looked freshly scrubbed, reminding Owen how filthy he yet felt. Fitzbaldric wore borrowed clothing, a tunic that fitted him ill, short in the sleeves and exposing too much of a pair of faded leggings. 'I must speak with you, Captain.'

'Then let us retire to the hall.' Owen had just caught sight of what was in the covered dish that had smelled of rotten meat – Magda was about to apply maggots to the worst of the burns, to clean away the dead flesh.

Kate scooped up the children and took them upstairs as Owen invited Fitzbaldric to sit at the table in the hall.

The merchant slumped down into a chair, propped his elbows on the table and covered his face with his hands. Owen stood uncertainly, wondering whether he should return to the kitchen, where Magda and Lucie were talking in loud, angry voices. He had never heard them argue before.

Fitzbaldric lifted his head. 'Forgive me, I am not accustomed to a sickroom. His arm – was it necessary to remove it?'

'If he is to live.' The voices quieted. Deciding it was best to leave Magda and Lucie alone, Owen sat down opposite Fitzbaldric.

'I cannot imagine his agony.' The merchant was growing pale.

'Do you need something to drink?'

Fitzbaldric shook his head. 'Who is she – that woman in there working on Poins?'

'Magda is the best healer in all York, perhaps in all the shire.'

'In truth?' Relief returned some of the colour to the merchant's face, but in a moment he was frowning, pressing a cloth to his forehead. 'We have lost all the household goods, I fear, and much of my merchandise. I do not know how I shall afford the best healer in the city.'

Magda often worked for nothing – but the Fitzbaldrics were not so needy. 'You might speak with the bishop. He may feel duty bound to assist you. If you like, when I go to the palace today I could mention your situation.' While Fitzbaldric considered the offer, Owen added, 'I must tell you, I mean to find another place for Poins. It is too much for my household, having him here.'

Fitzbaldric kneaded the back of his neck, then dropped his hand to the table as if it were too heavy to hold up. 'Adeline and I need to move as well.'

'Your welcome is already stale at Robert Dale's house?'

'That is what I came to tell you. They say that such disruption and threat to the household is intolerable – an intruder in the night, a desperate husband pounding on the door at dawn. Dear God, why is this happening to us?' Fitzbaldric dropped his head on to his hands once more.

Owen remembered Alfred's fears. 'Did someone break into Robert Dale's house?'

Fitzbaldric straightened. 'We were not long in bed when the cook began to shout – someone had slipped into the kitchen, then ran when he found the cooks of both our households sleeping in there, as well as a kitchen maid. The Dales' cook cried out. My cook took up the chase, but he was too slow, awakened out of a sound sleep. It is a house with many locks, Captain, being a goldsmith's, the kitchen the only vulnerable chamber. But it is understandable that the Dales are afraid for their livelihood. Such valuable materials.'

'They are certain the person broke in because of your presence?'

'It happened last night, the first night we spent under their roof – what else could they think? I must speak with my guild master.'

'He will surely be able to help, or Bishop Wykeham. But you said this morning someone came to the Dales' house?'

'A tawyer, pounding on the door, demanding to know whether his wife had been at the house – the bishop's house – last night. He was drunk, quite red in the face and impossible to calm. She had not come home.'

'Eudo the tawyer?'

'The very man.' Fitzbaldric looked surprised. 'How did you guess?'

'Where is he now?'

'I escorted him to the shed where the woman lies. He bent over her ruined body, searching . . .' Fitzbaldric put a hand to his stomach. 'It sobered him and he said that he wished to be alone with her.'

'So he was able to recognize her.'

'He *believed* it to be her, though she is so disfigured.' Fitzbaldric crossed himself. 'I honoured the man's wish for solitude, though I told the people in whose shed his wife lies of his presence. They said they would send for Father Linus of St Michael-le-Belfrey, the priest who gave the woman the last rites.'

Owen was glad of that. He had worried that Eudo might do himself or others harm – he was a passionate, sometimes violent man, if Cisotta's stories were true.

'When I returned, Julia Dale was telling Adeline about the man's wife. She was a weaver of charms, Julia said.'

'She was a midwife.' Owen was disappointed that the man looked baffled.

'Adeline and I knew her not, nor her husband. But you have not told me how you guessed who he was.'

'I brought a piece of clothing from the fire. My wife knew it.' Owen nodded towards Lucie as she came through the door from the kitchen.

'Mistress Wilton.' Fitzbaldric bobbed his head.

Lucie smiled warmly at him. Owen wished he knew what Magda had said to her.

'Poins is covered now, if you wish to see him,' Lucie said.

Fitzbaldric looked uncertain.

'I shall tell the bishop of your plight,' said Owen.

'Do not trouble yourself. I shall speak with him.' Fitzbaldric bowed to Lucie, to Owen and, with the posture of a man facing an onerous task, headed for the kitchen, letting the door bang shut behind him.

The smile faded from Lucie's face. So it had been a mere courtesy.

Owen took her arm. He wanted to make sure of her state of mind before he went on to his business of the day and he wanted to reassure her that Poins would be out of their house as soon as another place had been found for him.

Lucie tried to pull her arm away. 'You need sleep,' she said.

'And what of you? I can feel how you are trembling.'

'It is not just Cisotta, but the fire. I imagine it happening to us. What if we could not get the children out in time? What if no one thought to go up to the solar for them? It almost happened to the Fitzbaldrics' maidservant.'

'But it did not happen to us.'

'No.' Lucie did not look comforted. 'Yours is a rough touch for one who claims to be concerned for my welfare. What is this about?'

'What did you tell Fitzbaldric before I arrived?'

'Ah, that is what worries you.' Lucie jerked her arm out of Owen's grasp. 'What do you fear that I told him? That Poins strangled Cisotta with his belt? I am not a fool, Owen. I kept the conversation to Poins. And you? Did you show him the belt? Ask him whether he recognized it?'

'No. I am not certain how much to tell him.' He felt the fool, having voiced his worry without thinking how it would sound.

'So you distrust Fitzbaldric?'

'I have not yet decided how to approach him. His

79

visit caught me unprepared. Did he tell you that Eudo came to the Dales' house this morning, drunk?'

'No.' Lucie's arm went limp.

'No doubt that is why Eudo did not notice Cisotta's absence until morning.'

'Poor Anna,' Lucie whispered.

'Aye.' Owen realized the man's eight-year-old daughter must have taken care of her younger brothers through the night. 'Fitzbaldric took Eudo to the shed where Cisotta lies. Now he wants to know why the woman was at his house.'

'As do we all.'

'His visit this morning was just the beginning of the burden of keeping Poins here.'

'Are we to toss him out on the street?'

'We must find another place for him to be nursed. Do you think they would take him at St Leonard's Hospital?'

'They might. But Magda would not see to him there. Why do you want him gone?'

'It is too much for this household. I must spend my days searching for Cisotta's murderer, eh? Seeing to Wykeham's safety. I cannot help you here. You have enough with the shop.'

'I want to help you find Cisotta's murderer.'

'You can help best by giving me nothing to worry about.'

'Like a child, or a favourite lap dog?'

It seemed he could say nothing right. 'Lucie, you have been through so much with your injuries and the loss of our child. You cannot be unaware of the way you have been behaving since the accident.'

'Of course I am aware.' Her voice was tight, her lips pinched. 'But Cisotta is dead, the woman who sat beside me so many days, selfless as ever Magda was. I must do something to help. I cannot sit waiting for you. Let me do what I can.'

He did not like it. 'Do you trust yourself?'

Her eyes wavered a moment, but then she faced him squarely with the familiar level gaze that he had not seen since the accident. 'I do.'

There was something she might do, but he doubted she would agree. Still, if he suggested it and she refused, she could not accuse him of not considering her offer. 'Emma Ferriby – would you be willing to speak with her, discover her family's movements yesterday, and on the day of the accident at the lady chapel when the tile almost hit Wykeham?'

'The bishop cannot think the Pagnells might be behind Cisotta's murder?'

'The tile and Cisotta's death might not be connected,' said Owen. 'Perhaps not even the fire.'

'Then Wykeham has been visited by a string of random misfortunes.'

'Aye. And I am uneasy with that conclusion.'

Lucie looked uncertain. 'But Emma and her family.'

'I know. Would you feel a traitor to your friend?'

'Let me think.'

'There will be much to do in the shop with so many having helped at the fire last night – burns, sore throats, injuries. Perhaps you have not the time for this.'

'You want me to decline, is that it? How clever – ask me to do something you might be sure I'll refuse to do. I am not mad, nor so weak I cannot think, cannot read you. I am willing to do anything necessary to find Cisotta's murderer, even this, what you ask. And if that man who lies in our kitchen is the murderer, I pray he lives to suffer even worse than he has already.' Lucie's face was flushed, her chin high, her hands fists held tight to her body, as if they must hold her down.

He put his arms round her, not in restraint as before, but in affection. 'I shall be grateful for your help,' he said. 'I could not think how I might approach them without making them too aware of what I was doing.'

She relaxed her arms, then lifted them to encircle him and pressed her forehead against his shoulder.

'Promise me you will be careful,' Owen whispered.

'I meant to take Emma a sleep potion today and so I shall. She will want me to stay to tell her of the fire and of Poins.'

He did not warn her to watch how much she told Emma. He must trust her.

Brother Michaelo had interrupted Thoresby's morning prayer to tell him that Wykeham had a visitor, Godwin Fitzbaldric. It was no surprise that the man was distraught, but Thoresby wondered what he wanted of Wykeham, whether he was apologizing for the destruction of the house, or demanding new lodgings. Thoresby noticed the voices now, Wykeham's calm, reassuring; Fitzbaldric's loud, imploring. He did not like the sound of that. In a short while he learned that he had interpreted the voices correctly. Wykeham came to confer with him while his tenant waited in the hall.

'Might I assure Fitzbaldric that there is room for all his household here in the palace?' Wykeham concluded.

'Your tenant is proving to be a great burden.' Thoresby shook his head as Wykeham began to explain. 'I am aware of your noble feelings in this. They are your tenants, you are responsible for their welfare, it is possible that the fire was an attack on you. Yes, yes. But why such haste in inviting them here? York is a great city, crowded, yes, but there is always a way to find room. One of the archdeacons might have space for the Fitzbaldrics.'

Wykeham tapped his finger on the arm of his chair, impatient to get in a word. Thoresby found the sound annoying and gave way.

'If they had anything to do with the fire, the murder, is it not wise to have them under this roof, where we might observe their comings and goings, their tempers?'

'And be murdered in our beds, if they were the ones responsible for that woman's death.'

Wykeham ignored the comment. 'I am also concerned with Captain Archer's inconstant behaviour in this,' he said. 'To offer shelter to the injured servant last night, only to throw him out on the street this morning.'

'I shall speak with him about it. But it was never a good idea. His wife will be busy in the shop, Archer is busy with our concerns and the children must be frightened to see a crippled man in their kitchen. The household is just recovering from Mistress Wilton's fall and the loss of the child she carried. All in all, I am glad to relieve them of the burden.' Some of Thoresby's vehemence came from guilt, a feeling that Lucie had taken Poins in to help Owen in his investigation.

'You are very familiar with this captain of yours.'

'I am godfather to his children.'

'Indeed?'

Thoresby did not wish to pursue that subject. 'My greatest concern is having the Riverwoman at the palace. She is not a Christian. It is disturbing.'

'Then send for a physician.'

'Master Saurian is a gossip. All the physicians and surgeons in the city are. Magda Digby is not. She suits our purpose.'

'So we are agreed on this?'

'God help us, yes. Tell Fitzbaldric they may come.'

Owen returned to his chamber to dress more carefully, then tucked the belt and Cisotta's girdle in his scrip and set off to find Eudo and the priest he hoped would be with him. Although a mist still dampened the air, beading on eyelashes, dripping from hats and veils, folk were astir on Davygate, some going about their business, many clustered with heads together, no doubt reliving the night's drama. Stonegate, lined with the grand homes of goldsmiths and wealthy merchants, was abuzz with groups of neighbours exchanging gossip. Owen felt all eyes on him as he passed along the crowded street. In front of Mulberry Hall stood a cluster of some of the most important residents. They hailed him as he approached. After asking about Poins and expressing sympathy for him upon hearing of his injuries, they launched into the talk of the day, which was not only the fire but Cisotta's death in it – because of Eudo's early-morning visit to the Dales' house all now knew the identity of the woman who lay in the shed on Petergate. Owen wished he had known that before sending Lucie off. People had many questions about what had prevented Cisotta from fleeing the fire. He did not know how Lucie would respond.

'Trapped by someone meaning no good,' said a merchant.

This was met with nods all round but for one woman, a goldsmith's wife.

She shook her head as if listening to children stumbling over their lessons. 'Death by fire is the Lord's judgement.' She stood back, her face stern, while the others digested this. When she thought them ready, she continued, 'She wove charms, for good or ill.'

'Midwives do what they must,' said another woman.

'For good or *ill*, I said. That is not the way with other midwives.'

The merchant frowned in disagreement. 'Mark me, it is the serving man, lying in the captain's kitchen burned and lacking a limb – he knows what happened to Goodwife Cisotta. They say he lay with his arm stretched towards her.' He looked to Owen for confirmation.

'I arrived after he had been pulled from the fire.' And glad of it he was at the moment.

'Has he spoken?' a goldsmith asked.

'Not a word.'

'Some say it is the Duke of Lancaster wreaking vengeance on the Bishop of Winchester,' the goldsmith said.

'Do you mean the bishop's hearing Queen Philippa's deathbed confession that Lancaster was a changeling?' one of the women asked.

'No one who has ever seen the king and the duke together believes that,' said Owen. 'They are of the same mould.'

The woman sniffed.

Owen bade good-day to them all and continued up to Petergate and on towards the tawyer's house, relieved to escape the curious townsfolk.

Seven

UNDERCURRENTS

Crossing the garden to the rear door of the shop, Lucie paused outside, picking spent roses off the climbing vine while praying for strength to fend off the darkness. She had committed to helping Owen in this, but already doubt clouded her mind. *Holy Mother of God, help me fight against the devil who would crush me with despair. Give me the strength to see how I must proceed, how I can bring peace to Cisotta's spirit and protect innocent people from blame.*

Gathering a handful of dried petals in her apron, Lucie stepped inside. The workroom and storeroom for her apothecary shop had once been the kitchen and main living quarters of her home, with a sleeping loft above. A window overlooked the oldest part of the garden, which had been planned and planted by her first husband, Nicholas Wilton, adding to the small apothecary garden planted by his father and grandfather. Nicholas would have delighted in the space she had now, with room enough for half a dozen fruit trees and beds for more varieties of the herbs that they used

86

in the shop. Lucie's own father had bought the larger house next door in which they now lived. She wondered whether he would have regretted his generosity if he had lived to see her now, giving in to despair over the death of a child she had never known.

These were dangerous thoughts. She busied herself collecting a small jar and stopper for Emma's sleep potion and set out the sealing wax, lighting a spirit lamp to warm it. From a peg on the wall she took down a scrip in which to carry it all. As she worked, her hands steadied, her mind calmed.

Through the beaded door to the shop she overheard Jasper talking to a customer. 'I have set it here at my elbow because there have been so many asking for balms for the throat. Do you need a salve for burns as well?'

One of the tasks that Lucie had neglected of late was making more of the cough electuary, which would be much needed as the year passed into winter. She doubted they had enough to last through the next few days if already, in mid-morning, Jasper had dispensed enough to be keeping the jar on the counter. She waited until the customer departed, then joined Jasper in the shop.

He greeted her with troubled eyes, cheeks flushed with emotion. 'Is it true what they are saying, that it was Cisotta who died in the fire?'

The question took Lucie aback. 'Who told you?'

'Mistress Cooper. She came in for burn ointment for her husband and something to soothe his throat. And others have also been talking of it. Is it true?' His voice cracked.

'Yes, it is.' Seeing his distress, remembering how Cisotta had affected him, Lucie held her arms out to him and had a moment to comfort him before the next customer appeared in the doorway. 'I shall miss her, too,' she whispered, smoothing his straw-coloured hair from his forehead as she had not done in a while. He hugged her hard, wiped his eyes, and turned back to his work, greeting the customer with a gruff but stable voice.

While Jasper dispensed, Lucie mixed valerian root, fennel seed – for Emma had a tender stomach – crushed lemon balm and mint and, having tucked them in the jar, stoppered it.

'We need sweet vinegar and barley sugar to make more of the throat physick,' Jasper said as Lucie picked up the jar and headed for the workroom.

'And before the day is out,' she agreed. 'But we have the rest?'

'Steeped hock seeds and flowers, gum Arabic, dragagantum and quince seeds, aye.'

Something simpler might do for those not coughing, but the best remedies for the throat contained iris or violet vinegar and barley sugar. She had never allowed her supply of them to get so low.

'I shall stop at the market after I take this to the Ferribys,' she promised. No doubt the day after a fire the ingredients would be most dear, but she had no choice.

'I could take that to them.'

'I wish to see Emma. Do you mind so much, managing the shop by yourself?'

She could tell by the look on his face that he minded a little, but he assured her that he was content.

Quickly she sealed the jar and departed for Emma's house, hoping to set her thoughts in order as she walked to Hosier Lane. But on the street she found little peace in which to think. It seemed as if the entire population of York was abroad, exchanging tales of the fire the previous night. By the time she had made her way down Coney Street to Ousegate she had learned that the gossips, rather than talking of the good Cisotta had done, were listing her frivolous outfits, the men with whom she had flirted, the midwives she had stepped over to find work, how much she had charged for a birth when others did the work expecting nothing and, worst of all, the charms she had woven for profit.

By the time Lucie reached Emma's house she felt confident that she could rummage for information without sounding unnatural – her fury over the wholesale condemnation of Cisotta would cover any tension she might display.

The Ferriby house commanded Hosier Lane just beyond Pavement. Peter Ferriby was a merchant trading in a wide assortment of profitable goods, as his father had done before him, and the L-shaped house rose two storeys, gaily painted in yellow and red, a narrow end to the street with a wing jutting out behind the warehouse that shared the street end. She ducked through an archway which led into a small courtyard between the house and the warehouse and took a moment to appreciate the peace after her walk. She knocked only once on the door before Emma opened it. Lucie realized she must have been visible from within. 'I was enjoying your courtyard.'

'You may not wish to come in,' Emma said beneath her breath. 'Mother is in a fury.'

That was not unusual for Lady Pagnell. 'We are a pair, then,' Lucie said. 'But what is amiss? Is it her anger with the bishop? I thought they were about to come to a settlement.'

Emma winced. 'I thought so, too. But it is anyone's guess how long it will now be delayed. Peter heard this morning that some people are suggesting we are behind the fire at the bishop's house, that we did it in revenge for Wykeham's part in Father's death.'

'Lady Pagnell heard this?'

'Peter can be such a fool – he told me of this in her presence.'

'Oh, Emma, surely no one believes it?'

'Folk will believe what they like,' Lady Pagnell said loudly from somewhere within the house – what keen hearing the woman had – 'and the more who suffer for it the tastier it is. But you do not need to keep Mistress Wilton standing in the courtyard, Emma.'

Emma clutched her elbows with her stubby-fingered hands. 'Mother is my bane,' she said more quietly. 'But enough of her. I can guess what you are angry about. Folk are talking of nothing else this morning. What on earth was Cisotta doing at the Fitzbaldric house?'

'So far we do not know.'

'Well, come in, do,' Emma said in a louder voice, stepping back, her elegant green wool gown moving to show the pale-yellow undershift. 'You must tell me all about last night and the injured servant you have taken in.'

Lucie glanced down at her simple workaday blue gown, hoping she had not stained it while assisting Magda with Poins, or working in the shop. There was a tear at the edge of her left sleeve that she had not noticed before, a small spot on the skirt that might be blood and her hem needed a good brushing. She and Emma were both daughters of knights, but Lucie did not fuss with her appearance on workdays.

Lady Pagnell stood beneath a window, leaning over a large piece of embroidery in a frame, stabbing at it as if taking out her anger on the cloth. Though short like her daughter, she managed to be an imposing presence in the high-ceilinged hall. She wore a dark-purple gown with a matching veil over a white wimple and bib, a veil much crimped and curled and stiffened into an imposing square façade over her face. Murmuring something polite at Lucie's greeting, she feigned absorption in her needlework, as if her earlier outburst had never occurred.

At a table further back in the hall Emma's boys, Ivo and John, sat with their tutor, Edgar, writing on wax tablets as he dictated. Matthew, the Pagnell steward, sat further down the table with rolled parchments, tally sticks, and a ledger spread out before him. He did not look up at her entry, but seemed to bend his head even closer to his work. Lucie was curious about him after Emma's complaints regarding his relationship with Lady Pagnell. She had met him only once before.

'Mother has frightened the boys, talking of the rumours about our family with such anger, telling them they will be shunned by all.'

Since the tutor had paused in his lesson, Lucie felt free to offer a greeting to the boys. She remembered how painful it had been to be ostracized as a child. After the death of her mother, Lucie had been sent off to St Clement Nunnery where the sisters had watched her for signs of the weak morals they had ascribed to her mother, who had had a lover. The memory of that brought Lucie back to Cisotta and the reputation that was blinding people to the tragedy of her death.

The tow-headed boys greeted her with solemn courtesy. She had expected them to burst with questions about the fire, the rumours – they were intelligent and energetic. But after a brief acknowledgement of her presence, they both returned to their work.

While Emma drew up a bench so that they might sit away from the others and near the fire, Lucie took the jar from her scrip and set it on a small table. 'This should help you sleep.'

Emma glanced towards her mother, then shook her head slightly. 'She does not approve,' she whispered.

But it was too late. 'What is that, Emma? Are you in need of a physick? You might have said something to me. Is it for digestion?'

'If you must take part in our conversation, I pray you, join us, so you do not disturb the boys at their lessons.' Emma had flushed scarlet. 'Sometimes I think Mother has no sense,' she whispered to Lucie.

'I am busy with my embroidery,' said Lady Pagnell. 'Come, sit by me. I so seldom have a chance to see you, Lucie. There was no time to talk at the minster the other day. At least let me thank you for attending Sir Ranulf's mass.'

'My father counted Sir Ranulf a good friend, Lady Pagnell, and I remember his kindnesses.'

An opportunity to speak with both Lady Pagnell and Emma was more to Lucie's purpose than sequestering herself with her friend, though she prayed for patience in dealing with the two of them. She did not understand their conflict, but she understood that her impatience stemmed from envy. Neither Lady Pagnell nor Emma appreciated what they had in each other. Lucie did not even have a mother-in-law with whom to contend.

'We cannot very well deny your mother's request,' she said to Emma in a voice that even Lady Pagnell could not hear.

The boys' tutor directed Ivo and John to move the bench closer to Lady Pagnell. Again, they seemed reluctant to meet Lucie's gaze. Perhaps Emma had not exaggerated Lady Pagnell's negative effect on the household. As Lucie passed the long table, she noticed the steward watching her. He quickly glanced away, but not before she caught his irritated expression. She could not blame him, being interrupted in his work by all the bother her visit was causing.

'Come, Lucie, let me look at you.' Lady Pagnell held out her arms, then gestured for Lucie to pivot. 'A lovely gown. Blue is a good colour for you. But my child, how thin you are, and how pale.'

'Mother,' Emma warned.

Ignoring her daughter, Lady Pagnell continued, 'I was sorry to hear of your loss.'

This was nothing of which Lucie wished to speak to Lady Pagnell. But it was to be expected. And noting shadows beneath the widow's eyes, new lines etched on her face and her complexion less robust than usual, Lucie was reminded that Lady Pagnell, too, had recently suffered a painful loss. 'I was confined to my bedchamber so long it is no wonder I seem pale, Lady Pagnell. But I am much recovered.'

The widow shook her head. 'You are still young, do not waste your days grieving for a lost child. It was God's will. He will bless you with another if it is meant to be.'

Unable to respond, Lucie stepped closer to examine the embroidery. 'Is this for the chapel altar?' The strength of her voice surprised her. God was co-operating for a change. The cloth was narrow, a fine linen, draped over the embroidery stand and folded carefully on the floor behind. The end on which Lady Pagnell was working depicted a knight in armour sitting astride a prancing chestnut horse with black mane and tail. The ground beneath the pair was a carpet of tiny flowers. The knight's tabard was white with a large red cross, signifying a crusader.

'It is for the chapel altar. On the other end is a cross-legged knight. Though why I play to that foolishness I do not know.' Lady Pagnell's voice said otherwise.

'Father's wish to go crusading was not foolishness.' Emma spoke sharply.

Lucie prayed that she and Gwenllian never grew so distant. 'Sir Ranulf would be moved by your work, Lady Pagnell.'

'You see, Emma? Lucie does not find me heartless.'

'Do sit down,' Emma said to Lucie, 'and tell us about the fire last night.'

At last a subject of use to her. She settled beside Emma. 'I would as lief not repeat what you already know. What have you heard? Was anyone from your household there?'

'Matthew was out, but he missed the excitement,' said Emma, glancing towards the table where the steward bent over his work. 'It did not occur to him to come to the aid of the bishop.'

Now Matthew glanced up, his face moving from light to shadow so that Lucie could not see his expression, but his voice was quiet as he said, 'There were so many people in the street I thought I would only be in the way.'

'And right you were, of course, Matthew,' said Lady Pagnell. 'Emma, watch your tongue with my steward.'

'Then he should be so good as to watch his with my servants.'

Mother and daughter locked eyes, both with high colour born of anger, not health. Lucie had never witnessed such discord in the Ferriby house. Something was very wrong, but she could not believe Emma's suspicion, that the steward harboured hopes of winning Lady Pagnell. The Pagnells were too proud a family.

Lady Pagnell stabbed at the embroidery and pricked the finger she held beneath as a guide.

'You should follow your own advice, Mother. "Never place your fingers beneath your needles. The frame makes that unnecessary."' Emma did a perfect imitation of her mother's voice.

Lady Pagnell sat down on a stool beside the large frame and sucked her finger, pausing to say, 'Really, Emma, you are acting the petulant child. This is not like you.' She paused. 'As for our household helping in the fire, Lucie, I regret to say we were dining quietly here. It was Stephen's last night in the city.'

Stephen was Lady Pagnell's eldest son, the heir. Emma often complained of her brother's efforts to control all the family, so it seemed odd to Lucie that Stephen had departed for home before the negotiations with Wykeham had been completed. The manor was soon to be his own home.

'Will he be returning to meet with the Bishop of Winchester?' Lucie asked.

Lady Pagnell shook her head. 'Stephen said as he has little knowledge of our neighbour he would leave it to Matthew and me to choose what might be acceptable. I must say I was disappointed. I should have welcomed my son's guidance in this. I fear that I shall offer something too dear in exchange for the modest piece of property on which I wish to live. Stephen withdrew from the deliberations just to vex me.'

Emma had caught Lucie's eye at the mention of Matthew and made a face as if to say, 'You see?'

'It is fertile land with a stream of clear water,' said Lady Pagnell, 'and it will require an equally pleasant and useful property to wrest it from that man's clutches.'

'He was good enough to contribute to Father's outfitting,' said Emma, 'and he deserves a fair exchange. Stephen was in too much haste to return to his Pippa.' His wife was pregnant with her fifth child and could not make the journey for the funeral. 'It is not a steward's place to take part in such decisions.'

'Might I be of help?' Lucie asked, desperate to avoid another argument. 'Are any of the properties south of the city, near Freythorpe Hadden?' – her family estate.

'Some are,' said Lady Pagnell. 'Our neighbour means it for a new tenant, not himself, so it was not necessary to have it adjoining his land. Perhaps you might look them over?' She turned towards Matthew, who was in the process of gathering up his work and strapping the items together.

'That will not be necessary, My Lady. I plan to ride out to the various properties so that I might provide you with a full description of each, its prospects and amenities. It is impossible to judge such things from deeds.' Matthew was a well-spoken man, but though his words were courteous his scowl was not. He bowed, now, and clutching his bundle he made his excuses and departed by the rear door.

'Mother, you allow him to be too familiar.'

'Your father hired him, Emma. I have not often heard you question his judgement.'

To save them both from any more argument, Lucie launched into an account of the fire, of the servant Poins's wounds, Magda's remedies and this morning's gossip about Cisotta. 'Last night it seemed the fire had inspired the people of York to help their neighbours, but today they are intent on destroying her good name rather than praying for the dead and injured.'

'Amen,' said Lady Pagnell. 'They assisted in dousing the fire to save their own homes, not out of charity.'

Emma fussed with the keys that hung from her girdle. 'Can it be so bad as that?' she managed to say.

'I have heard hardly a word spoken in sympathy for Cisotta,' Lucie said.

Emma crossed herself. 'May God give her peace. She was a skilled healer.'

'Jealousy, that is what drives gossips,' said Lady Pagnell. 'I understand she was a pretty woman and dressed to be admired.'

'Mother,' Emma warned.

'She was, Lady Pagnell,' said Lucie.

'They do say Adeline Fitzbaldric is ambitious for her husband,' said Emma, 'and that is why she seized the chance to live in William of Wykeham's house rather than secure a more permanent residence.'

'What else do you know of the Fitzbaldrics?' Lucie asked. 'I had not met them until last night.'

'Misfortune follows them,' said Emma. 'They lost their son and daughter to the pestilence. Mistress Fitzbaldric was bedridden for months with her grief.'

'They do say that Lady Percy was so after her son drowned,' said Lady Pagnell. 'But you have seen how well she has refined the art of fainting to avoid unpleasantness.'

Emma nodded. 'Yet her gown is never soiled or torn.'

Lucie's thoughts had turned elsewhere.

'Do you know Lady Percy, Lucie?' asked Lady Pagnell.

As Lucie nodded, Emma asked what she had been thinking. 'You looked so sad.'

'I thought of Cisotta, how I admired her neatness. She worked so hard but always looked as if a servant had just dressed her.'

Emma and Lady Pagnell crossed themselves.

As Owen arrived at the tawyer's shop the drizzle gave way to a timid sun, glistening off the rooftops of

Girdlergate. Eudo's apprentice, a young man of perhaps twenty years, his curly hair kept from his face with a tight-fitting leather cap, was already at work at the counter that opened on to the street, softening a piece of leather by drawing it back and forth over a blunt blade set in a block of wood. A small child's plaintive cries came from the house beyond, answered by a man's angry voice.

'You are up and hard at work betimes,' said Owen. Though it was not so early now – mid-morning by the shadows in the street. It was difficult to judge time with so little sleep.

'I'd as lief work as lie abed listening to little Will screaming and my master in a foul mood. He went out searching for Mistress Cisotta. She was away the night, without leaving word that she would be so long. He came back alone and in such state – I called for a neighbour to come and help Anna quiet the boy.'

'The child is ill?'

The apprentice jumped at the sound of something heavy hitting a wall in the living quarters. A woman's voice now drowned out the boy's cries.

'Aye, a stomach complaint. It smelled foul in there last night at supper.'

Owen wondered how the lad could smell anything after spending his days working the hides, trampling them in tubs of alum, egg yolks, oil and flour. But the child's illness might explain Eudo's absence from the crowd last night at the fire. 'Your master attended the child all evening?'

'Nay, he drank and cursed the boy, shouted at Anna for being slow.' The apprentice rose abruptly as another visitor entered the shop – George Hempe, one of the city bailiffs, wearing his official livery.

Looking from Hempe to Owen, the apprentice said,

'This is no accident, both of you here. What is amiss?' He strained his neck to see the street behind Hempe, perhaps fearful of a guild searcher. Owen had noticed scrips, shoes and a belt that looked new, all items a guild tawyer was forbidden to sell.

'I am not here as a guild searcher,' Hempe said, responding to the apprentice though fixing his gaze on Owen.

'We must speak with your master,' Owen said to the apprentice. 'Would you tell him we are here? I would not walk in on his family without warning.'

The young man glanced behind him, his heading sinking down between his shoulders. 'He will want to know the matter of your visit.'

'I doubt he will ask,' said Owen.

'It is the mistress?'

'Aye, it is.' The apprentice would know soon enough.

'Mother in heaven.' The young man crossed himself. 'I feared that when he came back with such a face on him. Was it the fire?'

Owen nodded.

'Now go, tell your master we wait without,' Hempe said. His deep voice and hawklike appearance lent the slender man an authority that humbled the apprentice.

Shrinking, the young man made his way to the door, opened it and closed it quietly behind him.

Hempe picked up a shoe, turned it over. 'Pity the guilds go after Eudo as they do – this is good workmanship, better than many a cordwainer in this city.' He leaned back, nodded to Owen. 'What exactly are you about, Captain, taking in the servant, bringing word to the family, which I assume you mean to do here? You are the archbishop's man. The fire occurred outside the minster liberty. This is the city's concern.'

That was true. In following Thoresby's orders Owen was encroaching in the city bailiffs' territory. 'Mistress Cisotta died at the house of the Bishop of Winchester,' Owen reminded him.

'It does not matter. She lived and died in the city.'

'It matters to Archbishop Thoresby and to Bishop Wykeham.'

'They have no say in this.'

'I suspect His Grace has already sent word to the sheriff, the mayor and the council with Bishop Wykeham's request for this to be kept a Church affair.'

'A Church affair? Not by any stretch of . . .' Hempe stopped as the door opened and the apprentice slipped back in.

He shook his head at the two of them. 'The air is foul in there. But my master bids you enter. He says he is eager to speak with you.'

Owen followed the bailiff into a long, squat hall with a meagre and very smoky fire in the centre, a few oil lamps sputtering.

'Smells like all houses with young children,' Hempe said beneath his breath.

Eudo stood near the fire, holding a squirming, whining young boy out in front of him while Goodwife Claire, a neighbour, spread ointment on the lad's bare bottom. Eudo's eight-year-old daughter, Anna, left her place by the largest piece of furniture in the room, a dresser full of jars and bottles of Cisotta's potions, and crossed over to Owen and Hempe. She was small for her age, with little flesh on her tiny bones. But she comported herself with a mature solemnity, greeting the two men with courtesy and offering them ale.

Owen declined. Eudo might be quietly assisting his neighbour at present, but Owen had heard him earlier and knew he and Hempe were about to deal with a man at the end of his tether. Hempe was apparently of like mind.

The woman had taken the boy and carried him to a box bed in the far corner. He was quieter now, his cries softened to an occasional whimper. Eudo strode towards the guests, wiping his hands on his alum-stained leather leggings. He was dressed to work in the shop – Owen guessed he had never undressed last night. A squat man with a much creased and jowly face, ever scowling, Eudo was as homely as his wife had been beautiful, and at least two score years older than she had been.

'I want some answers, men. Are you here to give them?' Eudo pulled up a stool and straddled it, gesturing to them to find themselves something to sit on.

Anna approached, reaching out as if willing a bench to move towards them. Owen met her halfway and suggested she go to sit with her brothers while he and the bailiff talked to her father.

'When will they bring Ma's body home, Captain?' Anna asked.

So they knew. Owen crouched down and took her little hand in his. It was rough for the hand of so young a child. 'You cannot have your mother's body here, not with your brother so ill. She is being taken to St Sampson's. Father John will have parish women prepare her. But you will have your say in that, to be certain.'

She wiped her nose on her sleeve, but her tears were coming steadily.

'Anna!' Eudo shouted. 'Do as the captain said. Go and sit with your brothers, make sure they mind Goodwife Claire.'

Owen watched as the girl began to disobey, opening her mouth to ask yet another question. He was glad of

Eudo's interference – he would find it difficult to lie to such a solemn child, and he was certain she wished to ask how her mother had looked, whether she had suffered.

'Go,' he whispered. 'The little ones need you.'

Owen's knees ached as he rose, and his head pounded from the lack of fresh air and the reek of the child's sickness as well as the odours of Eudo's business. He noted that Eudo grew angry under Hempe's questioning. The bailiff's presence was most unfortunate.

'Can you tell us how your wife came to be at the Fitzbaldrics' house?' Hempe was asking.

Eudo had been sitting, one elbow on his knee, but with the question he shot up straight as a post. 'That is what you two were to tell me.'

Owen settled back on the bench beside the bailiff, picked up a child's top that lay at his feet.

'Where did she say she would be?' Hempe asked.

'She told me nothing. It is Anna she would have told, but . . .' Eudo stopped, mouth open, and shook himself as if waking himself up. 'I said such things to the children in anger last night while Cisotta lay in the burning house giving up her spirit. May God smite me.' He beat his chest and began to sob.

'We shall get little out of him today,' Hempe muttered.

Eudo might have been more forthcoming had the bailiff a less confrontational approach, Owen thought. He needed to distance himself from the man.

'What of the girl?' Hempe asked, beginning to rise.

'Let me speak with her,' Owen said. 'You might stay with Eudo in case he says anything of import.'

Anna had curled up on the box bed beside her little brother. The other two boys huddled together on the floor by her, watching Owen approach.

Crouching again, Owen placed a hand gently on the shoulders of the two boys. 'You have nothing to fear from me, lads. Your ma was a good friend.'

The boys twisted round to see Anna's response. She nodded to them. 'He is the husband of Mistress Wilton, the apothecary.' She met Owen's eye. 'I heard what you asked. Ma said she was to see someone, but she would be back early. She was worried about little Will. His stomach was already gripping him.'

Goodwife Claire cleared her throat to remind them she was close at hand, rinsing out rags in a pot over the fire. Owen straightened his aching knees and perched at the edge of the bed, facing the neighbour.

'There was a man waiting by the back door the other day,' the goodwife said. 'I did not know him. Dark hair, dressed well, but plainly.'

'I remember him,' said Anna. 'He was here when Ma and I came home. He frightened me. Ma told me to go inside.' Her eyes were swimming with tears.

Owen just nodded and gave Anna the linen cloth he carried in his scrip to dab at her eyes. Then he withdrew from the children, gesturing to the goodwife to follow him. 'How old was this man?'

'Her age, Cisotta's, I would say.' The goodwife searched his face. 'Is this important?'

'It might be. What else can you tell me about this meeting?'

'Sadly, I can tell you no more. I did not watch after that. I do not wish to know too much.'

'I don't understand.'

'She was a beautiful woman, Captain, in an unhappy marriage.'

'Are you certain of that last part?'

She regarded him. 'I heard Cisotta and Eudo quarrelling most evenings.'

'You're certain you had never seen this man before?'
The goodwife nodded.

'I am grateful for your sharp eyes. Can you stay a while for the children?'

'As long as they need me, Captain.'

Owen returned to Eudo, who was still weeping. He hesitated for a moment before drawing the belt from his scrip and asking the tawyer whether he could identify it. He did not explain its significance.

Eudo raised his head, gazed on the belt for a good long moment, reached out, drew it through his rough, tanned hands, looked up at Owen as he felt the burned edges. 'This was found at the bishop's house?' His voice was hoarse, tremulous.

'Aye. Found in the undercroft, where the fire began. As you are a tawyer, I thought you might recognize the workmanship.'

Eudo wiped his eyes on his sleeves, heaved a shuddering sigh, studied the belt. 'Nay. If I worked on such fine cordovan I would have a team of apprentices, not one.'

Owen had not noticed the quality of the leather, stained as it was and partially charred. 'What else can you tell me about it?'

'The buckle is good brass. The strap is narrow. A boy's belt, I would say.'

'So this would cost dear.'

Eudo nodded.

Owen put the belt aside. 'How did you know to go to the Dale house?'

'I went out for more ale, heard the gossip. Later, towards morning, I thought it could be . . .' He turned away, a hand to his eyes.

'Now I must ask you something far more difficult. I promise I'll then leave you in peace.'

'What peace can I have?'

Owen held out the ruined girdle. 'Was this Mistress Cisotta's?'

The tawyer's heart-rending sob was answer enough.

'Forgive me.' Owen rose as he placed the items in his scrip. It was time to leave. He did not like the bailiff's expression. If they were to argue, he wished to do it out on the street, not in this house of mourning.

In the shop, the apprentice sat slumped forward, his head on the pillow of his forearms. They left without disturbing him. Expecting Hempe to continue the argument, Owen headed towards the yard of St Sampson Church, where they might not be overheard. He sensed Hempe's hot breath on the back of his neck as he passed gossiping townsfolk who watched him with interest. Stepping out of the street, Owen felt an unfriendly hand on his shoulder and instinctively swung round. 'Never grab a soldier like that,' he said.

'The archbishop will hear from the council.'

Owen drew closer to Hempe, speaking as softly as possible. The churchyard was not as deserted as he had hoped and the bailiff's behaviour already drew curious eyes. 'The bishop was lately one of the king's chief counsellors. He has many dangerous enemies. What seems the city's concern may prove to be the realm's concern.'

'You have planned this from the beginning. That belt you showed him – what part did it play in last night's tragedy?'

It was true that Hempe had the right to know, but Owen was not about to discuss the crime in public. 'I did not say that it played any part. I found it near his wife's body.'

Even as he spoke, Owen was looking about, noticing a ripple of excitement passing through the crowd.

Down Girdlergate came a small procession, Father John of St Sampson's leading four men carrying the plank on which Cisotta's shrouded corpse lay.

'I don't believe you,' the bailiff said.

'Come to the archbishop's palace with me, if you like. But I shall not discuss it in such a crowd.'

'I shall come anon. First I'll report to the council.'

Owen thanked God for the man's sense of order.

Eight

A CONTRADICTION

The crowds had thinned by the time Owen made his way up Petergate again, but several people stopped him to ask after Poins, or about Cisotta. Speculation was rife about why she had been unable to escape the fire, whether she had been trapped, and one passer-by asked Owen whether she had injuries besides her burns. He said little, fearful that he might reveal more than he intended. One thing was certain – Wykeham would not be pleased by how much the city guessed.

Owen was saddened by the morning's task, questioning Eudo about his wife's death while not telling the truth. And yet he was uneasy about Eudo's temper. Without evidence to the contrary he could not rule out the possibility that the tawyer had killed his wife. He would not be the first spouse to lose control in an argument. They might have fought about the man who had frightened Anna. Owen resolved to post a guard at the tawyer's shop and in the yard behind his house both to watch Eudo and to protect him. It was always possible that the mysterious intruder in the

Dales' kitchen the previous night might seek him out.

Close to the scene of last night's fire, Petergate was much quieter than it had been earlier, although a few clusters of people lingered near the bishop's gutted house. The right corner of the roof had caved in – that was where Owen had seen the flames climbing when he had been inside. That entire corner was blackened, the boards burned through in places. It reminded Owen of a black lacquer cabinet with elaborate carving that he had once seen, he could not remember where. The steps to the living quarters had survived almost intact, up to the last few and the landing, where the boards were blackened and several hung down and swung gently, caught in a draft in the alleyway.

The undercroft door was gone – two wickets shoved into the opening were all that secured the remains from animals, theft, or the curious. Owen was considering where he might find a lantern so that he could ascertain whether a better closure was needed when someone joined him on his blind side. Remembering his earlier encounter with the bailiff, Owen turned slowly.

A short man with a shock of greasy hair stood beside him, hands clasped behind him, rocking slightly back and forth on his feet. 'Good-day to you, Captain Archer.'

'Good-day to you,' Owen said, searching his memory for the man's name.

'Such a fine house. It would be a pity if Bishop William abandoned it.'

'It would indeed.'

The man turned to Owen. 'Corm's the name. I live at the back of Edward Taylor's messuage.'

Now Owen remembered him, once a regular at the York Tavern, now married to a woman who embarrassed him by fetching him home when he strayed, thus training him to stay put.

'You must have said a prayer of thanks when the fire was contained,' Owen said.

'Aye. It was a night I'll not soon forget. Nor will any of the women of this parish. Are they safe, Captain?'

Here again was the assumption that Cisotta's death had not been accidental. 'Why do you ask?'

'Because of the man I saw hurry away from the undercroft.'

Owen tried to hide his excitement. 'Tell me about him.'

Corm stepped closer to Owen. 'He rushed out from the undercroft door.'

'Rushing from the fire?'

Corm shook his head. 'Nay. I cannot be certain, of course, but I do not believe the fire had yet begun. I heard voices before he appeared, angry voices they sounded to me.'

'You saw no fire behind him in the undercroft?'

'There was light, but I did not think of fire then. Later, after I carted my sacks of grain back to the house, unloaded them and returned the cart to Taylor's shed, that is when I raised the alarm about the fire.'

'What did you see then?'

'The door was ajar and smoke poured out, flames flickering behind.'

Owen backed up to the alleyway between the bishop's house and Edward Taylor's. 'You went down this way?'

'Nay, on the far side of Taylor's house, by the shed.'

'The shed to which Mistress Cisotta was taken?'

'Aye, the very one.'

'You heard voices raised in anger?' Owen wondered about that, with all the noise of the city of an evening.

'Aye. It was a quiet evening, until the fire. It was no accident, was it?' Corm rocked back and forth.

'Your tale makes me wonder. Have you told anyone else?'

'My wife, that is all.'

'I would ask you to keep it a secret for now, Corm.' The man nodded solemnly.

'Would you walk me through your movements that night?'

Four heavy sacks of grain the man had carried down the alley from the street and set them down at his door, one at a time, which was all he could manage. Long enough for a blaze to begin behind the departing man, but surely Corm would have noticed something amiss before all four bags had been stowed inside.

'Were they men's voices?'

'I couldn't say for sure, Captain, nor what they said.'

Upon turning on to Stonegate, Owen found the Fitzbaldric and Dale families gathered by the front gate of the goldsmith's house, with two of Wykeham's men standing off to one side. Except for the Dales' two daughters, who were clipping late roses, arranging them in a nosegay, it was a grim gathering. The lovely Julia Dale, looking tired and dressed in more sombre garb than Owen ever recalled her wearing, was urging Adeline Fitzbaldric to accept an armload of wool cloth – fine wool, by the look of it. Adeline wore the same gown she had worn the previous evening, damp spots revealing attempts to clean it. Her eyes were narrowed in temper, though her tone in addressing Julia Dale was cordial. The servant May stood back a little, leaning against the garden wall. Her face was sallow, slack-skinned. Owen wondered why she did not wait on the garden bench nearby. But perhaps that was not considered appropriate behaviour for a Fitzbaldric maidservant.

'Good-day to you,' Owen said. 'I hope you have

had no further trouble that has driven you from the house.'

Fitzbaldric, still suffering his ill-fitting clothes, would not meet Owen's eye, so it was up to Adeline to explain. 'His Grace has offered us shelter and we have accepted. We cannot continue to impose on the Dales. They have their family to think of.'

As I do. Owen must speak with Thoresby about moving Poins. 'His Grace is most generous,' Owen said. He wondered whose idea it had been to take in the Fitzbaldrics. Thoresby seldom mixed with the citizens of the city.

'It is better this way,' said Adeline, tight-lipped.

Julia Dale had shifted her gaze to her daughters. Tension was thick in the air. The girls had completed their nosegay and now watched Owen, bobbing their heads and blushing when they found him looking at them. Whatever had transpired among the adults, the daughters thought all this exciting. They would regret the abrupt departure of their guests.

Owen would like to talk to Robert and Julia about the Fitzbaldrics, but it must wait. Perhaps he might find them alone and expansive on the morrow. For now, as the Fitzbaldrics and their maid had salvaged nothing from the bishop's ruined house and had two of Wykeham's men to carry what little they had, Owen did not consider it his duty to escort them to the palace.

He made his farewells and departed, feeling all eyes on his back as he headed for the minster gate. Once in the close, he slowed his steps and considered whether he had the time to say a few prayers in the minster. He did not want to become so caught up in the investigation that he forgot the tragedy of last night – that a woman had perished and a man had been horribly injured. More than Owen's efforts to learn what had happened to them, they needed his prayers. Inside, in the chill dimness that echoed with the whispered prayers of his fellow supplicants, Owen knelt and prayed for Cisotta and her family, and for Poins. Before continuing to the palace he added a prayer for Lucie.

When Lady Pagnell and Emma fell to arguing once more about Matthew's behaviour, Lucie judged that it was time she took her leave. Emma escorted her out to the street, promising to pay her for the sleep powder when next she escaped from the house. She did not wish to draw her mother's attention to it by fetching her purse.

'Is Matthew not an unpleasant man, just as I said?'

'It is difficult to judge on so little evidence,' Lucie said, her mind elsewhere. 'Do you and your mother ever agree?'

Emma drew her hem away from a dog that had wandered into the courtyard, shooed it out to the street. 'Did our arguments disturb you?'

'No, it is not that. Only – you are so fortunate to have her here.'

'You mean I should honour my mother while she walks among us. I know. Father hated our bickering.' Blinking, Emma dropped her head, crossed herself.

'I did not mean to chide you.' Lucie understood how close to the surface her friend's emotions were in this time of mourning, how fragile her composure. She had noticed the solemnity of all the household. 'The boys were so quiet today,' she said.

'Do you think so?' Emma glanced back at the house with a sympathetic expression. 'They miss Father, too. He doted on them.' She embraced Lucie, stepped back to study her. 'You must have a care. Let Magda and Phillippa fuss over the servant while he is in your house. I shall pray that Owen finds another good Samaritan. You do not need the extra burden so soon after the loss of your baby.'

Emma was one of the few people who openly spoke of Lucie's miscarriage, and did not dismiss it as God's will as the older women tended to do.

Lucie pressed her friend's hand in thanks. 'Once Owen sets his mind to something, it is soon accomplished,' she said. 'I must hurry now – I promised Jasper sweet vinegar and barley sugar from the market.'

Only after she was out of sight of the Ferriby house did Lucie slow, worried about a deep, dull pain in her belly. She tried to distract herself from it by going over the conversations at Emma's house, searching for what she had gleaned. In doing so she walked past Thursday Market and down Coney Street, remembering the vinegar and barley sugar only when she crossed into St Helen's Square and passed a customer carrying a jar of physick. She was about to turn back, but thought better of it. She would send Jasper. He could do with an outing.

As Owen entered the palace garden, Brother Michaelo rose from a bench and joined him, his neat habit somehow shedding the leaves and dried blossoms that tried to cling to it. 'I thought perhaps you would escort the Fitzbaldrics,' said the monk.

'With two of Wykeham's men at hand they did not need me.'

'Ah yes. The bishop has spread his men all about the city today. Four were dispatched to bring the River-woman and her patient here. The crone came – can you believe it?'

That Magda and Poins were already at the palace was an unwelcome piece of news. The suffering man should have been left in peace for a day or two. And Lucie would take it ill, Owen was sure of it, thinking he had urged such speed. 'I did not expect them to be moved so soon. Who was in such haste?'

'Our masters. They thought it best to have them here. May God watch over us.' Michaelo crossed himself as he spoke the last words.

So be it. Owen had wanted Poins gone and so he was. Now he must make the best of it.

Michaelo flicked the hem of his robe away from a cat lying near the path. 'That wanton prevented me from hearing what Guy and someone in the Pagnell livery were arguing about the other day.'

'The cat did?'

'I'd caught her moving her kittens to the porch behind His Grace's quarters. They made such a fuss as I was carrying them back to the stables that they broke up the argument. Pity. It seemed quite heated.'

Owen smiled at the image of the fastidious monk carrying a litter of squealing kittens.

'Ah. Here come the rest of His Grace's guests,' said Michaelo.

Following the monk's gaze, Owen sighted the Fitzbaldrics and their maid approaching from the minster, flanked by Wykeham's guards. Adeline carried the nosegay from the Dales' garden, holding it at an awkward distance from her body, as if uncertain of its safety. Fitzbaldric still looked pathetic in his borrowed clothes. One of the guards carried a sack over his shoulder. The maid, pale and coughing, dragged behind all of them, carrying the cloth Julia Dale had urged on the Fitzbaldrics.

'Before I meet with them,' Owen said, 'I want to see Magda and Poins.'

'They are in the kitchen,' Michaelo said. 'A corner

has been enclosed with screens. It should be warm, and the sound of the cook and her servants might cheer the invalid.' He pressed his fingers to his temples. 'How he must suffer. I do not know how he lies so quietly. Do you think he will survive?'

'I pray that he does, at least long enough to tell us what happened last night.'

Michaelo studied Owen. 'Do you think he murdered the charm weaver?'

'I have no way of knowing that yet. I wish I did.' Owen bowed to him. 'I shall leave you to your guests.'

The morning's clouds had burned away. The midday sun felt warm on Owen's head and shoulders. Once he rounded the corner of the palace and slipped from observation, he paused, lifting his face to the radiance. If only it could burn away the scent of death on him. For several moments he stood there. When at last he opened his eyes the garden seemed bathed in a white light and as he moved into the shade of a linden he felt the sweat on his face cooling. There would not be many more days like this until spring, months away.

By the time Lucie returned to the shop there was a lull in customers, and a good thing it was, for only a few spoonfuls of the cough syrup remained. While Jasper was out at the market, Lucie assembled the other ingredients. The hocks seeds and flowers, the gum Arabic and dragagantum were all within easy reach on the bottom shelves in the shop and the storeroom, but the quince seeds, seldom used in physicks made while a customer waited, or asked for specifically, were stored on a high shelf.

Lucie hesitated – she had been fetching quince seeds when she fell. As if the memory were not enough, the cramp in her belly worsened. She rested on a stool, passed a few moments talking to a customer who bustled in – needing a toothache remedy, thank goodness. When the customer was gone, Lucie resolved that she would not spend the rest of her life fearing to climb to a high shelf. She was doing to herself what she had accused Owen of doing – assuming that once she'd had a fall, it would happen again and again.

Positioning the small ladder, she gathered her skirts and climbed, with more caution than usual and with her breath held all the way. The jar was large and smooth, and she would need both hands to lift it from the shelf. She must let go her skirts and her grasp on the shelves in order to pull out the jar. Taking a deep breath, she reached for it. Her hands were clammy, slippery on the glazed pottery, but she clutched it tightly to her side, freeing the hand that must keep her skirts from underfoot, and backed down the ladder.

Weak with relief and bent over with the cramp, she almost wept. But Jasper appeared just outside the shop door, greeting a neighbour. Catching her breath, Lucie set the jar on the counter and calmed herself by measuring out the seeds.

The kitchen sat between the two palace halls, Thoresby's and the more public great hall. Behind it, screened from the archbishop's chapel and the minster by a juniper hedge, a large oven rose out of a patch of packed earth, squat and blackened from years of baking for archbishops of York. That is where Owen found Maeve, the archbishop's cook, bent over a tray of fresh bread.

She greeted Owen with a broad grin. 'More mouths to feed.' She straightened with a sigh of contentment, wiping her large hands on her apron. 'I have made pandemain for the injured one. Easy to chew.'

'I hope he wakes to relish it. He will not have such a treat again, I warrant. No one makes bread so light as yours.'

'The Riverwoman tells me the poor man has said nothing, though he looked about him when they carried him in.'

Owen was glad to hear that Poins had at least awakened.

'How fares Mistress Wilton?' Maeve asked.

'No better nor worse than you might expect.'

Maeve clucked in sympathy. 'Tell me, what is Mistress Fitzbaldric like?'

'No more demanding than Brother Michaelo, I promise you.'

Maeve laughed. 'Go on, then, Captain. I must not keep you. Bishop William is within.' She gestured towards the kitchen.

'The Bishop of Winchester is here? In the kitchen?'

She nodded, then leaned towards him with a conspiratorial expression. 'Discussing the treatment of burns and the severing of limbs. I preferred the autumn afternoon.' She fanned her ruddy face. 'Maggots and butchering knives – such talk does not belong in a kitchen. But I shall enjoy the Riverwoman's company.' She eyed him up and down. 'You look hungry.'

'I am. And thirsty. But I have no time –'

'You have time for a cup of ale and a meat pasty, you will not gainsay me.' She nodded to a bench where a tray covered with a cloth had the inviting shape of the items she had mentioned. 'I brought it out for myself, but now I've no appetite. Talk to me for a moment while you eat. You will not digest a thing if you eat it in there.' She rolled her eyes towards the kitchen.

Owen had already settled on the bench and had drawn the cloth from the tray. The aroma of spiced meat tempted him to try that first, but with his mouth as dry as it was the food would choke him. He took a good long drink of ale. 'Tom Merchet's ale?' he asked, picking up the pasty.

'Aye. His Grace trades brandywine for ale from the York Tavern. Mistress Merchet is a stubborn bargainer.' She watched him take a bite, chew. 'How is that, then? Will that hold you until you can sit down to a decent meal?'

'It will indeed.'

'Good.' Maeve bent once more to the oven, wielding a paddle with long-accustomed skill.

Owen felt the food improving his mood. He washed the pasty down with the rest of the ale. 'How long has the bishop been in the kitchen?' he asked as he rose and brushed off the crumbs.

Maeve stood with hands on her hips, considering. 'Long enough for the bread to rise a goodly amount.'

Owen felt a lethargy in his limbs as he walked across the yard to the kitchen door. The afternoon was so warm that sweat trickled down through his hair and his clothes stuck to him. He guessed by the damp heat and the utter stillness of the air that a storm was coming. He was grateful to enter the coolness of the kitchen. Across the room, plain wattle screens enclosed a corner just beyond the one window. He crossed over the rush-strewn floor and peered round the screens. Dressed in his clerical gown, his bejewelled hands pressed to his knees, Wykeham perched at the edge of a stool, straining to watch Magda, who knelt on a stool beside Poins, applying the tanning unguent to a raw area on the man's right thigh. Poins flinched, then struggled to lift his head to see what Magda was doing. The bandage wrapped round his head and the swelling of his face made it impossible for Owen to interpret the man's expression.

'I understand that silver filings in an unguent speed the healing,' said Wykeham.

'Many claim that is so, but Magda uses no filings in wounds. They are too harsh.'

'They scour the flesh, perhaps? It would seem preferable to maggots.'

'Maggots attack only the dead flesh.'

Their tones were calm, conversational.

'If the maggots have consumed the dead flesh,' Wykeham said, 'what need have you of the unguent?'

'The salve cleans the wound and protects it while new skin is growing.' Magda glanced round at Owen. 'Hast thou come to enquire after thy houseguest?'

Wykeham swivelled, noted Owen and nodded.

Owen stepped past the screens and bowed to Wykeham. 'My Lord.'

'Captain Archer.'

Owen joined Magda. 'I did wonder at the haste with which you removed Poins. I see he wakes.'

Poins lowered his head to the pillow and turned away from them.

'Has he spoken?' Owen asked.

'He tried when he first woke. The pain stopped him.' Magda finished smoothing the salve, stepped back to consider her work. 'This is Owen Archer, the good man who gave thee shelter last night, Poins,' she said.

The patient twisted his head back to face them and grunted. His eyelids were heavy with salve, as were his lips.

'You are fortunate to have the Riverwoman watching over you,' Owen said.

Poins glanced at Magda, then over in the vicinity of the bishop.

Of Magda, Owen asked, 'Do you have all you need?'

'Aye. Go now, he must rest and thou hast much to do.'

Wykeham rose. 'I shall walk with you, Captain.'

The crinkles round Magda's eyes suggested laughter as she watched them depart.

'She is a singular woman,' Wykeham said as they entered the screens passage to Thoresby's hall. 'Confident of her skill, and rightly so, I am told, yet lacking all understanding of whence comes her gift. That troubles me.' He said nothing more for a few paces, then, 'Yet, having met her and observed her at work, I would not cast her out.'

'I am glad you recognize her worth.'

Wykeham made a sound in his throat. 'Her worth is yet to be proved.'

They paused by a door open to the garden. Wykeham stepped out and glanced around. 'Such an October day is rare this far north, is it not?'

Owen thought it an odd question. The bishop had possessed prebends in both Beverley and York, and not so long ago – he should know the weather in the shire. It revealed how seldom Wykeham had resided in either minster close.

'We treasure these last days, My Lord, but they are not so rare. Sometimes we are blessed with a mild, dry autumn through Martinmas.'

Wykeham tucked in his chin, studied the gravel path. 'Who is to be first in your questioning, Captain?'

'I think it best to allow the Fitzbaldrics time to settle themselves, so I would begin with your clerks.' Owen had only just decided that as they departed the kitchen.

Wykeham nodded. 'I shall come with you.'

When a page opened wide the bishop's chamber door, the clerk Alain hastened to greet his master and bowed

Owen in. Though Alain wore merely the bishop's livery, he still managed an air of elegance.

Guy rose from a table, setting his pen aside. He was not so elegant as his fellow, his gown bunching about his round middle, his hands stained with ink. He had lank, colourless hair, tiny, widely spaced eyes, a flat, broad nose.

After making his obeisance to Wykeham he bowed to Owen. 'Captain. We have awaited your visit.'

The bishop turned to Owen. 'My men will be more forthcoming in my absence. I leave you to them.' As the page opened the door, Wykeham took a few steps and then paused, regarding Guy, then Alain. 'Tell him all you know,' he commanded. 'Captain Archer has a reputation for bringing the truth to light. You have nothing to gain by dissembling with him.'

'Yes, My Lord,' Guy said.

Alain bowed.

'If you would not mind, Captain,' Guy said as the page closed the door, 'it will take but a moment for me to complete this letter.'

Owen nodded to him.

The guest chamber given over to Wykeham was a large room partitioned with carved wooden screens. The carving echoed the patterns in the window tracery above. The bishop's bedchamber with a small altar for prayer was furthest from the door. The section in which Owen stood was furnished with several tables, benches, a comfortable chair for the bishop and several chests. A tapestry depicting the boy Jesus with the elders in the temple hung on the wall facing the table at which Guy worked.

Owen settled in the comfortable chair.

Alain arranged himself on a bench near the table. He was a handsome man, sharp blue eyes, fair hair cut neatly about his ears and fringing his arched brows. Of moderate height, he was slender and straight-backed. He had long-fingered, delicate hands, with which he now smoothed the folds of his gown. According to Thoresby, the bishop had engaged Alain as a favour to his family, to rescue him from the clutches of a scheming woman who would have ruined his name.

After a final scratch of his pen, Guy put it aside, sprinkled sand on the parchment, shook it, then leaned away from the table to blow. 'I have just finished.' He shifted his stool to face away from the table, inclined his head towards Owen. 'Captain.'

'You have both heard of this morning's discovery, that the woman who died in the undercroft was not of the Fitzbaldric household?'

Guy nodded.

'We have,' Alain said, with a touch of irritation in his tone. 'A woman of questionable character, I understand.'

'Cisotta attended my wife during a recent illness. She will be missed.'

Alain dipped his head.

'My comrade's ill humor is his weakness,' Guy said. 'He means nothing by it.'

'Are you here to play cat and mouse with us, Captain?' Alain had reached back to the table for Guy's penknife and now began to clean his nails with it.

Owen ignored the question. 'I understand that both of you have been much at the house on Petergate, working in the records room in the undercroft.'

'Such a dungeon,' said Alain. 'His Grace wished us to record what was there, but everything was in disarray. We spent our time trying to create order so we might work.'

'Oh?' This was news to Owen. 'What records were kept there?'

'God have mercy,' said Guy, 'has the fire destroyed all trace?'

'I have not had the opportunity to make a search,' said Owen. 'But I suspect all is ruined.'

'I had not realized the extent of the fire.' Guy shook his head.

'They were records for the bishop's Yorkshire properties,' Alain said.

Guy nodded. 'Forgive me, yes, property records. We have been most concerned about them, particularly the deeds, which of course should not have been kept in such a place. When will we be permitted to survey the damage?'

'After such a fire, the undercroft must be shored up before any search begins. What other records were there besides the deeds?'

'Some accounts, letters.' Alain waved the penknife. 'Including accounts from properties no longer in my lord's possession, which explains our assignment.'

To Owen it explained nothing. 'Had you planned to come north for this purpose before Bishop William decided to escort Sir Ranulf's remains?'

'That you must ask my lord,' said Guy.

'By your questions are we to understand we are suspect?' Alain asked.

'Did either of you know Cisotta?'

Alain shook his head. 'Thank heaven, no. It is enough to deal with the fire.'

'What business would I have with a midwife?' Guy looked puzzled.

'Tell me what you saw in Petergate last night,' Owen said to Alain.

'In faith, I can tell you little that you did not see. I arrived to find a street full of people running this way and that with buckets and pots, shouting directions to the nearest wells, forming lines to pass the water along. I know few people in the city, so I cannot provide you with names.'

'And you were all the time in the minster in prayer?' Owen asked Guy.

The clerk bowed his head. 'I was, Captain.'

'Neither of you had been working in the undercroft yesterday evening?'

'We did not work there at night,' said Alain. 'Rats – I am brave about most things, but not those hideous creatures.'

He must have been brought up in a wealthy household in which he was protected from such creatures. It brought the Pagnells to mind.

'I understand you have been involved in the negotiations with the Pagnells. In fact, you delivered property deeds to them.'

Alain rolled his eyes. 'They mean to squeeze everything they can from Bishop William.'

'Were the deeds among those in the bishop's undercroft?'

'They were,' said Alain.

Owen wondered at Guy's silence in this. 'Have you also an unfavourable impression of the Pagnells?'

Guy blinked nervously. 'They have suffered a great loss in Sir Ranulf. I do not think it fair to judge them at such a time.'

'Well said.' Alain clapped his hands and laughed. 'Only the other day you were about to explode with indignation after an encounter with Stephen Pagnell.'

Guy winced. 'He is a most discourteous man. Even so, he has some cause for his anger.'

Feeling his lack of sleep clouding his thoughts, Owen hastened to conclude. He stood, leaned against the table and glanced at the parchment on which Guy had been writing. Wykeham's signature already graced it, although the bishop had not touched it. Guy must have the bishop's complete trust. Thoresby had mentioned that Wykeham had had charge of the clerk's education from the beginning and that they were as father and son.

'I cannot think how the son and heir tolerates the steward Matthew,' Alain was saying. 'I envision them spitting venom at one another over the accounts.'

'Enough, Alain,' Guy muttered, his balding pate pink with his discomfort. 'Might we have a look at the records room, Captain? See whether we might salvage some of the more important documents?'

'Resolve that there is nothing worth a cress,' said Owen.

Alain breathed a curse. 'Leather-wrapped boards and thick parchment, they do not burn so quickly. I cannot believe nothing is left.'

'You witnessed the fire,' Owen said. 'What is not ashes is sodden and unreadable, I warrant.'

'We might save something if –'

'I've told you it is not safe,' said Owen, interrupting Guy. 'But in time you will have access to what is there.' He straightened. 'If either of you remembers anything you have not told me, be so good as to send me word.'

As soon as Jasper returned with the vinegar and sugar, Lucie withdrew to the workroom behind the shop and began to make the syrup that formed the base of the electuary, standing the bowl in which she had mixed the ingredients over a pot of water so that the syrup warmed, but did not burn. As she worked she became aware of a feeling of light-headedness. Perhaps she had stopped taking Magda's tonic too soon. She should have considered how much blood she had lost. She found the jar on a shelf and mixed some in a cup of water, then pulled over a stool and relaxed with the drink, leaning over occasionally to stir the syrup. The warmth and the pleasant scent of warming sugar began to make her drowsy. She woke to find Jasper reaching past her to stir the syrup.

'It is good you were heating it in a pan of water,' he said, smiling to let her know there was no harm done. 'Would you rather stay out in the shop?'

Lucie's thoughts were muddled as she focused on Jasper.

His expression changed in an instant from teasing to worried. 'Are you unwell?'

'I am exhausted, that is all,' Lucie said, as her head cleared. Being caught nodding over her work made her feel like an old woman. Like Phillippa. She rose to stir the syrup, thanking God it had not burned. 'It is warm enough to add the rest. I shall bring it out to you in a little while.'

Jasper stood watching her for a moment, as if uncertain whether to believe her reassurances, but a hail from the shop decided him and he withdrew to see to the customer.

Lucie fell into a stew thinking about Cisotta. She must have been horribly disfigured by the fire for Owen not to have recognized her. *Merciful Mother, do not let Anna and the boys see their mother's ruined beauty.*

'Master Eudo!'

Lucie's head jerked up, hearing the tension in Jasper's changeable voice.

'Where is he? Where is the man who killed my Cisotta?' Eudo's voice was shrill, his words slurred.

'I do not know whom you mean, Master Eudo.'

'Tell me!'

Peering through the beaded curtain, Lucie saw the

tawyer, wild-eyed and flushed with rage, bear down on Jasper, who stood behind the counter. Eudo slammed his hands down on the wood. Lucie crossed herself, her heart pounding. Jasper backed away just enough to push shut the bolt that locked down the opening part of the counter. Then with one foot, his eyes still on Eudo, Jasper slid a wooden chest into the opening.

The man had no weapon that Lucie could see and Jasper was holding his own, but still she choked back a sob of fear. She must calm herself and think what to do. Eudo might come next to the house. Kate must be warned to keep the children away from the kitchen. She did not want them frightened. And Phillippa, dear God, Lucie had no idea what her aunt would do if Eudo stormed into the house.

Backing up, Lucie turned and slipped to the back door, opened it with quiet care, pulled it shut and hurried out through the garden, seeking the guard posted there. The stitch in her side slowed her for a moment, but she pushed past the pain, searching the garden for the guard who should be by the kitchen door. Finding no one, she ran round the house to the front gate, biting back pain and growing fear. She found no guard there, either.

Nine

A RAGING GRIEF

O wen crossed the hall from Wykeham's
chamber. He saw through the windows that it
was already mid-afternoon and cursed at how
much of the day was gone and he no closer to
understanding what had happened at the bishop's
house last night than he had been at dawn. That records
had been stored in the undercroft might prove
significant, but one fact seemed little reward for his
efforts. Avoiding the kitchen, he stepped out on to the
long porch connecting the two wings.

Wykeham stood opposite him just inside the
doorway of the great hall, tapping a slow rhythm with
long, slender fingers against the door frame. He was
looking off to his side, speaking to someone within.
Owen hesitated, thinking to retreat – but he was too
slow.

Wykeham noticed him and regarded him with his
hooded eyes. 'Captain Archer, I would speak with you.'

Resigning himself, Owen joined the bishop and
accompanied him into the great hall. The Fitzbaldrics
were nowhere to be seen, although the archbishop's

servants were setting up a table for a meal at this odd mid-afternoon hour. It must be for the newly arrived guests. At least that would cut short his meeting with Wykeham.

Wykeham drew Owen aside to a bench beneath the high south windows. The brief autumn sunlight had given way to leaden clouds. If the storm had come last night, might Cisotta have stayed at home, out of danger? The memory of Cisotta's corpse haunted Owen as he took a seat. His investigation had provided distance from her grisly image, as he had focused on others' expressions, tones of voice, gestures that might reveal lies, things left unspoken. But now, in this quiet moment, the horror of the deed flooded back and rendered him mute.

'Captain, are you unwell?'

Wykeham was leaning towards Owen, concern creasing his brow.

'I had little sleep last night,' Owen managed.

'You lost all colour for a moment.' Wykeham called to a servant to bring wine.

'If it is for me, I would prefer ale.'

Wykeham nodded to the servant, who bowed and hurried off. 'You must dine with the Fitzbaldrics.' He gestured towards the table. 'There will be plenty.'

The prospect of sitting at the table with those whom Owen must question dulled any hunger he might have had. 'Thank you. But I mean to talk to as many people as possible while their memories are clear.'

'Of course.' Wykeham sat back, still watching Owen closely. 'Just then, when you paled, of what were you thinking?'

'Of Cisotta, what she suffered.'

Wykeham held his eye a little longer, then shifted his gaze to the window. 'May God give her peace and may the Blessed Mother watch over her family.' He crossed himself.

Owen did likewise.

'I had not thought how painful this might be for you,' said Wykeham, 'that you might know the woman.'

'A month past she was a frequent visitor in my house, nursing my wife through a difficult time –' Owen checked himself. The bishop did not care about the details of his life, nor did Owen truly wish to share them. He took the cup offered by a servant, paused for a long drink, closed his eyes as it went down.

'It was a most horrible crime,' Wykeham said in a quiet voice. He shifted in his seat, shook out a silken arm to drape the dropped sleeve smoothly, but said nothing else until Owen set his cup aside. 'Fitzbaldric questioned some of Mistress Digby's methods.'

'Had she accompanied my old lord's army in France, we would have lost far fewer men.'

'That is where you lost the sight in your eye, I believe?'

Owen's scarred eye prickled – he did not like the way Wykeham looked at him, as if weighing what he knew of him. 'Normandy, My Lord Bishop.' *Where Owain Lawgoch is, is that what Wykeham is thinking behind that courteous mask?*

Lawgoch, a mercenary fighting for the French king, sought to prove himself truly the heir of his great-uncle, Llywelyn the Last, by leading a Welsh rebellion against English rule. It was Owen's brief flirtation with the rebellion while in Wales that he wished to hide from Thoresby.

Lucie's hands felt strange, almost numb, as she pressed them to the pain above her groin and looked up and down the street, searching for the guards. Davygate had quieted in the heat of the afternoon, though many people had found tasks they could do while sitting in their open doorways, enjoying the warm weather while they worked. Neighbours shifted on their stools and glanced her way. Suddenly she felt an arm round her. Her heart skipped a beat even though the touch was too gentle to be Eudo's.

'Mistress, what is amiss?' Kate asked. 'Are you injured?'

'Where are the children?' Lucie hurried back towards the house.

Kate followed her. 'In the hall. Why?'

Rushing inside, Lucie found Hugh sleeping on a mat, his fiery hair stirring in a gentle breeze from the garden window. Gwenllian sat beside him, resting her back against the wall, a slate on her lap.

'Take them up to the solar, Kate. Where is my aunt?'

'Tidying the kitchen. I pray you, Mistress, tell me what frights you so.'

'Cisotta's husband was in the shop looking for Poins. He is in a terrible rage. He started for the back of the shop. I think he means to come to the house.'

'He will find only Dame Phillippa in the kitchen, Mistress. His Grace has already sent for Poins and Mistress Digby.'

And the guards had thought their duty done, damn them. Lucie shook her head as Kate began to explain. 'There is no time. Take the little ones up. I shall send my aunt after you.'

Lucie found the kitchen door open. Within, Phillippa was raking up the soiled rushes. Unaware of Lucie's presence, she eased herself down with difficulty, reached for a basket, dragging it towards her and began to scoop the pile of rushes into it.

Lucie crouched down to help her aunt, cursing

herself for bringing this danger on her family. She tried to keep her voice level as she said, 'This work is too dusty for you, Aunt, and the day much too warm for such exertion. The children have gone to the solar to nap. That is what you should do.'

Phillippa patted her forehead with the back of a gloved hand. 'It *is* warm. How are Emma and her lovely boys?'

Lucie must get her out of the kitchen. 'Where is your walking cane?'

'Over there, by the table. It is of little use while I . . . Merciful Mother, you gave me a start!'

Eudo was in the doorway, his short, stocky mass blocking the light. He had lost his hat and his greasy hair stuck out in coarse tufts. His red eyes and slumped shoulders reminded Lucie of the grief from which rose his anger. 'I mean your family no harm, Mistress Wilton. I want the man who murdered my wife.'

'He is not here,' Lucie said, fearing that he would hear the tremor in her voice if she said more.

Jasper appeared behind Eudo, hands outstretched. The tawyer sensed him and rushed towards Lucie. Desperate for anything that might stop him without injury, she took up the bucket of water sitting ready for Phillippa's scrubbing and tossed it on him. As the tawyer sputtered and stumbled, Jasper grabbed his middle, pinning his arms to his sides. But anger and grief gave the man such strength that he broke away, knocking Lucie to one side, and disappeared through the door to the garden.

Jasper knelt to her.

'I am not injured,' she assured him. It was Eudo who needed comforting and her panic had merely fuelled his rage, making him more dangerous to himself. 'Where did the guards take Magda and Poins, Aunt?'

'To the archbishop's palace.'

Thank heaven. There were surely guards at the palace. Even so, 'Go, Jasper,' she said. 'Warn them!'

'You are certain you are not injured?'

'Yes. Go!'

He took off out of the door.

Lucie gathered herself up and, remembering the lamp burning in the workshop, gave Phillippa orders to lock all the doors and let no one in but Jasper or Owen. Her heart was still racing, but tears threatened as she returned to the shop.

'The viciousness of this crime makes it all the more crucial to solve, Archer,' said Wykeham. 'Such a thing occurring in a bishop's home . . .' He sucked in his breath, sighed it out as if willing himself calm. 'Were my men of help to you today?'

'Aye, My Lord. As much as they could be. But they could not explain why you had set them the task of organizing and listing the records kept in the undercroft of your townhouse.'

Wykeham hesitated, as if considering his response. He lifted a foot, studied the soft leather boot. 'We were coming north. It seemed an appropriate time to see to the matter.'

Owen grew impatient with Wykeham's vague responses. 'Did it have anything to do with the Pagnell ransom – or rather the part of the funds that went astray?'

Abruptly the bishop straightened, met his eye. 'You know of that?' He was not pleased.

'Aye, My Lord. His Grace understood that if I was to guard you, I must know from what.'

A momentary silence followed while Wykeham sat with eyes closed, his lids twitching with thought. 'I wished to have a clear record of what was stored in the house. And a few days ago I set them a further task of finding land of a certain value to offer Lady Pagnell. But His Grace the Archbishop could tell you of that – it was his desire that I do this.'

The servants whispered among themselves as they set the table. Faintly, Owen heard Thoresby's and Michaelo's voices in the garden.

'Would you be willing to walk the undercroft with me when it is shored up, My Lord Bishop?'

'I am flattered, but no. You must see – that this has happened in my house makes it likely an attempt to get to me. I should be a fool to walk into such danger.'

His sojourn as lord chancellor had taught him extreme caution.

'If you are so concerned for your safety, would it not be prudent to distance yourself from the danger, to leave York?'

'Prudent, yes. But first I must meet with Lady Pagnell and her son Stephen.'

'May I ask why?'

'You forget yourself, Captain.' Wykeham emphasized the last word.

'My Lord Bishop, you cannot insist that the fire was meant as a threat to you yet refuse to tell me why. One of York's bailiffs has already challenged my involvement.'

Wykeham looked away, quiet for a few moments. With a sigh, he said at last, 'I must convince the Pagnells that the circumstances in which Sir Ranulf died were beyond my control, that I was caught between the king's will and theirs. I must make them see that I am most grieved by what happened.'

'You have done what you could to appease them.'

'It is more than that. I believe it is my enemies, those

now close to the king, who have turned her against me. Lady Pagnell and her son Stephen have many Lancastrian friends. I intend to confront those who are ruining my name. But for that I need information.'

'You believe the Pagnells will confide in you?'

'I must try to reason with them.'

Wykeham glanced up with annoyance as Michaelo interrupted them, followed by Maeve, red-faced and wheezing.

'My Lord Bishop, forgive me,' said Michaelo.

'Captain, you must come at once,' Maeve cried. 'Eudo the tawyer is in the kitchen saying he means to murder Poins.'

Owen was well past both Maeve and Michaelo before the bishop could say anything. Weapons drawn, the guards swept into the hall and disappeared down the kitchen corridor at Owen's command.

'Be alert for companions.'

If Eudo were somehow involved with the Lancastrians, he might have support. Belatedly Owen thought to warn the guards not to attack except to save a life. He cursed the gossips of the city for telling the widower where Poins had been taken.

A great shriek came from the kitchen, an unearthly sound that sent a shiver through Owen and propelled him towards it. His heart was pounding in his throat by the time he heard the voice of Magda Digby, now raised in anger, but coherent.

His men stepped aside for him. One of the large screens had fallen, exposing Poins's area. Magda stood on a stool beside Poins's pallet, pointing a dagger at Eudo, who stood stock still at the foot of the bed, his arms spread out as if he had intended to throw himself on to the injured man. He held his head stiffly, his eyes locked in Magda's angry gaze.

'He murdered my wife,' Eudo said through clenched teeth, his jowls quivering. 'Why should I spare him?'

'What if thou art wrong?'

'They found him with her.' Eudo flicked a glance sideways as Jasper, panting, joined Owen in the doorway.

In the circumstances, Owen was not happy to see his adopted son. 'What are you doing here?'

'I came after Eudo. He'd been in the shop.' Jasper took off his cap and mopped his brow. 'Mistress Lucie sent me to warn you.'

'Go away,' Eudo shouted. 'He is mine! Away, all of you!'

'Stay back,' Owen said in a quiet voice to Jasper, then stepped forward. 'Be ready,' he said under his breath to the three men standing by him, then nodded to the bishop's pair who stood behind Eudo.

As Eudo turned to look on the bishop's men, two of Owen's lunged forward and grabbed the tawyer. He struggled in vain against the men as they bound his hands behind him.

Magda sheathed the knife. 'Thy wife's murderer will be found, thou shouldst have no doubt of that,' she said. 'Shame on thee. Thy children need thee and now thou art trussed like a game hen ready for the spit.'

Hearing the commotion in the kitchen, Thoresby opened the door of his parlour and listened long enough to catch the drift of the crisis, then commanded a passing servant to fetch his secretary. None of this had figured in his plans when he invited Wykeham to lodge at the palace while conducting his business in York. First the alienation of the Pagnells and Ferribys, then the falling tile, the fire, the murder, and now an attack in his very kitchen. Thoresby grew weary of the scandal that followed the bishop, weary of everything if truth be known. He was easing himself down into his cushioned chair when Brother Michaelo arrived, breathless and damp at the temples.

'Sit down and calm yourself before you attempt to speak,' Thoresby said. He settled back in his chair, fighting the instinct to steel himself for bad news.

Michaelo sank down in a backless chair, dabbed his temples with one of his scented cloths, cleared his throat.

'Now. Tell me what damage the tawyer has done,' said Thoresby.

'I saw little of the event, Your Grace. You might have learned more had you not summoned me.'

'Tell me what you do know.'

Michaelo described Maeve's interruption in the great hall, her account of Eudo rushing into the kitchen. 'When I arrived the man stood over Poins most menacingly, yet frozen by the Riverwoman's shriek. She stood upon a chair, threatening the intruder with a dagger.'

'It sounds as if the matter is under control.'

'Let us pray, else the man is a demon in the guise of the tawyer. Do you wish to speak to him before he is taken away?'

Torment him with questions in his grieving? Thoresby began to decline, thinking it one of his secretary's crueller ideas, but perhaps he should consider the matter. He knew that the city was abuzz with the rumour that the midwife had been murdered. It was not uncommon for a man to kill his wife, but to do so in Wykeham's house and then call attention to himself with an attack in the palace kitchen seemed too ridiculous an idea to entertain. Yet the man had broken the peace in Thoresby's palace, wanting vengeance, no doubt. He must be reprimanded, but also assured that Archer would find the guilty man and that Thoresby would punish him sufficiently.

'Yes, bring him to my hall.'

'What of the meal, Your Grace? The servants are setting up a table for your guests in the great hall. But with the state of the kitchen . . .' Michaelo lifted his hands and shook his head.

'Have a servant inform the Fitzbaldrics that Maeve will send for them when the meal is ready.'

Owen and Jasper slipped from the kitchen by the garden door. Thunder rumbled in the distance and a contrary breeze sent swarms of leaves swirling round them. The swift change in the weather chilled the sweat on Owen's neck, yet the air felt heavy. They paused at the crossing of two paths, one leading round the palace and off to the minster and the city, one to the rear entrance to Thoresby's hall.

'Are you sure your mistress is not injured?' Owen asked.

'I cannot say for certain,' said Jasper, 'but her voice sounded strong.'

'God be thanked.' Owen trusted the lad's powers of observation. 'I am grateful to you for coming to warn me.'

Jasper shrugged. 'I was too slow.' He poked at a fallen bird's nest with his toe. 'Do you think anyone would miss this?'

The prisoner and his guards would soon be in the hall.

'Take it and hurry home,' said Owen.

Jasper crouched and scooped it up. 'What will happen to Eudo?' he asked as he straightened, his hands gently cupping the nest. 'Is it a bad sign, being summoned by His Grace?'

'In truth, I do not know. Now go. Your mistress will worry until she sees you.'

Jasper nodded to Owen and set off down the path for home, his long legs covering a good distance in no time. Owen turned and entered the hall.

Thoresby and Wykeham waited in seats arranged near the hearth. The darkening day brought a gloom to the hall even with the window shutters flung wide.

'Light some lamps and close the shutters,' Thoresby ordered the servant who was trying to blend into the corner shadows. 'Have I lost all sense of time? Where is the sun?'

'A storm is gathering,' Owen said.

Wykeham sat a little back from Thoresby. In the sputtering lamplight Owen saw that the bishop's face was set in a frown befitting a judge. 'Was anyone injured?' he asked.

'No, My Lord,' said Owen. 'At least I hope that Eudo is unharmed.'

'Why such concern?'

'He has suffered enough, My Lord, and will continue to do so. It is the worst loss in a family, that of the mother.'

'Are you condoning his behaviour?'

'Not a whit. But if you punish him, you punish his children as well. My Lord,' Owen added, not wishing to be responsible for offending the two powerful men who were about to rule on Eudo's deed.

'Here they are, Your Grace,' Michaelo said quietly.

He stood aside to allow Wykeham's guards to enter. They came forward with Eudo thrust before them. He hung his head and hunched his shoulders as if hoping to protect himself from curious eyes. But it was an open room with no place to hide.

'Lift your head, Master Tawyer,' Thoresby said. Unlike Wykeham, the archbishop seemed in a gentle mood. Perhaps it was just the lamplight softening the sharp lines of his bony face.

Eudo hesitated, then lifted his head, blinking in the lamplight. His coarse, jowl-heavy face was made pathetic by the anguish in its lines. 'Your Grace.' He tried to bow, but the guards held his upper arms and his hands were bound behind him, so he could do little more than rock slightly forward.

'Unhand him,' Thoresby said. To Eudo, who made as if to attempt a bow once more, he added, 'No need. You are in mourning and sick at heart, I know.'

Wykeham leaned forward and whispered in Thoresby's ear.

Thoresby nodded. 'Was it your purpose to do violence in my kitchen?' he asked Eudo. 'Did you think to take the law into your own hands?'

'He murdered my wife, Your Grace, orphaned my children.'

'Hm.' Thoresby seemed to be elsewhere for a moment. Then he said, 'Let me remind me that your children are not orphaned while you yet breathe. And what makes you cry murder? Who has said your wife was slain by a hand other than God's?'

The very question Owen wanted to ask.

'The folk, Your Grace, I heard them in the streets. Why did she not run, they ask, and the answer is plain, I did not see it at first, but she must have been struck down before ever the fire began.'

'Do you so think of anyone who dies in a fire?' Wykeham asked.

Eudo glanced at Wykeham, over at Owen, back to

Thoresby. 'You are trying to confuse me.'

'We are trying to reason with you,' Thoresby said, 'although reason may be wasted on a man who would launch such an attack on the strength of idle gossip. Are you often befooled in such wise, Master Tawyer?'

'I – then is it not so, Your Grace?'

Owen did not like this. It was one thing to omit the detail of the strangulation, quite another to toy with Eudo's wits.

He stepped forward. 'What would you like us to do with this man, Your Grace?' He expected to be sent out of the hall, which would suit him, for he did not know how much longer he could hold his tongue.

But Thoresby sat back so that he might see Owen's face, held his gaze a moment, then inclined his head. 'Indeed.' He turned back to Eudo. 'Let me assure you that we are examining all that we can learn of the events leading up to the fire, Master Tawyer, and if we find that it was other than an accident we will hunt down the culprit and judge him with the stern hand of the law.'

'What do you care about my Cisotta?' Eudo mumbled as his tears began anew.

'We care, Master Tawyer,' Thoresby said in a gentle voice. 'Do not doubt that.' He sat back, rubbed his eyes.

Eudo hung his head.

'Untie him, men,' Wykeham said quietly.

His retainers knelt to the purpose. Once his hands were free, Eudo made good use of both sleeves to mop his face.

'Now,' Thoresby suddenly said, 'we have the matter of what to do with you.' He waited until Eudo raised his head before he continued, 'I propose that two of my men escort you home and take up a watch at your house, a watch that will be kept until such time as I judge your reason returned. In that time you shall see to your family, your work and your wife's burial, but no more. My men will escort you on the morrow to St Sampson's for the services. What do you say, My Lord Bishop?' He twisted round to face Wykeham.

The scowl on Wykeham's face spoke volumes. He was disappointed. 'He must be given some penance, Your Grace.'

'Penance. Yes. I leave that to you.' Thoresby turned back to Eudo, who stood most humbly now, his eyes glistening, his great jaw trembling. 'Do you deserve such trust?'

'God help me, I will do so, Your Grace, My Lord Bishop.' He bowed to each in turn.

That vow would stick in Eudo's throat in a short while, when Owen began to ask more questions about Cisotta's activities in the past few days, but for now it would get the tawyer home to his frightened children. Owen prayed Eudo did not take his frustration out on them. He bowed to Wykeham and Thoresby, then slipped away.

Two of his men stood waiting near the doorway to the garden, too damp from the rain to move farther into the hall. Owen had sent the pair to search the stone pile at the minster, thinking that four eyes might find more than his one.

'All we found were these bits of rubbish,' said one, handing Owen a sack. 'Nothing of use. We'll resume our search on the morrow, if it please you, Captain. We cannot do more in the storm.'

'Aye. I'll walk with you to the barracks.' Settling his cap, Owen pulled his hood up over it and bent to the tempest. While he walked he invited his anger at the guards who had abandoned Lucie to heat to a boil.

In the retainers' hall the fire circle lured him, as it

had beckoned the pair he was after. It was plain from the looks on their faces when they recognized the newcomer that they had heard of the incident at Owen's house. Making straight for them, Owen flung a stool aside that blocked his path to them and kicked over a flagon one had resting by his foot, letting the ale soak the young man's leggings.

'Who gave you permission to desert your posts, leaving my family unprotected?'

They interrupted each other trying to explain. Owen dragged one of them up by the collar and reached out to stop the other, who had begun to move sideways on the bench. 'You will take the first watch at the tawyer's house.' In the storm, it would be good for them. 'And you will not move from your posts until your replacements arrive for the night watch, is that clear?' He let go of them. 'You know the house in Patrick Pool? Good. I am going above to talk to Alfred. I do not want to see you here when I return.'

Being the top-ranking retainer living in the barracks, Alfred enjoyed the privacy of a solar room, though it was only partitioned off by flimsy wooden screens that did not keep out noise. As Owen had expected after Alfred's watch through the night and into the morning, he was in bed, though sitting up, grinning at the treatment of the renegades. Up here right beneath the roof, the rain thundered.

'They would have been looking forward to a good meal and dry beds.' Alfred rubbed his face, bringing the blood back to the sallow surface, then raked a hand through his fair, thinning hair.

'They will have their comforts in good time, but I want them miserable first. I need you to organize the watch list. We now have men here at the palace and at Eudo's house.'

'Aye, Captain. Did Eudo harm anyone in your household?'

'No.'

'Do you want another guard on your house?'

'The men will get little rest if we spread them further. Word will soon be out that Poins is no longer at my house. I shall trust to God and the gossips.'

Alfred looked uncertain.

'Eudo was looking for Poins and he found him.' It was now late afternoon and Owen's head grew heavy as he sat on the edge of Alfred's bed. 'I have more folk to see before I rest this day.'

Alfred's gaze had strayed to the pouch in Owen's hands. 'What is that?'

'Gleanings from the mound of tiles. They say they found nothing of worth, but I'll be the judge of that.'

'God go with you,' said Alfred.

An odd thing for him to say. Owen wondered whether his lack of sleep was showing.

He departed from the barracks, walking out into the storm, which he was disappointed to see was passing, the rain gentler now. The guards' punishment would not be as severe as he had wished. He must devise some further unpleasantness for the lazy pair. The earth smelled rich and loamy. Raising his eye to the great minster, he remembered scrambling on the pile of rubble. It seemed so long ago, and so unimportant now. But it was with that incident that Wykeham's fear had taken root. Perhaps he should not ignore it.

He paused in the palace kitchen to enquire how Poins had weathered the intrusion. The screen had been righted and the injured man was asleep.

'He understood that Eudo might have killed him,' said Magda. 'He stared after the men for a long while and would drink nothing for his pain. But in the end, he cried out for relief.'

'He must fight hard to survive,' Owen said. 'Does he have the will?'

'Thou knowest better than to pose Magda such a question. Only time will tell thee what Poins intends.'

'You will spend the night here?'

'Aye. A few nights, perhaps. Then Magda will teach the Fitzbaldrics' cook to watch over him.'

Owen had settled on a bench and opened the pouch. Magda joined him. A button, a battered shoe, a crushed tin cup, a penknife.

'Hast thou a use for these?' Magda was amused.

Not so Owen. He lifted the penknife towards a lamp, studied the crest carved on the sheath. 'For this, aye.' He rose abruptly. 'Perhaps I do not need Poins's witness, now I have this.'

He passed out into the strange half-light of the sun setting beneath the clouds, heading for the masons' lodge on the south side of the minster.

Ten

THE STONEMASONS' TALE

The storm had driven people into their homes, giving Lucie quiet time in the shop. While she poured the cough syrup into pots she kept hearing the tune of a Breton ballad in her mind's ear. It was the first song Owen had ever sung for her, of love and betrayal. She remembered only some of the words, picked up over time, though the language was unknown to her. It was the tune that haunted her now, filling her with sadness. She could not remember when Owen had last picked up the lute that had been her mother's. That, too, saddened her. Though the children often clamoured for a song, they grew impatient while Owen plucked and listened, adjusted the tension of the strings and plucked, proof of how seldom the instrument was played.

Her fingers must have moved with the memory and the pot she was filling began to slip in her hand. She jerked to catch it, regretting the sharp movement as her shoulder twinged, her groin ached.

She thought about the last time Owen had played the lute. She had been lying abed a few days after her fall.

He had played to cheer her, but succeeded only in making her weep. Cisotta's effort to explain to Owen how the memory of joy might sadden Lucie had irritated him, as he took it to imply that he did not know his own wife. He had kissed Lucie and withdrawn.

Setting the pots aside, she sought the open door to St Helen's Square and breathed in the damp, rain-fresh air. The storm had passed but for a fine mist. In St Helen's churchyard the stones glistened in the brightening sky. Lucie spied Jasper at the end of Stonegate talking to a neighbour. Seeing her, he waved and came running through the churchyard, his clothes clinging to him damply, his face aglow. He began at once to tell how Eudo had been captured in the palace kitchen.

Hearing how close the tawyer had come to attacking Poins, Lucie crossed herself and said a prayer of thanks that he had been stopped. Had he succeeded, Thoresby would not have shown mercy in dealing with him. But there was yet hope.

Standing on the rush-strewn floor, dripping and steaming, Jasper became aware of his surroundings, noticed Lucie's progress on the electuary – and also her tear-streaked face. His expression changed to one of concern – or perhaps embarrassment, for he did not ask Lucie what had made her cry, but instead offered to take over the sealing of the pots.

'Yes, do,' Lucie said, wishing he would ask about her tears, but understanding that a fourteen-year-old boy did not discuss such things. 'While you are busy with that, I shall explain the working of dwale to you, as I promised, how it is that the briony purges the patient of the dangerous hemlock and henbane, leaving the quiet sleep of poppy.' It was a safe topic for both of them.

The stonemasons' tale gave Owen no joy. As he left the lodge and headed back into the city he had no appetite for what he must do. But he was determined that when he stepped across his own threshold for the night he would know whether or not the falling tile had been an accident.

Walter, the assistant to the master mason, had come forth from the lodge to enquire what Owen wanted, intent on preventing him from intruding. But when Owen had shown him the penknife and explained the significance of where it had been found, Walter had escorted him into the shelter. Luke, the mason who had co-operated with Owen on his search of the pile, glanced up from the rough stone along which he had been guiding a young man's hand. Two other masons paused in their discussion of a corbel.

Walter's tone and expression were grim. 'The captain is here on the archbishop's business.' He nodded to Owen. 'Go on, then. Ask them what you must.'

Six eyes avoided Owen's. 'You know of last night's tragedy at the house of the Bishop of Winchester,' he began. Two nodded, one shrugged. 'It was the second threat to the bishop this week. The first was the falling tile.' Owen glanced round at the masons, caught Luke's eye, watched the colour spread up his face. 'You may have heard of the enmity between the bishop and the family of the late Sir Ranulf Pagnell.' Bert and Will studied the packed earth floor. 'I have evidence that someone in the Pagnell household was recently atop the mound of tiles.'

Luke started. 'But it was –' He covered his mouth.

The others glared at him.

'Go on,' Owen said.

But Luke ducked his head and would not go on.

'They cannot have had aught to do with the fire last night,' said Will.

'I have worried about our silence, though,' said Bert.

'They're just boys,' said Will.

'The new master is not like his father,' said Bert. 'He has a temper.'

'It takes more than temper to set a house afire,' Luke said.

'But what if we might have prevented the death of the midwife and the serving man's injuries?' Bert looked to Owen. 'They say he lost an arm.'

'Aye, and his burns have him in agony,' said Owen.

Bert prevailed and the three told Owen what they knew, a tale that had now brought Owen to Hosier Lane. Too quickly. He felt unprepared. Emma was Lucie's good friend, Jasper was fond of the boys. *Dear Lord, guide my speech, my bearing, so that I say what is needed, no more.*

Peter Ferriby opened the door with an absent air. 'I still do not think it wise,' he called to someone over his shoulder before he turned to see whom the evening had brought to his door. 'Well, Captain Archer. Come in, tell us the news.'

Peter was a tall, stout man with a prosperous paunch that his dark, loose robes did little to hide. He dwarfed Emma, who had joined him and now reached out a hand to Owen.

'I hope you did not expect to find Lucie here,' she said, 'for you have missed her by several hours.'

'No. I hoped to find your family together,' Owen said.

Emma gave him a puzzled look as Peter led him into the hall.

'You are come in good time,' said Peter. 'My wife and I were just debating whether either of us should attend the midwife's funeral tomorrow.'

'Cisotta was so good to Lucie,' said Emma. 'But with the rumours about my family's connection to the tragedy I fear we might be . . .'

Her voice trailed off as Owen kept moving past her to the boys, who stood near Lady Pagnell's embroidery frame. Ivo held a squirming puppy in his arms, John stood stiffly beside him studying Owen's boots with a grave face.

'The lads can guess why I've come.'

Lady Pagnell stepped out from behind her work, placing herself between Owen and the boys. 'What business have my grandsons with the archbishop's guard?'

'Lady Pagnell.' Owen bowed.

Emma had followed him. 'What do you mean, John and Ivo know?'

Owen moved so that he could see the boys. Both stared at him as if he had cast a binding spell. The puppy barked.

Peter ordered a servant to take it away. 'Are my sons in some trouble, Captain?'

Owen drew out the penknife, showed it first to the boys, then their parents, and lastly to Lady Pagnell. Ivo looked as if he were choking back tears.

'John's penknife.' Peter looked down at his son, who stared stonily back.

'I lost it,' John whispered.

'Atop the pile of stones at the minster's lady chapel,' Owen said.

Ivo, chin down, biting his lower lip, peeked over at his brother. John stood straight, meeting Owen's gaze now with a defiant steadiness. There was a tale there and perhaps not so innocent as Owen had hoped.

'That is where I lost it,' John said.

'Aye, the day before your grandfather's funeral,' said Owen.

'No, surely not,' Peter said.

'Dear God,' Emma cried, 'they *were* at the minster that day. I sent them with a message for the stonecutter.' She sank down on to a chair, leaned towards her sons. 'Did you climb the pile? All those loose stones and tiles? The masons allowed you up there?'

Lady Pagnell's silk gown rustled as she paced a few steps, then turned back to her grandsons. 'And you said never a word –'

'Mother –' Emma warned.

'How did you learn of this?' Lady Pagnell demanded of Owen.

'My men found the knife. I questioned the masons who had witnessed the accident.'

'Why go to them? If you recognized the arms you should have come directly here.' With every word she heightened the tension in the hall.

Owen turned to Peter and Emma. 'Perhaps I might question your sons in private? I merely need the details of the accident so that I might give Bishop William a full accounting.'

Peter put a hand on Emma's shoulder. She looked at the boys, at Peter, then reached a hand towards Lady Pagnell. 'Let us withdraw to the solar, Mother.'

In a surprising gesture, the grandmother turned suddenly to her grandsons, bent to kiss them on the forehead, first John, then Ivo. 'You know the captain from St George's Field. You have nothing to fear from him.' Straightening and nodding to Owen, she took her daughter's hand and progressed across the hall.

Emma hesitated in the doorway to the stairs. 'Peter?'

'I'll sit quietly in a corner, but I will listen.'

The women withdrew.

Owen accepted the compromise. 'Let us sit at the

table,' he said to the boys. He settled across from them. 'Where is your tutor this evening?'

'On an errand for Ma,' said John, clearing his throat afterwards. He was a stout lad with a round face, rosy cheeks, and pale brows and hair.

'And Matthew, the steward?'

'He rode out to a property Bishop William has offered Grandmother.'

'It is a serious matter, this negotiation between the Bishop of Winchester and your family,' Owen said. 'You are both aware of its importance?'

Two fair heads nodded. Ivo was slender, dark-eyed and browed, though his curly hair was as pale as his brother's.

Owen set the penknife down on the table between them. 'It is a fine knife. You must have regretted losing it.'

John nodded.

'Suppose you tell me how you came to lose it where you did.'

Again, John was the speaker, folding his chubby hands on the table before him. He focused on them as he precisely enunciated his tale. After delivering their mother's message to the stonemason the boys had stopped to watch the masons at work on the lady chapel.

The masons and their apprentices had been friendly, answering all their questions. But as the shadows lengthened John had warned Ivo that they must return to their lessons – they'd had leave only to deliver a message to the stonecutter who was polishing their grandfather's tomb for the funeral the following day. Ivo had argued that he was learning far more than he would in a day's work with their tutor. After John issued a second warning, Ivo requested one last thing: that they climb up on to the hill of stone and tile, for they would then enjoy a view that no one would ever see once the chapel was complete. John turned to the masons for permission.

Luke had told Owen that he was against it at first, thinking it too dangerous, but Will and Bert had argued for the boys, reminding their fellow that some of their helpers were not much older and he thought nothing of sending *them* scrambling on the pile. So Luke had agreed.

The boys climbed the pile, with one of the apprentices calling out advice about the best footholds, and once at the top they took turns attempting to stand, but gave that up when Luke shouted a warning that some of the tiles at the edge had begun to shift.

The boys dropped to their knees, then sat down to enjoy the view, and the masons and their crew left them to their play, forgotten until Bert, working higher on the scaffolding than the others, called out that the Bishop of Winchester approached.

'Did the bishop hear him?' Owen asked John.

The boy shrugged. 'If he did, he chose not to raise his eyes to us, nor did he hesitate.'

The lads lay flat on their bellies and began to slither forward to see the bishop pass by.

'The tiles started moving beneath us,' said John, 'and one began to fall. Someone cried out for Bishop William to drop down, and he did so, dropped to his knees, covering his head with his hands. He must have heard the stones, too.'

'So more than one fell?' Owen asked.

'I think only one went all the way,' said John. 'Then the pile shifted and settled.'

Bert had described the boys splayed atop the mound like they were clinging on for life, though John made little of it.

'And then the bishop was surrounded by guards,' John continued, 'and the masons said nothing. Later they said that since the bishop was unharmed, there seemed no need to expose us to questioning.'

John's account followed the masons', though the boy added some small details, such as Ivo's inability to control his bladder as he lay flat on the pile, a weakness he related with much blushing on Ivo's part, and his own loss of the penknife as they scrambled off what they then understood was a dangerously unstable mound.

'Why did you not tell us?' Peter cried. 'How could they allow you up there?'

Owen turned to Ivo, with whom he had much more eye contact than with the stolid John. 'Do you agree with your brother's account?'

The boy nodded energetically. 'It was as he said.'

Owen believed him – so far. But John's dispassionate accounting was disturbing.

'I am sure you have been taught to own your errors, face your penance with good grace, eh?' Owen paused, waited for the nods, which were slow in coming. 'Why then did you not climb down and admit to the bishop what had happened?'

Ivo was increasingly uncomfortable, pressing his arms against his sides, playing with a button just above his belt. 'I was frightened. Bishop William is a wicked man.'

'Who told you that?'

Ivo glanced over at his brother with a look of dread. John did not acknowledge him.

'It is a simple question, Ivo,' Owen said. He caught the boy's eye, held the gaze.

'He heard it from my mother-in-law, to be sure,' said Peter from behind them.

Ivo nodded. 'And I was afraid,' he mumbled.

'No doubt you were. But if the falling of the tile was truly unintentional, I think the bishop would have believed you. He had no cause not to.'

'Will he have us put in the stocks on Pavement?'

'I do not think so, Ivo.'

The boy sighed.

'And you, John.' The elder boy raised his eyes to Owen. 'Why did you not speak up after the accident? Why did you wait for someone else to reveal your part in the incident?'

The elder boy covered a nervous cough with a trembling hand. 'Dropping the tile was an accident. We had no purpose in climbing the pile of stone but to see the view.'

'Answer the captain's question,' Peter said, in a quiet but firm voice.

The boy glanced back at his father, who nodded to him.

John took a deep, shivery breath and, pressing back his shoulders, faced Owen squarely. 'All the time we waited for Grandfather to come home, thinking King Charles refused to negotiate, the bishop was offering him only half the ransom we sent, so little he insulted him, while the bishop spent the other half on his palace in Winchester.' He paused for a breath. 'For the suffering he has caused our mother, he deserves punishment.'

'Dear God,' Peter groaned.

Owen observed the boy in silence for a moment, then turned to Ivo. 'Do you agree with your brother?'

The boy pursed his lips, looked down at his hands. 'Aye, Captain. My family has been wronged.'

'You have no need to lie for me,' John said evenly. 'Ivo thought it was cowardly. But I am the eldest and he follows me. He would have told the truth of the matter that very day if I had not sworn him to secrecy.'

'Tell me this, John. Had the bishop been injured, would you still have stayed silent?'

'No.' John shook his head. 'No. Because then my family might be blamed for it.'

'But your family has by rumour been blamed for what happened.'

'The bishop was not hurt. And no one believed that a Pagnell would have left it unfinished.'

'They did believe it, John, they did,' Ivo cried. 'You heard what Grandmother said.'

Now John's reserve began to crack, colour rose in his cheeks. He was a stubborn lad, set in his opinions. True heir to Lady Pagnell. He turned to his brother. 'Well, now it will be all the worse.'

Ivo looked up at Owen. 'The bishop will let it be known that we dropped the tile?'

'I cannot think what purpose it would serve him. Still, I cannot speak for him.'

'It would serve him to darken the Pagnell name,' John said. It seemed a bitter attitude for one so young. 'He let my grandfather die.'

'It is for your elders to deal with the bishop.'

Peter came forward, shook his head at the boys. 'Go up to your mother now. I have heard enough.'

The boys stumbled out to the stairway and disappeared.

Up in the solar, Lucie and Phillippa had two gowns out on the bed, discussing which Lucie should wear to Cisotta's funeral on the morrow. Her light-blue one, the better of the two, might seem too cheerful for such an occasion, but the dark-blue was missing several buttons near the waist, where she had stressed it while pregnant. She did not want to spend the evening sewing on buttons. She had hoped to rest a little, talk to Owen of his day and hers.

'Sewing on buttons is a chore I can yet manage,' Phillippa offered. 'I must tidy my better gown. I so seldom go out, folk will be curious, they will inspect me and I do not want them to think I am no longer presentable.' She patted her cap as she said it, smoothed her apron. 'A few buttons will not take me long to sew.' Her face was alight with anticipation. It seemed to Lucie that the elderly took funerals in stride.

Phillippa's words gave her pause. She had not considered the possibility of her aunt accompanying her to the funeral. She had planned to go early in the morning to Eudo's so that she might help ready the children. It seemed the least she could do. But her aunt dragged one leg a little and, though not as much as a year ago, still she was a slow, awkward walker, dependent on her cane for support, having much to do to watch where she placed her feet and what she needed to avoid with the rest of her body.

'I thought to help Cisotta's children dress in the morning,' Lucie said. 'Can you manage the extra distance?'

'I can, and I shall be happy to be of use.'

Jasper appeared, carrying a lighted lamp. 'Kate asked whether you want to eat with the children or to wait until the captain is home.' He set the lamp on a shelf by the door.

Lucie wished to dine with Owen so that she might ask what was to become of Eudo and whether anything yet pointed the finger of guilt towards a particular person, and so she told Jasper.

'Could I join you at dinner? I would hear the captain's news,' Jasper said.

'Of course you may.' Lucie tucked a lock of his straight, fair hair behind his ear, but it slipped out at once. 'You thought quickly today, bolting the counter, pushing the box in Eudo's way. And I saw you were ready to fight him when you followed him to the kitchen.'

Jasper ducked his head, a boyhood gesture she seldom saw these days. 'I did not want to hurt him, but I could not let him hurt you, or any of the family.'

'I was thankful to have you there. Go now, tell Kate not to wait for us.'

Lucie noticed how dark the house was beyond the doorway, wondered at Owen's delay. By now he must be tripping over his own feet with weariness. Gathering the darker dress, she offered to carry it down to the hall for Phillippa. 'I am on my way there, it is no effort. I mean to sit with Gwenllian and Hugh while they eat. It has been a confusing day for them.'

Cursing himself for spending hours unravelling an accident, Owen stood in St Helen's Square debating whether to go into the house or to keep on walking. Everything seemed more muddled than ever. What he needed was a quiet hour in a corner of the York Tavern with a tankard of Tom Merchet's ale.

Bess Merchet was near the public door of the tavern when Owen entered. Already the room buzzed with voices. 'You look in need of ale, my handsome friend,' Bess said. Her dusty red hair had escaped from her cap in tendrils that clung damply to her neck and cheeks. She freed them with little flicks of her fingers.

'Sleep is what I sorely need, but ale will do for now. I could pour it myself, if it please you.'

'Go through to my parlour. I shall fetch us some ale.'

Companionship was not what Owen had planned,

but at the moment he could think of no one with whom he would rather discuss the day. Time and again Bess Merchet had proven a trustworthy and helpful confidante. So he moved on to the kitchen and slipped behind a screen to an alcove with a small table and two high-backed chairs – Bess's parlour. He took his own tankard and Bess's down from the top of a cupboard.

In a moment she joined him with a large pitcher of ale. He poured while she fussed with her sleeves, taking off the cloths that protected them, pushing them down, buttoning one, then the other. She lifted a hand to her cap, thought better of it and let it be. She took a drink, then settled back, arms crossed, nodded to Owen. 'In need of sleep, you said. Was it the fire that kept you awake last night? Or the wounded man?'

'Both. My head was too full to settle. Tonight might be much the same but that I'm too tired to think any more.' He told her about his day.

Bess made sympathetic noises throughout his accounting and took a long drink when he was finished. Owen drained his cup and sat staring at the table for a few moments, letting the ale numb him.

'You are wrong about a day wasted,' Bess said. 'Now you know you need not worry about the tile. To think those lads made such mischief. Ferriby's is a joyless house this night, I warrant. How is Lucie?'

'Better until she found this in my scrip when she was dressing this morning.' Owen drew out the girdle. 'It was she who identified it as Cisotta's. It fell from her as she was pulled from the burning house.'

'Oh, my poor lass,' Bess said, fingering the ruined leather, the charred beads.

'Lucie took it very hard.'

'Aye. God has much to answer for of late.' Bess lifted the girdle and turned it over and back so that the glass beads twinkled. 'I recall how this caught the light as Cisotta walked.' She laid it on the table, pushed it towards Owen. 'Was it murder?' she asked, her voice catching. 'Is that why you are so grim?'

'Aye.'

They were silent a moment.

'You are one of the few who know,' Owen said as he tucked the girdle back in his scrip.

'I shall keep my ears pricked, my tongue silent.' Bess sighed. 'To hear some talk of her, well, they were jealous, eh? Beautiful and gifted. Some folk cannot bear another's fortune. The gossips had never crossed her threshold, seen the state of Eudo when he was not insulting someone in the shop, watched poor Anna minding the children while struggling for breath. No wonder Cisotta cheered herself with bright colours.'

Owen had not been aware how well Bess had known Cisotta. 'Jealousy, aye, I believe it. But can you think of anyone who hated her enough to murder her, and so brutally?' He drew out the other belt now, handed it to Bess.

She set it down on the table and tilted the buckle towards the lamplight, ran her fingers along the leather. As Owen explained how he had found it, she pushed it aside and withdrew her hands, clenching them to her breast. 'I cannot think who would have done such a deed.'

'Do you recognize the belt?'

'Sweet heaven, I see many buckles in a day, I cannot remember them all.' Her fisted hands and red eyes belied the brusqueness of her response.

'Forgive me. I did not come here to torment you. I had intended to sit in a corner with a tankard and my thoughts.'

Bess leaned on one elbow and with her other hand

stroked the wood in front of her, as if smoothing away the waters to see herself. 'What you need to hear is the rumours about Cisotta, God give her peace.'

'That might help,' Owen said.

Bess pushed the belt towards Owen and shivered. 'I have it well in my head now, put it away, I would not look at it more. If I see aught like it, you will know.'

Owen removed it from her sight.

'Many folk feared the charms Cisotta wove,' Bess said.

'She wove what they requested.'

'Aye, the problem was the charms she called her fending charms – some considered them curses. Knowing that, they feared she might curse them some day. I do not think many folk believed it of her, but there was talk.' Bess watched Owen over the rim of her tankard. Setting it down on the table, she added, 'I disappoint you.'

'I see no passion in that, nothing that could lead to such a murder.'

'Passion. As for that, wives did not like the way their husbands eyed Cisotta.' Bess gave Owen a weary smile as he began to ask a question. 'Had they cause to distrust her? Now and then she strayed from Eudo, I think. I do not know how she kept it quiet – her lovers must have been a loyal few. It is possible a woman might have had the strength to strangle her.'

Owen instinctively touched the patch over his left eye, thinking he knew well what a woman was capable of. 'It is not a woman's belt.'

'It is small, though. Is this all of it?'

'You saw how the edge was burned. I do not know how much longer it was.'

Tom called to her from the tavern. Bess pushed her

chair back. 'Can't leave my husband alone all the evening.'

'Just one more question. One of the bishop's clerks claims to have eaten here last night, then departed with all the others to help with the fire. Alain. He would have been . . .'

'Handsome and almost as tidy as Brother Michaelo.' Bess nodded.

'Aye, that would be him.'

'He sat so straight and ate so well I did not believe he could truly be a cleric, but his hands are soft and elegant, and he owned he was part of Wykeham's household. I thought better of him for joining the others who rushed out to the fire. He did not hesitate, though he is a stranger here.' She touched Owen's shoulder gently as she passed. 'Sit here as long as you like, have some quiet. We must find the man who did this terrible thing.'

Owen felt his energy ebbing. He should go home. But he could not bring himself to waste the gift of peace, something he had enjoyed precious little of since Lucie's accident – even longer, now he thought about it, with Jasper's occasional threats to ask to be accepted into St Mary's as a novice, Dame Phillippa's incoherent days, Gwenllian's stubbornness, Hugh's delight in disappearing and sending the entire household searching the streets, and most of all Lucie's difficult pregnancy, for it had given her far more discomfort than her earlier ones. Now and then he missed the simpler days, when he was captain of archers and his men all jumped at his command. Owen pushed his tankard aside and rested his head on his arms.

Eleven

NIGHT THOUGHTS

By the time Owen returned, the children had been tucked in for the night and Lucie had run the gamut of emotions about his absence from irritation through anger to fear, the latter having won out. Phillippa had given up and eaten with Kate, then gone to bed. Jasper was not so easily discouraged, though he sat nodding across the table from Lucie. When Owen stepped into the lamplight Lucie saw the deepened lines on his forehead and down alongside his mouth, the shadows beneath his eyes, the slump of his right shoulder, where an old wound bothered him when he was weary, and she tried to hold her tongue about the guards who had disappeared when she most needed them.

But she snapped when he gathered her into his arms and she smelled ale on his breath. 'All the while I worried and prayed, you were drinking?' Hearing her own voice, she hated herself for sounding like a shrew, but the words were out, there was no taking them back now.

'You know what I have been about, my love.' Owen's

voice was gravelly with a long day of talking. 'Let's not quarrel over the time. The day began badly – if I can even consider yesterday to have ended.' He drew up a stool near the brazier at the end of the table, doffed his cap and shook out his hair, which was curled from the damp. Lucie took the cap, asked Jasper to help Owen with his boots. 'You know I slept precious little.' He leaned back to brace himself for Jasper's tugs. 'In truth, I wanted to put my thoughts in order so that we might talk of what I have heard today, so I stopped at the tavern. But I fell asleep where I sat. Bess just now discovered me and pushed me out of the door. Jasper said you were unhurt. Was he wrong?'

'No, Eudo pushed me aside and I stumbled, but I was not hurt.'

One boot dropped with a thud.

'God's blood that feels good,' Owen said as he lifted the still booted foot to the boy.

'I was so frightened for Jasper,' Lucie said. 'Eudo was so angry I did not know what he might do. I ran for the guards, hoping they might scare him into his senses.'

Owen rubbed his hands over the brazier. 'They should not have deserted their posts. They will be punished for it, do not doubt it.'

Lucie noted how he kept his eye averted. He sensed an argument in the making. 'I should not have spoken to you like that,' she said.

He glanced up, nodded. 'My arms make a sorry pillow. I have suffered for my truancy.'

'We have not yet eaten. Have you?'

'You waited for me? No wonder you were angry. Jasper, too?'

Lucie called after Jasper, who was headed for the kitchen with Owen's boots. 'Ask Kate to serve us now. Come, sit with us.' To Owen she said, 'He is anxious to hear what happened after he left the palace, what is to become of Eudo.'

'I can eat in the kitchen,' Jasper offered.

'No, eat with us,' said Owen. 'Then I need tell my tale but once.' When Jasper had disappeared through the door, Owen leaned over to take Lucie's hand. 'I confess I am glad to be rid of Poins tonight. Perhaps at least the time we are together will be peaceful.'

'Aye.' She kissed his hand. 'How is he?'

'Much the same, despite Eudo's intentions. Are you not relieved to have him gone?'

'I am, my love.' Lucie knelt beside him and kissed him warmly.

Jasper and Kate interrupted them with a steaming pot of stew, two trenchers of brown bread a few days old and a pitcher of ale.

'The ale is from Tom Merchet,' said Kate. 'He brought it over – said you had little chance to drink at the tavern tonight.' She bobbed a curtsy. 'I'll go up to the children and see that they are not a bother to Dame Phillippa.'

Lucie, Owen and Jasper talked as they ate.

Owen recounted his altercation with George Hempe, the bailiff. 'We shall hear more from that, I warn you,' he said in such a weary tone that Lucie wondered he did not speed his meal and seek his bed.

But Owen waited until Jasper could no longer keep his eyes open, then suggested to Lucie that they take the remainder of the ale up to their bedchamber. Sitting on the bed, sharing the last cup, they spoke of the storm, and the cost of the sweet vinegar and barley sugar at the market. As Lucie was beginning to think Owen would fall asleep with his next sentence, he perked up a little, downed the rest of the ale and told her what he had learned from the masons.

'Ivo and John were the culprits? Merciful Mother, what were they thinking?'

'They were having a bit of fun and were not thinking. It is the masons I fault, they should have spoken up at once.'

'They would have saved themselves much trouble, for now Wykeham will wonder at their silence.'

'Did you have any sense that Emma was worried about the boys?'

'I saw no sign that she knew of it. But I had noted that John and Ivo were unusually subdued and solemn today. Emma ascribed it to their missing Sir Ranulf.' Lucie thought of Gwenllian, how anxious she became about hiding anything from her parents for long, her imagination creating a far worse punishment than a parent could bear to inflict. 'What must the boys have suffered, isolated with their secret? They must have been affrighted – and no one to comfort them.'

Owen set aside the cup, rubbed some salve into his scarred left eye, a little more into the puckered skin on his shoulder. 'Aye. Peter seemed most worried about their silence.'

'What did he say?'

'He fears Lady Pagnell is poisoning the boys' minds. He asked whether I would tell the bishop. Which I must, of course.'

'Of course you must.'

Owen slid down on to the pillows.

'I am more sorry than I can say for my temper this evening,' Lucie said, slipping down beside him.

Owen pulled her to him. 'And in the morning I face Wykeham with the tale – *after* Cisotta's service.'

'You will attend?'

'Aye. I loved her for what she did for you.' Owen kissed Lucie on the neck.

They lay quietly for a moment.

'What *will* the bishop do with John and Ivo?' Lucie asked.

'I pray that his abiding interest in the education of boys will guide his decision.' Owen's voice had softened to a rasping whisper. 'I must sleep.'

Lucie settled her head in the crook of his arm, enjoying the warmth of his body.

A dog barked outside, a church bell tolled, fiddle music drifted from the tavern next door. When Lucie had first come to the city from Freythorpe Hadden to live at the convent of St Clements the night noises broke her sleep, or if she did not waken they grew and invaded her dreams. The bells swelled, filling the sky; faces thrust out from the walls screaming and shouting curses; animals with teeth bared chased her down endless avenues of trees. She had not expected ever to grow accustomed to the night sounds of the city. Now she found them reassuring, a sign of life, the promise of tomorrow.

It was also oddly comforting to have Owen fall asleep before she did – a touch of normality in a hideous time – but Lucie had hoped she would sleep well tonight. She had been up since before dawn, more active than in many a day, yet although the pain in her lower abdomen had eased with several cups of wine and her body was heavy with fatigue, her mind spun through the previous night and the day past, round and round, as if by frequently circling past her anxieties she might control them.

She folded her hands and whispered a 'Hail Mary', and another, but by the third prayer her mind was wandering again and her cheeks were aflame.

Pushing back the covers, she sat up at the edge of the bed, dangling her feet over the side. As she slid down to touch the cool floor she felt a warmth between her legs and all at once realized what she had been feeling – her flux had begun once more. How her fear had blinded her. Smiling to herself, she pulled a shift over her head and draped a wool scarf over her shoulders. She must fetch a rag to absorb her flow. Then she would make a warm tisane of gaitre berries and wild lettuce to soothe the cramps, perhaps adding a little valerian to help her sleep.

The stair landing was dark. She felt her way down and was crossing the hall to the kitchen door when the hairs on the back of her neck prickled. The door that led to the street stood ajar. No one in the household used that door at night. The privy was in the other direction, out behind the kitchen. Remembering the prowler frightened away from the Dales', Lucie held her breath, pressing her hands to her heart to muffle its pounding. She could hear no one in the hall, but if anyone was within they would be able to see her most clearly, for the moonlight spilling in from the doorway picked out her pale linen shift as if beatifying her. But now, from beyond the open door, she heard gravel crunching in an uneven rhythm, and a softer susurrus. Staying low, she crept towards the open door, pressed herself against the wall beside it, then peered out. A woman in a dark gown paced back and forth on the path to the street, limping a little and speaking in a soft voice. It was Phillippa, sleepwalking.

Lucie crept out through the door, moving into the shadows beneath the eaves while she waited for her heart to quiet.

'. . . riding at night. So dark. He has fallen from his horse. He is lying somewhere, bones broken. I must send Adam to search for him.'

Lucie stepped on to the path and called her aunt's

name softly, then took her arm and led her into the house.

Thoresby lay in bed listening to floorboards creak, shutters rattle, a door slam shut somewhere in the palace. The page who slept near the door wheezed in his sleep. What an irony it was that in old age, when one's body yearned for rest, one slept but a few hours at night. Which led to drowsiness by day, nodding off while listening to a speech, while sitting in the garden, while praying. There were sleep potions, of course. Thoresby prided himself on never having used them, but to everything there was a season. The Riverwoman must know many sleep cures. He might speak with her on the morrow.

For now he rose, slipped a simple gown over his nakedness, padded over to the small altar in his chamber, knelt on the prie-dieu, bowed his head, closed his eyes. 'Our Father, who art in Heaven . . .'

The page's snoring forced Thoresby's prayer into an unaccustomed rhythm. Irritated, he left the prie-dieu and bent over the sleeping boy, prodding his shoulder. The lad flung out an arm in defence. Thoresby caught it. 'Accompany me to the chapel for prayer,' he commanded. He let go of the page's arm, seeing him wide-eyed and struggling to sit up, and went in search of his sandals. His preference for the open shoes was just another indignity of his advanced age. Of late his feet swelled horribly by evening and his toes had begun to twist at the joints. Sandals were easy on his aching feet, though he did not wear them when anyone outside the immediate household was about.

By now the page awaited him at the door, lamp lit, a light cloak over one arm, for Thoresby's old bones, he guessed. His increasing frailty had been noted, though never mentioned. Down the corridor their footsteps whispered, through the hall past sleeping servants, out on to the porch, where Thoresby assured the guards all was well, through the great hall and into the screens passage.

The page stopped suddenly by the door leading to the chapel. 'Someone has passed through here, Your Grace,' he whispered. 'I smell lamp oil. Shall I inspect the chapel first?'

This business made everyone edgy. 'We have a house full of guests, including several clerics, as well as those of our household. I do not wonder that someone is there before me.' It had been a long time since Thoresby sought out the chapel for his night prayers.

The page pushed open the chapel door. Inside, one of Wykeham's clerics knelt before the altar. Guy – the name seemed inappropriate for a cleric, yet he seemed by far the more devout of the two, praying in the minster all last evening, the chapel tonight. Thoresby knelt down beside him. Guy glanced up, bowed his head in obeisance. Thoresby acknowledged his greeting, then, dropping his head in his hands, turned his mind to Sir Ranulf Pagnell.

The death of his old friend weighed on him with a heaviness for which he had been unprepared. He had been fond of Ranulf, had been humbled by his piety, admired his goodness. But they had often been out of touch for years at a time. Thoresby did not understand why he felt such a void. It had occurred to him that God had given him this pain for a purpose, perhaps to draw his thoughts to the example of Ranulf's life, one well lived in God's grace. And so his prayers for Ranulf were meditations on his friend's goodness.

In comparison, Thoresby found his own life lacking. He had accomplished some, perhaps even much, good, but more often than not he had been irritated by the necessity of breaking from his routine to see to others. Yet there had been a time, not long ago, when he had assisted in feeding the poor outside St Mary's Abbey at least once a month and he believed his commissioning of a catechism in the vernacular would reach many lay souls. These days he did little more than what was necessary as archbishop. He lived quite a solitary existence. His household had once been large and noisy – knights, clerics, wards, their tutors, visiting dignitaries, retainers – which was only proper in an archbishop's palace, and he had been full of plans for reaching out to more of the faithful. In the past few years he had interacted little even with his wards, dining with them when he was at Bishopthorpe, seeing them in his parlour when they needed permission to travel or receive guests, conferring with their families on occasion, but he left their education to their tutors, a trio he paid more than they could possibly be worth. Perhaps he should give his wards more of his attention. Wykeham had tutored Guy closely as a boy and the man had grown into a devout, efficient member of his household.

He glanced over to the balding Guy. His two shortcomings were that he mumbled and that he overindulged at the table. No wonder he sweated so – even now, in the chilly chapel, the lamplight reflected off a sheen of sweat on his forehead and upper lip. He would die young with such bad habits.

Alain was another matter, fastidious in person and speech, and yet lacking the solidity Thoresby sensed in his fellow clerk. Alain had not been educated in Wykeham's household.

Thoresby's thoughts had strayed far from his purpose, and his hands and feet were chilled beyond his ability to ignore them. Giving up the effort, he woke his dozing page and headed back to bed.

Lucie had stoked the kitchen fire, heated water, and now sat in the warmth and light, her head bent over the steam from her tisane. Phillippa had been too distressed and disorientated to climb the stairs to her chamber, so Lucie had guided her instead to the kitchen, coaxed her into drinking a cup of wine laced with valerian, then made her comfortable on the pallet on which Poins had lain the night before. It hardly seemed possible that the woman lying there in such state had spent the afternoon stuffing the pallet with clean straw, sweeping the old rushes from the room, scrubbing stones, putting down fresh rushes and dried herbs. Firelight flickered over Phillippa's pale, bony face. Her mouth was pressed tight, her brows drawn down in unhappy thought, even in sleep. She had confided to Lucie how much her spells frightened her – and how humbling they were. They had struck her less often of late and Lucie had hoped that perhaps she was free of them, though she had not believed, as Phillippa did, that it was Cisotta's charm against elf-shot that had driven away the confusion. She wished the charm had worked. To suffer such confounding of one's wits in old age seemed a cruel ending.

Phillippa was given little reward for her unwavering faith in God. Magda was not so afflicted, despite her refusal to step foot in a church. But at least Phillippa had been blessed with a longer life than Cisotta.

Dear Cisotta, God grant you peace.

Lucie had tried all day to push away the image of the cold, hard buckle pressing into Cisotta's throat. But such horrors gained strength in the middle of the night. She imagined the man seizing Cisotta – had he come from behind? He dropped the belt over Cisotta's fair head. She reached up, opening her mouth to scream, but he pulled the belt tight. She clutched at the air, at her throat, slipping down all the while. Now the man's face was exposed – it was Poins.

If he is guilty may his pain torment him this night.

But if it was not him – no, Lucie was certain. That was why God had so punished him.

Lucie's hands were shaking, her heart racing. Her stomach ached and where the discovery of her flux had given her joy only a while ago, now she feared it for the disappointment it would bring. For surely, surely she grew too old to conceive and bear a child through all the long months. It would have been better had her flux not returned, better not to hope again. She set the cup aside, still half full, and dropped to her knees. *Heavenly Mother, Holy Mother of God, show me what to do, help me banish this despair, quiet my devil.* She buried her head in her arms and wept.

Something brushed past her elbow, and again. A cold nose nuzzled her hand, a rough tongue licked it. Lucie sat back on her heels and Melisende climbed on to her lap, butted her head against Lucie's chin. Gathering the skinny elderly cat in one arm, Lucie eased up and settled back in to the chair by the fire, Melisende on her lap. At first the cat stiffened, but as Lucie petted her she relaxed, finally settling down, her chin resting lightly on one of Lucie's forearms, a warm, purring comfort. She was just a wisp of a cat now. Lucie had not been aware of how Melisende was fading.

In the morning, Lucie was puzzled to awaken to Kate's gentle prodding. 'The captain is out in the hall, Mistress, breaking his fast with Gwenllian and Hugh.'

Lucie lay alone on the pallet before the fire. Some

time in the night she had slipped beneath the blanket next to her aunt. 'Where is Dame Phillippa?'

'She is in the hall, too, but she will not eat. She is confused today and does not know me.'

More was coming back to Lucie now – she feared she had added too much valerian to her tisane last night, so slowly was she waking. 'Cisotta's funeral. Am I too late?'

'No, Mistress. I woke you in time to help ready Mistress Cisotta's children, as you wished.'

'How will you manage with my aunt unable to help you? Perhaps I should not go. Someone must see to the chores while you watch the children. Jasper will be busy in the shop.'

'You have nothing to worry about, Mistress. Alisoun Ffulford is here. The Riverwoman sent her, just as she promised, though I had not expected her so soon. She says she has much experience minding children.'

'Alisoun – I had not thought of her.' The girl had taken care of several sets of young cousins since she lost her family in the last visitation of the plague, even though she was young – a year younger than Jasper. 'I do not recall Magda offering to send for Alisoun.'

'She told me as she departed yesterday. She said Dame Phillippa was due for a troublous time, and you and the captain would be too busy to help with her. I forgot to tell you last night, but I thought it would be days before she came. I can comb your hair when you are dressed, Mistress.'

'So you can.'

Magda had said nothing of being able to predict Phillippa's spells.

Kate gave Lucie a hand up from the low bed. 'Already Alisoun has Gwenllian and Hugh in hand.'

'From what I remember she was as wilful as my

Gwen – perhaps my daughter has met her match.'

Kate handed Lucie her shift. 'I put your clothes by the fire so they would be warm.'

Seeing the dark-blue gown, Lucie remembered the missing buttons, how calm and content Phillippa had looked as she sewed by the window last night.

'Dame Phillippa sews buttons so neatly,' Kate said, kneeling to help Lucie with all the fastening. 'I did not think old folk could see well enough to do such work.' She laced one of Lucie's sleeves to the shoulder of her gown.

When Lucie was dressed, she slipped out to the privy. The dew was heavy on the grass, the sky striped by fast-moving clouds. A penetrating breeze set her shivering. By the time she returned to the hall the chill had cleared her head.

At the table set near the garden windows Owen sat beside Phillippa, one hand cupped beneath and one over her folded hands, talking to her in a comforting tone. The elderly woman, with her better ear cocked towards him, wore the ghost of a smile. *Bless him for his kind patience.* As if he had heard her prayer, Owen glanced up and wished her a good morning.

'Who is she?' Phillippa demanded. 'Was she invited?'

In the far corner beneath the windows Alisoun held Hugh on her lap and Gwenllian sat beside her. Alisoun was singing in a high, clear voice while nodding to the children to clap as she did to the rhythm. Gwenllian held her hands stiffly up towards her face as she focused on Alisoun's hands, struggling to catch the beat while stumbling over the words as she tried to sing along. Hugh seemed more interested in Alisoun's hands than his own, giggling and squirming.

How the girl had grown since Lucie last saw her. She had been a sullen, skinny child with wild hair and ill-fitting clothes. But there she sat with her hair tamed by a crisp white cap, the bodice of her gown fitted to her slender frame, the skirt draping well and the hem tidy.

'Good-day to you, Alisoun,' Lucie said.

Gwenllian jumped from her bench and ran to Lucie, hugging her legs. 'I was singing.'

'I heard you.'

'God be with you, Mistress Wilton.'

Alisoun's eyes were as Lucie remembered, dark and wary, and the chin defiant. But she moved with Hugh's squirms, gently containing him.

'You can stay today? You are not expected back at your aunt's house?'

'No, truly, I intended to begin at once. The River-woman said you needed me.'

'We do. God knows that we do.'

Gwenllian ran back to Alisoun to ask for another song. The girl looked to Lucie for leave to resume.

'Your voice is cheering – we have need of that today,' Lucie said, withdrawing.

'I did not guess what new troubles the day would breed,' Owen said as Lucie sat down beside him at the table. 'I thought I had done with Alisoun Ffulford.'

'We need someone to watch the children.'

'What are you doing in my dress?' Phillippa demanded.

'You mended this gown for me yesterday, Aunt.'

Phillippa frowned at Owen. 'Who is she to call me "aunt?"'

'This is Lucie, Sir Robert's daughter, your niece,' said Owen.

'No no no.'

Kate served Lucie bread and cheese, then asked Dame Phillippa to help her in the kitchen.

'Is cook unwell again?' Phillippa asked in a shrill

voice as she placed her walking stick firmly on the floor and leaned on it to rise, Owen helping with a hand to her elbow. 'I told you it was a mistake to permit her to marry.' Phillippa shook her head at the past as she followed Kate to the kitchen.

'Poor Phillippa,' Lucie said, 'she was looking forward to going out today.'

'Was it truly because of her that you slept in the kitchen?' Owen asked.

'What other reason could I have?' Lucie put her hand over Owen's, stared at him until he met her gaze. 'She is entirely to blame.'

'I did not know what to think when I woke before dawn and found your side of the bed cold.'

'You could have come to fetch me.'

He watched her as she ate, and only when she began to slow did he speak. 'I must tell Wykeham about the Ferriby boys before he hears it elsewhere. More time wasted.'

Lucie touched his cheek with the back of her hand. 'It cannot be worse than telling Peter and Emma.'

'No. But that is small comfort this morning.'

She worried to see him exhausted at the beginning of his day.

Twelve

TROUBLING
DISCOVERIES

A s Owen approached the Dale residence he
slowed, thinking it a good time to talk to Robert
and Julia. He would not keep them long and he
might feel better having accomplished something
before facing Wykeham, who was sure to be difficult.
He should have time for both before the requiem mass.

The goldsmith shop occupied the ground floor of the
Dale dwelling. A young man, an apprentice by the look
of his clothes, opened the door and invited Owen to sit
while he found his master and mistress. Already at this
early hour the apprentices and journeymen sat at their
work at two tables, one near a great hearth, chiselling,
hammering, polishing. Along the walls were racks with
various types of hammers, chisels and tongs, shelves
holding earthenware pots, trays, sticks of wax. The side
of the room with the hearth was warm, the air acrid
with the scent of hot metal. But the breezes from the
open windows, front and back, freshened the air on
the opposite side.

The apprentice reappeared, his face flushed with the
activity. 'My mistress requests that you attend her in

the hall above, Captain Archer. My master will join her in a moment. The stairs are just outside the door, on your left.'

Up in the hall, which stretched the length of the shop below, Julia Dale rose from a cushioned bench, framed in the light of several oil lamps. She was a vision in a blue silk gown that matched her eyes, her dark hair caught up in delicate filigree netting beneath a gossamer veil, a gold circlet crowning all. She had bold features and a powerful voice, tempered by her beauty and warmth. Had she married a man who could afford to provide her only the simplest of ornaments, she would have shone no less. Her daughters passed through the far end of the hall, pushing one another and giggling. They had her colouring, but not yet the presence that drew one's eyes and held them. Owen cleared his throat.

'I trust this will be a more comfortable place in which to talk than the shop,' Julia said. 'Certainly my husband will be less distracted up here.' She lifted her chin at the sound of her daughters greeting their father. 'There he is now.' She awaited him, quietly composed.

So Lucie once was, full of smiles for Owen, welcoming, soothing, loving. Was it the children who had changed her? This last child, so eagerly awaited, so violently lost? Was the shop too much? Perhaps the strain of motherhood and work were too much. And yet he could not imagine Lucie without her work. He rose abruptly when he noticed Robert Dale extending his hand.

Julia's husband was a pleasant-looking man except for the poor vision that drew his face into a perpetual squint. Owen often wondered why Robert did not use some of his wealth for a pair of spectacles such as Thoresby's.

Robert greeted Owen amiably and sat down beside Julia. 'You are here about the evening of the fire,' he said. 'It is good you have come so soon, while it is fresh in my head.' He nodded to his wife. 'You might name the guests.'

She ticked them off on her fingers.

'How long had the evening been planned?'

Julia glanced over at her husband, who shrugged and shook his head. 'I had spoken with Edwina Hovingham,' she said, 'and she agreed that we must introduce Adeline and Godwin to our acquaintances. Being connected in Beverley and Hull as well as York, they are good people to know.'

'Julia, the captain asked when, not why,' Robert said in a fond tone.

'Forgive me. It was that Monday. The laundress arrived just as I was leaving.'

'Tell me about the evening,' Owen said.

Robert nodded. 'All the invited guests had arrived, save William Hovingham, who is ailing. We were a dozen for dinner, as Julia said, which is why Bolton, the Fitzbaldrics' cook, was assisting ours. We had completed the fish course when Hovingham's servant came to fetch Edwina home. William was asking for Master Saurian.' Robert pressed the bridge of his nose with his fingertips, sighed. 'May God watch over his family.' He fell silent, staring at nothing.

'We were about to have the cakes when Godwin excused himself,' Julia said. 'I should think that is the most important detail. He was so long about it – I had finished a piece of cake and saw that the sauce on his was separating. I sent a servant to check the yard, fearing he had taken a fall, or was ill, and he returned with news of the fire.'

Robert had shaken himself from his fears for William

Hovingham and sat forward now. 'Adeline Fitzbaldric was first to the door, crying out for her husband.'

'Yes,' said Julia. 'I thought it strange at the time. She cried out, "Dear Lord, not Godwin! Have I not given enough?" But afterwards I remembered she had lost both children to the pestilence.'

Robert caught her hand and they looked at one another for a few moments.

A happy marriage. Three healthy children, the boy at the minster school, the girls showing promise of their mother's beauty.

'And that night, where did the Fitzbaldrics sleep? How was your household arranged?'

'We put Godwin and Adeline in the solar, near us,' said Robert. He rose, took a few steps to the hearth. 'The children slept here – it is chilly in the evenings now, though the hearth in the workshop below warms the floor through the night. The servants were sleeping behind a screen just over here.' Robert strode a few paces. 'Except for the cooks and the scullery maid – they were out in the kitchen. And my apprentices down below in the shop. That is what troubled me so, we were all spread out. If the intruder had come through this door . . .'

'The servants would have caught him, husband,' Julia said, rising to coax him back to his seat.

'But he came only to the kitchen and fled at once?' Owen asked.

Robert nodded. 'I shall walk down with you and show you where he climbed the wall.'

'It needs repair,' said Julia. 'One can scramble up with little trouble. The children have done so many a time.'

'It shall be mended,' Robert said, nodding energetically.

'What of May, your guests' maidservant? What did you notice about her injuries that night?' Owen spoke directly to Julia.

'She had a few scratches on her legs, a good bruise forming on one knee, a grazed wrist and she said her hip was tender. Her eyes were smeared with blood. Dried, caked. She kept blinking and I washed them out. I urged Adeline to send for a physician, someone, thinking she must have injured her eye and we could not tell. But she assured us that her eyes were fine, she saw well enough. And Adeline was content with that. Fretting over her loss, I am sure, and her manservant's terrible injuries.'

'How did the Fitzbaldrics behave after the intruder?'

'Crossing themselves and praying,' Robert said. 'It was too much for them in one evening. And then that poor man in the morning. Though I can tell you I cursed him from here to the devil when he woke me. I had just managed to fall asleep after spending the night checking the doors and windows over and over again.'

'Robert could not rest, that is true,' said Julia, touching his arm lightly.

Perhaps it was Owen who had changed, not Lucie.

'Is that all, Captain?' Robert asked.

Owen straightened. 'I've no doubt you found it difficult to rest after the fire, the intruder. Have you any idea whether the Fitzbaldrics slept?'

'I do not believe Adeline did,' said Julia. 'But Godwin had the red, creased face of someone who had slept deeply.'

'You are most helpfully observant,' said Owen. 'How did they respond to Eudo the tawyer?'

Julia looked to her husband.

'Godwin thought it best simply to take him to the

shed, let him see for himself whether it was his wife,' said Robert.

'We held Adeline back. She feared the tawyer would attack Godwin. He was coarse with drink, but I assured her that he had too many witnesses to be such a fool, and that Godwin was no weakling, he could protect himself.' Julia had grown uncomfortable, toying with a ring on one finger, avoiding eye contact. 'It was kind of him to take the tawyer. Godwin Fitzbaldric is a good man.' Her voice trailed off.

'Julia is full of remorse for how the two households parted.'

'I was thinking of the children.' Her eyes pleaded for understanding.

'So, too, was I when I told Master Fitzbaldric that we could not keep Poins in our home.'

'Oh yes.'

Owen had nothing else to ask at the moment. Robert escorted him to the yard, showed him the tumbled wall, which would have been an easy climb, probably the way the intruder had arrived as well.

Owen was glad to be away from the Dales. Their ease with one another had brought home to him how he and Lucie had drifted apart.

The counter at the front of Eudo's shop was closed, the door shut. Overhead, the tawyer's sign creaked in the breeze. Somewhere further down the street a door or shutter banged in an uneven rhythm. Lucie turned down the alley towards the kitchen entrance, giving a cry when she stumbled over a man in the archbishop's livery sitting with his back against the wall, dozing.

'Who goes there?' he called out as he scrambled to his feet.

'Mistress Wilton. I have come to help Eudo ready the children for the funeral.'

'The captain will have my hide for sleeping,' the young man said.

Lucie did not know him. 'I, too, should find it difficult to stay awake in a dark alley. Perhaps you would fare better standing where you were posted, out in Patrick Pool.'

'Aye, mistress,' he mumbled, lowering his gaze to the ground.

It was not her habit to reprimand Owen's men, but her abandonment yesterday still rankled. Ignoring the young man's exclamation as he stepped out into the windy street, Lucie hurried on down the alleyway, the sound of her footsteps echoing between the two buildings. The quiet unnerved her. She was glad to hear a child's petulant wail as she stepped into the kitchen yard, a sound of normality.

Eudo and a guard had their eyes trained on the alley as Lucie appeared.

The guard sheathed his knife. 'Mistress Wilton,' he said, bobbing his head.

'Good-day to you, Mistress Wilton,' said Eudo. He had shaved and combed his thinning hair, and wore his best tunic and leggings. A pair of boots with no creases or scuffs in the polished leather were either new or had been oiled for the occasion.

The guard nodded to her.

'I have come to help with the children,' Lucie explained.

'Goodwife Claire is helping Anna,' Eudo growled. 'Not a moment to ourselves, folk inside, outside.'

It was no mystery why the tawyer had trouble finding support in the guild with such outbursts when offered help.

But it was the guard who said so. 'You should be grateful that neighbours are coming to your aid, Master Tawyer. They might have shunned you after your folly yesterday.'

'Are you my protector or my warden?' Eudo demanded.

The guard shrugged and turned away.

'Come within, Mistress Wilton, I meant nothing by my complaint,' said Eudo. 'I can hear Anna and the goodwife struggling with the lads.'

What Lucie heard most keenly was Anna's cough. She stepped inside, pausing to adjust to the dimness, then crouched to catch the youngest who was careening towards her, one leg kneeling in a low, wobbly wheeled cart, the other pushing alongside. He saw her at the last moment and tried to brake, but the rushes slipped beneath his bare foot. The impact almost knocked Lucie backwards. She lifted him by his skinny shoulders and set him on his feet. He felt feverish and his breath indicated a sick stomach.

'Will!' The shout came from a woman who held tight to a naked boy squirming to escape. Lucie thought it was Henry, though he and Ned looked much alike. 'Oh, Mistress Wilton, I am sorry.'

Anna had run to grab little Will. 'Bad boy, you almost knocked Mistress Wilton over.'

The boy screwed up his face and stuck a fist in his mouth.

'He did not hurt me,' Lucie assured Anna and the goodwife. She bent to hug the girl. 'I am sorry about your mother.' It was not the thing one might say to most children, but Anna was a grave girl, old before her time. Still, Lucie was glad the din of the other boys hid the tremor in her voice.

'I keep hoping it was a mistake, it wasn't Ma in the

fire, she's just away at a birthing, maybe outside the city.' Anna smoothed her brother's hair. 'He's in a temper,' she said. 'Because of his fever he is going to Goodwife Claire's for the day.'

'But the rest of you are going to St Sampson's?'

Anna nodded. 'Pa is not pleased. He says we'll embarrass him.'

No more than he does himself. 'What can I do to help?'

'Would you fuss over Will while Mistress Claire and I dress Henry and Ned? Pa just shouts at Will and makes him worse.'

Lucie tested the boy's weight, judged him light enough for her to carry – he was much smaller than Hugh, who was about his age. 'Go on, see to the others.'

Will held himself stiff in her arms, watching her with an uneasiness that could quickly turn to tears. She walked over to the dresser with him, where a lamp glowed warmly, and searched for something to enter-tain him. The shelves were full of Cisotta's jars and bottles, but it was a thin string that she chose. Setting him down while she drew a stool over, she then lifted him up to sit astride it and sat facing him, knotting the string and stretching it between her hands. 'Do you know any string games, Will?'

Still with one fist in his mouth, he shook his head.

Though he mastered none of the games it wasn't for lack of trying.

Soon Mistress Claire came to scoop him up. 'Anna is dressing. I shall take little Will next door. Come, Will,' she cooed.

The boy shoved his fist into his mouth once more.

Lucie tidied the dresser while she waited for Anna. The jars and bottles lined up on the main shelf had no markings on them; though she had known Cisotta could not read, she had expected some symbols or marks. Opening them at random, she found rosemary, a powder mixture with valerian root as the strongest scent, rue, a jar of feathers, a bottle of lavender oil, a jar with a small amount of blood at the bottom, a tray of stones. She moved on to the other items on the dresser. A scale was tucked on a higher shelf, along with small rolls of cloth tied with laces and strings. Lucie did not fuss with them. A dozen or more small boards tied together caught her eye. Untying them, she found pressed flowers, hairs, what looked like fingernails. She pressed them back together and tied them, wanting no part of Cisotta's charms. The boards would not slide back where she had found them. Pulling the bench over, she climbed up to inspect the obstruction. Tucked at the back of the shelf was a delicate pair of gloves, made of butter-soft leather. Stepping down from the stool, Lucie held the gloves towards the lamplight. Tooled leather, with jet beads on the outer wrist of each and, tracing some of the tooling, they seemed too fine for Cisotta.

'I should give them to Papa, I guess.'

Lucie started. 'These are your father's work?'

Anna shook her head. 'Ma said they were a surprise for Papa, a pattern he could copy.' Her eyes were on the gloves.

'Was she saving them to give him for a special day?'

'Nay. Just until she had the hides to give him, so he could make a few pairs using these for a pattern. I thought that was where she was going that night, for the hides.'

Lucie turned the gloves over and back. 'They are very fine, Anna. Where did your mother get them?'

'As payment, I suppose.'

'From whom?'

Anna did not know. 'She showed them to me a few days ago.'

'When, Anna?'

'I think it was the afternoon we found the stranger waiting out in the kitchen yard.'

'Was he a stranger to your mother?'

'Anna!' Eudo shouted from the doorway. 'If you must come, come now.'

'Henry! Ned!' Anna called.

The boys hurried up to take her hands, squirming in their good tunics, their hair slick from an unaccustomed combing. They would be handsome lads, when the terror in their eyes faded.

A sharp wind whipped down the narrow, shaded streets, irritating Anna's cough. Through the maze of signposts and overhanging storeys Lucie glimpsed high, thin clouds scudding across a blue sky. The city streets were not so crowded today, it not being a market day, and most of those passing along were too busy holding on to their hats and manoeuvring with billowing clothing to gossip, though they did notice Cisotta's family, especially when the boys grew bold and veered away, returning only after much shouting by their father. But all the party hushed as they approached the door of St Sampson's. Anna used both hands to muffle her relentless cough. Bowing their heads, they entered the candlelit nave, standing still for a few moments to become accustomed to the gloom.

There were a dozen lay people standing about, a few others kneeling in chantry chapels in the north aisle. Two couples approached Eudo, both women with arms outstretched, weeping. He moved away from their embraces while introducing them to Lucie as Cisotta's sister and her husband from Easingwold and his own cousin with her husband who lived in York. Once

Cisotta's sister began to speak, Lucie saw the resemblance. Though stouter and a good five years older than her sister, the woman had her liveliness, her musical voice.

Eudo's cousin looked nothing like him, sweet-faced and petite. She knelt to the children and hugged them one at a time, then scolded her cousin for bringing them. 'It is too much for them, can you not see?'

'It is all too much for all of us,' Eudo mumbled. 'They begged to come.' He nodded to his sister-in-law. 'Where is Mistress Agnes?'

'Our poor mother cannot eat or sleep for grief. I did not think it wise for her to risk the journey.'

'If she had wished to come she would have found a way.'

'You would not have wished her here,' she said, stepping closer so as not to be overheard by the folk milling past them.

Eudo's response was lost in the noise of others who wished to express their condolences.

Lucie gathered the children and took them up close to the front of the worshippers. As the mass began, Eudo joined them.

Anna handed Lucie the embroidered cushion she had brought with her. Lucie shook her head, thinking Anna's knees were far bonier than her own. But the girl insisted. 'I always carried it for Ma,' she whispered.

Lucie accepted, but in return she gathered the boys, one on either side of her, to give Anna and her father some peace during the mass. As it proceeded, Eudo fought a fierce battle with his emotions. Anna slipped her hand in his but he shook it off and lifted it to shade his eyes, even though the interior of the church was but dimly lit. What had Lucie been thinking, to fear Eudo

189

so when he came to the house? He would not have harmed her or the children.

By the time Owen arrived at the church the Eucharist was past, the mass nearing an end. There was not such a crowd as to hide the mourners at the front. Eudo's hunched shoulders reminded Owen of how lost he had felt when he feared Lucie was dying. The pain had been physical, a tearing through the centre of his being, as if his heart were being ripped from him. It frightened him to think of it, more than the memory of any battle, for he had glimpsed the void that would open up and swallow him if Lucie died before him. His children had been a comfort, but they could not replace their mother.

Realizing he was staring at Eudo, Owen turned his head. Near the centre of the small crowd of mourners stood Alain, Wykeham's clerk. Approaching him, Owen caught sight of Lucie kneeling with Cisotta's boys on either side. Anna's slight figure stood woodenly between the trio and her father, her head lifted towards the ceiling of the church, tears glistening on her cheeks. Owen wondered at Lucie's involvement with Cisotta's family.

'You are here representing the bishop?' he asked Alain.

'Bishop William wishes to know the temper of the people.'

'He expects something other than sorrow at a funeral?'

'He is concerned that the people might blame him for the tragedy.'

'Why should he worry? He is surrounded by guards.'

'He is afraid of much these days, Captain Archer.'

As the priest intoned the final blessing, the wind

moaned without and from the open church doors a draft sent the candles around the nave flickering, the guild banners snapping. As the worshippers crossed themselves and bowed their heads, the stained glass rattled and the sacristy door slammed shut. Heads turned and a murmur passed among the people. Perhaps it was because the coffin bearers had lifted their burden and begun the procession to the churchyard, but Owen sensed a shift in the mood of the mourners, as if the wind had brought to mind the gossip about the woman whose body was being borne past them.

At the edge of the churchyard a group of women held their skirts and veils, watching the procession. They had not been in the church, and one of them Owen recognized as a midwife. Suspecting trouble brewing, he approached them, but at the same moment George Hempe entered the yard and nodded to the women, who bobbed their heads briskly and dispersed.

Lucie had noticed Owen at the edge of the mourners as she had turned to follow the coffin from the church. Now she started as he reached for her hand. When the priest had withdrawn and Eudo knelt with his children beside the grave, Lucie and Owen moved away from the mourners. Owen had just begun to tell her something about midwives watching from the market place when Henry and Ned ran past, with Anna in pursuit. Lucie abandoned Owen for the chase, cursing the need, for she had seen such concern in her husband's eyes that it had frightened her.

'Here, lads. What will your mother think if she is gazing down upon you from heaven?' Hempe crouched by the boys, each hand firmly gripping the shoulder of a tunic.

Henry tilted his head back and searched the clouds with frightened eyes. Ned held his hands out to Anna, who backed away, then ran to Lucie.

Perhaps it was the bailiff's presence that worried Owen, as Hempe clearly frightened the children. 'You have nothing to fear from the bailiff,' Lucie assured them.

'Here now,' Eudo called out, brushing off the knees of his leggings. 'They are good lads, there is no need to frighten them.'

Hempe let go of the boys, looking bemused as Eudo's extended family joined them, his cousin and Cisotta's sister scooping up the boys, who looked cowed and on the verge of tears. 'I merely thought it would be best that they quieted down and did not run from the churchyard.'

'It was kind of you to help,' said Lucie.

'Aye, I did not understand,' said Eudo, his face averted. 'I am grateful you kept them from the street or the market.' He bobbed his head towards Hempe.

Lucie looked round for Owen and saw him striding away. Could his job never rest, even at the burial of a woman they had known so well? She returned to the mourning family, knelt to Anna and warmed the girl's hands in her own.

Thirteen

a lady's composure

As Owen made his way towards the palace he tried to push aside thoughts of Eudo's emotion, his frightened boys, his daughter's frail dignity. He was impatient with the need to spend the rest of the morning pandering to Wykeham and Thoresby when Cisotta's death and the grief it had caused were so fresh in his mind. But Owen must tactfully tell them of the Ferriby boys' role in the tile incident and reassure them that it had been an accident. No doubt Wykeham would refuse to accept the boys' innocence, but Owen must try to convince him. As he mounted the steps of the palace porch he passed Alain descending. The clerk nodded to him and Owen had just begun to ask where he might find His Grace and the bishop when Wykeham called out to him from the doorway of the archbishop's hall in a peremptory tone. Owen swore beneath his breath. Alain must have failed to convince his lord that those attending the funeral were mourning, not plotting against him. Owen began to think parliament right in blaming Wykeham for the setbacks in the war – the war that had cost him his eye. The bishop could not act for all his anxieties about his good name.

'We must talk,' Wykeham said.

'My Lord Bishop . . .'

'Now, Captain.'

As soon as Owen shut the door behind him Wykeham rounded on him and demanded, 'When did you intend to tell me the truth about the falling tile?'

'The truth?' Owen muttered, wondering what Wykeham had heard.

'The Ferriby boys.'

'I have just come to tell you the truth of it.' *Damn the gossips.*

'Walter, the master mason's assistant, came to the palace last evening,' Wykeham said. 'Why did I hear it from him first, Captain, why not you?'

Cursed mason. 'I considered it important to get the tale from the lads before I came to you, My Lord. And to tell their parents.'

'And then you went home?'

'I have had much else to attend to. You were in no danger.'

'In no danger?' Wykeham's voice crackled with anger. 'They are the grandsons of Sir Ranulf Pagnell and his widow, that viperous woman who would suck me dry if she could. Their uncle Stephen Pagnell has Lancastrian connections. I should have been told at once.'

'My Lord, they are but boys. As a father I thought how frightened they must be.'

'How kind of you. And their parents feigned surprise, I've no doubt.'

'My Lord, they did not know.'

By the time Wykeham released him, Owen was shaking with anger. He headed for the barracks and drank his fill from a barrel of ale, then slept it off on Alfred's bed.

Owen woke in mid-afternoon with a headache and marched back to the palace, telling a disapproving Michaelo that he must speak to the archbishop.

Interrupting a meeting with the mayor to speak to Owen, Thoresby was plainly irritated to hear Owen's story of the Ferriby boys and complaints about Wykeham. 'I don't expect you to like the bishop. Your mission is to investigate the recent incidents involving him and his property.' He held up his hand to stop Owen from interrupting. 'If you are satisfied that the tile incident was an accident, then that matter is closed. Now I must return to Mayor Gisburne. Have a care, Archer. Convince me you are yet trustworthy.'

Still cursing under his breath, Owen came upon Godwin Fitzbaldric in the palace garden, sitting on the very bench from which Wykeham often studied the minster. The merchant sat stiffly straight, his hands resting on his thighs. His eyes were not fixed on the magnificent structure, but rather downcast. He looked despondent – as he should, having almost cost his serving woman her life. More likely he mourned the goods lost in the fire. Owen slowed his pace and studied Fitzbaldric. According to the Dales, the merchant had disappeared to the garden for a long while before the servant brought news of the fire. Here was someone on whom he might exercise his irritation. He continued his approach with more energy than he truly felt, allowing crunching pebbles to announce him. Fitzbaldric brought his head up, nodded once at Owen and then rose with care, a cautionary hand on his lower back.

'Good-day to you, Master Fitzbaldric.'

'And to you, Captain Archer.'

'I am glad to find you alone.' Owen settled down at one end of the bench, straddling it, gesturing for Fitzbaldric to resume his seat.

'I cannot think what else I might tell you, Captain.' The merchant eased himself down, allowing Owen his profile as he moved gingerly, finding a comfortable balance.

'Do you play me false, Master Fitzbaldric?'

The merchant bristled with indignation, turning too suddenly. 'What is this?' But his eyes were more wary than angry, or perhaps it was pain Owen was reading.

He felt no sympathy. 'It is about the evening of the fire. You left the Dales' hall for a long while, your fellows have said. What were you doing all that time?'

Fitzbaldric's breathing altered slightly. 'I . . . I was in the Dales' yard, relieving myself. It was dark, the yard unfamiliar.'

'And?'

'I heard a shout, or a cry. Or I thought I did – that is why I have not mentioned it before, I am not certain what I heard.'

'Continue.'

'I ran to the Dales' gate off Stonegate and saw someone running off towards St Helen's Square.'

Corm's running man. 'You have not spoken of this before.'

'Everything happened at once.'

'Could you tell whether it was a man or woman?'

'A man, I am sure of it. The shout – or whatever the sound was – had come from Petergate, in the direction of my house – or the bishop's, of course – so I stepped out into the street, rounded the corner and it seemed to me the air was too smoky. By the time I reached the house, Poins was being pulled from the burning undercroft.' Fitzbaldric wiped his brow.

If the shout had been Corm's alarm, the running man had taken a long while to run round the corner from the bishop's house to the Dales'. Corm had seen the running man, then carried the four sacks of grain down the alley one at a time. All that before noticing the fire and shouting for help. 'You are certain of how it happened? You heard the shout, then saw the man?'

'I am. I had no cause to look out on the street but for the shout.' Fitzbaldric grew uncomfortable under Owen's study. 'Others must have seen him, surely,' he said in a weak voice.

'One person has mentioned a man running, but you disagree on the sequence of events.'

'What are you implying, Captain?'

'You should have told me of this at once.'

'I told you, I was unsure what I had heard.'

'His Grace the Archbishop is uneasy about the fire, as is the bishop.'

'I cannot fault them in that. But what of us, what we have suffered?'

'Did you keep the undercroft locked?'

Fitzbaldric turned slightly on the bench, dipping his head to look into Owen's eye. 'We did.'

'Did your wife keep the key on her person?'

'No, we kept it on a hook in the hall, as we do at home in the country. Now look, you . . .'

'How long has Poins been in your service?'

'What are you getting at?'

'The bishop kept records in the undercroft, as you know. It is possible the fire might have been no accident.'

'But you cannot think Poins would set fire to the house? What would he profit by such a deed?'

'What might anyone?'

Fitzbaldric began to rise, but sat back down with a groan, pressing his hands on his thighs. 'Cursed back. What are you saying? Is it me or Poins you are accusing? I might ask you why you took Poins in, only to pack him off the very next day.' He caught his breath, eased it out slowly. 'Forgive me. The pain steals all courtesy from my tongue. I am not myself. But by the rood, Adeline and I have lost everything we had brought with us to York, Captain.'

'It is more than a fire that I am investigating.'

Fitzbaldric wiped his brow. 'What do you mean?'

'Cisotta was dead before the fire began.'

The merchant froze, hand halfway from brow. Even his wheezy breath paused. 'Christ have mercy,' he whispered at last. He held his back and shifted his weight so that he could look Owen in the eye. He looked haggard and frightened. 'We speak of murder?'

'We do.'

'Oh, dear Lord.' Fitzbaldric took off his velvet cap, dabbed his balding head with a cloth, set it back on his head. 'A murder,' he mumbled as if to himself.

Owen noticed Adeline Fitzbaldric standing in the porch doorway. She nodded to him and approached, her servant May at her heels.

'Godwin, Captain,' Adeline said, joining them.

May placed a stool near the bench, but Fitzbaldric had turned too quickly to see his wife and his face now crumpled with pain. Adeline bent to him. She was a sallow-faced woman with a shadowy down on her upper lip and dark hair that dipped into a widow's peak above her brows. She was finely dressed, in autumn colours, gold and brown. As far as Owen knew, the couple had not yet been given access to the ruined house, yet Adeline had an elegant wardrobe. Perhaps

Julia Dale had loaned her the gown. He could imagine her in it.

'What upset my husband?' Adeline demanded.

As if all had been well for Fitzbaldric until Owen appeared. 'I regret imposing on him when he is in pain, but my business cannot wait, Mistress Fitzbaldric.'

'The body in the undercroft.' Fitzbaldric frowned and shook his head as if searching for the right words. 'Mistress Cisotta was not accidentally caught in the fire, Adeline. She was – she had been murdered before it began.' His voice had grown so quiet that his wife moved towards him to hear.

The maidservant groaned, then covered her mouth as if embarrassed to have made a sound.

Adeline glanced from her husband to Owen. 'In truth? You know this?'

Owen nodded.

She took a few steps to the side, reached out to a late rose, cupped it in her hand. Owen had noted that her movement and voice were measured, her eyes shrewd. With a sigh she let go of the rose, turned to regard Owen. Her expression was troubled. 'We did not know her, Captain. How did a stranger come to be murdered in our house?'

'Adeline,' Fitzbaldric said softly, 'that we did not know her does not make her any less dead.'

'For the love of God, I am not simple.' She pressed a hand to her forehead. 'But how can we help the captain if we did not even know the woman?'

'Had you been unwell, perhaps mentioned the need for a healer to someone?' Owen asked.

'I had no need for a midwife.' Still Adeline pressed her forehead. 'I must think.'

'She did not confine herself to midwifery,' said Fitzbaldric.

Adeline turned to her husband. 'We had no need of a healer before the fire, Godwin.'

'Perhaps one of your servants?' Owen suggested.

Adeline glanced over at May. 'My servants know to come to me, is that not so, May?'

May stood with folded hands, her eyes averted, and nodded shyly. She was a plain woman past the blush of youth. Her breath sounded laboured, her cheeks unhealthily flushed in her pale face.

'What is the condition of the bishop's townhouse?' Adeline asked, filling the momentary silence. 'Will it be possible for us to return at all? At least to salvage some of our clothing, our furniture? Or is it all gone?' Now she looked less chilly, less distracted.

'I have not been in the house since the fire,' Owen said. 'The bishop will be seeing to that. He will certainly keep you informed.'

'Of course.' Adeline paused beside her husband, glanced at the space on the bench Owen had vacated and smoothed the back of her gown as if to sit, but did not. Instead she surveyed the garden while idly fingering the buttons that ran down the bodice of her dress. Owen had guessed her to be close to his own age, but in the daylight he thought her younger, as young as thirty. Her hands were certainly those of a younger woman than he had at first thought her. 'I should think the bishop is concerned about the records his men were working with,' she said.

At least she had brought the conversation round to something useful, but her lack of emotion was more interesting to Owen at the moment than anything she said.

Fitzbaldric gleaned something from Owen's expression. 'Have you quite understood, Adeline? The bishop had more important things on his mind than the old records in the undercroft, and so have we. A woman was murdered in the very house in which we were living.'

'I have heard you, Godwin, and I thank the Lord that we are not still in a house where someone was murdered. But our lives must go on, and I am certain the bishop will also wish to retrieve what he may.'

Owen wondered at the woman's indifference. If it was an act meant to hide her true feelings, she was a consummate actress.

'Did Bishop William's clerks have access to the undercroft?' Owen asked. 'Did Guy and Alain have a key?'

'Of course,' said Fitzbaldric, 'the bishop's key.'

'How often were they at the house?' Owen enquired, looking at Adeline.

She gave him a blank look. 'I would not know.'

Fitzbaldric shook his head.

Owen addressed May, who now stood behind the bench before which her mistress still hovered. 'You perhaps spent more time in the undercroft?'

May crossed herself. 'I did, Captain, but I did not like it down there, it was so dark and –' She clamped her mouth shut when she glanced at her mistress and saw the frown she was throwing her. 'That poor woman,' she murmured.

'We were speaking of the bishop's clerks,' Owen reminded her, though he was sorry not to hear what else she had wished to say.

She glanced at Adeline, who nodded once. 'Yes, they were often there in the undercroft, Captain, in the records room.'

'Would they stay long?'

'I was not often down there so long as they, Captain.'

Adeline at last settled on the bench beside her

husband. She smiled at Owen. 'You will find us most co-operative.'

'I am grateful, Mistress Fitzbaldric.' It was a polite lie. He felt he had lost control of the situation the moment she joined them. He drew the belt out of his scrip. 'Is this familiar?'

Adeline glanced at it. 'No. Not at all. Should it be?'

'Have you ever seen this belt, May?'

The maid leaned towards it slightly, shook her head. 'No, Captain.'

He glanced at Fitzbaldric, who merely shook his head.

Owen was satisfied for the moment. He put the belt away, his thoughts elsewhere. 'When did you tell your servants of the feast the Dales were hosting in your honour, Mistress Fitzbaldric?'

'That is it?' she said. 'We are to be left mystified about the belt?'

'For now, yes.'

She rolled her eyes. 'How annoying.' She smoothed the skirt of her gown. 'But perhaps that is your purpose.'

'I asked if you could . . .'

'Yes, you are asking when they knew the house was to be empty for the evening.'

'Or spoke of it to others,' Owen said, glancing at May, who was gazing upwards, shading her eyes with one hand, her expression unreadable.

'My servants are trustworthy, Captain.'

'A passing comment is all someone seeking the information might need,' said Owen. 'May?'

The maidservant straightened and moved her gaze to Owen, with a reluctance, it seemed to him. 'Sir?'

'Do you recall mentioning the dinner to anyone? Perhaps proud that your master and mistress were being so honoured?'

She was facing the windows, the sun in her eyes. She lifted a hand to shield them. 'Oh no, no, I know no one here, nor would I boast among fellow servants.' She took a breath. 'I am most grateful for what you did, carrying me from the fire,' she added softly.

'Well spoken, May,' said Adeline. 'Is there anything more, Captain?'

'For May, yes. How did you come to be trapped up in the solar?'

'I was asleep. I knew Poins was in the house, so I thought I might lie down . . .' Her voice trailed off as she dabbed her eyes with her apron.

'You'd cut yourself that evening,' Owen said. 'There was blood on your face. Yet I see no evidence of it now.'

May had moved to a better angle but still needed to shield her eyes. 'I have many scratches on my arms and legs – the blood must have come from them.'

'I remember the blood, Captain,' Adeline said, glancing back at her maid. 'Surely there are stains on your gown, May?'

'There were many stains, most of water and ash, Mistress. I scrubbed them out as best I could that night with Bolton's help.'

'May is a good laundress,' said Adeline, but her expression was one of puzzlement.

Owen wondered whether it would be useful to speak with Adeline privately about the maid. Something bothered him, but it might merely be the unusual resilience of Adeline that unsettled him. 'Did Poins have a visitor that evening?'

May shook her head.

'Had he been working in the undercroft?'

'No. He was in the hall when I went above.'

'Is he fond of women?'

The maid blushed. 'I would not know.'

'Are you friends with Poins?'

'I tolerate nothing improper, Captain,' Adeline said, her voice sharp.

'How is Poins today, May?' Owen asked, trying another path.

The maid looked down at her hands. 'I have not seen him since that night,' she said in a quiet voice.

'What is this? When he is here at the palace? Are you not concerned for him?'

Her head came up. 'I am!' Her face was flushed.

'Captain' – Adeline rose abruptly – 'that is enough.'

'Patience, Adeline,' Fitzbaldric urged, reaching for her elbow.

Adeline bristled. 'May has been busy helping me settle here. I thought it best that she not upset herself with Poins's condition.'

'And you, have you sat with him, Mistress Fitzbaldric?' Owen asked. She was already angry, so he saw no benefit in mincing.

Gracefully resuming her seat beside her husband, Adeline shook her head, dropped her eyes to her folded hands. 'God help me, but I cannot bear to see his suffering.'

'Nor should you need to,' Fitzbaldric said, putting a protective hand over hers.

Adeline smiled up at her husband, tears shimmering in her eyes.

Owen doubted that the woman required the protection Fitzbaldric seemed so anxious to give her.

Despite Eudo's frequent rebellion against his guild's rules, his fellow tawyers had arranged for the mourners to dine in the hall of an alewife, with guild dues paying for the small feast. Cisotta's sister, Eudo's cousin, and their spouses, the master of the tawyers' guild and several members, as well as some of Eudo's neighbours accompanied the family to the house on Girdlergate. Lucie offered to take the children home, but at their looks of disappointment their aunt insisted they partake in the feast. 'They deserve a reward for tolerating Father John's unpleasant voice,' she said, 'and what they have been eating for the past few days I do not care to think about.'

'A neighbour has been seeing to such things,' Lucie said.

'It is not for neighbours but for family to see to such things,' the cousin said.

Lucie had hoped to resume her conversation with Anna about the gloves Cisotta had hidden in the dresser. The information might be of use to Owen. She considered departing and returning later, but in the end she remained, honouring Cisotta's memory. Anna stayed close to her, but it was not the place in which to talk of such matters, with too many curious ears.

At first the girl seemed reluctant to partake in the feast, but her brothers' cries of delight soon stimulated her appetite. Lucie imagined the children had never had eel, pigeon, and venison in a single week much less a single sitting. By the end of the meal Henry and Ned had fallen asleep with their heads on their aunt's lap and Anna with her head on Lucie's.

It was not until the family returned home that Lucie was able to talk to Anna. Eudo settled into a chair near the fire circle, with little Will on his lap, and picked up a tankard of ale to resume the drinking he'd begun at the meal.

Lucie and Anna sat well away from him, talking about the relatives and their promises of help. Anna expressed concern that help would translate to interfering, but Lucie reminded the already exhausted child that it was difficult even for an adult to run a household. Gradually Lucie led the conversation back to the gloves and the hides.

'I told you all I knew of it, Mistress Wilton. Ma didn't say any more.'

'After your mother spoke with the stranger in the kitchen yard, how did she behave?'

Anna shrugged. 'She was glad I had put away the things we'd brought from the market.'

'Did she seem excited? Upset?'

'She just went on with chores.'

'When she went out the evening of the fire, what did she take with her?'

'Her basket.'

'Did you see what she put into it?'

Anna shook her head. 'Little Will was crying and Pa was shouting from the shop to keep him quiet because he had a customer.' She took a deep breath, blotted her eyes with her apron. 'It would help if I could remember what she put in the basket, wouldn't it?'

She was a remarkable child, both clever and courageous.

'It might.'

Anna faced the dresser, ran her hands slowly along the row of jars and bottles. 'I remember her picking up some cloths, then putting them back.' She lingered over a jar, moved on, backtracked, then at last dropped her hand to her side. 'I was too busy with little Will.' Her voice broke.

Lucie crouched down and gathered Anna in her arms. 'Forgive me for making you try to remember.'

The girl clung to Lucie, her reserve gone.

Eudo put down his tankard and carried Will, now sleeping, to the corner bed, then came over to them. 'What is this? Why did you make her cry?'

'It is good for her, Eudo. She has had to be strong for the boys. Just for now, she can be a child, weep for her mother.'

He held Lucie's eyes for a moment, then turned away as his face began to dissolve in his own grief. 'Aye, well, don't you leave her like that. See that she's calmed before you go.'

'I shall.'

Eudo crossed the room, reaching up to punch one of the ceiling beams as he passed beneath it, then the lintel before stepping out into the kitchen yard.

Anna had quieted. Lucie lifted her chin. 'Would you mind if I took the gloves away for a few days? I should like Captain Archer to see them.'

The girl wiped her eyes with her sleeves. 'Was Ma doing wrong? Is that why she died?'

'We have no cause to think she did wrong.'

Anna glanced over at her father. 'Should we tell Pa about the gloves?' He had returned to the doorway, leaning against it as he talked to the guard.

'Not yet, Anna. He has enough sorrow to bear. Let him rest this evening.' There was no predicting the man's temper.

Getting up on to a stool, Lucie took one of the jars from the bottom shelf and drew out the gloves, tucking them inside her girdle, beneath her surcoat. When she stepped down, she crouched and gave Anna a hug. 'Little Will is cooler tonight. But if he worsens again, send for Goodwife Claire.' The woman had gone home to see to her own family.

'He will get better?'

'I believe it is a catarrh, nothing more.'

Lucie felt Eudo's eyes on her as she made her way past Henry and Ned, and the overturned toy wagon they were repairing. The tawyer stood in the doorway, hands on his hips, legs spread, effectively blocking her way. His face was ruddy with drink, his eyes flinty.

'I thank you for including me at the table today,' she said. 'It was good to hear how beloved Cisotta was by her friends and your fellows in the guild.' Her breathless speech did not move him.

'What did you tuck into your girdle?' He moved his head, trying to see anything showing beneath the surcoat, which was cut low at the sides, allowing a glimpse of the girdle at her hips. 'Something of my wife's, was it? What are you and my Anna conspiring?' Eudo brought his face uncomfortably close to Lucie's, his jowls thrust forward, the pain of his loss visible in every line, every patch of swollen, reddened skin.

Lucie hesitated. Anna had joined her and watched her with a frightened expression. She must think of the child in dealing with Eudo, not herself. If he did not believe his daughter, he might beat the truth out of her. 'I did not wish to give you any more to worry over today, Eudo. It is Cisotta's day, when we remember her and pray for her soul.' Though he was not doing much of that while tippling. But as he had asked, Lucie showed him the gloves and told him what she knew.

He stepped back and fell to studying the gloves. He held them close to his face, sniffing the leather, squinting at the decorative beads and stitching; then, with a gentleness she had not guessed possible with his large hands, he turned one of the gloves inside out, patiently working several of the fingers inside out as well. 'Deerskin, tawyed by someone with skill. I thought at first it might be from a hide I had worked, but the oils are not mine. The stitching is fine.'

How he changed when talking of his work, what he knew well. How at ease he seemed, confident. 'See how smooth the tips of the fingers are. These have been worn a long while.' He held the glove up to Lucie.

Indeed, the nap had been worn smooth and darkened.

'Though there is wear within, the stitching has held – the glover fitted these well,' said Eudo. He turned the glove right side out again.

'Can you identify the glover?' Lucie asked.

Eudo shook his head. 'Jet and silver thread – these were made to order, I'd wager, not the glover's common work.'

'If you wished to make gloves like these, to whom would you go for the hides?'

Eudo handed her the gloves. 'I can tell you two merchants who trade in such hides – Peter Ferriby and of late Godwin Fitzbaldric.'

Fourteen

THE DEVIL'S SPORT

O ut in Patrick Pool, Lucie found herself uncertain whether to return home or continue on to Emma's house. She was anxious to see how her friend was taking the news of her boys' transgression. But she was worried she would be tempted to show Emma the gloves and she was not yet convinced it was the time to do so. It was best that Owen saw them before she showed them to anyone else. She dreaded telling him that Eudo had seen them.

Yet she had learned much from Eudo's comments, and Emma and Lady Pagnell knew far more about fine clothes such as the gloves than Lucie did. It would be helpful to Owen if they identified the glover or the former owner.

And if the gloves had belonged to Emma or her mother? There was the rub.

She turned down the street, heading for the Staithe. Watching the river might quiet her mind enough to think more clearly.

*

The rear door of the palace kitchen was wide open to the sunshine and what had calmed to a pleasant breeze. Inside, Owen found Maeve bent over a small brazier as she stirred a sauce and spoke in quiet tones to a maidservant who was cracking nuts and digging out the meats. They seemed absorbed in their work and Owen thought he might reach the screened corner unnoticed.

But he had not taken two steps when Maeve cried out, 'Captain! Did you mean to pass through without so much as a greeting?' Instructing the maidservant to take over the stirring, the cook hastened towards Owen while wiping her hands on her apron.

'I did not mean to take you from your work,' he said. 'You have a large household to feed.'

'That is the least of my worries, Captain.' Her rosy face was pulled together in a troubled frown. She leaned close and whispered, 'I do not like what is ado in my kitchen. The devil is in that poor man who lies beyond that screen, mark me, I am right about that, and the Riverwoman sees naught amiss in it – indeed, she encourages him in his evil confusion.'

Owen began to ask her what she meant, but she put a finger to her lips and motioned for him to follow her to the screen, then stayed him with an imperious hand while she peered round it. Drawing back, she whispered, 'Look you, and hark what they say as well.' With a last glance towards the screen, she crossed herself and left him to his spying.

He heard Magda's voice. She spoke softly, with immense calm. He felt a humid warmth even before he spied a small brazier with a pot of water simmering on the top, caught the scent of lavender and mint. The elderly healer was gently unwrapping Poins's stump while coaxing him to stretch out his fingers, ease the cramp in his hand. The stump moved a little. Poins groaned. As Magda turned to dip the cloth in the simmering water, she nodded to Owen. With a stick she stirred the cloth through the water so that it might soak in heat, then lifted it and held it dripping over the water to cool a little before wringing it out.

'Rest a moment,' she said over her shoulder to Poins. 'When thy shoulder is warm again it will be easier to move thine arm.' She regarded Owen. 'Thou knowest this pain, Magda thinks. Thy friend Martin Wirthir suffered it when his hand was severed.'

'Aye, his thumb it was that woke him in the night. It does so still, so he says. And if he hits his right elbow, he swears the fingers tingle.'

So this was the devil work Maeve feared, that Magda accepted Poins's claim of pain in the severed arm.

'I witnessed this in the camps as well, after a limb was severed,' Owen added. 'Not all suffer so. I never understood the cause.'

'Neither does Magda, but the pain is real, thou canst be certain of it.' She wrung out the warmed cloth, laid it gently on the stump.

Owen sat down on a bench and stretched his legs. Noticing the injured man regarding him from the depth of his bandages, he said, 'Good-day to you, Poins. I pray God you make a full recovery.'

Poins turned away.

'Does that ease it?' Magda asked.

When Poins nodded, Owen rose and approached him. 'Are you able to talk?'

Poins glanced towards him, then closed his eyes.

Owen wished there were a way to trick him into talking. But though he could think of ways to elicit a scream or a shout, he doubted he could make the man actually communicate until he so chose.

'Would you walk out into the sunlight with me, Magda?'

'Aye.' Magda eased herself to her feet, whispering to Poins that she would return, then headed for the closed door. 'Best not to pass through the kitchen. Maeve has much to say and none of it what thou seekest to know.'

On the sunlit path between the kitchen and the great hall Magda paused, blinking in the brightness, then headed to the cool shadows behind the hall. 'He has not spoken again since that first night,' she said.

Owen noted that she looked pale. 'Have you left his side since then?'

Magda wagged her head. 'Now and then. But Poins is thy concern, not Magda.' She glanced away, summoning her thoughts. When she spoke again her tone was quiet, as if even out here the patient might be affected by her words. 'His body will mend, but the burns will leave terrible scars, flesh that will pucker and misshape him even with daily salves. And the lack of an arm –' She touched her right shoulder with a vein-patterned, wrinkled hand. 'As he heals, worries will gnaw at his heart. What occupation can he have, a man who has been a servant, fetching and carrying, helping his master to dress? What woman will wed him?'

'Aye.' Owen remembered his own awakening to the change the knife of the jongleur's leman had made in his life. He felt again the upwelling of anger that had carried him along for a time, and eased only to leave a void more terrible than either the anger or the physical pain. Death had beckoned, and he had decided to pursue it by sailing to the Continent to take up the life of a mercenary. Thoresby had offered him an alternative just in time.

'Thou art deep in thy past,' Magda said, settling down on the ground beside the hedge, where the afternoon shadows had lengthened.

Owen crouched down beside her, noticed how straight her fingers were, despite the age of her hands. 'I would talk to Poins, hear his tale of the fire.'

'Aye, Magda knows what thou needst. Thou wilt be called at once when he is ready.'

'So he truly has not spoken?'

'Thou knowest well that Magda does not lie.'

'Is it that he cannot, or that he will not?'

'To Magda, there is no difference between the two, not in speech.'

'Would that were true of sight as well.'

Magda tilted her head to study him. 'Dost thou so wish? And what wouldst thou do? Take up thy bow and fight for Lancaster? The crow thou dost serve needs no captain of archers.'

'I may have erred in valuing the archbishop above the new duke, but I made the choice, my life is here now.' Owen had been devoted to the former Duke of Lancaster, Henry of Grosmont. He had gladly followed him into Normandy and fought with confidence that his was a righteous cause. But the present duke was not Henry's son; he was the son of King Edward, son-in-law to the old duke, and far from his equal. Over time, Owen had grown to respect him despite his shortcomings. How Thoresby had guessed his change of heart he did not know.

'Thou didst not trust thy aim, that is truly why thou didst not stay with Lancaster. If thou couldst use thy left eye, what then?'

'I would change nothing in my life.'

Magda wagged her head. 'Easily said, Bird-eye.'

Her teasing unsettled him. 'Have you changed your

mind about my eye? Do you think I might yet have the use of it?'

Magda chuckled. 'Would Magda not tell thee?'

'I wish I knew.'

'Thou wouldst do well to search thy heart before wishing for what thou hast lost.'

Owen's knees ached. He rose slowly, silently cursing his weariness. 'I have much to do. When should I come again to talk to Poins?'

Magda reached up a hand. Owen took it and helped her rise, wincing at the strength of her grip.

'Come tomorrow,' she said. 'Whether he will talk or keep his silence, that Magda cannot prophesy.'

The gentle breeze and plentiful sunshine lifted Lucie's mood a little as she neared the river. Though she had hoped the walk would quiet her mind, instead she worked on the problem of how she might present the gloves to Emma and Lady Pagnell. Little by little, she pieced together a lie that might work quite well with two women so devoted to elegant dress. Checking her steps, she headed back up Ousegate to Hosier Lane.

A servant greeted Lucie at the door and led her through the hall. John and Ivo barely glanced up from their lessons as she passed the table. Their tutor took more note of her, but when she caught his eye he nodded curtly and went back to the lesson. Ever since the family had received word of Sir Ranulf's imprisonment there had been a pall over the house, but never so thick and soul-dampening as this.

Emma sat alone beneath an apple tree, paternoster beads in her hands. The old tree shone golden in the sun and a quince glowed a fiery red. Catching sight of her visitor, Emma kissed the beads, laid them aside and came forward, arms outspread. 'Oh, my friend, it is good of you to come.'

The warm greeting heartened Lucie, but Emma's bloodshot eyes and poor colour concerned her. 'The sleep draught is not helping?'

Emma shook her head. 'But your physick is not to blame. Even the most potent elixir would not have helped me sleep last night, not after learning that my sons kept such a secret from me.' She pressed her square hands to her cheeks. 'What are we to do? What will Wykeham do? Has Owen spoken to him?'

'I have not heard.'

Emma drew herself up, motioned Lucie to join her on the bench where she had been sitting in the shade of the apple tree. 'Come, sit down, do. Are you thirsty?'

'No. And I should not stay long. I have left Jasper alone in the shop too much of late.' Only as she settled beside Emma did Lucie realize how tired she was, and she sighed with the relief of being received with affection by her friend.

'Whatever time you can spare, I thank God for it,' Emma said. 'I had not thought to see you today and I am sorely in need of your counsel.'

Lucie felt uneasy, coming there as she did with the gloves, and the dread that they might link Cisotta with Emma or Lady Pagnell. 'My counsel? I do not know the Bishop of Winchester, not in the way you need. I do not see how I might guide you.'

'We slept little last night. Peter believes that John is frightened about something greater than what we learned of. He has been so quiet of late, and has no appetite.'

'He was so fond of Sir Ranulf. Could it not be that?'

'I believe so. John wept most bitterly when Father departed for France. And when word came of his imprisonment, both he and Ivo spent many hours at St Crux praying for Father's safe release. That must be what tears at his heart. And that he almost injured Wykeham – he understands the damage this will cause to our name if it becomes widely known.'

'Ivo is not so disturbed?'

'He is a child of quick moods. It is his nature. John is different, stolid, unflinching.' Emma pressed a hand to her forehead for a moment. 'Perhaps there is more to it – I cannot understand their not telling us. It has made it all so much more serious. I pray that Wykeham is wiser in this than he was with my father's ransom.'

'You can be assured that Owen will speak well of the boys.'

'I am grateful for that.'

Emma shifted on the bench and in doing so knocked the Paternoster beads to the ground. She was retrieving them when Matthew the steward stepped into the garden. Seeing Lucie, he bowed curtly and began to withdraw, but paused when Emma straightened.

'So you have returned?' Emma said with such an edge to her voice that Lucie glanced at her. 'Surely by now you have covered all the properties under consideration, walked every bit of ground, climbed every tree. It seems to me the choice should be left to our neighbour, as it is he who must be pleased with the trade.'

Expressionless, Matthew bowed deeply to her. 'My lady has entrusted me with this task, Mistress Ferriby, and I mean to be thorough, weighing all with care, in the hope that Master Tewksby will be pleased with the first offering. Is my lady above?'

'She is not to be disturbed.' Emma dropped her attention to the beads, wrapping them round her wrist.

217

Matthew bowed once more to her bent head and withdrew to the hall.

'He is a worm,' Emma said.

'He works hard for Lady Pagnell. And your father never had complaint.'

'The worm turned upon Father's death – he plots to gain by Mother's widowhood, I am certain of it.'

'What has he done?'

'Last night he argued with Mother, insisting that she take the boys away to the countryside, save them from the gossip.'

'Some would consider that good counsel.'

Emma leaned closer, grasping Lucie's hand as if to ensure her attention. 'He spoke as if he were her equal, Lucie. As if Mother were bound to heed his words.'

Lucie could see that Emma expected her now to comprehend the nature of Matthew's transgression. Perhaps the steward had overstepped his position, but she did not see anything improper in his suggestion. 'The boys are yet here, so Lady Pagnell must have stood her ground.'

'Not without some effort to appease him with gentle words. But yes, she did stand firm. "A Pagnell never runs away," that is what she told him, and she would not be moved by anything further that he said.'

'Then what is your worry?'

Emma let go of Lucie's hand as she rose and walked a few steps away from the bench, hugging herself. 'I do not know why I fret so about her. She never has a civil word for me.'

Nor did Emma for her mother. But Lucie kept her counsel. 'I came on a trifling errand,' she said. 'Seeing your distress, I am almost embarrassed to bring it up. But perhaps it will distract you.'

Emma sat down on the bench once more. 'Something to do with the garden?'

'No, the matter is a pair of fine gloves.'

'Do you require a good glover?'

'I hope to find a specific one. Aunt Phillippa had a pair of my mother's gloves in her chest. I should love to have a pair like them, and I thought you might recognize the glover's mark or the workmanship.' Lucie drew the gloves from her scrip.

'How beautiful they are,' Emma breathed, holding them in her outstretched hands as if they were made of the most delicate lace. 'Do they not fit you?'

'Not as I would like.'

'What a pity. To wear them would be like slipping your hands in hers, I'd think.'

Her words made Lucie ashamed of her deception. But she could not undo it now. 'I don't want to risk damaging them. I have so little that was hers.'

Now Emma began to examine them, turning up the edges, holding the underside to the light searching for a mark.

'I recall some cut-work like this at the wrists, but I do not think the gloves had been made by a York glover. And the mark is not familiar. Might your mother have brought them from Normandy?'

If they had truly been her mother's that was possible, indeed. But the suggestion would not help Lucie. 'What about the cut-work?' she asked.

Emma ran her fingers beneath the scalloped wrists, each outward curve containing a small cut-out diamond shape. 'Your mother took care not to pull the gloves on by the wrist, or this delicate edge would have stretched and eventually torn. Ah – that is it. I have seen gloves such as these that were not so well cared for.'

'Who wore them?'

Emma shook her head. 'I cannot remember. But do not despair, it may come to me.'

'Might Lady Pagnell recognize them?'

'She is not to be disturbed this afternoon. The trouble with John and Ivo has kept her in bed with a dizziness.' Emma looked again at the glover's mark. 'I'll describe the gloves and the mark to Mother when she wakes. If we remember anything, we'll let you know.'

It must be enough for now. Lucie was making her excuses when she remembered what Eudo had said about who sold the type of hide for gloves like these. She had not considered how that would work with her lie, but perhaps it need not. 'If I find a glover who might make a pair like this, where would I find such a hide? Might Peter find one for me?'

'I am certain he could, though I confess I buy hides elsewhere if I see ones I like. It is not a great part of his trade, and he does not always fight for the best. But you must not tell him that I said so!' She handed Lucie the gloves. 'I am cheered to see you thinking of such a gift for yourself.'

Lucie needed to escape before she admitted her deception. It felt wrong to lie to her good friend. But in so doing she had been comforted – it was plain the gloves meant nothing to Emma. With Jasper as her excuse, Lucie soon departed.

The breeze strengthened around the soaring bulk of St Crux Church. Lucie held on to her veil with one hand to keep it from blinding her as it caught the wind, and with the other hand she lifted her skirts to keep them from tripping her. She had so dreaded a look of recognition on Emma's face, or worse, a withdrawal, a lie. Over the past few years Emma's friendship had become dear to Lucie. She had never had a close friend of her own age and station – Bess Merchet played more the role of an adviser than a confidante, and she did not understand the tensions Lucie experienced as a knight's daughter married first to an apothecary, then a steward and captain of the archbishop's retainers. Sometimes Lucie felt neither here nor there, and so some folk treated her. Emma knew all this without Lucie needing to explain. They were easy with one another. Had Emma turned out to be hiding something from Lucie . . . She could not complete the thought, for it brought the mirror up to her own behaviour in lying to Emma.

The door to St Crux stood open and the scent of incense and candle wax beckoned Lucie into its dim, echoing nave. She had spent much time in churches recently, praying for her children, both living and dead. Several people stood near the door, talking in low voices. A baby played noisily with a rattle while his nurse or mother knelt with her paternoster beads. Lucie headed towards the altar of the Virgin Mary, but saw that someone already knelt on the prie-dieu before it. She knelt on the stones nearby and, bowing her head, prayed for her children, Cisotta, the Ferribys, Phillippa, Poins. She prayed that Emma would forgive her deception, would understand. The lie had served its purpose, but eventually Emma would know of her friend's falseness. Lucie should have taken more time to plan what she meant to say. And already she regretted having left so soon, without seeing Lady Pagnell.

But Lucie's place was at home this afternoon. Alisoun was with Gwenllian and Hugh for the first time, and Kate might be caught up in easing Phillippa's confusion.

Having thought of that, Lucie grew anxious about

the children. Her quickest way to St Helen's Square from St Crux was through the Shambles, the street in which the butchers lived and worked. She hurried from the church and crossed the yard to the Shambles, only to find a crowd all but blocking the street. 'What has happened?' she asked a tall man whose eyes seemed caught by something far ahead.

'Harry Flesher caught a lad thieving, held him up off the ground by his collar and belt, and a customer said Harry was a cruel man, there was no cause for him to lay hands on the lad. They're calling each other such names!' He chuckled and rose on the balls of his feet.

Lucie gathered her skirts and pushed her way past several people. As she moved deeper into the crowd she was jostled and pricked by packages and pins. She paused for a moment, lifting her chin in search of some air, then plunged ahead.

'A dog took the meat!' a woman near her shouted.

The pitch of the crowd grew louder, the pushing and shoving more brutal. Something tugged at Lucie's girdle. She reached for it, thinking it had caught on something, but drew her hand back in pain. Blood bloomed along a gash on the back of her hand, and she felt the girdle slipping away, scrip and all. She turned and heard a woman a few people away shout as she was pushed aside. For a moment, as folk shifted in the thief's wake, Lucie caught sight of cropped blond hair and a rusty brown cap.

'Thief!' Lucie shouted, trying to lunge after him. 'Stop him!' She elbowed her way towards the disturbance in the crowd, her fury lending her strength.

'You'll never catch him,' a man muttered as he tried to make room for her, but failed.

Another growled to her to be quiet.

A woman offered Lucie a cloth in which to wrap her

hand. 'It's bleeding all over you. You've ruined your gown.'

'I've lost sight of him. I've lost . . .'

'Come, give me your hand.'

As Lucie lifted her right hand, she saw that blood had soaked her sleeve to the elbow. 'God help me,' she whispered.

'I'd say he's the one started the fight, or the comrade of the one,' said the woman as she wrapped. 'Then it's easy pickings.' She looked up at Lucie. 'You're Mistress Wilton the apothecary, aren't you? Well, you'll know what to do with this hand when you reach home. Folk are moving away now, the play is over. Can you make it home?'

'Yes,' Lucie said, though she had begun to tremble so badly it had been difficult to keep her hand still, and there was a roaring in her ears that made her unsure of her balance. 'Did you see the thief's face?'

'Young one, he was. I've seen him before, always watching for a chance at a purse.'

Lucie began to move away, shielding herself from the shifting crowd with her left arm. Someone bumped her wounded hand as they passed and she almost crumbled to the ground in pain, but with a deep breath she kept going. Something was wrong at home, she felt the prick of fear. She must get home.

Having failed to change Maeve's belief that Magda was encouraging the devil's work, Owen made his way home, where he found Phillippa napping in the kitchen and Alisoun Ffulford in the garden working on an embroidery while Gwenllian and Hugh slept on a blanket beneath the fruit trees. Kate was tidying the apothecary workroom.

'Is your mistress in the shop?'

'No, Captain. She has not yet returned.'

Through the beaded curtain Owen peeked into the shop. Jasper was seeing to Master Saurian, a physician with a loose tongue. Wishing to give him no new gossip, Owen departed through the workroom door and took the side pathway out of the gate and round to the York Tavern.

Tom Merchet greeted him from the doorway. 'Wind is rising again. Rain by nightfall.'

Owen paused, torn between asking for Bess so he might gather some information and sitting down to talk with Tom about Lucie and the household. Bess won out.

'Wife is up above, searching for a cushion that has vanished.' Tom shook his head. 'Her efforts will come to naught, I trow. But she will not believe one of our best customers would steal a cushion. Ruined it and hid the damage, that is what I think.'

Owen mounted the steps, following the sound of furniture being dragged across creaking floorboards. Finding Bess struggling to move a heavy chest, he hurried to her aid, lifting one end. And there lay the ruined pillow, torn and spilling its down and straw.

'Bless you, Owen.' Bess crouched to the mess. 'It can be mended. In truth, the straw needed changing. But the coward who put me through this will pay, I promise you. He will learn to face up to the damage he does sleeping with a knife beneath his pillow.' She sat down on the bed, dabbed her forehead with the cloth wrapped round her sleeve, protecting it. 'God bless you for lifting the chest. Did Tom fetch you, or are you God's blessing?'

'The latter, though I do not feel I am God's chosen today.' Owen moved to replace the chest.

'No, leave it where it is for now, I pray you. Look at

the dust beneath it.' She fanned herself. 'I pray it isn't Lucie who cast such a pall over you. Is she unwell?'

'She seemed much improved this morning, though Dame Phillippa gave her a difficult night.'

'Walking in her dreams again?' Bess tsked when Owen nodded. 'And you've not found the man who used that belt on Cisotta?'

'No. I came to ask where I might find the midwife Margaret Dubber.'

'Why?'

He told her of the group of midwives who had stood outside St Sampson's churchyard. 'I thought she might tell me things about Cisotta that a fellow midwife might know. Though why should anyone confide in me, eh? Do I look trustworthy?'

'In my eyes you look as tasty as sin itself.' Bess smiled as she regarded him. 'Trustworthy is another matter. But John Thoresby would not retain you had he any doubt of your talents, my friend. You've been his salvation many a time. You are weary, that I can see, and no wonder. Let me think now. Margaret lives in Lady Row, the second door in the row.' She lifted her chin, sniffed the air. 'That man will burn down the kitchen one of these days.' She groaned and held the small of her back as she rose from the low bed. 'Good fortune walk with you, my friend.' As she departed she was muttering, 'I have never known a cook so bemused by drafts.'

Owen lingered in the room, caught in the memory of his sojourn long ago at the inn, when he was still adjusting to the loss of his eye, restless with the physical idleness of his new life as Thoresby's spy. He had been quick to tell Magda yesterday that he would change nothing in his life, but sometimes he missed his soldiering days, when women delighted and confounded him but never let him see their devils. He remembered how beautiful Lucie had been, and how exciting, untouchable. Cursing himself for yearning for the past, he abandoned the room.

As he descended the steps he could not only smell but see the smoke wafting from the kitchen, where Tom's voice roared in uncharacteristic anger. He went quickly to assist, but saw from the doorway that the fire had been dowsed. He judged it best to leave them alone to deal with the offender. Besides, he had enough on his mind.

He would see Margaret Dubber in what was left of his day, then relieve Lucie in the shop so she might have time to talk to Alisoun. Jasper would appreciate time away from the counter, too. They all needed some semblance of life as usual.

He made his way from Petergate to Goodramgate via an alley between the buildings that crossed over one of the great ditches of the city. The water was clearer than usual thanks to the run-off from the buckets thrown on the blaze a few nights before.

Margaret Dubber was sitting in her doorway, stretching a stained fustian tunic between her hands. It had a ragged hem and as she held it up to the light several slashes round the middle were apparent. She nodded to Owen. 'To be mended,' she said, dropping it on to a small pile. 'My nephew the dubber pays me a pittance for my sorting of what are truly rags from what might be mended and given to the poor. He is of late concerned for his soul.' She rolled her shoulders about, stretched her back. 'You are here about my presence at the funeral today, I'd wager.'

'I am.'

She lifted another piece of cloth, frayed and thin, dropped it on to the larger pile beyond the mendables.

'Rag.' Then she folded her hands on her lap and raised her fleshy face, veiny cheeks and nose flushed, the late afternoon sun silvering her eyes. 'We thought to pay our respects to one of our own, but the looks we received from some made it plain we were not welcome. We are not the ones spreading rumours of her charm weaving, Captain. Others may be, but not my companions of the morning.'

shambles

On tiptoe Lucie could see the house that bordered the cross street of Little Shambles. With that as her goal, she clutched her bandaged hand to her chest, bent her head and slowly shouldered her way through the folk. Some pushed back, most did their best to move out of her way. The woman had been right, the crowd was lightening. Lucie raised her head several times to get her bearings. Her mouth was dry, her breath painful – she could not get enough air. Reaching the edge of the crowd at last, she let down her guard and promptly stumbled, pitching into a friar, his brown robe coarse and smelling of smoke and river water, like Magda's clothes. He steadied her and then assisted her to the corner of Little Shambles, bending close to ask her how he might help her.

'God bless you,' she whispered, 'I shall be fine now.' She leaned against the house and took great gulps of air.

With a blessing, the friar moved on.

Lucie's wounded hand throbbed and the cut burned. The blood had seeped through the thrice-wrapped cloth. But worse than her injury was the loss of the gloves. She should have known better than to carry them in such a crowd. Yet she walked through the crowded streets every day, or very nearly, and had never been robbed. Why today? In such a press the thief could not have seen the scrip hanging from her waist unless he had been next to her, but she did not remember a blond boy among those close to her in the crowd. Even had he seen it, why hers? It was a simple piece, containing nothing of value but a few coins and the knife she used when eating. The gloves were important only to her. Perhaps the thief had noted that she had been wearing a woven silk girdle, not easily cut, but more easily than a leather one.

She must find Owen. Abandoning the support of the wall, she straightened her veil and brushed off her surcoat with her good hand. She waited a little while, until she felt steadier, then moved along into the shadows of Little Shambles. When she emerged in Silver Street the late-afternoon sun blinded her and she stumbled to one side as she heard a cart rumbling towards her. Shielding her eyes with her bandaged hand, she saw a man leading a donkey and cart. It was the friar who had been so kind. He stopped beside her and held up his hands in peace. 'I am come to take you home, Mistress Wilton.'

She thanked him as he helped her into the cart. She did feel light-headed and would be glad to get home.

Owen and Margaret Dubber had fallen into conversation, talking of the city dwellers' fear of fire, the ease with which rumours spread, the worth of a skilled tailor, gardens. Eventually Owen reintroduced Cisotta.

'Women there are who did not look on her with charity,' Margaret said. She lifted a piece of yellow cloth, and a red one. 'She drew all eyes to her with her gay attire. And her bonny smile made men foolish.'

'And her ambition?'

Margaret dropped the cloths. 'The young midwives must learn while the old yet live. It is better to work with an elder, but except for Adam the Cooper none found fault with Cisotta. Some might have felt slighted, but to murder? Nay, I never heard that anyone hated her so much as that.'

'What of Adam?'

'He blamed her for his first wife's death, said the charm for an easy delivery was a curse killing both mother and babe. Folk gossiped, Eudo took a fist to Adam, their parish priests and guilds put an end to the quarrel, and Adam remarried and fathered two healthy children.' She groaned as she lifted one of the baskets of cloth. 'The shadows are settling. I must stoke the fire, cook my dinner.'

Owen helped her with the baskets, stooping to pass through the low doorway of her house. As he stepped out for the last of the three, he saw the groom from the York Tavern standing in Goodramgate counting the doorways of Lady Row. Owen hailed him, dreading his errand.

'Captain!' The groom hastened to him. 'Mistress Merchet says you are to go home at once, you are needed.' He bobbed his head and began to leave.

'Stay a moment. What has happened?'

The young man shook his head. 'A friar brought Mistress Wilton home in a cart and helped her to the house. That is all I know, Captain.'

Margaret, standing in her doorway, crossed herself and said, 'You're both in my prayers, Captain.'

Owen caught up with the groom. 'Is my wife injured?'

'I've told you what I know, Captain.'

Kate met Owen at the door with a confusing account of the friar, who nodded to Owen as he passed him sitting in the hall.

'And Magda Digby had come to see Alisoun, thank the Lord –'

'Where is your mistress?' Owen demanded.

'In the kitchen.'

Owen was there in half a dozen strides and almost choked with relief to see Lucie's eyes opened. She lay on the pallet, close to the fire, Magda bending over her.

'Now that thou art here, thou canst hold this tight.'

Magda had a stick twisted in cloth to cut off the blood flow to Lucie's hand.

Owen saw the gash as he sat down beside Lucie and took the stick. 'Who did this?'

'I was trying to catch a thief.' Lucie tried to smile. 'I caught his knife with the wrong side of my hand.'

'Where did this happen?'

'In the Shambles.' She closed her eyes, licked her lips.

Magda lifted her head and helped her drink something that smelled of honey.

Owen noticed Lucie's gown lying on the rushes next to the pallet, rumpled and torn. A sleeve was stiff with dried blood. 'I thought you were with Eudo and his children.'

Haltingly, she told him what had happened, while Magda cleaned the wound and then stood by, casting impatient looks at Owen. When he had heard all that Lucie had the breath to tell him, he asked Magda how bad the wound was.

'The bleeding is the worst of it,' said Magda. 'She has lost too much blood of late. It will be a long time before she has need of leeches again.' She drew closer. 'Begin to ease the pressure now, let Magda see whether the bleeding has stopped.'

Owen eased the tourniquet and watched, hardly daring to breathe. Droplets appeared, welled and grew no more. 'God be thanked.'

'Good. Magda will continue.'

Owen rose to give her his place. One twist at a time she loosened the bandage, pausing after each turn to see whether the bleeding would resume. At last she drew out the stick and began to clean the wound once more. 'It is seeping a little, but not enough to worry Magda.'

Owen paced the kitchen while Magda finished cleaning and dressing Lucie's hand. He kept his silence, for Lucie's breathing was shallow and he did not want to make her strain to talk to him. He did not know what to think of the incident. Lucie seemed so certain that the gloves were important. Yet nothing in her tale made him so sure. He wondered why she had pushed her way into a rowdy crowd. As with her fall from the stool, she had been injured because of her own carelessness. It was not like Lucie.

'Thou art to stay in bed a week, drinking as much of Magda's blood tonic and Phillippa's concoctions as thou canst bear, and thou must have meat once a day.'

Seeing Magda gathering the bowls and rags, Owen resumed his seat near Lucie, took her uninjured hand and kissed it.

'I must redeem myself,' Lucie whispered.

Owen smoothed back the hair from her forehead. 'You are my redemption.'

'I lost the gloves. I should have brought them home at once. I cannot be trusted.'

'If thou canst not speak without making thy heart race, Magda must forbid talk.'

Lucie closed her eyes. 'I *am* tired.'

Magda muttered something unintelligible as she took away the tray she had filled, then retreated to the hall.

The firelight warmed Lucie's face. 'Can you forgive me?' she whispered.

Owen kissed her hand again. 'There is nothing to forgive.'

'I lost the gloves.'

'Why are they so important to you?'

'They were important to *you*. Eudo knows. He must have sent the boy after me. Only he and Emma know of the gloves.'

Owen smoothed her brow. 'Eudo cannot leave his house. There is a guard at either door.'

'There is no one else.'

'What makes you so certain the gloves will help me find Cisotta's murderer?' Owen asked.

'It is the way she hid them, and swore Anna to secrecy.'

'But that is all in keeping with a surprise for Eudo.'

'Anna thought Cisotta was to get the hides the night of the fire.' Lucie did not open her eyes. Her voice was faint, her speech slurred.

'It may prove to be nothing but a child's imagination that connects the gloves with that night,' he said.

Lucie fought to open her eyes. 'I am not a child.'

'I did not mean *you*.'

'You think I am mad. I see it in the way you look at me.'

The door opened and Magda came in, followed by Alisoun. 'Enough talk,' Magda declared. 'I must show Alisoun what she must do.'

Owen pressed Lucie's hand. 'Send them away.'

'You'll see,' she whispered.

He kissed her on the forehead and withdrew, feeling

useless and filled with an anger that had no target. He did question her judgement these days. She seemed to move about in a dream, motivated by her feelings, not her head. Her insistence on the importance of the gloves was a good example – Eudo could not slip past his men. Or could he? Perhaps Owen should not be so certain of that. But even if the tawyer could find a way past the guards, he would be a fool to attack Lucie. It was too obvious. She had shown him the gloves.

The friar had risen from his seat in the hall. 'Mistress Merchet's groom has this moment kindly taken the cart from me to return to its owner. I must leave.'

'God bless you for what you did.'

The friar bowed his head. 'The owner of the cart is equally to thank.'

'Would you be willing to show me where the theft occurred?' Owen asked.

'It is on my way.' The friar preceded Owen out on to Davygate. 'It was the Lord who put me in Mistress Wilton's path when it seemed she could walk no further. There she was, lit up by the sun when I reached the crossing of Little Shambles and Silver Street. God watches over her.'

Not enough, Owen thought. 'Did you see what happened?'

The friar shook his head. 'I caught sight of Mistress Wilton pushing through the crowd, trying to give chase to the thief. By the whiteness of her face I knew she was in pain. I followed, calling out to her time and again, but she did not hear me.'

Owen was only half listening, worrying that perhaps Eudo had found a way out. He turned north from Thursday Market so they might pass Eudo's in Patrick Pool. He was relieved to see the tawyer working beside his apprentice in the shop, a guard sitting nearby.

As they entered the Shambles, the friar pointed to Harry Flesher's shopfront at the far side. 'That is where the argument took place.' Moving further up the street, the friar finally paused. 'I believe this is where Mistress Wilton was standing, perhaps a little closer to the shop's side of the street.'

Owen noted that it was in fact quite close to the butcher's shop itself.

'I must leave you now, Captain. May God be with you. Mistress Wilton will be in my prayers and those of all my brethren.'

Owen thanked him, though Lucie seemed to be in all of York's prayers by now and it had done little good.

The shopfront in the Shambles was still open, though all the others were shut. A young man whom Owen recognized as one of Jasper's friends was raking up blood-spattered rushes. 'We are closed for business, sir,' he said without pausing.

'I have not seen you for a long while, Timothy. How do you find your apprenticeship?'

Now the boy raised his head. 'Captain!' He leaned his rake against the door jamb. Glancing back at the shop and seeing they were alone, he said, 'I think I would rather do anything else. I smell of the slaughterhouse. Dogs follow me in the streets. But my master is kind, and fair.'

'I understand there was much shouting in front of the shop this afternoon.' The boy was already nodding and, by the light in his eyes, eager to tell the tale. 'What was it about?'

'My master caught a boy thieving and lifted him up by the neck of his tunic, and a customer took offence, preaching at my master that he should be lenient with the poor. "Poor!" my master shouted. "Half the wealth of the city passes through his hands. Poor indeed." And

235

they fell to arguing with such intent that the thief got away and the customer dropped a good piece of beef on the ground. Worse, a dog made off with it.' Timothy laughed, then looked round to make sure he had not been heard and continued more softly, 'When my master said the customer must pay, that is when the fighting truly began. Such names they called one another!' Timothy stopped to catch his breath.

'The thief. Could you describe him to me?'

'Weedy, like my little brother, sprung up too fast for his clothes, all wrists and ankles. Long, dark hair tied back in a piece of string, and he's lacking a bit of one ear.'

Lucie's thief had been blond, or so she thought. So there were two at work in the street.

'How did you hear about it?' Timothy asked.

Owen told him of Lucie's loss.

'Faith, you will wish to talk to my master, then, since he knows the cur.'

'Aye, if you could find Master Flesher.'

Timothy tossed aside his rake and disappeared into the shop. He returned a moment later accompanied by Harry Flesher, a short, muscular man with a bush of white hair. He had his sleeves caught up above his elbows, exhibiting strong forearms. 'I fear Timothy has given you false hopes, Captain. I've seen the thief before, aye, we all know him by sight on the Shambles, filching coin from our customers. But to tell you his name or his abode . . .' Harry shook his head.

'Do you know if he works with another lad, short, fair hair?'

'Well, they oft work in pairs, eh? I would have wondered about the customer who caused all the trouble, whether he was working with the lad and the dog, curse him, but the man was well dressed, with clean hands and hair. A thief could not scrub all the filth from his hands for one jest.'

'He was a stranger to you?'

Harry nodded. 'It is not so rare as you might be thinking. York is a big city.'

Owen thanked him. As Harry withdrew, he remarked that Timothy was slow in cleaning up the rushes. The lad took up his rake again.

'Is Jasper much in the shop these days?' he asked when his master had shut the door behind him.

'Aye, he has been busy of late.'

'He is lucky, working with sweet-smelling potions.'

'He measures out pig's bladders, blood and dung as well as lavender and mint.'

'At least he never stinks of it.'

'What did you think of the man who spoke up for the thief?'

Timothy leaned on his rake and studied the rushes. 'I did not take him for a charitable man.' He made a face. 'I have not been of much use. If I hear anything, I shall come to you right away.'

'Aye, keep your ears pricked, Timothy. God go with you.'

Owen walked slowly up the Shambles, glancing into the shadows, but all was quiet. He walked a little way down a narrow alley that might have been a continuation of St Saviourgate to the west of St Crux, but had been overbuilt so much a cart could not fit down it. Wattle fences alternated with stone walls of all heights and condition, and a few doorways opened on to the alley. He saw a woman suckling a babe in a small garden, an elderly man cleaning a fish in his doorway, two children kicking a ball back and forth in a yard. If a thief had run down here a few hours ago, he had left no worried souls in his wake. Nor had he dropped Lucie's scrip. Retracing his steps, Owen slipped into St Crux Church, but it yielded no clues and he finally admitted to himself that he had no idea what he was looking for. Thefts happened all the day and folk accepted it as a part of living in the city. Which brought him back to the significance Lucie placed in the gloves.

He found Emma Ferriby in her courtyard. She was holding pieces of silk up to the dying light but her expression was anxious as she greeted him. 'Have you spoken to the bishop?'

'Aye, and the archbishop, who is satisfied that it was an accident.'

'God is merciful.' She crossed herself. 'Thank you. My mind is much eased.'

'I've come about another matter.' He told her about the theft of the gloves.

She crushed the silk in her hand. 'I cannot believe it. Her mother's gloves, something so precious to her.'

Owen prayed that his face did not betray his surprise.

Emma tucked the silk squares into her girdle and held out her hands to grasp his. 'Such a loss is hard to bear.' He saw sincere concern in Emma's face and was glad Lucie had such a friend. 'And her hand. It is too much, all she has been given to bear this autumn.'

'Your family has also had sorrow.'

Emma squeezed his hands and bowed her head. 'Yes.' A world of sorrow echoed in that one word.

'I hoped you might help me. I have never seen the gloves, or I made no note of them if I have – that is what I fear. Could you describe them to me?' He thought by Emma's frown that she saw through his ruse.

But then she laughed. 'Peter is the same. Even though he sells the silks and wools with which my gowns are made, he will express surprise again and again at the same garment.' She closed her eyes and described the gloves in such detail it was as if she could see them inside her eyelids. 'Do you mean to catch the thief before he can sell them?' She had opened her eyes and now studied his face so intently he felt himself blush.

'Would they be worth selling?' he asked.

'They were a little worn, but a dubber might pay tuppence, perhaps more. The jet beads alone are worth something. You are angry – is Lucie badly injured?'

'She is wounded, that is enough, and weak –' He turned away, uncomfortable under her keen regard. 'She has lost so much blood of late.'

'Mother would say that is good.'

'Magda thinks it too much. She says Lucie must stay abed for a week.'

'I shall come to her tomorrow, Owen.'

'I cannot imagine why anyone would steal them.' *Except Eudo, but how?* 'Still, might anyone have seen her showing you the gloves?'

'Come with me to the garden. I shall show you where we sat.' Emma led him out of the courtyard and into an alley bordered on one side by the warehouse, on the other by another multi-storey house – Hosier Lane was an affluent street, as was Pavement beyond, despite the presence of the city stocks.

As Emma opened the gate in the garden wall Owen noted a lock on the iron grille, which seemed a good caution. 'When do you lock the gate?'

'At night, or when we are all away. But as you will see, no one could have entered the garden without one of us seeing them this afternoon.' She led him to a bench that did indeed have a complete view of the small garden. 'Sit down.'

He found himself grateful to rest his legs, but the sun was setting and the damp was rising. It would not long be pleasant to sit here. 'Do you know Lucie's mind in this? Why she showed the gloves to you today?'

'She thought it might cheer her to have a pair made like them. She asked whether I recognized the glover's work, which I did not, and whether Peter might have such hides.' Emma drew the silk squares from her girdle. 'It grows too dark. I was going to ask your opinion.'

'Might Peter have the hide to make the gloves?'

'I asked when I borrowed these from the shop. He has no hides at present.' She turned fully towards him. 'Do you think to have a new pair made for her?'

She looked so delighted at the thought of a conspiracy that would please Lucie that Owen was caught up in the idea. 'I fear she thought of that first.'

'But I could help you. I remember them so clearly.'

He noticed Emma's son John standing in the doorway to the hall, anxious about Owen's presence, he had no doubt. In the shadow of the house the details of the boy's clothing were indistinct, but Owen and Emma, sitting in the late-afternoon sun, would be clearer. 'What of someone observing you from the house as you talked?'

'Do you truly think the thief wanted the gloves?'

Owen inclined his head towards John, who withdrew at once.

'Peter has forbidden them to step outside the gate.' Emma rose. 'Perhaps we should leave them to what little land they are permitted to walk on.' There was disapproval in her tone.

Owen's legs felt stiff as they walked to the gate. 'So no one interrupted your conversation with Lucie?'

'My mother's steward, Matthew.' A sharpness entered Emma's tone as she paused to open the gate. 'But he stayed near the doorway to the hall.'

'Were the gloves visible to him?'

He felt her eyes on him, though it was now grown too dark near the alley to read her expression clearly.

'I am not certain.' She said it softly, as if to herself.

He made his way home in the gathering darkness, alert to every footfall, every shadow. He found a quiet household, the children listening to one of Phillippa's long tales before bedtime, Alisoun assisting Kate in the kitchen.

Lucie was sitting up and reached her arms out to him as he approached her. 'Forgive me for my temper,' she said.

He bent down and tried to embrace her, awkward in his attempt to avoid her bandaged hand. He thanked God for Magda's skill and her timely presence. 'You had been frightened.' The change in her mood made him uneasy.

'Did you speak to Emma?'

'Aye, and glad I was that I did not say more than a few words before she mentioned a different tale of the gloves and who had worn them.'

'Sweet heaven, I had not thought to tell you. Does she know of my lie?'

'No. And I reassured her that Thoresby is relieved that the tile was not meant as a threat to Wykeham.'

'Meaning Wykeham is not so comforted.'

Owen shrugged. He touched the bandage, saw no stain. 'Are you in much pain?'

Lucie shook her head. 'And the shivering has passed, so I feel more easy in myself. I want to sleep in my own bed tonight, Owen. Could you help me up the stairs?'

Owen caught Alisoun's look of concern. He was not about to let the children's nurse rule their household and, if it cheered Lucie, it would be done. 'I'll not stop at helping you, I'll carry you. But first you must eat, and I'll take my meal with you.'

They did not speak of the theft and their separate investigations until they were alone in their chamber, and by that time Lucie was fighting sleep, though she tormented herself so about the loss of the gloves that he wondered how well she would rest.

'For all we know the thief has searched the scrip, taken the few coins, perhaps the knife, and left the gloves and scrip where someone may find them. With your initials and the apothecary rose burned into the scrip's flap, it might be returned to you. And perhaps the gloves with it. Or the finder could show us where they are.'

He handed her the cup of honeyed physick.

She pushed it away. 'I have drunk enough of that for many a day.'

'You have not.'

'Honeyed words, honeyed drinks. Perhaps I should not have been so quick to apologize. You do treat me like a child now.'

'Lucie, I want you well.'

'So do I,' she snapped, then lay down, with difficulty, avoiding the use of her right hand. She pulled the covers over her head.

Owen turned down the lamp and sat for a long while, wondering whether Lucie was truly beset by some devilish spirit. Perhaps it was time he went to his friend Archdeacon Jehannes and asked his advice in this. He fell asleep listening to the sounds of the night.

'Owen, wake up.'

Lucie stood over him, shaking his arm. Morning ligh streamed from the open shutters. 'The bailiff, Georg

Hempe, is sitting in the hall with a grim face. He will not tell me all until you have come down.'

Owen groaned. 'What has he told you?'

'He has shown me my scrip, my cut girdle and the gloves. But he will say nothing of how he comes to have them.'

'He has a rigid sense of order, that is all,' Owen said, pulling on his leggings and slipping into his tunic.

She handed him a cup of ale. 'I thought you might need some strength.'

'Aye, it seems the day begins apace.'

Sixteen

AN UNYIELDING MAN

As Owen entered the hall, he saw through the garden windows that it was later than he had imagined, for the children were already at play. Alisoun sat calmly by and Phillippa, who tended to be a late riser, was seated as close to the windows as she could manage and yet still move, seeking light for her sewing.

'Tell Alisoun to take the children to the kitchen,' Owen said quietly to Lucie as they paused at the bottom of the steps.

'I thought we might talk in the kitchen.'

'No, it's best we see Hempe in the hall, else he will suspect a slight. Where is Jasper?'

'In the shop, where I should be but for my hand.'

'You were to remain abed for a week.'

Lucie was ashen, her face pinched with pain. She held her bandaged hand protectively close to her. 'After the bailiff departs I'll lie down. Jasper, Alisoun and Kate do seem quite capable.'

Hempe perched on the edge of a chair a distance away from the children and Phillippa, hat in hand, his eye fierce in his hawk-nosed face, his balding pate doing nothing to dispel the impression of a predator. At his feet was a hide sack.

He rose as Owen crossed the hall to him. 'Captain Archer.'

The children glanced back at the bass voice as Alisoun herded them to the kitchen door.

'Good-day to you,' Owen muttered, distracted by the sound of Lucie and her aunt in an argument. Phillippa did not wish to withdraw from the daylight.

'I did not think to find you yet asleep at this hour,' Hempe said.

Like a predator, he struck before Owen got his bearings.

'I have had little opportunity for rest since the fire,' Owen said, drawing himself up to full height so that he was more than a head taller than the bailiff.

Hempe's face hardened.

Owen checked his mood. He did not yet know the man's purpose. A more courteous tone might be to his advantage. 'I pray your pardon for the wait. I know you are a busy man.'

'I *am* busy of a sudden,' Hempe said.

Lucie joined them. 'Master Hempe, I pray you, tell us now how you recovered what was stolen from me yesterday.'

The bailiff fixed his gaze on Lucie. 'Your injury, Mistress Wilton. Would you describe for me how you received it? Did you attempt to stop the thief?'

'I was not aware that he had . . .' Lucie began.

Owen could see that Hempe meant to bully her. 'What is your purpose in questioning my wife?'

'I had not thought it necessary to discuss this with Mistress Wilton in private. Was I wrong?'

245

'You waited until I was present, Hempe. What game are you about?'

'I am a city bailiff, Archer, it is my duty to arrest those who break the laws of the city.'

'Owen, I pray you, let Master Hempe be about his business.' Lucie sank down on to a stool, all colour drained from her face. 'Forgive me, I am not well.'

'I am sorry to disturb you,' Hempe said in a quieter tone.

'For what offence are you questioning my wife?'

'I merely wish to understand the order and the character of yesterday's events.'

'First let us see whether you do indeed possess the goods stolen from my wife, and tell us where you found them,' Owen demanded.

'That does seem reasonable,' Lucie agreed. 'But I can tell you briefly, I thought my scrip had caught on something in the press of the crowd. I reached for it, something sliced my hand, and my girdle with the scrip was gone.'

Hempe nodded, resumed his seat, lifted the sack, opened it and drew out the contents. They were indeed Lucie's scrip, the girdle – cut neatly – and the gloves. But the latter were now stained.

Lucie lifted them. 'They were so soft. What did the thief do to them?'

'That is blood, Mistress Wilton,' Hempe said coldly. 'The blood of a lad with cropped blond hair, a skinny fellow perhaps a head shorter than you. Your thief?'

'He was blond and smaller than I am,' Lucie whispered. 'This is his blood?'

Hempe gave a curt nod. 'He was found in a ditch near the King's Fishpond this morning, with his throat slit. The weapon still lay beside him.' He drew a little knife from the sack.

It was Lucie's knife.

'God help us,' she whispered, crossing herself with her bandaged hand, which was shaking so badly that she truncated the gesture when Hempe looked her way and tucked the hand behind her.

'Do you recognize it?' Hempe asked.

'Of course she does.' Owen could not bear the man's taunting when the horror of his revelation was writ so clearly on Lucie's pale face.

'It is uncommonly sharp for a lady's knife, is it not?'

'That is enough.' Owen bent to Lucie and lifted her in his arms.

Caught by surprise, Lucie did not begin her protestations until they were across the hall and on the first step. 'Owen, please, you are only angering him.'

Indeed, Hempe rushed after them. 'I am not finished.'

Neither was Owen, but he had no intention of allowing Hempe to subject Lucie to more of his interrogation. He continued up the stairs. 'I won't have you treated in such wise.'

Hempe stopped at the foot of the stairs.

Owen eased Lucie down inside their bedchamber and kicked the door closed behind him, holding her until she was steady on her feet. 'Lie down and stay warm. I'll come up when he is gone.'

Lucie sat down on the edge of the bed holding her injured hand. 'My knife, Owen. Someone slit the boy's throat with my knife and left the gloves to soak up his blood.' Her eyes were wells of sorrow in a face pinched with pain. 'His questions – does he think I murdered the boy?'

'If he does he's a madman. Why would you have run off without your possessions?'

She dropped her head.

'It is proof the lad's murder has nothing to do with

you,' Owen went on, speaking the words as the thoughts came. 'Whoever went after him knew nothing of the gloves, else he or she would have taken them, surely. It was thieves fighting among themselves, no more. Rest now.'

God had been watching over Lucie, that she was not the corpse.

As Owen descended to the hall he went over what Hempe had told them so far and questions curled round each other. The bailiff did not bother to rise when Owen took the chair opposite him.

'The gloves are bloody, but not the scrip,' Owen said. 'So you did not find both items together?'

Hempe's eyes bored into him. 'Are those the first questions that come to your mind on hearing about a boy's murder, where were the gloves, where was the scrip?' He shook his head as at a foolish child.

'Your time would be better spent asking such questions than finding fault with all I say,' Owen snapped. 'It may be important.'

Warring emotions played across Hempe's face. He turned away for a few heartbeats, then settled back, facing Owen. 'The gloves lay on the lad's chest, the scrip, emptied, at his feet. The blood did not pool so far as his feet.' He glanced towards the steps. 'What is your wife's complaint?'

Owen wanted to shout that it was none of Hempe's business, but he, too, would be better to set aside his dislike. 'She had a fall a while ago and lost the child she carried. The Riverwoman says she lost much blood then, and yesterday's wound has drained her further. She is weak and still mourning the loss. I too am in mourning.' With his eye and his posture he dared Hempe to make an inappropriate comment.

But the bailiff rubbed his balding head and looked aside. 'I did not know about the child.'

'Aye.'

Hempe sighed. 'Are you certain these items are Mistress Wilton's?'

Owen lifted the flap on the scrip, pointed to the initials and the apothecary rose. 'And the knife, aye, she always carries that. I shall buy her another. I doubt she'll ever eat with that again.'

'The belt and the gloves?'

'They are hers.' Owen ignored his conscience, which nagged him with the truth about the gloves. How could he say whose they were, not knowing himself? Still, the lie made him uneasy.

'You must see that you and Mistress Wilton are at present the only suspects in the thief's murder.'

'What?'

'I am headed for the archbishop's palace now to present the case.'

'The council will not care about the death of a thief.'

'I am being fair with you, Archer. If Archbishop Thoresby vouches for both of you, I shall look elsewhere.'

'Anyone in York could vouch for us, Hempe, and you know it.'

'Then I waste my time. It is mine to waste.'

'The aldermen might not agree. And while you chase the innocent, the guilty one goes free. Have you thought of that?'

'I shall attend my business in my own way.'

'Aye, no doubt. I can imagine what His Grace will say about this.'

'Accompany me now and you need not merely imagine it.'

'I must see to my wife.'

Hempe shrugged. 'As you wish.'

When the bailiff was gone, Owen asked Kate and Alisoun to see to Lucie. 'And take these items up to our chamber, tell your mistress they are safely away from the children.' The gloves he stuck in his scrip.

Thoresby was standing in the porch between the halls having a discussion with Wykeham when they were interrupted by George Hempe. He looked a shrewd man, but he proved to be a simpleton with a ridiculous claim that Owen and Lucie had executed a thief. Thoresby sent him away with little courtesy.

'Such an angry man,' said Wykeham. 'A poor choice for a bailiff. I do not like the mood of the city.'

'All the more reason to withdraw from York for a few days.'

Thoresby had proposed an expedition to his manor at Bishopthorpe, wanting Wykeham's advice on a building project he was about to undertake. More importantly, he hoped a brief absence would provide some relief from the uncomfortable tensions in the palace and Wykeham's paranoia. He also planned to take Maeve, who was complaining about the River-woman's presence in the kitchen, wanting the healer and her patient moved above the kitchen. It was too smoky up there for a man in such condition.

Unfortunately, Wykeham was hesitant to leave until after his meeting with Lady Pagnell, to which she had not yet agreed.

Thoresby resumed his effort to reason with him. 'You had been planning a longer trip to the ruin of All Saints in Laughton-en-le-Morthen, taking Archer along.'

'He is needed here now. So much has changed since the fire. I am uneasy, John, Lancastrians are all around me.'

'You were a fool to lash out at the Duke of Lancaster. What did it profit you?'

'I regret it every waking moment. But I was so angry – they'd taken everything from me, all I had worked for.'

'Far from everything. You are Bishop of Winchester – do you forget so soon how hard won your bishopric was, how the king fought the pope for you?'

Wykeham paced to the edge of the steps, his hands clasped behind him, his eyes on the minster that rose just past the walled garden.

Thoresby did not wait for his response. 'There were already the rumours of his lowly birth between you.'

'I had nothing to do with that.' But he had done little to discount them. 'I should have thought you would weigh every word in the duke's presence.'

'All the more reason to go to Bishopthorpe,' said Thoresby.

'Perhaps. I have this morning sent a messenger to the Ferribys suggesting a meeting with the boys tomorrow.'

'The lads? Why?'

'Only after I make peace with them will Lady Pagnell likely agree to see me and settle our business. But if she still holds to keeping me at bay until after her husband's month's mind, I shall gladly ride with you to Bishopthorpe.'

'Come into the hall, we shall . . . Ah, here comes Archer.' *Good Lord, let him bring news of some resolution, the murderer caught, Lady Pagnell ready to meet with Wykeham.*

'Perhaps we have news at last,' the bishop said.

Thoresby disapproved of the ashy stains on his captain's livery, but he said nothing, seeing a smouldering anger in Owen's eye and his fisted hands.

'I guess by the condition of your clothing you have examined the ruins of my house this morning,' Wykeham said.

'Aye, My Lord.' Owen's tone was sharp.

Thoresby informed him of Hempe's visit and their vouching for him and Lucie. He thanked them grudgingly, it seemed to Thoresby.

Owen described the layer of damp ash covering everything in the ruins, the parts of the upper floors that were compromised, where the roof and walls needed shoring up. All reported in a toneless voice. 'So far I've found nothing in the house to assist my investigation,' Owen concluded, then withdrew to the great hall to tell the Fitzbaldrics that they might enter the house with caution.

John Ferriby's feelings about Wykeham and the possibility that parliament was right in blaming him for the setbacks in the war that had cost Owen his eye, this and more had been brewing in Owen's head as he approached the palace. He had fought to speak courteously to Thoresby and now he saw he must proceed without a respite in which to cool his anger, for Godwin Fitzbaldric stood in a corner of the hall, watching the door, his eyes wide with interest.

On the table beside the merchant was a chessboard with the gaily painted pieces in place. 'My wife thought this might distract me from my worries. Adeline will be here presently.'

'They are handsome pieces,' Owen said, trying to sound at ease.

'Bishop William is a man of taste,' Fitzbaldric said.

Owen felt the merchant's eyes on him as he fiddled with one of the knights.

'Why was the bailiff here?' Fitzbaldric suddenly asked. 'What has happened now?'

'It was merely a territorial dispute,' Owen said.

When the silence had stretched on for a while, Fitzbaldric asked, 'Do you play?'

'Would that I had the leisure.'

'You studied it so closely, I thought perhaps it was how you honed your skills. Did you wish to speak with me?'

'Aye. Forgive my silence. It is not yet mid-morning and already the day seems long. I have been at the bishop's house. I am afraid I can tell little of what was in the undercroft.'

'I feared it was all a loss.' Fitzbaldric sounded as if he had held some hope, now dashed.

'It could be of use to me to know what you had stored in the undercroft of the bishop's house. Might we sit?'

'Oh yes, of course.' Fitzbaldric nodded towards the chair across the table and dropped into his. 'I would be a poor merchant not to know my goods. I had wool cloth, wine, jet, hides – some furred – a few silver bowls and a dozen spoons stored down there. I hope to recover at least the bowls and spoons.'

'Hides, you said? Are you certain that Cisotta had not approached you about trading her services for hides? Or buying some? Small hides, suitable for gloves? Perhaps you do not remember the name –'

Fitzbaldric was shaking his head. 'I have not yet established a shop, Captain. I trade with other merchants, not individuals.'

Owen held out the gloves. 'Have you ever seen these before?'

Fitzbaldric shook his head. 'They are not familiar.' He felt the scalloped edge, his gesture hesitant, but whether it was because he recognized the gloves or because he realized what had stained them, Owen could not judge. 'They are well made,' he said, 'the workmanship and the materials.' He glanced up at Owen with a wary look. 'First you showed the belt, now these. What is the significance of these items, Captain? What has stained them? Is it blood?'

'Aye, it is. The thief who stole these has been murdered, left to bleed to death in a ditch near the King's Fishpond.'

'Another murder?' Fitzbaldric searched for a place to set his gaze. He did not seem to wish to look on Owen or on the gloves. 'I never dreamed when we decided to move to York that violence was such a common occurrence. Is that why the bailiff was here?'

'He protests His Grace's authority in all of this.'

'Do you think this latest incident has aught to do with the other . . . ?' He stopped as Adeline joined them.

Owen rose and greeted her.

'Captain.' She nodded, then resting a hand on her husband's shoulder, asked, 'The other what, Godwin?'

Fitzbaldric patted her hand and rose. 'The captain was admiring Bishop William's chessboard and pieces. We shall not be long – I am providing him with a list of what I'd stored in the undercroft. I'll come for you in the garden.'

For once May did not accompany her mistress. It was an opportunity to discuss the maidservant that Owen was loath to pass up. 'In truth, your husband has told me all I need to know. Might I have a private word with you now, Mistress Fitzbaldric?' He anticipated Fitzbaldric's objection – had he not just prevented Hempe from further questioning Lucie? 'Forgive me, but it would be most helpful if I might speak with your wife alone. They have finished the scaffolding at the bishop's house. You may enter now with care.'

Adeline had noticed the gloves. Her eyes just passed over them, but a hand to her throat suggested to Owen that she recognized them.

'What can my wife have to say that cannot be said in my presence?' Fitzbaldric demanded.

Before Owen replied, Adeline put a hand on her husband's forearm and said, 'Perhaps you might go with Bolton to the house, see what you can retrieve.' She looked at Owen. 'We may be able to salvage some of the clothes and furniture on the upper floors.'

'Bolton is sitting with Poins,' Fitzbaldric grumbled. 'The midwife was called away. I thought we were to play chess.'

'Not at the moment, husband. You might at least go and see the condition of the upper storeys.'

'Aye, I will. I spoke to a guild member who might have a property for us to rent. It would be good to see how much we must fetch from Hull to furnish another house.' He bowed to both of them and departed.

Adeline took the seat Fitzbaldric had vacated and, leaning towards the chess table, nodded to the gloves where they lay at the edge. 'Do those have to do with your investigation, Captain?'

'They might. You have seen these before, I think.'

She tilted her head, shook it. 'I once owned a pair of gloves much like these, so for a moment I thought they were familiar.' She touched two of the jet beads. 'But it was many years ago.'

'What did you do with them?'

'I cannot recall. I did not care for them. Perhaps I gave them away.'

'If you would try to remember, Mistress Fitzbaldric.'

'It is important? Mine had been made to my order by a glover in Beverley. What could this have to do with the death of that woman? Such a woman could hardly afford such clothing.'

Owen found Adeline's attitude a puzzle, both disarmingly open and defensive. 'Might there be other pairs like the ones you once had?'

'Of course. Once a glover has a pattern, he will use it again. Why would he not? Though as they were costly, I cannot think there would be many such pairs.'

'Where did you last see yours?'

'In our house near Hull.' Her manner had changed again. There was a vagueness in her eyes, as if she were remembering something and by her voice it was troubling. 'A long while ago.'

'You remember the gloves very well. How is it that you do not recall what you did with them?'

'Do you enjoy pestering people, Captain Archer?'

'No. It is the part of an investigation that I dislike most.'

Adeline touched the gloves again, gently, with her fingertips. 'Are these bloodstains?'

'They are.'

She pulled back her hand, made a fist. 'I believe I added them to some clothes I was giving the priest, for the poor. My children's clothes.' She turned her head away, but Owen could hear the emotion in her voice, recognized the rigid posture of someone hiding pain. 'I had quarrelled with my daughter about the gloves a few days before the pestilence took her. She went so quickly. I never had the chance –' She took a deep breath. 'I could not bear to look at them again.'

Owen bowed his head and said nothing for a long while.

Adeline broke the silence, asking a servant for some watered wine. 'And for you?' she asked Owen, the servant waiting.

'Some ale would suit me.' When the servant withdrew, Owen said, 'I am sorry for your loss, Mistress Fitzbaldric, and sorry to make you remember it.'

'It is a wound that never heals, Captain. I am called indulgent for mourning my children so long, indulgent in my pain.'

The servant returned and they sat in silence for a little while.

But Owen feared Fitzbaldric would return before he had finished questioning Adeline, so once again he interrupted her peace. 'Did you take the clothes to the priest, or did you give them to someone to take for you?'

'That I truly cannot recall, Captain.' Adeline picked up a pawn, turned it round in her fingers, set it down, then looked Owen in the eye. 'Are you thinking that someone in my household might have kept them?'

'It is possible, is it not? What of your husband? Might he have kept them, thinking you might regret your action, or perhaps because for him they conjured up good memories?'

She had grown angry as he spoke. 'Listen to yourself. You are weaving a tale to make Godwin appear guilty. What does my husband have to do with the gloves?'

'I seek the truth, Mistress Fitzbaldric, not a scapegoat.'

'No?' She held herself so taut the pulse was visible in her long neck. 'Where did you find those gloves? Whose blood is on them?' Her voice grew tenser with each question. 'You are trying to blame my husband for the fire.' Owen's silence brought blotches of colour to her neck. 'Dear God.' She rose. 'Mother in Heaven, you cannot believe . . . Whose gloves were those?'

257

'You said "were". And you are right. They were in Cisotta's house.'

'And you believe they are the ones I discarded? Then how did she get them?'

'I hoped you might know.'

'I . . . I cannot imagine.'

At last Owen saw honest fear in Adeline's eyes.

'How long has May been in your household, Mistress Fitzbaldric?'

'Since we married. Seventeen years.'

'And before that?'

'She was in my mother's household, the daughter of the gardener. Mother had –' She stopped herself, shaking her head, sitting down again to sip at her wine.

'May had blood on her face the night of the fire, yet she has no wounds on her face. What do you make of that?'

'Oh, dear God, I do not know what to make of it, Captain, any of it. She is a good woman, though of late she has been clumsy and distracted.'

'What of her relationship with Poins?'

Adeline glanced up at him, all subterfuge gone. 'Have you looked at them? No, of course not, he is in bandages so thick you cannot see his youth, his beauty. Yes, I have gone to see him since yesterday. Poor man.' She closed her eyes. 'I had not understood the extent of his burns.'

'So May is too old and plain for him?'

'Yes. It is uncharitable, but it is true. They say the dead woman was beautiful and flirtatious. Perhaps Poins –' She covered her face. 'I do not want to believe it of him, that he could do such a thing to his leman.'

So she thought Poins the murderer. 'This is the most difficult question of all, Mistress Fitzbaldric, but I must ask it. Are you and your husband happy in one another?'

She gave a little sound like a laugh, but she had tears in her eyes and her voice trembled with emotion as she said, 'You cannot believe Godwin was in some way connected to the dead woman?'

'He is a man like any other.'

'Are you happy in your wife, Captain?'

I was, Owen heard himself respond somewhere deep inside, and the answer shook him.

'I see you, too, find it a difficult question to answer, Captain. Godwin and I have rejoiced in our children and lost them, we have built a business and lost most of our goods, we have aged, quarrelled, loved and hated. Am I happy in him, and he in me? We are accustomed, Captain. And some days more than that. I did not lie with Poins, and I doubt that my husband lay with either May or Cisotta.' She rose with a commanding dignity, though she was trembling with emotion. 'I shall say no more, Captain.'

'I wish to speak with May and Bolton. Do I have your permission?'

Adeline had already turned from him. She inclined her head, whispered, 'Do what you will' and crossed the hall to the screens passage.

Owen sent a servant for May, tucked the gloves in his scrip and sat back to finish his ale. He did not feel good about cracking Adeline Fitzbaldric's façade, particularly as he had been wounded in the assault. Of course he was happy in his marriage. Lucie's pregnancy had been difficult and had ended in sorrow. He had been so frightened he might lose her. Of course he loved her. But that momentary doubt unsettled him.

The archbishop entered the hall, in better colour than he had been of late. He approached Owen, but

259

when he caught sight of May making her way towards Owen he simply nodded and said, 'Come to me before you leave the palace. I shall be in the chapel.'

As Thoresby passed her, May stumbled against a piece of furniture, which so flustered her that as she sat she hit her knee on the chess table, then brushed her sleeve over the chessboard, sending several pawns spinning. Owen caught them. She was indeed a clumsy woman. As he leaned close to replace the pieces, he smelled her fear, saw terror in her eyes. That was not good. It was easier to draw information out of someone angry or secretive than someone so frightened.

He would go slowly, try to put her at ease. 'I am glad that you do not seem to have suffered injury in the fire,' he said.

'I . . . I am so grateful to you. I don't know how I can ever repay you for saving my life.' She blushed crimson and kept her gaze on the chess pieces.

'Are you comfortable in the palace? Have you everything you need?'

She nodded.

'It is a lovely chess set, is it not?'

'Yes, Captain.' She put a hand to her chest, as if trying to quiet her pounding heart.

He could think of no more idle talk. He had never been good at it. 'I need you to tell me what you remember of the night of the fire, what your actions were, say, from the time your master and mistress departed.'

'There is little to tell, Captain. I had not slept well for a while. I am not accustomed to the noise of a city and my bedroom was so high up in that house.'

'You were uncomfortable there?'

'I should not say so – my mistress dearly loved th house – but I am glad to be out of it.'

'Closer to the ground.'

A shy smile and a glance at him. 'Aye.'

'So, you were tired that evening.'

'I was. And as Bolton was out, and my mistress, I had little to do. So I went up to nap.'

'That is all?'

She nodded. 'Then I heard you calling and breathed in a mouthful of smoke.'

'What of the blood on your face?'

May touched a temple absently. 'I told you, I suffered many scratches and cuts.'

'Have you been feeling well of late?'

She glanced up, her eyes huge with fear. 'A little tired, Captain, as I said.'

He drew out the gloves, laid them on her side of the chess table.

May sat so still that Owen could hear her breath rasping as she stared at the gloves.

He said nothing for a little while, waiting for some reaction. But at last he asked, 'Have you seen these before?'

She nodded.

'Where?'

'They were my mistress's. She would not wear them after little Sarah died. She gave them to the church for the poor.'

'Are you certain of that?'

May nodded.

'And you have not seen them since?'

May shook her head.

'Aren't you going to ask how they came to be stained?'

She lifted her other hand to her chest, then dropped both in her lap. 'Much might have happened to them since they left my mistress's house,' she said.

'Did you have need of a healer, May?'

She shook her head.

'Did you see Cisotta about a charm, perhaps?'

'No.'

It was uncanny how she resisted glancing up to see his expression. It was unnatural.

'Tell me what frightens you so, May.'

Silence.

'May?' he whispered.

She took a deep breath. 'You think evil of me. I've done nothing.' Still she did not meet his gaze.

'Do you know who murdered Cisotta?'

May shook her head.

Owen felt in his gut that she was lying. But so far she had not run away. He doubted she would now. He would give her some time to stew in her fear.

'They are bloodstains, May. A lad was killed for those gloves, but the murderer left them with him. Why do you think a man would do that?'

Now she looked up at him. 'What lad?'

'A thief, who had stolen the gloves from my wife.' He could see the confusion on her face, but also that fear. It seemed a good time to stop. Perhaps she would come after him with questions. He reached over. She leaned back away from him as if fearing he was reaching for her. He took the gloves and, as he stood, tucked them in his scrip. 'I have kept you from your duties long enough. Thank you for giving me your time.' He bowed to her and crossed to the screens passage, listening to May's stumbling rise from her seat. There was something about her clumsiness that bothered him.

Seventeen

a change of heart

What troubled Owen about May's behaviour was that Adeline Fitzbaldric did not seem a woman to tolerate much clumsiness in a maid. But she had spoken as if it were a recent change. Which begged the question of what had brought on the change; whether it might be something for which May had consulted Cisotta. Or it was possible that May truly found the move to the city distressing. He remembered how their maid Tildy had feared leaving York for the first time, having never before gone past the city walls.

'That maid is a danger to herself.'

Owen started. He had not noticed Wykeham approaching. Once more he wore a simple robe, but contrary to his recent behaviour he was smiling.

'My Lord Bishop.' Owen bowed to him and tried to push away his resentment of the man.

Wykeham's smile had faded by the time Owen lifted his head.

The dark clothing accentuated the bishop's greying temples and shadowed his doubling chin. 'I shall need you and your men watching the palace more closely than usual tomorrow. Particularly from midday. Lady Pagnell is coming here to settle matters between us.'

This was a sudden shift. 'She has agreed to meet?'

'She has.'

'I do not understand. What need have you of extra guards for such a meeting? What trouble do you expect?'

'If the Lancastrians are behind all that has befallen me of late – the worst of it murder in my townhouse – and if they believe Lady Pagnell means to make peace with me, they may make a move tomorrow.'

The bishop's fears became more convoluted by the day. 'What would be their purpose?'

'They mean to keep me from the king, to prevent my ever resuming the chancellorship.' Wykeham's voice was high with tension.

'It seems a matter for diplomats, My Lord, not soldiers.'

Wykeham moved closer, his jaw thrust towards Owen, eyes wide with indignation. 'Do you serve Lancaster or Lawgoch?'

For a moment Owen froze. 'Neither, My Lord,' he managed to say at last. 'I serve His Grace and King Edward.'

'Do you?'

'Aye, My Lord. And you while you reside here. My men and I shall be ready for whatever befalls.'

Kneeling in the chapel, Thoresby thought about Sir Ranulf and prayed for guidance in how he might best bring peace to his household – or whether peace was the wrong state to wish for towards the end of one's life. For several years before offering his services to the king, Sir Ranulf had been a shadow of himself, handing over to his son Stephen all business of the manor while suffering from a lethargy that weakened him in body and in soul. But as the preparations for his mission for the king had begun, the years had fallen away. During his last days in York, Ranulf had spoken in a freshly vibrant voice, his eyes had cleared and lit on everything with interest, his steps lengthened, his back straightened, his memory sharpened. Of Ranulf's last days in France Thoresby knew nothing. He wondered what had gone wrong. A slip in his persona witnessed by someone already suspicious? Had his memory faltered? The latter is what Thoresby suspected, yet he had nothing on which to base that. Perhaps the youthful moment had been merely that, a passing moment, a teasing improvement before the end. He wondered what his own end would be like. He had done nothing of late that would suggest he had still some great achievement ahead of him, the crowning glory of his considerable career. He had not wielded a weapon since helping Archer against a murderer years ago. He had participated in no significant councils – indeed, had not even been invited to the council in Winchester to advise the new lord chancellor. It felt a paltry life, without purpose. Perhaps he should seek out a quest, as Ranulf had done.

He groaned at the thought. Aches in all his joints, difficulties with sleep, failing sight, a suspicion that he did not hear as well as he had only last year, all these were signs of a body that was incapable of derring-do. But that did not mean he could not produce something of worth. The lady chapel would be a fine monument to his archbishopric. And it was almost complete. Within the year he could move his predecessors to their new tombs and work on his own would begin. And then what? He must do more. He must move back into the realm of action, use his power for the good of mankind. Perhaps he should ride to Westminster, or wherever King Edward might be, and offer his service as Ranulf had done.

The thought exhausted him and he was easing himself up when Owen entered the chapel, knelt beside Thoresby, crossed himself, bowed his head. Thoresby settled back down on his knees, but his feet were beginning to tingle, which was a sign they would soon be numb. 'When you have finished your prayer, come along to my parlour. I would speak with you, Archer.' He rose and retreated to his high-backed chair to wait.

Owen did not keep him waiting long. Thoresby noted as his captain and steward joined him that he looked as if he had not slept in several days. He had never seen Owen so haggard. Together they walked in silence down the corridor to the screens passage.

'You do not look well this morning, Archer,' Thoresby said when they stepped into the daylight from the high windows in the hall.

'Awaking to the bailiff's accusations was unpleasant, Your Grace. I am worried about Lucie, and I have not yet broken my fast. I've no doubt I am not at my best.'

Thoresby clapped for a servant, who came in his own good time, damn him. He ordered food and ale brought to his parlour for Archer. 'It appears I feed my servants too well,' he said so that the servant might hear, 'and they grow lazy.'

Owen said nothing.

In one corner of the hall the sun shone on Wykeham's colourful chess pieces. 'I see the Fitzbaldrics have abandoned their game,' Thoresby noted as they passed it.

'They have access to the bishop's house.'

'Ah. Yes.'

Owen resumed his silent walk through the great hall. Thoresby followed. 'I sat with the Fitzbaldric manservant for a while last night.'

That sparked an interest. Owen paused on the first step, his hawk eye on Thoresby. 'You sat with Poins and the Riverwoman?'

'Mistress Digby had been called away late in the afternoon. I took the opportunity. I have never seen such injuries outside of battle. The man is in great agony.'

'Aye. What made you . . .' Owen began, but cut himself off. 'Did he speak to you?'

'He asked for my blessing.' Thoresby could see that Owen was surprised. 'Guy and the Fitzbaldrics' cook were also puzzled that he spoke to me. But when I asked him what he remembered of the fire he turned away from me.'

'So he is concerned for his soul.'

'Does that give you pause?'

'No. With his injuries, it is fitting.'

There was an autumn chill in the air, a dampness that did not suit Thoresby's joints. 'Your food has doubtless preceded you to my parlour.' He led the way across the porch. He hoped a meal would revive Owen.

A small table had been set beside one of the comfortable chairs, spread with cold meats, cheese, bread and fruit. A jug of ale and a cup sat to one side.

'Maeve is in a generous mood,' Owen said. 'But I should not eat in front of you.'

'I sent for it and you will eat it. While you do, we shall talk.'

Thoresby was glad when Owen took a seat, slipped his knife from its sheath and stabbed a piece of meat. Settling nearby, he poured himself a cup of equal parts hot water and wine.

'You spoke of Guy,' Owen said. 'He was present at Poins's bedside?'

Thoresby could see by Owen's frown that this disturbed him.

'He has offered to sit with Poins when neither the Riverwoman nor Bolton the cook is able to do so. I thought it strange, such a sullen man, to be so charitable. But Wykeham says he has a kind heart.'

'I've seen no sign of it till now.'

That did not require a response. 'The bailiff overstepped his duties. But I am concerned whether there is any connection between the thief's murder and the midwife's.'

'Would that I knew, Your Grace.'

Thoresby wondered at the weariness in his captain's voice but forgot that as Owen drew a pair of women's gloves from his scrip. They were pretty things, or had been before being stained and stiffened.

'Lucie was carrying these. She had found them hidden behind Cisotta's potions. She believes it was no accident that the thief chose her.'

'But the recovery of the gloves is surely a sign that neither the thief nor his murderer was after them.'

'Lucie would argue with that.'

'Why?'

Owen paused, elbow on the table, a piece of bread in his hand. 'Much of what she says is against reason of late.'

Thoresby knew that Owen depended on his wife's good sense. To have her lacking it must seem a great void. 'Mistress Wilton has suffered much. Perhaps when she regains her health she will regain her wit also. Tell me what you know of the incident.'

Owen pushed away the food and leaned his elbows on the table as he related the events.

Thoresby listened with growing concern. 'What is this city coming to, a man attacking a woman for a pair of gloves?'

'The gloves were not visible.' Owen raked a hand through his unruly hair. 'I can make no sense of it.'

'Are you certain that her only injury is the hand? Did she fall?'

'And addle her pate?'

Owen's eye grew so dark that Thoresby rose and went to his writing table. Atop other documents for his consideration was a note in Brother Michaelo's hand saying that Wykeham wished to discuss arrangements for a meeting with Lady Pagnell to take place the next day.

'So Lady Pagnell has relented,' Thoresby murmured. Life might soon return to a calm rhythm, God willing.

'Aye,' said Owen. 'The bishop wants a full guard on the palace tomorrow, in case Lady Pagnell alerts the Lancastrians of it.'

'This feud he began in self-righteous anger will be his undoing.'

'So fall great men,' Owen agreed. Setting aside his cup, he prepared to rise.

But Thoresby was still disturbed by Owen's mood. 'I am fond of Mistress Wilton, as you know, and I ask this in that light. What is her condition, Archer? Is she pressing herself to work when she needs rest? Has she seen the best physicians?'

Owen studied him but said nothing for a while. Thoresby kept still, allowing the man to decide whether or not to confide in him.

It was Owen who shifted his gaze at last, casting his eye at some point just beyond Thoresby. Despite the food he looked more haggard than before. 'If anyone can return my wife to her true self it will be Magda Digby,

I think. I trust the Riverwoman with my life. But Lucie claims that work is her solace, that lying abed as Magda has ordered is agony for her. God knows what she is thinking, what she is suffering.'

'Does she suffer in both flesh and spirit?'

'Aye, Your Grace. But the spirit is the worst.'

'Might it be good for Jehannes to see her?' The Archdeacon of York was a close friend of the family.

'She has sought him out as confessor and guide, Your Grace. He has comforted her, but nothing eases her for long.'

'I am sorry Wykeham's problems have drawn in your family, Archer. Let us pray that tomorrow's meeting is satisfactory, and then we'll be free of him.'

'Amen.'

Lucie woke to a knock on her chamber door. Her mouth was woolly, her eyes swollen. She had cried herself to sleep, God's curse on her at last crumbling all her reserves. Self-pity was ignoble, sinful, yet she preferred it to the self-hatred that had poisoned her days and nights of late. Now she woke with a new emotion – anger.

'Come in,' she called out, coughing at the effort.

Alisoun entered with a cup of Magda's tonic. 'You had a visitor, Mistress Wilton. The bailiff George Hempe.' Lucie looked up sharply, saw the distaste in Alisoun's expression. 'He stayed only a moment, saying he did not wish to wake you. He begs your pardon for his unpleasant behaviour this morning.'

'George Hempe said that?'

'He did, Mistress.'

Lucie stared out of the window. The day had grown wanly fair but the breeze still held dampness. 'How long have I slept?'

'It is midday, Mistress.'

'Are Gwenllian and Hugh behaving themselves?'

Alisoun's colourless face lit up. 'They are the best children I have ever minded, clever and cheerful. They are no trouble at all.'

Lucie smiled. They were good children. Heaven knew what they must think of their mother, always abed, always in bandages. She drank some of the tonic, then pushed back the covers.

Alisoun brought a bedpan from beneath the bed. 'Do you need help with this?'

'I do not need it. I am going out to the privy.'

Instead of backing away, as Lucie had expected, Alisoun shook her head. 'Mistress Digby said you were to stay abed, that you are weak, and only rest and a good appetite will strengthen you.'

'I shall have little appetite if I do not move about.'

'May I look at your hand?'

As Lucie lifted it, a pain shot up her arm. She clenched her teeth. 'Dear God.'

'I'll pack the wound with the Riverwoman's paste that will cool it and draw out the bad humours.'

'First help me with the chamber pot,' Lucie said. 'An injured hand does not make me a cripple. And when we are finished, bring the children up to play for a while.'

Alisoun's hands were strong and her presence comforting.

'Do you know the ingredients of the tonic Magda made for me?' Lucie asked.

'I do, Mistress.'

'I would have you and Jasper remix it without the sleeping potion, which is valerian and something else – sleepwort? It is difficult to taste.' The girl had paused in her ministration. 'Did I guess correctly?'

'Aye, Mistress. But the Riverwoman says it is important that you rest.'

'Rest I will, when I have seen to my affairs. Will you give Jasper the instructions to make the tonic without the sleeping draught?'

Alisoun, tucking the rag bandages and ointment in a basket, hid her face from Lucie. 'The Riverwoman is watching me for signs that I am not a healer born, Mistress. If I disobey her . . .'

'Then it is best that I go without the tonic until I am ready for rest.'

From the set of the girl's shoulders Lucie could see that she was annoying her.

'That is not doing as the Riverwoman wishes, either,' Alisoun groaned in the pure tones of a child weary of unpleasant responsibilities.

'But I shall disobey, not you.'

'What do you mean to do?'

'When Magda tells you to do something, do you question her intentions?'

'Aye, Mistress.'

'And does she allow it?'

'No, Mistress. I'll bring the children to you now.' Alisoun departed.

Bolton, the Fitzbaldrics' cook, was a bald, well-fleshed man with scars that suggested he had experienced a much more adventurous life before becoming a domestic. He was sitting cross-legged on the rushes beside Poins's pallet, singing a bawdy ballad when Owen entered the screened-off section of the kitchen. Poins lay with eyes open, staring at the ceiling.

Bolton swallowed the end of a note and scrambled upright. 'Captain,' he said, bobbing his head.

'I'll relieve you for a little while. But first, have you

ever seen these before?' Owen drew the gloves out of his scrip.

Bolton bent close, making an odd sound in his throat. 'I don't like it when gloves dry like that, like claws ready to grab you.' He crossed himself. 'No, I've never seen such fancy gloves. Ladies are not commonly dressed so fine when they're in the kitchen.' He retreated to the screens.

'I'll stay long enough for you to go to the privy and have something to eat.'

'Bless you, Captain.'

Poins had closed his eyes.

The kitchen had high ceilings, and a small window was open near the bed. Even so, the man's burns smelled like rotting greens and made Owen's recently filled stomach queasy. Thoresby had been kinder than Owen realized in sitting with the man last night. Poins's face was partially visible now, the bandages only covering his right eye and upper cheek, the scalp over his left ear. His lips were still swollen and cracking. Owen found the ointment for them and smoothed some on.

'Poins, do you remember me?' he asked as he worked. 'I'm Captain Archer. My wife and I took you in after the fire.'

Poins's lips trembled, and a tension in his jaw suggested that he heard and held himself back from responding.

Before a battle the best commanders envisioned the thoughts of the enemy, trying to predict their movements. Owen sat back and thought about how he would feel if he had suffered the wounds and the burns Poins had, the loss of a limb. Magda said that some of his deepest burns were painless. Did that mean he was numb in those places? Owen thought that might be almost as frightening as pain. And there was the pain in the limb he no longer had, as well as the pain of his burns and the stench of his own decaying flesh. He wondered whether Poins was aware that he had moved from Owen's house to the palace. And what he thought their purpose was in their attempts to question him about the fire. He must be frightened, confused, despairing, and perhaps angry that Magda had removed his arm without telling him what she was to do. It was no wonder Poins did not choose to talk. But he might be the key to that night. Owen must find a way to reach him.

He wondered whether Magda had told Poins anything about Cisotta's death. Owen had not. Perhaps it was time to speak of it. Softly, so that his words carried no threat, Owen told Poins how he and Cisotta had been found, and that she had been murdered, but not how, watching all the time for signs that he understood. Again there were subtle changes in Poins's face, and as Owen described Cisotta's burns tremors ran down Poins's ruined side.

'We know nothing of what happened that night, how you both came to be in the undercroft,' Owen continued. 'Did you argue with her?'

No response.

'Did you catch her stealing your master's goods?'

One side of Poins's mouth twitched.

'Small hides, perhaps? Goatskin? Rabbit?'

Another shudder ran through Poins's body and his throat began to work.

'Is that it, Poins, you caught her, and in your surprise you dropped a lamp?'

Poins contorted his mouth and a sound came out half groan, half sigh. 'Not . . . my . . . lamp!' he managed, his voice hoarse, his words barely coherent because of his swollen tongue.

'What happened then?'

Poins moved his head back and forth weakly.

'Did you kill her?'

Poins turned away, moaning as he tried to roll over on to his right side.

Owen slumped down on to a stool, head in hands. He must be patient though it drove him mad. When his heartbeat returned to normal, he straightened and watched Poins for a short while, but though the injured man breathed more quickly than he had before, he was motionless.

It seemed to have been Owen's mention of the hide that had roused Poins, and that he had acknowledged that a lamp had set the fire, though someone else's lamp. It would not be for nothing that Poins had broken his silence in Owen's presence, not after all this time. He also seemed keen to deny his guilt. Yet his refusal to say more seemed a token of some measure of guilt.

'I am sorry if I caused you distress, but you must see how important it is that I learn what happened that night. A murderer walks among us. He must be found before he kills again.'

Poins opened his eyes. 'He struck me down.'

Owen dropped to his knees beside the pallet. 'Someone was there? A man? Did you see him?'

Poins barely shook his head. The pain in his eyes made Owen want to believe him.

'Why was Cisotta there?'

Poins shook his head and turned away.

'I beg you, Poins, tell me.'

Silence.

Hoping for another chance, Owen sat with his attention focused on Poins until Bolton returned, but in all that time Poins did not move. It was even more maddening to Owen than before, knowing the man could speak, remembered the night and refused to tell him all he knew.

Gwenllian and Hugh had grown bored playing in Lucie's bedchamber, begging Alisoun to take them out to the garden.

Lucie told herself it meant nothing, she should rejoice in their delight in play, their enjoyment of the garden, but she felt the rejection deep within. They were right to prefer the young, energetic Alisoun to her. Lucie's hand throbbed, as did her head, and her balance was precarious when she stood. But worse than all that, the darkness was creeping back. She must busy herself.

She slipped out of bed and waited until the room stilled, then, with the mincing steps of the elderly, she made her way across the boards to the chest in which she had locked her scrip and the items Owen had brought from the fire. Unlocking it, she found the scrip, the knife she had wrapped in a rag, the belt used to murder Cisotta and her friend's ruined girdle, but not the gloves. If Owen had taken them it must mean he thought them of some importance. Perhaps in finding them she had redeemed her mistakes of the previous day. She tucked the belt into her scrip, took her paternoster beads from a shelf and crossed back to the bed, annoyed by how weak her legs felt. Her pulse pounded in her head. The loss of blood could cause some of this weakness, but she suspected that most of it was the effect of the tonic, that Magda had meant it to enforce the rest she had ordained. But it was a half-hearted effort, for Magda would know Lucie might discover the cause of her exhaustion and set the tonic aside.

Sitting propped up against pillows, Lucie examined her scrip. Nothing but a greasy smudge suggested it had ever been out of her possession. Opening it, she passed her fingers over her initials and the apothecary rose, proud of such a fine piece, then dipped her hand within and retrieved her own ruined girdle. Uncurling it she saw that the fabric had been neatly sliced, the result of a sharp blade. With the items spread out on her lap for inspiration, she took up her beads and prayed for God's guidance in helping Owen. By the end of the first round of prayers she still lacked inspiration. A second round was equally fruitless, though she felt steadier, more alert than before. She was setting the scrip and belt aside when Emma Ferriby appeared in the doorway.

'Is that what I hope it is? Have you recovered your scrip and your mother's gloves?'

Lucie wished she had not lied to Emma about the gloves, for surely she would slip with the truth. She distracted her friend by telling her of the bailiff's visit and his later apology.

Emma had settled on the edge of the bed while Lucie talked, studying the items strewn on the covers. At the last part she glanced up. 'George Hempe contrite? I wonder what Owen said or did to him?' Her gaze wandered back to the items on the coverlet. Picking up the burned belt she studied the buckle, looked closely at the leather. 'I could swear – but it cannot be.'

Lucie's pulse quickened. 'Do you recognize it?'

Emma traced the brass pattern with a stubby finger. 'It looks very like one of a pair of straps Father used to hold rolled documents together. They were made of a fine cordovan leather that had been salvaged from a belt he had worn as a soldier.'

'Who has them now?'

'As Mother has handed over all business to Matthew, he has them. I thought he had used them to strap together the property documents from Wykeham.'

A fragment of memory teased Lucie, a table with a number of items, including a strap such as this might have been when whole. Tally sticks, too.

'But I cannot recall when I last saw them,' Emma said. 'There was something wrapped round the rolls, I'm sure.' There was an excitement in her voice, but her veil obscured her face as she bent over the belt fragment.

Now Lucie saw it, the table with John, Ivo and Edgar at one end, Matthew at the other.

'I saw one of the straps the morning I came to your house with the sleep draught.' Lucie remembered Matthew rising from the table, gathering his work, securing the rolls. 'He used only one strap that day.'

As Emma lifted her head she was almost smiling. 'Are you thinking he might have been in the burning house? With documents?'

'Or he had left documents there and someone else used the strap. We do not know where he was that night.'

Emma lifted the strap higher, tugged it taut. '*Used* this? What do you mean?'

Lucie had forgotten that Emma did not know how Cisotta had died. It was difficult to keep track of what people knew, what must be kept secret, who might be after what she knew and to what ends.

Her silence led Emma to demand, 'What are you hiding from me?'

Lucie needed Emma's insights, her information. It was too late to back away from her now. Already one lie stood between them. Lucie would not tell another. 'Owen found it round Cisotta's neck.'

At first Emma did not seem to understand. Then she dropped the strap on the bed, raised her hands to her neck. 'She was strangled?'

Lucie nodded.

'Dear God.' Emma stared at her upturned palms. 'I thought him evil, but not so evil as to murder.'

'I cannot make sense of it,' Lucie said.

Emma had dropped her hands to her lap and sat contemplating them in a silence that troubled Lucie. It was so quiet she could hear Gwenllian's laughter in the garden, Kate speaking loudly so that Phillippa could hear her over the splashing water in the laundry tub.

'How long have you known how Cisotta was murdered?' Emma asked in a voice that echoed the tension of her former silence. Her eyes accused Lucie.

'I have known all along. It is a secret, Emma. I pray you, tell no one of this.'

'Is that why you kept it from me this long?'

'Of course it is. What need had you to know? I have only this moment learned that the strap might belong to your household.'

'My mother's household.' Emma slipped from the bed, moved to the window, where she looked without, her back to Lucie. 'Or do you fear that the rumours are true, that my family had a hand in the fire?' She did not move, did not turn to regard Lucie.

'I have never thought your family to blame. I told you, no one knows how Cisotta died. Emma, please, you must believe me.'

Emma did not respond.

Lucie slipped the strap and the beads into her scrip, pushed back the covers and rose, using the bedpost to steady herself. Her balance felt better than before, but the floorboards were cold. 'It is time to hang the bed curtains,' she murmured to herself, dispelling the uncomfortable silence.

'You should keep them up throughout the year,' Emma said, glancing at the plain rails connecting the posts. 'Drafts in summer are as dangerous as those in winter.' She noticed where Lucie was. 'Standing there in bare feet and just a shift is doubly foolish.'

'I should be grateful for less criticism and your help in dressing.' Lucie lifted her bandaged hand. 'This makes the simplest task difficult.'

Emma gently took the bandaged hand. 'Are you in pain?' she asked, avoiding Lucie's eyes. Her voice was strained.

'Yes. But it matters not whether I lie abed or sit in the garden, and I am not as fond of this chamber as I once was. I've spent too much time in it of late. I should enjoy some air.'

'Why did you have all those things on the bed?'

Lucie heard concern in Emma's tone. 'I thought to learn something from them. I prayed for guidance in how to assist Owen – and God answered me with your identifying the strap. Now I feel impatient to tell Owen, but he may be out all the day. I must do something. I cannot sit here any longer.'

Emma had already taken the gown Lucie had worn in the morning from a hook on the wall and collected her shoes and linen-lined hose.

'Those are too warm,' Lucie protested.

'You have lost much blood and your humours are ill-balanced. Warmth is important at such a time. I shall instruct Kate to spice your food.' Emma still seemed stiff in demeanour.

Lucie did not wish to argue about her humours at the moment. 'Owen must talk to Matthew, find out the truth.'

Emma lifted the gown and helped Lucie pull it down, then began on the buttons. 'If he murdered Cisotta and has been clever enough to hide his guilt so far, he is not likely to confess.'

'Where does Matthew sleep?'

'With Edgar, the boys' tutor.'

'I would speak with Edgar.'

Emma sighed and held out a sleeve for Lucie's arm, then fumbled with the laces at the shoulders.

Lucie tried not to complain about Emma's jerky movements.

'Owen will not be pleased if you go abroad in the city,' Emma said.

Nor was Lucie ready today. 'Then would you speak with Edgar, ask him whether he has noticed anything in Matthew's behaviour, whether he knows where Matthew was the night of the fire, or at least whether he was out, when he came in?'

Emma pulled over a low stool and sat on it, wrapping her arms round herself. 'My stomach aches to think of going home. How can I look upon Matthew?'

'Remember that we have no proof that he is guilty. Faith, we do not even know whether he knew Cisotta.'

'That is so. I cannot imagine how he would have made her acquaintance.'

'Men have a way of finding beautiful women.'

Emma shook her head. 'He is chasing wealthier and more powerful prey.'

'Cisotta might have been a past conquest. Or merely a dalliance, a distraction. But at the moment we know nothing to accuse him of.'

The two women looked at each other, their faces sober.

'Except that she was strangled with a strap very like hose in our house,' Emma said slowly.

'Speak with Edgar.'

Emma slipped one of the hose up Lucie's leg and helped her fasten it, then the other. They were warm on Lucie's chilled feet.

'Mother is meeting with Wykeham on the morrow,' Emma said as she picked up Lucie's shoes. 'Have you heard?'

'No. How did he convince her? Was it the boys' accident?'

'He sent a messenger asking to meet at our house with John and Ivo in the morning. Mother took it as a sign of trouble, though I thought the bishop took care with his words to sound reassuring.'

'Has she invited him to the house?'

'No. She proposed to meet at the palace.'

'But that is perfect! At what time do they meet?'

Puzzled, Emma said, 'Just after midday.'

'I shall come to your home in early afternoon.'

'Why?'

'To search Matthew's belongings.'

'Oh – but surely Magda wants you to rest.'

'I cannot rest until we have found Cisotta's murderer.'

'Lucie.'

'I have been lying in that bed day after day, night after night, thinking of the child I lost, worrying about God's purpose, whether he means to take more from me. When I am not fearing for my children I am mourning the friend who nursed me. I cannot bear it, Emma. I must have occupation.'

She could see in Emma's eyes that she had touched a chord.

physicks

O wen sank down against the wall outside the
palace kitchen and let the sun soak into him.
He felt his failure with Poins in his bones.
The man had little more to lose, so there was precious
little chance of coercing him into talking more
about the fire. To come so close to knowledge only
to have it incomplete – Owen's jaw hurt he clenched
his teeth so, and his stomach churned from the
stench of Poins's decaying flesh that seemed to have
seeped into his skin. So Owen sat, letting his head,
chest, arms and the front of his legs grow warm while
those parts of him not directly in the sun stayed
chilled.

His head spun with questions that might never be
answered. He needed to work up a sweat, purge the
stench, ease his aches. He thought about the practice
yard at Kenilworth where he would fight until his head
buzzed and afterwards dowse himself with a bucket of
cold water, then sit in the sunshine enjoying a tankard
of ale with his men. Lief was dead now, Ned exiled.
Bertold still led Lancaster's archers and Gaspare had

gone on a mission for Lancaster and never returned. There was no going back.

The best he could do now to work up a sweat was to split wood or do the garden chores that required a strong back, neither as satisfying as the practice yard. Magda's voice drifted from the kitchen. He should speak with her. But he found himself walking in the opposite direction, into the palace garden.

With Emma steadying her at the elbow, Lucie walked the paths of her garden and thought about her new piece of information. It was God's gift to her, of that she was certain, for had Emma not walked in when the strap was lying on the bed Lucie doubted she would have shown it to her at all, and would never have known its use. That the Lord had answered Lucie's prayer with such clarity and speed had cast out her devils for the moment. Gwenllian and Hugh had seemed much comforted by her smiling face. Alisoun had said Magda might have erred in giving Lucie such a strong tonic, for she seemed far better without it. Lucie fought to hide her unsteadiness. Slowly though she was walking, still her heart pounded and her legs felt as if they might buckle beneath her with each step. But it was worth the effort.

A strap for documents. It changed the way she imagined the scene on the night of the fire. And that gave her an idea. 'Emma, I would see Bess Merchet. Would you fetch my scrip and walk with me to the tavern?'

Pulled from her own thoughts, Emma at first agreed then took a good look at Lucie. 'Your colour is much better for being out in the air. But do you have the strength to go so far?'

'It is not so far, just past our garden wall,' Lucie said

In a short time they were crossing the yard at the York Tavern. Lucie tried not to lean too much on Emma, though her balance was unsure and her hand was throbbing. She should have supported it in some way, but she disliked the encumbrance of binding up her arm. Once within the tavern, she sank down on a bench and let Emma search for the innkeeper.

Bess's ruddy face darkened as she saw Lucie. 'I heard what happened in the Shambles.' She stood back and studied Lucie, shaking her head at what she saw. 'You are not so feeble as I feared, but your face boasts of its bones and I can see your veins through your skin.' She sat down on the bench opposite Lucie. 'I am making a pottage with meat for you. You need your strength. And Tom will bring a cask of ale to put some flesh on you.'

Bess's mothering of Lucie was one of the reasons she did not know as much as Emma did about the past few months. Lucie wearied of advice. She did not wish to hear more about what she should be eating and, seeing that Emma was about to voice her own opinions on that, Lucie took out the strap and laid it before Bess, pre-empting a lecture.

'I've seen that,' Bess said, 'and I know why you are so keen to know who wore it. I've already told Owen that I see so many belts, I cannot say whose it might be.'

'But what of a strap round rolls of parchment?' Lucie asked.

Arms crossed before her as if to restrain herself from touching it, Bess bent close to the buckle, then leaned back to gaze round the room.

Emma moved to speak, but Lucie silenced her with a touch and a shake of her head. She could see by the movement of Bess's eyes that she was reviewing her memories. Suddenly Bess rose, crossed to the door of the tavern, paused with an ear cocked as if listening, frowned and shook her head, then crossed to the kitchen door and looked around.

With a great sigh she returned to the table, where she propped up her elbows and rested her forehead on her hands. 'There is something, but –' Her head snapped up and she pointed to a corner table. 'Aye, there was a man that evening, before the fire, an hour or two before, so he was an early customer. I'd seen him before, and since, and know to say naught to him, for he will not speak to the likes of me except to demand service. He had a leather strap like this round three or four rolls, perhaps two straps now I think of it, though I cannot be certain. He tapped on a buckle to his own tune – I thought him strange to fight the rhythm of the man who was singing in exchange for supper.'

'Can you describe him?' Emma asked.

'A proud bearing, cold eyes and a mouth that I've never seen smiling, light-brown hair that lies straight beneath his cap, dressed in the colours of earth, nothing to draw attention, but of good cut and cloth. Who is he, then?'

'My mother's steward.'

'Is he the murderer?' Bess crossed herself.

'We do not know,' Lucie said.

'But if he is . . .' Bess glanced at Emma.

'You wonder whether the fire was my family's vengeance after all.' Emma shook her head. 'If Matthew did this, he acted on his own, for his own purposes.'

'I am glad to hear that,' Bess said, but there was doubt in her voice.

Lucie and Emma departed in an uncomfortable silence, nodding to passers-by in St Helen's Square returning to the house rather than the garden. The hall was deserted, everyone still outside. Lucie took refuge in a well-padded chair, resting her head against the high back and closing her eyes.

'Shall I help you up the stairs?' Emma asked. 'You should lie down.'

'What if Matthew lit the fire to gain your mother's gratitude?'

Emma sank down near Lucie. 'I have thought of that, don't think that I haven't.'

'If he is guilty . . .' Lucie sat up, took Emma's hand. 'A man who could kill so ruthlessly might do so again to hide his guilt. Your household – all of you are in danger.'

'He had no cause to murder Cisotta,' Emma said. 'That is the sticking point.'

'Such a crime committed in Wykeham's house –'

'The blame would more naturally fall on the tenants.'

Emma was right. Lucie's thoughts were growing muddled.

'I have poisoned your judgement with my distrust of Matthew,' Emma said.

Lucie was searching for what felt wrong to her. It was the timing. 'On the night on which your family was dining with Stephen, who is now Matthew's lord, Matthew dined or at least drank at the York Tavern, carrying with him rolls of parchment. Why?'

Emma did not respond at once. 'I don't know,' she finally admitted.

'You must ask Edgar what he recalls about Matthew that night. And I must speak with Owen.'

Emma crossed herself.

Owen found no solace in the palace garden, partly because his conscience kept pushing him back towards Magda Digby. In order to heal Poins she must understand his state of mind as well as his body. He returned to the kitchen.

'Here again?' Maeve said. 'Has the crone cast a spell on you now?'

'She casts no spells, Maeve.'

'That is what you all pretend. But I trust my own eyes and ears.'

Magda greeted Owen from the small entrance between screens.

Maeve said a 'Hail Mary' as she bent back to her work.

Safely out of Maeve's sight – and hearing, Owen hoped – he told Magda of Poins's reaction to his questions.

She seemed impressed. 'Thou hast coaxed much from him. Magda has heard so little of his voice she would be unable to pick it out among the voices of others.'

'He sleeps a great deal?'

'Aye. He escapes his pain by retreating from his ruined body. Nor does he have aught he wishes to say to Magda.'

'Will he survive?'

'Not if he continues to despair. It is the great destroyer. Already one of the burns that had begun to heal is oozing bad humours.'

'Is that what causes the stench?'

'Aye, as well as some of the healing burns.'

Owen left the palace feeling responsible for Poins's failure to thrive. His presence as an inquisitor – surely that caused Poins despair as well as the wounds. Or it could be a guilty conscience. He was tired of questions and ready to work in the garden, touch the earth, get soil beneath his fingernails, but his conscience nagged that Jasper had been left in charge of the apothecary by himself too much of late.

The hall was quiet. Lucie sat on a bench, her back resting against the wall beneath the garden windows, playing string games with Gwenllian and Hugh. Through the window he could see Phillippa and Kate spreading laundry on the lavender hedge to dry.

He had expected Lucie to be abed. 'Why are you watching the children? Where is Alisoun?'

Lucie smiled to see him. 'How pleasant to see you here in mid-afternoon.' The children hurried to him, demanding hugs. Lucie rose, her movements stiff. 'Alisoun is helping Jasper modify Magda's tonic to allow me more waking hours. I am merely sitting here playing with Gwenllian and Hugh until she returns. It is not tiring.'

'Magda ordered bed rest. You will undo yourself.'

'Put that aside. I have news. The fragment of belt that you found – it was not a belt but a strap, one that keeps rolled parchments together. Matthew had been using a pair of them to hold the documents Wykeham's clerks brought to Lady Pagnell, but now has only one. Bess . . .'

They both turned as someone knocked on the door.

When Owen opened it, Adeline Fitzbaldric swept past him and into the hall clutching May by the arm.

Adeline's face was brittle with tension, her posture that of one holding much back. May appeared to move solely by her mistress's will. 'Forgive me for intruding, Mistress Wilton, but I must speak to your husband.'

'What has happened?' Owen asked.

Adeline glanced at Lucie and the children who had paused in their play to study the newcomers.

'Might I see you alone, Captain?' Adeline asked.

'My wife is privy to all my business,' Owen said.

Lucie bent down to the children. 'Gwenllian, take Hugh to the shop and stay there with Alisoun until

Kate or I fetch you. Make certain he touches nothing in the workshop. I am entrusting him to you.'

Gwenllian rose and bowed to all of them, then took her little brother's hand and moved away slowly.

With an uncertain glance at Lucie, Adeline hesitated, then laid a small bundle on the bench beside her. 'Servants were able to enter the bishop's house today and bring out much of our clothing and some of the furnishings. Among May's things I found this.' She unwound the wrapping, revealing a bloodstained cloth, two jars and a small cup.

Owen wondered how he had missed the rag. 'What are they?' he asked.

Adeline turned to May. 'Tell him.'

The maid ducked her head and came forward, blinking and giving her head little shakes. She pointed to one jar. 'There was blood in that – it's caked now.' She pointed to the other. 'Cisotta called it a colliry.' She touched the cup. 'This was the little cup she used to hold the blood to my eyes.'

So it was a physick for the eyes. Lucie opened the jar of blood and sniffed. 'Could this be bat's blood?' she wondered aloud. 'Do you have difficulty seeing in the dark, May?'

May pressed her eyes. 'I did not know it was the blood of such a creature,' she cried.

Owen understood now. 'Your clumsiness – your eyes are failing, aren't they?'

May was on the verge of tears. 'Aye,' she whispered.

'Not just at night?' Lucie asked.

May shook her head. 'Would that it were.'

'That is not all she has concealed behind that timid countenance,' Adeline said, taking a seat with a little huff. 'May, tell them the rest.'

Lucie motioned for May to sit. She seemed in need of

support. The maid sank down and for a moment buried her face in her hands.

'She has been like this ever since I confronted her,' Adeline said.

'You did not know of her condition?' Lucie asked in a tone of concern, not accusation.

Owen took note of it, for Adeline did not bristle, but only sighed.

'I did not know the cause of her recent accidents. There has been so much to do with the move, and since May had never been so far from home, I thought it a passing problem. May, speak up, woman.'

Owen held his breath as Lucie moved the jars and cup closer to May and sat beside her. He feared May would be silenced by Lucie's nearness.

'May, have you told the Riverwoman about your eyes?' Lucie asked.

May shook her head.

'Do you fear her?'

Another shake of the head.

'Do you visit Poins?'

Owen was about to tell Lucie that he had already asked May about that, but the maid raised her eyes to meet Lucie's.

'I don't know what happened, what caused the fire.'

It was an interesting answer to the question.

'I pray you tell us whatever you do know,' Lucie said. 'I was Cisotta's friend. I would know what happened that night.'

Tears streamed down May's cheeks. Lucie pulled a cloth from her sleeve and handed it to the maid.

'My mistress's visitors spoke of how Cisotta had sat by you day and night after you lost your child.' May spoke in such a choked voice that Owen crouched down to hear. She started at his nearness.

'He is my husband, May, and no one to fear,' Lucie said softly. 'So what you heard led you to seek Cisotta's care?'

May pressed the cloth to her eyes, then wiped her nose. 'I had given her my mistress's old gloves in payment. I was so afraid when I saw them today.' She sniffed. 'That night she brought me the remedies and showed me how to soak my eyes in the blood, then rinse them once a day with the wash. Then I was to lie still with my eyes closed until I heard my master and mistress return.'

Owen asked, 'Did you escort Cisotta out of the house?'

May shook her head. 'She said she knew the way.'

'Where was Poins?' Lucie asked.

'I don't know.' May shivered and hugged herself. The room was almost too warm for Owen, the brazier burning because of Lucie's weakness.

'Was anyone down in the undercroft that evening?' Lucie asked.

May shrugged. 'I was frightened about having Cisotta there. About what my mistress would say if –' She cut herself off.

'But if you were so concerned, did you not check to make sure no one saw her arrive or leave?' Lucie asked.

May looked down at her hands. 'I did not think of that. I have never before lied to my mistress. I do not have the knack for it.'

Lucie looked up at Owen, her eyes questioning whether she should continue.

Adeline understood the expression. 'She claims to have no idea where Poins was or whether anyone was in the undercroft at that time,' she said. 'So I thought to question Poins. But the Riverwoman would not let me see him.'

'I was just there with him,' Owen said.

'Yes, I know. I watched you leave. I had hoped to keep this private.'

Lucie lifted the other jar and sat for a time sniffing and thinking. Adeline rose and began to pace. May kept her head down, sniffling now and then.

'Fennel and ground ivy,' Lucie said. 'And a little nettle seed. You were to dampen the mixture and apply it to your eyes?'

May nodded. 'She was to make more. She said it would take a while because she must soak it in wine and then let the sun dry it. I was to go to her in a few days. She said in a week I would see better. But the fire kept me from the medicines. And she –' The maid held her stomach and gulped air, as one about to vomit.

'I shall fetch you something for your stomach,' Lucie said. 'I'll send it with the captain when next he goes to the palace.'

'That would be kind of you,' Adeline said. 'But how can I take her back there? What am I to do with a servant who is going blind?'

May stared at her mistress, her eyes glassy with tears and horror.

'Comfort her,' Lucie said. 'Have Magda Digby examine her.'

Adeline Fitzbaldric was not one to comfort a servant and her expression said as much.

Owen thought it time to be blunt with her. 'If May leaves your household before this matter is resolved, the gossips will declare one of you guilty of Cisotta's death and the destruction of the bishop's house.'

Adeline drew herself up straight as a board. 'We shall leave the jars with you,' she said. 'Come, May, we have said all we came to say.'

'Is that truly all of it, May?' Lucie asked softly.

The maid was fiddling with the jars and the cup on the blood-stained cloth. 'Yes, Mistress Wilton,' she whispered.

After Adeline and May departed, Lucie and Owen stood by the window staring out at the garden for a long while without speaking.

Owen tried to piece together all he had learned just now of that fateful evening. 'Despite her timidity, May is a determined woman to have found her way to Patrick Pool to bargain with Cisotta,' he said.

'It is the sort of mistake Cisotta might make, thinking bat's blood good for any problem of the eye.' Lucie's voice shook with emotion.

Owen gathered her in his arms, listening to her ragged breathing, trying to imagine what Cisotta's death meant to her. In his mind Cisotta had been a poor substitute for Magda, and he had thought her efforts to cheer Lucie and encourage her to resume her life inadequate. He was certain Lucie would have recovered much sooner had Magda cared for her from the time of the fall – a part of him even thought the baby might have lived. He wanted to find Cisotta's murderer more out of a sense of justice than as a personal vengeance. But he understood that for Lucie it was the latter.

'What were you telling me about the belt? Have you been about with it asking questions of folk?'

'Emma recognized it.' Lucie stepped away from him told him what had transpired and what Bess had remembered. While she talked, she wandered over to the things May had left. 'I'll take these to the shop an see whether I can pick out any other ingredients.'

Her strength was returning and Owen was glad of i But he worried that she was doing too much. 'You mus rest now. From what you've told me you've been out o bed for a long while. Let's go up and you can lie down while we talk.'

'I should prefer to do this.' Her voice was uncertain.

'Come. Up the stairs. I must confess to you how close I came to knowing Poins's heart before I failed in my talk with him.'

As often of late, Thoresby grew drowsy as the sun set, in the hour or so before the evening meal. He fought to concentrate on the letter Brother Michaelo was reading to him, but it became impossible and he allowed a velvet stillness to envelop him. He found himself in a moonlit room scented with roses. His dear leman Marguerite slept with her head on his shoulder, radiating such warmth that his arm was soaked in sweat. As he slipped it out from beneath her, she woke and turned to him. Suddenly the bed pitched and yawed. He woke at sea, bereft of his dream of his love. The pile of rope on which he reclined cut into his back, but how beautiful were the stars overhead, how peaceful the sigh of the ocean and the gentle rocking of the ship.

'Your Grace!'

The voice pulled Thoresby from the dream. Someone leaned close.

'Your Grace, the Riverwoman begs an audience.'

For a moment Thoresby was not certain where he was, in what time. The scent of lavender reminded him of Brother Michaelo. But he had not been Thoresby's secretary during his years with Marguerite. He reached round and plucked the crumpled pillow from behind him, held it in his lap and studied it, then looked about the room, slowly remembering. He was in his parlour in his York palace, listening to letters from supplicants, avoiding the strangers to whom

Wykeham had so presumptuously extended his hospitality.

'Who?'

'Mistress Digby, the Riverwoman.'

'She would not beg.'

Michaelo sighed with impatience. 'Will you see her?'

'She will have my head on a platter if I do not.'

Michaelo leaned close again and, reaching out his long, slender hands, paused. 'Might I adjust your cap and surcoat, Your Grace?'

'Do you think she will be offended by my appearance?'

'You are the Archbishop of York. It is not fitting that you be seen in disarray.'

'It is you who are offended. You do not like that I am old.'

Michaelo looked pained. 'Your Grace, I am devoted to you.'

'The crone has been here for days. Why must she see me now?'

Michaelo drew a comb through Thoresby's thinning hair.

Thoresby rose and crossed to his high-backed chair, noticed they were alone. 'Where is my page?'

'I thought perhaps you would prefer to speak with the Riverwoman alone.'

There was something in his secretary's tone. 'You know what she wants, don't you?' By Michaelo's blush he saw he was right. 'Is that why you have kept everyone out of the room above the kitchen? You've been spying on the sickroom?'

Michaelo cleared his throat. 'Your Grace, she wait without.'

His secretary was a sly creature.

'Very well. I shall see her.'

He felt himself tense as Michaelo opened the door and bowed to the wizened woman. Magda rose from the guard's chair with a limber grace unexpected in such an ancient of the labouring class, a commanding figure despite being a good four hands shorter than the monk. As she stepped across the threshold she did not gaze round the room as one would expect but sought Thoresby at once and bowed to him. 'Thy Grace.' Her voice seemed to echo in the room.

'Mistress Digby, we are all grateful to you for the life of the servant Poins.' Thoresby began to raise his hand in blessing, but thought better of it. She nodded to him, for all the world as if thanking him for not embarrassing both of them. He wished her gone as quickly as possible. 'What is your request?'

'Poins fears he is dying, Thy Grace, and according to thy customs wishes to be shriven. By thee.'

'Me?'

The white-haired crone nodded once. 'He says he will have no other. Thou wert kind to him and he trusts thee.'

'He wishes to be shriven now?'

She shook her head. It was a queer cap she wore, of so many colours they blurred when she moved. Her gown was the same. Perhaps that was what made him feel odd in her presence.

'He sleeps now, but he will wake in an hour.'

'How do you know when he will wake?'

'Magda mixed his physick and she has watched him these few days, noting when he wakes.'

It might prove frustrating. Anything Poins told him in confession was useless to the investigation. But so be it. Thoresby might think of some way round it. 'I shall be there.'

Magda bowed to him. 'Thou hast a good heart.'

297

*

After her afternoon of air and exercise, and a draught of the modified tonic, Lucie slept for a few hours, waking when Phillippa came to ask whether she wished to take her meal with the family in the hall. Dropping her legs off the bed, Lucie found that her head felt clearer, and as she rose her balance was surer than it had been earlier in the day. 'Yes, I'll eat with the family tonight, Aunt.'

Lamps now lit the hall and the children had been put to bed.

Owen already sat alone at the table, staring into a cup of ale. When Lucie joined him, he put an arm round her and pulled her head close. 'I have been thinking.'

'I could see that.'

'Did you sleep?'

'Aye. Very well. Have you resolved anything?'

Owen sighed, withdrew his arm and, leaning his elbows on the table, set his head down in his hands. His fingers fanned through his curls, then clutched them. She knew the gesture as one of defeat.

'What is it, my love?'

'The strap, the documents – I have overlooked two of the most obvious suspects – Wykeham's clerks.'

'You told me you had spoken to them about that evening.'

'Aye, but the truth is I know little about them. And if the strap round Cisotta's neck had been securing the property documents from Wykeham, it's possible one of them is guilty.'

'Or Matthew the steward.'

'Oh, aye, Emma would like to hang him, I know.'

'You must question him, Owen.'

Kate interrupted them with trenchers and a good sized fish, as well as a fragrant pottage.

The four at table were a subdued group. Jasper seemed weary, and both Owen and Lucie were quiet in fear that they would reveal too much too soon, so Phillippa entertained them with a monologue of laundry days at Freythorpe Hadden.

Afterwards Jasper disappeared into the kitchen.

Lucie smoothed Owen's hair. 'Will you speak with Matthew?'

'Aye, but I must also speak with Wykeham about his men, and the sooner done the better.' He reached for his boots.

'You're going to the palace now?'

'I am. I must ready the men for tomorrow.'

When she looked confused he told her of Wykeham's demands.

'Have you changed your mind?' Lucie asked. 'Do you think he has cause to fear?'

'God's blood, I wish I knew. Nothing we have learned suggests that he has anything to fear. But one man working for Lancaster's followers – that is all it would have taken.'

'You dislike him more and more.'

'Aye, he sours the air he breathes.'

'Watch yourself. Remember you do all this for Cisotta.'

'Aye. He cares nothing about her, but I do.'

'God go with you, my love.'

'And you. Now to bed with you. You are too pale.'

She watched him leave, then slowly climbed to their chamber.

Nineteen

REVELATIONS

Thoresby paused over the garb in which he would hear Poins's confession. It was unlike him to expend such time on a trifle, yet he wanted neither to frighten the servant nor to disappoint him. Poins wished to confess to him – he did not know whether it was because he was archbishop, or because he was John Thoresby, the cleric who had been kind to him.

'Your Grace?' His page stood by the wardrobe chest holding up the houppelande that Thoresby had chosen earlier for dining.

'Yes, yes.' Thoresby motioned the page over with the gown. He would not look a beggar in any case.

Michaelo handed Thoresby a lavender-scented cloth as he passed through his private hall to the kitchen.

'God bless you,' Thoresby said. 'I had forgotten how the man's wounds stank.'

He caused a flutter in the kitchen.

'Be at ease,' Thoresby said, 'I am but passing this way to visit the invalid.' He caught a disapproving spark in his cook's eyes.

Magda Digby stepped out from the screened area and bowed to him. 'Poins is ready for thee.'

She sat down just outside the screens, a formidable guard. Thoresby wondered whether Michaelo was in place in the room above, but he did not dare look up for fear Poins would notice. The injured man was propped up on pillows. The bandage across his face was clean, as was all the visible flesh. His left hand lay outside the covers, pressed to his chest. He made a movement with his right shoulder, then closed his eyes for a moment.

'I cannot make the sign of the cross,' he whispered.

Thoresby felt the comment deep in his chest. Such a simple gift for which man never gives thanks until it is taken from him. 'It matters not, my son. May the Lord bless you, and may His peace embrace you.'

'Bless me, Father. I . . . do not know whether . . . I am guilty of the sin . . . of which they accuse me . . . with their eyes.' So little speech, yet Poins lay back, fighting for breath.

Thoresby eased down on to a chair that had been placed to the left of the bed, where the infirm man might hear and be heard with ease. An infirmarian had once told him that the dying straddle two worlds, that of the spirit and that of the flesh, and that holding their hands or merely touching their arms often draws them more firmly back into this world. In Queen Philippa's last illness she had often reached for Thoresby's hand, seeming to find comfort in his touch. He touched Poins's forearm.

The man seemed to straighten a little, his eyes focusing on Thoresby.

'Father, I fear . . . I am dying. I cannot bear . . . the stench . . . of my own flesh. I . . . do not know myself.' He paused for breath. 'The Riverwoman said . . . I must fight if . . . I wish to live –' His breath trembled on the exhale.

Thoresby took his hand.

'For what should I . . . live, Father? What work . . . might I do?'

Even the gestures of prayer were lost to him. He was unlettered, too scarred to seek a wife. Thoresby could say only, 'Despair is a sin, my son. It is not for us to choose our passing. God will take you when it is your time.'

'God.' Poins almost spat the word. 'My arm is gone . . . and still . . . He gives me pain. Have I not . . . suffered enough? Should I . . . fight to live . . . so I might . . . beg on the streets?' Poins clutched Thoresby's hand, and though his chest heaved with sobs, his eyes were fierce.

'We cannot know God's intentions,' Thoresby said.

Poins groaned and lay back again on his pillows, closed his eyes and struggled for breath.

In the long silence, Thoresby jumped at a tell-tale creak up above and began murmuring prayers.

At last Poins said, 'May must not be . . . blamed for the fire, Father . . . or for Cisotta's death.'

'Are you to blame, then?'

'Bless me, Father . . . for I have sinned.'

Thoresby bowed his head and listened.

Alfred and those guards not on duty were sitting round a table in the barracks finishing their supper when Owen joined them. On his walk over he had sought a way to impress on the men the importance of defending Wykeham the following day, but it was difficult when he was not convinced of the danger. Lancaster' hatred of Wykeham was the key. Yet since the fire, a had been quiet.

Owen need not have worried – the eyes that looke

up from the ale cups were all grave with the knowledge that tomorrow they might face a powerful enemy.

'Captain.' Alfred came forward. 'I am right glad you are here. The men have questions, and some suggestions for the morrow.'

This part did not require Owen's conviction, only his experience. He leaned against one of the aisle pillars and set his mind to strategy.

Thoresby had stepped back to bless and absolve Poins.

With his one good hand, Poins pulled up the edge of the blanket and mopped the sweat dripping into his left eye. The bandage across his forehead was soaked. The stench was enough for Thoresby at last to lift the scented cloth to his nose, inhaling shallowly so as to receive only the perfume, not the odour that permeated the room.

'For your penance, my son, you must repeat all that you have told me to Captain Archer.'

'I am tired, Father.'

'I cannot divulge what you have told me in confession. If you wish to clear the maid's name you must tell your story openly.'

Poins closed his eyes. 'I'll sleep now.'

Thoresby was exhausted. He wanted wine, fresh air. 'You must tell Captain Archer.'

Poins's head sank to the right, his breathing deepened.

Sleep. It was the only pleasure left to the man.

Magda Digby rose as Thoresby came out from behind the screens.

'Does he yet live, Thy Grace?'

'Yes, though for how long only God can say.'

'He grows weary of the struggle. Magda can only do so much.'

She glanced over to the doorway into the hall, where May stood with her head strained forward, her eyelids fluttering. Weighed down by Poins's despair, Thoresby sought the evening garden.

'Your Grace.'

May had come to him. She stood with head bowed.

'He wants your name cleared of all blame,' he told her before she asked.

She lifted her face to his, her chin trembling. 'Then he has confessed?'

'He has made his confession and that is all I may tell you. To be absolved he must tell Captain Archer all he has told me.'

'My Lord Archbishop cannot absolve him otherwise?'

'I will not. And you should tell Archer of your actions that night.'

'I have, Your Grace.'

What? What else is Archer holding back?

'Your Grace?'

'Then you have cleared yourself.'

'I am partly to blame. I called Cisotta to the house, Your Grace,' May whispered.

'Did you?' *And so did Poins.* Thoresby sighed. 'Who tells the truth here?' He shook his head and crossed the kitchen, waving a quick blessing as he passed Maeve and her assistant. He glanced back once as he reached the door, saw May step through the screens and Magda emerge, returning to the bench on which she had awaited him.

Who is lying, Thoresby wondered as he breathed in the night air. It revived him, perhaps too well. The desire to hear what Poins and May said to one another suddenly seized Thoresby like a fist in his gut. He wanted access to the room above that part of the kitchen. But he was a stranger in his own palace. With little cause to spend time in the kitchen wing, he did not know where the steps that led upstairs might be. He crossed back through the kitchen and opened the one door in the passageway to the hall. It was the buttery. It must be outside, then. He strode back through the kitchen, not bothering to acknowledge anyone, and almost collided with Michaelo in the garden.

'Your Grace.'

'Take me to your listening place. The maid is with Poins and I will hear what they say.'

Lucie started awake as Kate crept into her chamber, the lamp she carried lighting the room.

It was not Kate's custom to enter without knocking. 'What is amiss?' Lucie winced as she put pressure on her injured hand and rolled to the other side to raise herself up. As Kate approached, Lucie smelled the laundry lye on her clothes.

'There is a man to see you,' Kate whispered. 'Edgar of Skipton, he says, sent by Mistress Ferriby. He begs you to see him.'

'Is it very late?'

'I was still tidying the kitchen, Mistress. And Jasper has not yet retired.'

Lucie wondered why Emma had sent the tutor here tonight when she would be at the house in the afternoon. Perhaps Emma doubted Lucie would follow through with her plan.

By now Lucie was fully awake. 'Help me dress. I cannot manage by myself with this bandage.'

Jasper stood outside the door when they emerged. He peered over Lucie's shoulder into the chamber beyond. 'The Captain has not returned?'

'No. Why?'

'Are you armed?'

'Jasper, our visitor is only Edgar, the Ferribys' tutor.'

'Why should you trust someone who comes in the evening, unexpected?'

'Because I asked Emma to speak with him about her mother's steward Matthew.'

'Then someone is worried what he might tell you. There is someone in the garden.'

Lucie caught her breath. 'Are you certain?'

'I sensed them as I came from the shop.'

'Thank God you were not attacked. Did you call out?'

'I thought it best to fetch my dagger.' Jasper patted his right forearm. 'Do you want me in the garden, or in the hall with you?'

Perhaps Edgar had been followed, or had brought a companion. 'Stay with me until I have a sense of him.'

'Merciful Mother,' Kate muttered as she lit the way with the lamp.

Satisfied that his men were ready for the worst on the morrow, Owen crossed the garden towards the palace to assure Wykeham it was so. The guard at the rear door of the great hall stepped aside as Owen approached.

'Have you noted anything out of joint?' Owen asked.

'No, Captain. All is quiet.'

'Good. Pray the peace continues.'

In the hall he found the Fitzbaldrics, Wykeham and Alain discussing the whereabouts of Thoresby and Michaelo. It seemed they had not appeared for dinner.

Sitting just outside the pool of light that a lamp threw on the benches near the brazier, Edgar, in his dark clerk's gown, seemed determined to blend into the shadows.

He rose as Lucie approached. 'Forgive me for waking you, Mistress Wilton. Mistress Ferriby sent me to tell you what I know about the night of the fire. And the behaviour of Lady Pagnell's steward since then.' Sweat beaded the stocky man's forehead.

'It is so important that you come at night? Surely if you have waited this long . . .'

'My mistress believed Captain Archer might wish to hear my tale before Lady Pagnell goes to the palace with Matthew on the morrow.' Edgar glanced towards the windows.

'Does something worry you?'

'Matthew has ways of hearing things. I thought – but it was the echo of my footsteps as I hurried here.' He blew a strand of hair from his brow.

'Sit down, I pray you.'

Again Edgar chose a spot just beyond the light.

'Tell me about Matthew. I know you share a bed in the hall.'

'Matthew was out all the night of the fire. Just before dawn he crept in with his shoes in his hands and slipped into bed. He smelled of sweat – I thought he had been with a woman – and he was stripped to his shift. He had worn a tunic when he departed the evening before. I have not seen that tunic since. But I believe it is among his things – he has been uneasy about me going near the chest in which he keeps his belongings.'

'Why did you not mention this before?'

'I am a coward, I have no other excuse, God knows. I told myself that I did not wish to cause more strife between my mistress and her mother. Lady Pagnell already blames me for Ivo's and John's accident at the lady chapel. She says I have not given the boys sufficient moral training. Mistress Ferriby has defended me.' He pressed his temples as if the situation gave him a headache. 'But in truth, fear kept me silent.'

Lucie excused herself a moment to confer with Jasper, who sat in the shadows seemingly with one eye on Edgar and one on the windows.

'Have you seen anything?'

'It is quarter moon and cloudy, so it is even more difficult than usual to see from within. But something woke Melisende. Look.'

The cat lay on a cushioned chair, her ear cocked, one eye opened slightly.

'Pretend you are crossing the garden to the shop. Try to do it exactly as you are wont to do. If you sense anyone out there, go through the shop and out to the tavern. Fetch Tom.'

Jasper nodded solemnly and began to move away.

Lucie feared she was asking more of him than she should of a lad but fourteen. She caught his forearm. When he met her eyes, his gaze was calm, confident.

'Remember all that Owen has taught you,' Lucie said. 'And God go with you.'

Jasper bobbed his head. 'Make a racket if he proves false.' He departed by the door that led to the passageway from house to kitchen.

'Where is he going?' Edgar asked.

'To the York Tavern, for help. You were uncomfortable walking here alone, were you not?'

'I feel a fool for even mentioning it.'

Lucie hoped her smile was reassuring. She thanked God she had not taken the tonic with the sleepwort and valerian.

At first Thoresby found it impossible to hear anything over the clatter of Maeve and her maid, the creaks i the floorboards, the grumbling in his stomach, even his own breath. But as he calmed, he distinguished the sound of a woman weeping.

'I am in hell . . . and all for you,' Poins said, straining his voice to a hoarse shout, 'and you point the finger . . . at me, accusing me . . . of murdering Cisotta? Then damn you. Damn you!'

'No, no, I never spoke! I said nothing,' May sobbed.

'All night . . . I see her lying there . . . in the flames . . . beautiful Cisotta. I could do nothing.'

Other things were murmured but Thoresby could not make them out. He motioned for Michaelo to kneel at the knot hole.

'My hearing is not what it was,' Thoresby whispered.

Michaelo lowered himself until he was lying prone on the floor, his ear to the hole.

Thoresby fought the urge to pace and held himself motionless.

Wykeham had stepped aside with Owen, listening with attention to the plans for the defence of the palace. When he had exhausted his questions, he motioned to Alain. 'Fetch Guy. We must discuss our strategy for tomorrow's meeting.' As the clerk departed, Wykeham said, 'I do not understand what has come over Guy of late. I cannot depend upon him as I have in the past.'

'How well do you know your clerks, My Lord?'

Wykeham cocked his head. 'Why do you ask?'

'The deeds of the properties Lady Pagnell is considering –' Owen was distracted by the sight of Thoresby rushing into the hall from the kitchen corridor, his elegant gown, the colour of lapis lazuli, flapping in the breeze of his passage. His long, bony face was pink with exertion, his eyes anxious.

'Archer, come with me,' Thoresby said breathlessly.

He bowed to the gathered diners. 'I have told Maeve to serve dinner. Do not wait for me. I shall come when I can.'

Owen bowed to Wykeham and followed Thoresby, who had slowed his pace and was breathing hard. To Owen's surprise the archbishop led him out into the garden at the rear of the hall. They were joined by Brother Michaelo.

'Michaelo is to be our sentinel while we talk,' Thoresby said. 'You must go to Poins. I heard his confession, but I have told him that in order to be absolved he must tell you all he knows.'

'The seal of confession.'

Thoresby nodded. 'May heard that I was with him. She went to him. When he understood that she feared him guilty, he cursed her.'

'Did he confess to her? Can we learn the truth from her?'

'From May we might learn her truth, but not his. Go to him. He kept silent to protect her. Perhaps now that he knows she believed him a murderer he will speak.'

Or decide to slip away, succumb to the pain and, by succumbing, escape it. Owen crossed himself and prayed for God's grace.

Lucie offered Edgar a cup of ale, which he accepted with an embarrassed smile.

'Is it Matthew you fear?'

The mere mention of the man seemed to deepen the shadows beneath Edgar's eyes. 'I have not enjoyed a night of sleep while he has shared my bed for the nightmares his presence inspires. Even in slumber there is such an anger within him.'

Lucie listened while thinking Jasper must be at the

310

tavern by now. Perhaps he and Tom Merchet had returned to the yard.

'Do you think Matthew capable of setting the fire? Or of murder?'

Edgar put down his cup with a clatter. 'That is for God to judge, Mistress Wilton. I know only what I have told you.'

'Can you guess what so angers him?'

'It would be easier to point out what does not. The smallest inconvenience puts him in a temper. He is critical of everything in my master and mistress's household. His loyalty is with Lady Pagnell. He dislikes the Ferribys.'

'Including the boys?'

'Them most of all.' Edgar's eyes widened and he jerked towards the window. 'I heard a cry.'

Lucie rose with care, her exhaustion dizzying. *Blessed Mother, protect my family.*

Edgar hurried towards the front door. 'I must go.'

'Stay. You must have an escort.'

Someone pushed open the door from which Jasper had departed as Edgar vanished out of the front door. Jasper led a dishevelled boy into the room. Alisoun followed them, bow in hand. Lucie had forgotten that the girl was a skilled archer. The boy lifted his head and Lucie cried out.

'John Ferriby!' She ran back to the front door. 'Edgar! Wait!' She turned to Jasper. 'You must find Edgar.'

Jasper was already at the door, running out into the night.

Lucie sank down, cupping her face in her hands.

Twenty

COMPASSION AND GREED

Magda was at the bedside, cradling Poins's head in one hand, with the other helping him sip from a shallow cup. She saw Owen, but did not speak until she had settled Poins back on the pillow. 'What he has drunk will keep him wakeful for a good while,' she said, 'though he wishes for nothing so much as sleep.'

'Were you in here with him and May?'

'Nay. Magda sat without, but she could hear him forcing his voice to shout at the maid. Hear him now if thou wilt, for tomorrow he'll not be able to speak for the swelling in his throat. Thou shouldst prop him up with more cushions so that he has the breath for speech.'

Poins groaned as Owen arranged cushions beneath his upper back, though he made no more complaint. When Owen settled beside the bed, Poins regarded him with keener eyes than he had the day before, and almost at once he spoke. 'I meant to protect her,' he rasped.

'Who?'

'May.'

'We already know her part. She has told us of her failing sight, Cisotta's remedy.'

'And my part?'

'Not yours. She said she did not know why you were in the undercroft.'

Poins dropped his gaze to his swollen fingers, curling and uncurling them. Magda handed Owen some warm honeyed water to offer him. He took a sip and then lay back for a moment, catching his breath at the pressure against his blistered back, though only cushions touched it. Owen held the cup.

'I offered Cisotta . . . my mistress's cast-off gloves . . . but she wanted more . . . to come to the house.' Owen did not interrupt Poins's pause for breath. 'She asked for hides . . . I promised her some . . . if she would come that night.' He took a deep breath.

'Why did you do this?'

'May was patient with our . . . difficult mistress . . . She made it . . . easier . . . for Bolton and me. I wanted to . . . make it up to her.' Sweat soaked Poins's bandages.

'Where were the hides?'

'Just inside the undercroft door. I left it unlocked. Told Cisotta to . . . take them . . . as she left.'

Owen helped Poins sip the water.

'And what happened?' he asked when Poins's breathing seemed easier.

'I heard something . . . Too long after Cisotta left . . . Went down to check . . . lock the door. There was smoke.' He closed his eyes, shook his head slowly when Owen offered him water. 'Inside there was a fire . . . not big yet . . . I saw . . . her golden hair . . .' – his voice broke – 'near the flames . . . fanned out.' He closed his eyes and shivered. 'A man pushed me aside . . .

pulled the barrel down on me.' Poins gave a rough sob. 'I screamed. . . Flames licked at her . . . She never moved . . . never a sound . . . Beautiful Cisotta.' He wept.

Owen leaned close, whispered, 'Tell me what you see, Poins.'

'For a moment – something. A figure.'

'Clerk's gown? Something shorter?'

Poins coughed, shook his head. 'Water.'

Owen helped him again, then asked, 'Is that all you can remember?'

Poins slowly nodded. 'I said nothing because . . . I did not want . . . May blamed.'

'I understand.'

'Did it work? Can she see now?'

Owen could not bring himself to tell Poins how little all his suffering had helped May. 'More clearly. You must rest.'

'I could not move,' Poins sobbed. 'I could not save her.'

'She was dead before you reached the undercroft, Poins. There was nothing you could have done.'

'I should have . . . taken the hides . . . to her . . . I was frightened. If I did not . . . hand them to her . . . I could say I knew . . . nothing . . . of them.'

Owen thanked Poins and left his side, feeling his own breath shallow and ragged. So much suffering for so little. Such good intentions ended in horror. He crossed himself as he left the room and prayed for understanding. It seemed a brutal punishment for such insignificant transgressions.

Alisoun withdrew to the table and began to unstring her bow.

John Ferriby stood in the centre of the hall, his eye

searching for something other than Lucie to light on. One of his leggings pooled round his ankle, the flushed, dimpled knee like that of a baby. 'I meant no harm,' he said.

'Gwenllian woke and saw him creeping along the wall,' Alisoun said in a matter-of-fact tone, not taking her eyes off the string she was winding.

'Go up to her and tell her it was nothing,' Lucie said.

'But I'm –'

'Now.'

Alisoun gathered her bow and quiver and withdrew.

Tomorrow Lucie must talk to the girl about her duties, how to comfort children in the night without hurting anyone. Lucie crouched down to help John with his leggings, then left him warming himself by the brazier while she went to fix him a calming drink. She sent Kate off to bed, assuring her that there was no danger in crossing the garden to her room above the shop. Too late she remembered that having but one functional hand slowed her. She called John into the kitchen to talk with her while the camomile and balm steeped. The boy relaxed in the warmth and told her without prodding how he had overheard his mother's conversation with Edgar and resolved to follow his tutor to see whether he was false or true. But he grew silent when Lucie asked why he would distrust Edgar.

'Could I stay here?' John asked after a while. The drink had him yawning.

'Your parents would be beside themselves with worry. Are they very angry about the lady chapel?'

'It's not them, it's Matthew. I don't want to go home until he's gone.'

Hearing the fear in the boy's voice, she asked gently, 'What has he done?'

But the boy had jumped up at the sound of voices in the hall.

'It is Jasper and Edgar,' she told him, silently cursing them for returning just as John was confiding in her. 'Come, we'll join them in the hall.'

'I found him crossing the market square,' Jasper announced, raking back his hair and blotting his sweaty brow with his sleeve.

'In the time you were gone you might have run all the way to Hosier Lane and back,' Lucie noted, her voice sharper than she had intended. 'What kept you so long?'

'One of the Ferriby servants was out calling for John. So we hid until he passed by.' Jasper looked pleased with himself. 'There will be explanations asked, and I thought it best if everyone thought Edgar and John had gone out together.'

Edgar went to John, who sat huddled on a chair. 'What were you thinking, Master John? Lady Pagnell will blame me, no matter what your mother says.'

John glanced over at Lucie as if asking for her help.

'He fears Matthew as much as you do, Edgar,' Lucie said, joining them, crouching to hold the boy's hands.

'But he lacks only patience with you and Ivo,' Edgar said.

John was shaking his head. 'He caught me following him. He wants to kill me.'

'John, you cannot mean that,' Lucie said.

'It's true. He was selling the tunic he wore the night of the fire to a dubber. He said he'd kill me if I told anyone.'

'Dear God.' Lucie rose and tried to think what to do. 'Jasper, go to the palace. Fetch Owen. He must know of this.'

316

But John and Edgar must return to the Ferriby house or Matthew would know something was up. It took much reassuring to convince John to go home with Edgar.

'Speak only with your mistress,' Lucie coached the tutor. 'Neither Matthew nor Lady Pagnell nor any of the servants must know that you came to see me.'

Edgar put on a brave front for the boy.

Owen had settled on a garden bench away from the doorway torches, glad of the long grey shadows, the low clouds that hid the stars. He prayed that God would release Poins from his suffering. The flesh beneath the man's bandages was rotting away, even Magda Digby could not save him from terrible disfigurement. And his heart appeared unbearably heavy with grief and self-recrimination. Life seemed the worst of prisons for him. May, too, needed his prayers, but he thought she would gradually settle back into life. Magda might even improve her lot.

Something pressed against him, then grappled up his leg. He caught the purring ball of fur and settled it in his lap. It must be from the stable cat's litter that Brother Michaelo had complained about. Owen had forgotten the tale till now.

The others were dining when Owen returned to the hall. Michaelo left his place to enquire whether Owen wished to join them.

'No. But stay a moment. Have you ever met the Pagnell steward?'

'Matthew? Only once that I recall. His arrogance did not befit his station.'

'When was that?'

'The day before Sir Ranulf's funeral. He had been sent to request that Wykeham not attend.'

'What of the time you saw Guy arguing with someone in the Pagnell livery?'

'It might have been him . . .' Michaelo closed his eyes. 'They were in the shadow of the yew hedge and I was coming from the stables.' He shook his head. 'No, I was not close enough to see the face of the one in livery.'

'What day was it?'

'The day of the fire – I remember that well. His Grace and the bishop were to dine alone that evening and I wished everything to be peaceful, no kittens mewing outside the windows.'

'Morning or afternoon?'

'Late in the day, for I was concerned about moving them all before I had to instruct the servants in setting their places in the hall.'

If Alain had delivered the property documents to the Ferriby house that morning as Owen had been informed, it seemed rather soon for Lady Pagnell to send a messenger to the palace in the afternoon. But perhaps a document had gone missing, or there were questions that required a meeting in the records room.

'Where is Guy?' Owen asked.

'Alain says he is lying on the floor of the chapel in prayer. Have you heard that he has asked to be excused from the meeting tomorrow?'

A servant joined them. 'Captain, Jasper de Melton begs to speak with you.'

'Shall I fetch the holy clerk?' Michaelo asked.

'No. Let him pray,' Owen said. Nodding to Michaelo he followed the servant to the hall door, fighting the desire to send word that he was too busy to be bothered by troubles at home. Jasper paced on the hall porch. When he looked up at Owen it was plain the movement kept sleep at bay.

'You look tired, lad. It must be important.'

'Mistress Lucie has much to tell you, Captain.'

'Can it wait?'

Jasper grabbed his forearm. 'Come. You need to hear this.'

The urgency in the gesture moved Owen to give one of the guards instructions to pass round the word that Guy must not be allowed out of the palace precinct until further notice. Then Owen hurried off with Jasper. They found Lucie in her chamber with Gwenllian tucked in beside her.

A finger to her lips, Lucie drew them out to the landing. 'Alisoun has much to learn,' she whispered. She led them back down the stairs, to the still-warm kitchen. What Owen heard convinced him that he must return to the palace and question Guy. Lucie agreed that the argument between Guy and Matthew might be the key to all that had happened on that fateful day.

Two lamps flickered in the drafts of the chapel, animating the body lying prone before the altar with the illusion of unnatural movement. For a moment Owen feared Guy had escaped in a more permanent way than running. He knelt, reached out to touch the clerk's neck. Guy jerked. Owen withdrew just in time. Guy rolled over and up into a crouch. He was more agile than he looked.

Owen whispered a prayer of thanksgiving that the clerk was alive. 'I did not mean to frighten you.'

'You came upon me with such stealth.'

'You were so deep in prayer you did not hear me.'

Guy's eyes looked wild in the flickering light. He huddled into himself.

'The stone floor is a cold place to lie,' Owen said.

Guy began to rise.

'Stay a little,' Owen said.

'I am cold,' Guy said. 'I need some mulled wine . . .'

'I have just a few questions.'

'More?'

'What business did you have with Matthew, the Pagnell steward, the afternoon of the fire?'

Guy frowned and looked aside as if searching his memory, then shook his head. 'I had none. Alain took the papers to him . . .'

'. . . in the morning,' Owen said. 'Brother Michaelo recalls seeing you with Matthew in the garden that afternoon.'

'He must be mistaken.'

'Perhaps Lady Pagnell had some questions?'

Guy shook his head. 'If she did, I do not recall.'

'Michaelo said it was not a cordial meeting.'

'If there was such a meeting, it was likely unpleasant. There is much ill feeling between the Pagnell household and the bishop's.'

'What was the issue on that particular day?'

'I tell you I don't know what you are talking about and I am cold.' Guy made a swift move for the door.

Owen grabbed him, wrenching back one of his arms.

Guy let out a scream. Owen pressed a hand over his mouth and half carried, half dragged the clerk to the pair of chairs behind the prie-dieu, spun him forward and shoved him into one. Guy clutched the armrests, his face a mask of fear.

Owen leaned down and set his hands on Guy's forearms, forcing them down. 'What did Matthew say to you that afternoon?'

'I tell you you're mistaken.'

'You've been playing the gentle soul with Poin

sitting with him – you mean to be there when he remembers that night, don't you?'

'You are mad!'

'I've come to tell you that you missed your chance. This evening Poins told me of your presence in the undercroft that night.' It was all Owen had, his strong suspicion.

'*Christus*,' Guy whispered.

'Well?'

'I did not strangle Cisotta. In God's name I am innocent of that.'

'But guilty of other things?'

Guy shrank from Owen's eye, dropped his chin to his chest. 'Nothing so terrible as that. Matthew noticed changes in one of the property deeds.'

'What kind of changes?'

Guy fidgeted, muttering about bruises.

Owen gave him no additional space, just waited, ignoring the complaints, the sourness of the heavy man's sweat.

'It had stated a certain rent,' Guy said at last. 'I lessened the amount so that I might keep some of the money the tenant believed he owed. I took the money only for a few years, while my lord came regularly to the north and I was in charge of the rents.'

'You had debts?'

Again, Guy lapsed into silence.

'So Matthew threatened to expose you?'

'Yes. I begged him to let me have the document. He agreed, for a small payment.'

'So you came to this agreement the afternoon of the fire?'

'Yes. He came to the palace to press for payment.' Guy closed his eyes.

'And?'

'I knew the Fitzbaldrics were to be out that evening, and my lord bishop had some coin stored in the records room. Dear God, one little theft and I could not stop it.'

'So you met in the undercroft.'

'Yes. He took all the coin, more than I had intended. We argued. He told me he knew far worse of me, that I had stolen the ransom money and he could prove it.'

'You stole the Pagnell ransom money?'

Guy dropped his eyes.

'What debts do you have that were worth the life of Sir Ranulf?'

The sour odour increased. 'How could I know the old man would die?'

Owen fought the urge to strike the clerk. 'Surely Bishop William gives you all you need.'

'I . . . have a sister. She was not so fortunate in her household. The money helped her.'

'You could not ask the bishop for help?'

'He has so many in his care.'

'He thinks of you as his son.'

Guy looked Owen in the eye. 'I have been a great fool.' His gaze was too steady. Owen saw no emotion on the sweating, swinish face.

'Bastard,' Owen growled, giving the chair a good shake, making Guy gasp. 'Go on, tell me the rest.' His grasp on the arms of the chair was so tight that his wrists ached. He could not let go.

Guy took a moment to collect himself. 'He bragged of his power over Lady Pagnell, how he meant to have her, she was smitten with him. He had the strap in his hand, playing with it, wrapping the ends round his hands, tugging it tightly. That is when I began to fear him.' He paused, breathing hard. '*Deus juva me.*'

Owen relaxed his grip, moved the other chair to face

Guy, sat down, leaning forward, ready to block any attempt at escape. 'What then?'

'Something moved outside the record room. I told him there were some well-fed rats down there, but he grabbed the lamp and left me in the dark. I followed, hearing a woman's cry. She stood next to a barrel with some hides piled on it, one hand on the hides, one out before her like one does when calming a dog. She said she had just come from above and wondered at the light in the undercroft. I blurted out that she could not have seen it. "You were listening," Matthew said. He set down the lamp and grabbed her. I did not wait to see what he did. I ran. Dear Lord I ran for my life.'

'And left her in his hands.'

Guy crossed himself. Only now did he look up, his face contorted with sorrow and shame. 'He is evil. I knew it that night. But I swear I never thought he would kill her. Frighten her, perhaps –' he looked away – 'other things. But not strangle her with the strap.'

'Who told you how she died?'

'My master.'

'You have let a murderer walk the streets, live with a family who trust him.'

'For my part in it I'll lose everything I have worked for.'

'Do you deserve better?'

Guy shook his head. 'I was frightened. I did not understand why he didn't come for me.'

'Did he return the property document with the altered rent to you?'

'I left it there. I stopped for nothing.'

Owen rose to pace and think.

Guy did not move for a long while. Then he asked in choked voice, 'What will you do now?'

'We'll say nothing. Matthew will be here in the

afternoon, the palace will be surrounded by guards, and we'll take him.'

'I cannot see him.'

'Stand up,' Owen commanded. 'If he is not abed, the bishop should hear your story.'

Guy moved with the hesitant steps of one going to his execution. Owen felt no pity for him. He had thought only of himself that night, fearful lest his master learn that he had stolen from him, the man who thought of him as a son, who had trained him and given him a calling. Guy might have saved Cisotta. Matthew had flourished no weapon, only a strap.

In the chapel corridor, a dark figure caused Guy to cry out and press himself back against Owen.

'It is very late, Captain,' said Brother Michaelo, moving so that he no longer blocked the light from the torch. 'His Grace has suggested that you sleep in the palace tonight.'

'Has the Bishop of Winchester retired?'

'No. He is closed in the archbishop's parlour with His Grace.'

'Good. Will you announce us?'

Michaelo glanced back and forth between Owen and Guy, then nodded and turned to escort them.

Guy glanced back at Owen. 'Can it not wait until morning?'

'How could you rest with the prospect before you? Once you have unburdened yourself you will sleep and wake refreshed and able to assist us. I count on you tomorrow.'

Guy stumbled. Owen found a grim pleasure in roughly righting him and moving him on. He let go only once, to have a quiet word with one of his men about an extra guard on Poins.

Twenty-one

THe DeVIOUS ONe

A lamp by the parlour window flickered wildly in a draft, rearranging the planes of Wykeham's face as he looked on the clerk whose greed had caused him such embarrassment and perhaps cost Sir Ranulf his life. 'I thought of you as my son.' The hands with which he clenched the arms of the chair were white-knuckled, the veins swollen and angry.

Thoresby thought he knew what went through Wykeham's heated head. *He would slay Guy, but that it would give his enemies another tale to tell against him.* Thoresby motioned to Michaelo to replenish the bishop's cup.

But before Michaelo had lifted the pitcher Wykeham set the cup aside, rose and crossed to the window, setting his back to Guy. By the movement of his sleeves and the bowing head Thoresby guessed Wykeham was covering his face. He thought to give him some peace in which to compose himself.

'Why do you think we can trust this clerk to assist us tomorrow, Archer?' Owen's plan seemed fraught with risk. 'Why should he?'

'He will wish to be present to defend himself if Matthew contradicts his story,' Owen said.

Thoresby considered Guy, who slouched in his chair, his hands pressed together over his belly, his unlovely face creased into a penitential sadness. 'Can we trust you to do as we have instructed you?' Thoresby asked.

Guy dropped his gaze to his hands. 'I am your servant, Your Grace, though I would as lief sit in a dungeon than face that murderer.'

A dungeon is where you belong. 'If that is what you want, then that is precisely what you must not have, eh, Archer?'

'As you will, Your Grace.'

Thoresby would not have liked to be Guy, with Owen's rough face expressing so much loathing.

Wykeham suddenly spun round. 'Trust him? No, we know that is foolhardy. But he will sit at that table tomorrow. He will be present when I tell Lady Pagnell of his deceit, and how King Charles's unwillingness to release Sir Ranulf was no doubt due in part to the paltry sum put forth in the letters that my trusted clerk prepared for him.'

'I did not change the letters to France,' Guy protested.

'No?' Wykeham gave a little shrug, a very French shrug it seemed to Thoresby. 'How do I know that? I cannot send a messenger to King Charles requesting the letters returned, now can I?'

'Your Grace,' Owen said, breaking a charged silence, 'is Guy to move freely about the palace?'

Thoresby turned to Wykeham.

'You need not fear laxness in me, Captain,' said the bishop. 'I shall instruct my men that he is to be under their escort at all times. We would not wish to lose our witness to Matthew's crimes.'

Owen bowed and prepared to leave, but Wykeham stopped him. 'I would talk with you in private.'

'You may use this parlour,' said Thoresby. He nodded for the guard to take Guy away. 'You will be staying in the palace tonight, Archer?'

'I'll sleep with my men, Your Grace.'

'As you wish.' Thoresby departed.

Wykeham had knelt down at the prie-dieu in the corner of the room. As the silence settled, Owen poured himself a much-needed cup of wine and tried Thoresby's great chair. He felt he deserved some comfort this night. Easing back into the cushions, he began to reconstruct the evening of the fire.

'I never suspected Guy.' Wykeham had joined him, seated now across the table where Owen usually sat.

'Tell me what you know of him.'

'Alain is the devious one. Guy has always been a model of virtue. I took him in when he was ten, an orphan who showed promise, educated him personally with an eye towards his service in the household. He disappointed only in his slovenly appearance, his inability to be light and joysome. But it did not affect his work. Tidy in conception and execution, he was all one wishes for in a clerk.'

'I have seen him copy your signature,' Owen said.

'Of course. That is one of his gifts, a mastery of many hands.'

'A gift which proved too tempting, My Lord.'

'I see that now. It must have been simple for him to evise the accounts regarding Sir Ranulf's ransom. Damn him!' Wykeham cried out and looked away, truggling to control his breathing. 'He had no need to heat,' he said softly. 'He was well provided for. He has een with me for so long, Captain. He has moved up vith me, accompanied me everywhere, even to my prebendaries before I gave them up for the bishopric. He always served me well. Now Alain . . .'

'You called him devious.'

'Oh, yes. And his family moves in Lancastrian circles.'

'What? You had hoped to buy some support from the enemy?'

'Lancaster was not yet my enemy when I took in Alain. All this time I thought Alain was behind the Pagnell trouble.'

'And said nothing to me? Why? You requested my assistance.' *Damn you.*

'I had no proof. I wanted proof. Which is why I chose him to accompany me north.'

'To flush him out.'

Wykeham nodded.

'Before the Pagnell troubles – why retain Alain if you disliked and distrusted him so?'

'Better the enemy before me than behind.'

Owen slept little, his mind swarming with variations on the outcome of the day ahead.

Magda had assured him that Poins was sleeping quietly, that the evening had not taken the last of his strength, but she had warned Owen that if he hoped the man would remember more of that night in the undercroft he might well be disappointed. 'Oft-times a man will remember little of such an event. Thou knowest it, that soldiers oft forget the moment of their wounding.'

'I have never forgotten mine.'

'Mayhap thou didst need to remember it.'

He pressed his blind eye into the pillow and tried to still his mind with prayer.

So much depended on timing once Lady Pagnell an

Matthew were at the palace. And he did not trust that Guy had told him all the truth.

As the sky through the chinks in the shutters paled, he rose and dressed, and found a servant to take a message to Lucie explaining why he had not been home to bed, though she probably had not expected him to return. Then Owen stepped out into a morning loud with birds welcoming the dawn. The guard greeted him with sleepy respect. Owen made his way round the palace, reviewing the guard stations. Satisfied with the number and readiness, he moved on to the barracks to don a long leather surcoat with metal plates and a helmet. If Wykeham's fears proved justified, that Lancaster saw him as a Becket, a too-powerful prince of the Church who stood in his way, Owen would need the protection.

A few men still sat over their morning bread, cheese and ale. Owen joined them, preferring to eat with them than at the palace. The building was largely deserted, so quiet that Owen told the page who assisted him with his heavy surcoat after breakfast not to rattle it so. He headed back to the palace as soon as he was suited, stopping only to remind the guard at the kitchen that his duty was to keep peace in the area round Poins.

All along the palace the guards stood alert at Owen's approach, then relaxed as he passed. As he moved up the steps of the great hall Alfred came forth to greet him, his lank hair hidden beneath a light helmet.

'Is the household up?'

'Aye, Captain, though I trust they did not plan such an early rising. Sir Ranulf's son Stephen has just arrived – he must have been first at Monkgate this morning.'

'Stephen Pagnell is in the great hall?'

'Aye. He is demanding to participate in the meeting between Lady Pagnell and the bishop.'

Owen muttered a curse. He had given no thought to Sir Ranulf's heir, believing him to have wiped his hands of the business. Yet as heir he had a right to be there. 'Is he alone?'

Alfred shook his head, his expression grim. 'He rides with a party of young nobles. Brother Michaelo says they are all from families known to hold Lancastrian sympathies.'

'Are they armed?'

'Knives for the table are all they carry now. They gave up their weapons without quarrel.'

'I do not trust it.'

'Nor should you. They have a quarrel, that is plain.'

'What have you heard?'

'Gossip about Lancaster, his imminent arrival with his Spanish wife, Constance, and how he will desire details of the proceedings here in York. That Lancaster truly hates the bishop. That Stephen Pagnell is here to observe Wykeham and his clerks at the meeting, hoping to find some indication of who might have stolen the ransom. Friends await a signal at a farm outside the city gates.'

'Do they know you heard all this?'

'I did not, it was Brother Michaelo.'

'Why did you not send me word at the barracks?'

'Forgive me, Captain. I thought you would be here as soon as you were ready . . . Meanwhile, I gathered information for you.'

'Aye. And I am grateful.' Owen tried to think what to do first. 'Has the bishop received them?'

'He has not yet appeared.'

Awakened by a stripe of sunlight centred over her left eye, Lucie lay for a moment confused, groping for the memory of what she had been doing before lying down for a nap. Her limbs felt leaden, her mouth dry, her bladder full. Gradually she realized it was morning, and far later in the morning than she was accustomed to rising. She sat up with a jolt, remembering the events of the night before, the mounting evidence against the Pagnell steward. She must go to Emma's house. But Matthew and Lady Pagnell would not leave the house until after Nones and the sun was not yet so high in the sky. She sank back into the pillows, turned to Owen's side and saw no sign of his having come to bed. Rising, expecting dizziness, she was relieved to experience none. The room showed no trace that Owen had passed through in the night.

A knock took her to the door.

Phillippa entered with a cup of Magda's tincture. 'I heard you stir. I shall be your lady's maid this morning. Then Alisoun will change your bandage.' There was a strength to Phillippa's voice that Lucie had not heard in a while. 'A messenger came from the palace early this morning. Owen had much to do there and spent the night.'

'I thought as much.'

'Lady Pagnell is at last meeting with the Bishop of Winchester, did you hear? Long before Sir Ranulf's month's mind. I am sorry for that, truth to tell. I thought it a fitting sentiment.'

Lucie sniffed the tincture to check that Alisoun had not given her the original version. She could not afford to be drowsy this day.

By mid-morning the guards were fidgeting beneath the weight of the metal-clad surcoats. Owen shifted their posts to keep them occupied. His major concern was to prevent any of Stephen Pagnell's company from slipping a message outside the palace walls, informing comrades of the guards' positions, their strength and number.

He was irritated to realize he'd begun to share Wykeham's belief that he was Lancaster's Becket, that the duke's henchmen might think the only means of ridding their lord of his irritating churchman was to murder him. What was worse was a sudden certainty that Lucie would go to Emma Ferriby's house in the afternoon to learn more about Matthew. And there was no way Owen could prevent her from doing so, short of posting a guard at his own home. He prayed to the Virgin to protect Lucie, then forced his mind back to his duties.

Michaelo had suggested that the meeting take place in the archbishop's own hall, as Stephen Pagnell's companions were occupying the great hall. Owen found them a quiet quintet, two playing chess with Wykeham's board and pieces, two others playing backgammon. Stephen sat watching the chess game, but quickly abandoned it when Owen approached. Though small and slender, he had his mother's skill at creating an imperious presence with stance and clothing. He walked with a wide-legged gait, as if spanning a river from bank to bank with his well-muscled legs.

'I started for the minster to visit our chapel and your men prevented me,' Stephen said, coming to a halt far closer than Owen liked. 'I told you we have no purpose here other than to see that the Bishop of Winchester plays fair with my mother.'

'My orders are that no one stirs from the palace grounds until the meeting is concluded.'

'My mother can enter but I cannot leave?'

'That is correct.'

'I demand to see Bishop William.'

Owen inclined his head. 'You have only to clap for a servant and give him a message for the bishop.'

'I want you to deliver it.'

Owen glanced down at his military garb. 'I am not dressed for such an errand. I should frighten all the servants coming through the corridors.'

'You are not amusing.'

'It is not my business to be so.'

Stephen tried to stare Owen down. He lost in the end, spun on his heel and clapped for a servant. Owen took the opportunity to slip away.

It proved a tedious morning for all after such a tense beginning.

Despite the drizzle, Thoresby sat by his parlour window, the shutters open to the garden, a pile of petitions lying forgotten on the table beside him. Owen was glad of the draft as he stood before the archbishop describing the preparations. He regretted wearing the heavy surcoat and helmet – his role was to organize his men, not fight, and as the day warmed and the drizzle continued it was damned unpleasant. The whole palace seemed to be waiting for the long-delayed confrontation.

Lucie sat on a bench in St Crux churchyard watching for Lady Pagnell and Matthew to leave the Ferriby house. The walk had left her with little breath despite a stop at the market and at Harry Flesher's butcher shop with the excuse that she wished to tell Jasper's friend Timothy that her scrip had been recovered, though she knew he would have heard about it – a theft and a murder were just the sort of grist that kept the gossip mill grinding. Her weakness irked her, but did not frighten her the way it had. She began to believe that God had answered her prayers and cast out her devils.

At last she saw Lady Pagnell step out on to Hosier Lane, followed closely by Matthew, his hand ready to support her elbow if she stumbled. A servant trailed them, carrying a sheaf of documents secured with straps. Lucie held herself still as they walked slowly towards Whipmawhopmagate, then she hastened to the house.

Owen and Michaelo straightened as a servant flung wide the door to Thoresby's hall.

Lady Pagnell sailed in, imperious in her purple robes. But something was wrong. Matthew did not accompany her.

'My lady,' said Owen, bowing.

'Captain.' She inclined her head a little.

'*Benedicte*, Lady Pagnell,' Michaelo said while bowing with a fluid grace.

'Has my son arrived?' she asked.

'He has, My Lady,' said Michaelo, 'and all unexpected by us. I am afraid he did not receive as cordial a welcome as he might have hoped.'

'I did not invite him to attend, if that is what you think. It was my meddlesome steward. I learned of it only this morning.'

'You are not attended by your steward?' Owen said, growing anxious.

'Matthew will join us. He forgot a document and has gone to fetch it.' She shook her head as if annoyed.

A servant followed behind with a cluster of rolled documents held by two straps, a leather thong threaded between them as a handle. The straps did not match. One looked like the one Owen had found round Cisotta's neck. Something seemed wrong about that. Matthew had sold the tunic that might prove much witness to his presence in the undercroft that night, y he had continued to use the matching strap.

Lady Pagnell paused just past Owen and turned back to him. 'Why are you and all your men in war gear, Captain? Is the bishop fearful that my grandsons will drop another tile in his path?'

'My lord the Bishop of Winchester will explain, My Lady.'

She gave him a little bow and moved on. Thoresby entered the room and moved to greet her.

Owen watched the strapped documents as the servant moved past, frantically reviewing what must be done. There was no time to warn Lucie, Matthew was probably already back at the house. But he could not wait here, wondering whether she was in trouble.

'I am called away to the Ferriby house,' Owen told Michaelo. 'Have Wykeham's men watch Guy and Alain. Something is not right. I've no time to explain.'

He called to one of his men to help him out of his leather surcoat. He could not run through the city with it weighing him down.

Thoresby was irritated by Owen's hasty departure, leaving him with a hall full of Lancastrians and a delicate meeting over which he must preside, Wykeham's clerk ready to confront a murderer, but no one to confront. He was about to excuse himself for a hasty consultation with Michaelo when Lady Pagnell proposed to change the seating arrangement so that she and Wykeham would be eye to eye. It promised disaster. Michaelo had planned it so that Thoresby was directly across from her, Wykeham at an angle, thinking peace might prevail if they were not scowling at each other.

'My Lady, in the interest of peace –'

'And my son Stephen must sit beside me.'

'Lady Pagnell, that is not advisable.'

Her eyes flashed. 'I come here in good faith . . .'

'My Lady,' Brother Michaelo said, bending down towards her from behind. She shifted to glare at him, but his deferential demeanour softened her. 'I should be happy to explain all my reasoning in arranging the seating.'

Thoresby silently blessed him, but it left him with no one to ask about Owen's abrupt disappearance.

A tense quiet descended on the Ferriby house as Lucie and Emma knelt in front of the large trunk in which Matthew stored his belongings. Edgar was stationed by the front door, John the garden door, and Ivo was out in the garden by the gate to the alley.

'Remember,' Lucie said to Emma, 'we are searching for something he did not dispose of that might prove he had been near the fire, or anything that might reveal his intentions – stolen documents, money, a note from your mother. . .'

'She would not be so stupid as to write to him,' Emma said as she lifted the lid – Edgar had already proved useful in picking the lock.

Lucie hesitated at the sight of the first layer, a comb, worn leggings, a pair of riding boots oiled and wrapped in a cloth. Matthew had no home of his own. This chest contained all his property. She was invading it for what had seemed good cause, but now she felt a trespasser. Emma appeared to have no such reservations about the task. She had already laid aside the top items and a mended shirt as well, beneath which she had uncovered some letters carrying the royal seal.

'What is this?' Emma breathed, sitting back on her heels and opening one of the letters.

'Put it away!' Edgar cried from the doorway. 'Matthew is crossing the courtyard!'

Lucie snatched up all the items and placed them in the trunk, but Emma shook her head and slipped the letters beneath a box sitting beside her. There was no time to argue. Lucie dropped the lid and clicked the lock into place as Edgar exclaimed loudly over Matthew's early return.

But the steward's eyes had gone straight to the chest, then to Lucie and Emma standing near it.

'I forgot a document. My lady awaits me at the palace.' He was moving towards Lucie and Emma when John exploded from behind them, throwing himself at Matthew, a dagger in his right hand.

'John! No!' Emma cried.

Matthew crashed backwards. As the two hit the tile floor, Matthew howled in pain.

Edgar and Emma plucked at John as he and Matthew rolled over and over, leaving a trail of blood behind them. When Edgar and Emma finally succeeded in lifting the boy between them, Lucie bent to help Matthew move out of the way of the boy's kicks – he was bleeding freely from one forearm and his chin – but he snapped his arm out of Lucie's grasp and rolled towards his attacker, grabbing him by the ankles.

'You think you're a man, do you?' Matthew shouted at John, who was struggling to free himself from his tutor and his mother.

'Stop this!' Emma shouted. By now several clerks from the shop had joined them and the five managed to pull John and Matthew apart.

'Leave him alone, he's just a boy,' Emma said to Matthew, who lay sprawled on the floor.

The steward struggled to sit up a little, trying to support himself on his elbows, but his wounded arm failed him and he moaned as he fell back to the floor. Lucie knelt behind him. This time he did not push her away. With her hands beneath his arms she hoisted, then pushed his upper body into a seated position. From there he was able to use his legs to help her drag him to the wall, which would support his back. Lucie's hand throbbed.

'I threatened him and so he hates me,' Matthew said to no one in particular.

'Murderer!' John cried. 'Thief and murderer!' He strained to escape the firm grasps of Edgar and Emma. His voice trembled and yet trilled with defiance.

'A murderer? A thief? What are you talking about?' Matthew demanded.

Seeing that her friend was preoccupied with her son, Lucie began a litany of the evidence on which the boy based his accusations. The shop clerks and Matthew stared at her in disbelief. She faltered as she began to doubt all that she thought she had known.

Lady Pagnell rose and curtsied to Wykeham as he approached the table. Alain walked beside a servant who carried a writing desk.

'What is this?' Wykeham said, looking around at those already seated. 'What are you doing here?' he demanded of Stephen Pagnell.

'Representing my father, who could not attend,' Stephen said, visibly enjoying Wykeham's discomfort.

'He is Ranulf's heir,' Lady Pagnell said, a challenge in her eyes.

'I pray you, be seated,' Thoresby murmured to Wykeham. Everyone at the table seemed to be holding their breaths. 'Sit,' Thoresby repeated.

As Wykeham finally settled, Thoresby enquired after Guy, who had not accompanied him.

Wykeham leaned close and whispered, 'While at the garderobe he tried to slip away. He will be escorted in when we are ready for him.'

Thoresby had expected Guy to prove a coward, lacking honour, but he was not gratified to be right.

'Where is the steward?' Wykeham asked.

Thoresby explained curtly, not wishing to prolong the whispered conference. Lady Pagnell already grew curious. Owen's plan to seize the Pagnell steward seemed to be failing before it was ever put into play.

As Owen crossed Hosier Lane to the Ferriby house he was hailed by George Hempe, who strode towards him from Pavement.

'I thought I might expect you. I noticed your wife waiting here earlier. What's afoot?'

'Have you seen the Pagnell steward?'

Hempe nodded. 'He arrived a little while ago. I've found the thief's murderer, Archer.' He caught Owen's arm as he continued towards the house. 'Don't you want to know who it was? A fellow thief, after your wife's purse.'

That was it! Merely thieves fighting among themselves? Owen cursed and hurried past him. He heard Hempe following.

339

Twenty-two

RESOLUTIONS

The door to the Ferriby house was open, but no sound met Owen in the courtyard. His heart was pounding when he stepped across the threshold into the dimly lit hall.

The tableau before him was not at all what he had expected. In a far corner of the room, Matthew sat against the wall, pressing a cloth to his head. His right sleeve was empty, hanging from his shoulder on some laces. Lucie knelt beside him, wrapping his bare forearm in a bandage that was already blooming with blood. Emma sat on a bench cradling John's head against her shoulder – he was crying, his entire body shaken by the sobs. His younger brother sat on the floor near him clinging to his mother's skirt, looking confused but uninjured. Edgar and two unfamiliar men stood a little to one side. Edgar spoke quietly to the others, who glanced now and then towards the wounded man.

Hempe strode past Owen and demanded, 'What has happened here?'

'Lucie, I pray you,' Emma said, 'tell them what fools we have been.'

John straightened as his mother shifted on the bench. The boy's face was swollen, not only from his tears but from what appeared to be a broken nose, a bloody cloth pressed to it and one eye already darkening. John lifted his chin to slow the bleeding and gulped air, then held it, trying to quiet hiccups.

'Edgar, see that Tom and Paul shut the shop and wait for my husband to return,' Emma said. A corner of her starched wimple was bloodstained where the boy had rested his head.

Owen crouched down by Lucie as Edgar escorted the clerks towards the shop.

'Are John and Matthew the only wounded?'

'I have some bruises, I am sure, as I am certain Emma and Edgar do.'

Owen touched a bloodstain on the bandage round her hand. 'Did you open the wound?'

'No. I used my hand too much, but the blood is Matthew's, not mine.'

Hempe had settled on a bench nearby. 'Mistress Wilton, I pray you, speak up so that I might hear your account.'

'Why is he here?' Emma asked Owen.

'It was plain to him that something was afoot, so he joined me,' Owen said, trying to ignore his feelings. 'You must begin with Emma's identification of the trap,' he said to Lucie, 'or the bailiff will not understand what this is about.'

Lucie began as requested.

Hempe listened without comment, and when the tale was complete he said only, 'I see.'

Owen regarded Matthew, organizing the questions not yet answered. The one uppermost in his mind he asked first. 'What made you return to the house today?'

341

Matthew closed his eyes, leaned his head against the wall, as if too weary to speak. His upper lip was swollen. But without opening his eyes, he said in a voice just above a mumble, 'I watched my lady as we walked to the palace, her chin up, her eyes set on the unpleasant matter ahead, swallowing her pride to protect her family from more gossip. And I felt ashamed.' He drew up his knees, wrapped his good arm round them. 'I came back for some letters. Ones in the hand of the bishop's clerk, Guy. The ones acknowledging to my lady the receipt of the ransom money. The bishop has only to see the amounts on the letters to realize that they do not agree with the copies he holds in Winchester. I am certain of it.'

Owen was sorry Hempe had heard this, but the man was determined to learn all.

'May I see them?' Owen asked.

'They are in my trunk.' Matthew drew out a key.

'There is no need for that,' said Emma. 'Here they are.' She handed Owen a pair of documents bearing royal chancery seals.

'What?' Matthew sat forward, looking from Emma to Lucie, his colour rising. 'What right had you to search my trunk? And to remove those?'

'What right had I?' Emma raised her voice in disbelief. 'They concern my father's ransom. What of you? What are you doing with them among your personal belongings?'

'I am steward.'

'And what of the tunic you sold to a dubber? The one you wore the night of the fire?'

Matthew pressed his hands to his head, his elbows to his thighs, and sat very still.

'He may be innocent,' Lucie whispered to Owen.

At present that was not a comforting possibility. F

if Matthew was not guilty, Guy was, and he would be desperate to escape.

'Matthew is expected at the palace,' Owen said to Hempe. 'I propose we escort him there.'

Now Matthew looked up. A bruise was developing beneath one eye. Little John had done much harm. 'My lady does await me there.' He rose with a groan, holding his wounded arm close to him.

Lucie helped him into his torn sleeve.

'I should like to come,' she said to Owen.

Owen could see from the smudges beneath her eyes and the way she moved that she was exhausted. 'I will not have you walk into the middle of even a remote danger of attack.'

'You will send word of what has happened?' Lucie asked.

'To both you and Emma, I swear. Have you the strength for the walk home?'

'I shall rest here a while, then go.'

Lady Pagnell had tired of waiting for her steward and begun the negotiation by proposing two of the properties to Wykeham, who had quietly said that was out of the question.

'Alain and Guy considered the offerings with their customary care, My Lady, and each one is of equal value to the piece of land your husband forfeited. Your part in the decision is to choose which one your neighbour would prefer. I thought that had been explained.'

Thoresby would usually enjoy such combat, but he was uneasy about Owen's disappearance and the Pagnell steward's absence. Guy had been brought in discreetly, although Stephen Pagnell had not missed the guards on either side, and Thoresby's nod that they might return to their posts. It did not seem as if peace would settle on the palace this evening, as he had hoped. Perhaps it would have been just as well to begin with Guy's confession to his forgery and embezzlement. Thoresby found himself watching the son more than the mother. Stephen stared at Wykeham with such intensity that Thoresby expected him to lunge at the bishop at any moment.

Lady Pagnell's voice startled him. 'This property, then, and that's an end to it.' She shoved a deed across to Wykeham.

The bishop sat back with the document in hand, nodding solemnly. Alain whispered something to him. Guy had been silent throughout the proceedings. Thoresby could not guess what he was feeling, but when Wykeham handed Alain the document to copy and present to Lady Pagnell before she left, Guy's expression was clear – pure and simple jealousy. But he said nothing and dropped his head before most at the table caught the flash of emotion. Alain excused himself and retired to complete the transaction.

Lady Pagnell began to rise.

'There is another matter of business,' Wykeham said.

'I said that was an end to it.' Lady Pagnell motioned for the servant who stood behind her.

'Lady Pagnell, it is about the discrepancy in St Ranulf's ransom money.'

She turned back towards Wykeham, her face white. She looked ill. 'What?'

'I trust you will be pleased to hear that we have uncovered an embezzler who forged documents regarding your husband's ransom.'

Lady Pagnell swayed and Thoresby feared she might faint. But she propped her hands on the table and hissed, 'Will you stop at nothing to deny your guilt my husband's death?'

'I do nothing of the kind, Lady Pagnell. We have him in custody,' Wykeham began.

There was a commotion at the door, and suddenly Owen, Hempe, and Matthew entered the hall.

Lady Pagnell sank down in her chair.

'You have come in your own time, Matthew,' Stephen said, using all the power in his voice, which was considerable for a man of his stature.

Thoresby's eyesight was unimpaired regarding distances and he noted at once the steward's torn sleeve, his head wound, the thick lip.

As Owen brought him forward, the others rose, no doubt as relieved as Thoresby to shake off the tension in the room, and exclaimed about the steward's condition.

'Have these men laid hands on you?' Lady Pagnell cried. She had regained some of her colour.

'No, My Lady,' Matthew said, his words oddly shaped, his voice rasping, which was not as Thoresby remembered his speech at Sir Ranulf's funeral. 'Your grandson sought to punish me for my transgressions.'

'What?'

'Might he be seated?' Owen asked. 'He is none too steady on his feet.'

Michaelo showed Matthew to his seat beside Lady Pagnell, who called her servant over to see to him.

As Thoresby resumed his seat and the others followed, he noted that Guy was last to settle, glancing round the room with a wild look in his eyes. Thoresby caught Owen observing the clerk as well. Their eyes met and Owen gave him a nod so slight that Thoresby wondered whether he had imagined it. But he whispered to Michaelo that all doors should be well secured against anyone attempting to flee. Michaelo slipped away to spread the word among the guards,

Hempe and Stephen Pagnell straining to observe his circuit round the hall.

'Are we to be enlightened as to the cause of the boy's attack?' Wykeham asked.

'As to the immediate cause, it might be best left to another time, My Lord Bishop,' Owen said. 'But Matthew has come to take his place in this negotiation and to explain his part in the recent fire at your house.'

Lady Pagnell turned in her seat to study her trusted steward. He cradled his wounded arm against his torso and kept his eyes on the table edge before him, avoiding the curious stares set on him from all angles.

'We did not wait for you. We have settled on the land,' said Lady Pagnell. 'The clerk is copying the deed. What is this about, Matthew? Were you involved in that tragedy?'

'If I might begin before the event,' Matthew said. 'On the morning of that day.'

'Can't this wait?' Stephen demanded. He looked at Wykeham. 'You spoke of my father's ransom.'

'This is part of the tale,' Owen said.

Stephen sat back. 'Go on.'

Matthew nodded. 'My Lords, My Lady.'

Thoresby motioned to a servant, ordered honey water for Matthew. He would not speak long with such a hoarseness.

'As I examined the deeds to the properties you have just discussed, I noticed changes in one of them. Several numbers and other items concerning the rent had been scratched out and redone, and in several cases it was quite clear from the spacing that what had gone before had been of a different length. One might have been evidence merely of a scribal error, but three numbers and other items of rent were clearly evidence of intentional changes. I examined the deed in different lights. The changes had been made with great care. But the lettering was not precisely the same. In fact, it looked familiar. I checked the letters regarding my lord's ransoms, and there I saw the same hand. So I went to Guy.'

'I have told them all this,' Guy said.

'I have not heard it,' Lady Pagnell said coldly.

'I pray you, let him speak,' Thoresby said.

'I told Guy I knew something he would rather keep quiet. He told me to meet him in the undercroft, that the bishop kept a coffer there from which he would pay me well.'

'I trusted you!' Lady Pagnell exclaimed.

'My Lady, I meant to present you with the letters, the deed and the money as proof of the man's guilt,' Matthew said.

'You fool,' said Stephen Pagnell. 'He would have taken the deed.'

'But a woman appeared at the door as we were counting the coins,' Matthew continued.

'She did,' Guy interrupted, 'and it was plain he feared she had heard him bragging of his importance in the Pagnell household, of how it was but a matter of time before he won the widow. Her appearance put everything he had worked for in jeopardy.'

'What do you mean, "won the widow"?' Lady Pagnell murmured.

'I did fear that, I will not deny it.' Matthew raised his battered head. 'But then I realized she was not paying attention to me, she was looking at him.'

'That is not true,' Guy said.

'She said she had not known he was in York. He said he had not known she still abided here.'

'I did not even know her,' Guy protested.

'She asked about his sister. I felt a great anger in him

and fear in her, and I was afraid. I grabbed the documents, but he already had one of the straps in his hand and was moving towards her. I should have intervened, but the sounds coming from him – he was raving. God help me, I ran.'

'Ran right for her,' Guy interrupted. 'He was desperate to silence her . . .'

'Quiet!' Thoresby roared. 'You have told your version of the night, let Matthew tell his.'

'The documents were unwieldy with but one strap, they began to fan out and one rolled out. In turning to catch it –' Matthew stopped, looking at all the eyes trained on him. 'Tell me that she was dead before the fire, tell me I was not responsible.' His face was covered with sweat, the blood seeping again from the wound on his forehead. He looked a demon.

'You knocked over the lamp,' Owen said.

'Even then I did not stop.' Matthew gave a strangled sob. 'Even hearing the struggle. I turned – but seeing his wildness I kept running.' Tears coursed down his cheeks.

Owen turned to Guy. 'Why did you take the time to place the strap just so, centred on her throat, crushing it? Was she not already dead?'

Guy was watching Matthew, not Owen. 'You set the fire to kill me.'

'Was she already dead when you placed the buckle over her throat and pressed, Guy?' Owen asked again, hoping to trick him into a confession.

Now Guy turned to him. 'Why do you believe his word over mine? My lord bishop will vouch for me.'

'God help me if I ever trust you again,' Wykeham said in a choked voice.

'Matthew, why did you do it?' Lady Pagnell asked. 'You had only to ask for all you needed.'

Matthew turned away from them, heaving with sobs. 'The money was not for me. I sought to prove his guilt.'

'Easily said,' Stephen muttered.

'What is this play-acting?' Guy said. 'Will his lady comfort this steward knowing what he did? How he grabbed the woman and wrapped the strap round her neck, tightening it so quickly that her scream died in her crushed throat?'

Thoresby saw in the man's eyes that he was reliving the act, not narrating the act of another. 'Last night you said you ran. But now you describe her murder as if you were there.'

'That is how it must have been, Your Grace, it is plain,' Guy said in a more subdued tone.

Lady Pagnell, her face chalky, fumbled with her chair and rose with a moan. Michaelo quickly helped her to withdraw from the table, leading her towards Thoresby's quarters, her servant hurrying behind. Stephen Pagnell rose halfway, uncertain whether to follow or stay.

Guy searched the faces round the table, and seeing no support he flung back his stool and ran for the retreating couple. Thoresby shouted for the guards, but Owen had been watching, ready to spring, and spring he did, tackling the clerk to the ground. His fists pounded into the man, pounded, pounded, until the bailiff drew Owen off.

'Guy is a man of the cloth, no matter what his offence,' Wykeham cried.

Thoresby had seen this bloodlust in Owen only once before, when they had fought side by side at a manor near Ripon. The woman Cisotta must have meant much to Owen. He was glad the bailiff had been there after all.

Wykeham looked bewildered as he bent to Guy.

349

'This man's justice belongs in the ecclesiastical courts.'

Owen's lungs felt as if they would burst as he worked to catch his breath. His knuckles burned. Guy, his face bloody and his body limp, moaned as Hempe and a guard lifted him on to a bench to be carried out of the hall. Owen's fever of rage had died as suddenly as it had flared and he thanked God he had not killed the man. It was the Church's duty to dispose of him.

'Here, drink this.' Thoresby thrust a cup of brandy-wine into his hand. 'Then leave the grounds. Do not let Wykeham see you tonight. I shall send for you when he is calmer.'

Leaving Wykeham to deal with Lady Pagnell, Thoresby told Stephen Pagnell to summon his companions.

'You would tell them what happened here?' Pagnell asked.

'They have troubled to come so far, they should be satisfied.'

'Matthew's designs upon my mother – you will not mention that.'

'How else can I explain his motivations?'

'They will not notice the lack.'

'But the duke will.'

'What do you want, Your Grace?'

'Your word that Wykeham will have no trouble departing from York with Guy in his custody.'

'The duke would not care.'

'I think that he might,' Thoresby said. 'The clerk will be punished, and harshly, have no doubt of it.'

Twenty-three

ᴆepartures

At the Ferriby home, Owen's, Hempe's and Matthew's departure left a shocked household. John was escorted to the boys' chamber, Ivo hurrying behind him. Emma thanked Edgar for his help, then sat down heavily on a bench and doubled over, retching. Lucie brought her a bowl into which she was promptly sick.

'What was he thinking, to attack a grown man like that?' Emma groaned, then started at a sound above, rising but quickly sinking back down, pressing her hands to her temples.

'You must calm yourself before you can be of any use to John,' Lucie said. 'I'll go up to see that they are cleaning his wounds properly and send someone to you with wine. Then I'll go to the shop and have Jasper return with an ointment for John's nose, and herbs with which to pack it, as well as a tincture for pain.'

'How shall I explain all this to Peter?'

'All you can do is tell him the truth. Your mother will surely be full of the tale when she returns.'

'She will. Sweet heaven, I almost pity Matthew.'

Emma's colour was returning. Lucie doubted that she even needed the wine. But it would settle her stomach.

'Where is Peter today?'

'One of his ships has docked. He is always there for the unloading.'

'I pray he found no problems, so that he is in good cheer when you tell him of all this.'

In the days that followed, Wykeham alternated between grief-stricken prayer and furious pacing as he deliberated about how to dispatch justice.

Thoresby was blunt in his disapproval of Wykeham's eventual decision. 'Journeying all the way to Winchester to try Guy there is foolhardy. Why take such risk?'

'Thanks to your captain, Guy is unable to cause much trouble on the way.' Wykeham seemed unable to move past Owen's attack on the clerk to acknowledge the debt he owed the captain. 'I hope to talk with Guy more. I am not satisfied with his explanations. He said the king siphoned money, as did I, so he believed it was common practice, that he would be a fool not to seize for himself a small portion of the funds going through his hands. And he was confident that his forgeries were so subtle he would never be caught.'

'He is a thorough knave, prideful and defiant,' said Thoresby. 'But worse than that, he is a murderer. How does he defend himself with that?'

'He called the midwife a whoring, thieving witch who was trespassing in the Fitzbaldrics' house. But his voice broke when he said that. He knows his sin deserves death.'

'He has not explained his former acquaintance with the victim?'

'No.' Wykeham pressed his hands together, bowed over them for a heartbeat. 'But I do not wish him to die before he has understood all that brought him to his fall and repented.'

Thoresby thought it was Wykeham who needed to understand.

'I wish him to die in peace with the Lord,' Wykeham said. He fell silent again.

'You were so fond of him?' Thoresby wondered aloud.

Wykeham straightened, anger replacing the pain in his eyes. 'All this transpired because of Sir Ranulf's desire to go forth into danger in the king's name one last time. It is as with the king – the elderly are never wise.'

'I can name many greybeards and grey-headed ladies who have exhibited much wisdom,' Thoresby said, disliking this turn in the conversation.

Wykeham shook his head. 'For every one of them there are a hundred, a thousand, with addled minds.'

On the morning of the bishop's departure Owen ordered his men to line the drive while he stood near the palace doorway. Thoresby seemed confident that Stephen Pagnell's party would cause no trouble, but Owen meant to take no chances. When Wykeham stepped from the palace his gaze moved at once to the cart in which Guy sat trussed. Seeing the anguish in the bishop's eyes, Owen looked away. It was a subdued company that rode down the drive.

When the last of the bishop's men were out the gates, Thoresby summoned Owen to his parlour.

'You are not smiling,' the archbishop said, settling to his great chair. 'Are you not glad to see the backs that troublesome party?'

353

'Their departure does not undo the tragedy, Your Grace.'

'You must not mind Wykeham's seeming ingratitude.'

'He would have much preferred that I'd proven Lancaster was his nemesis. The truth held up the mirror to his own weaknesses.'

'Hm. He feared you were Lancaster's man and all the time you disliked his person, not his affiliations. Interesting. Was Lawgoch's appeal also personal?'

Owen stopped breathing.

'Come, come, you must not look so. You cannot be so naïve as to think Friar Hewald asked no questions in St David's.' Hewald was the messenger Thoresby had sent to escort Owen from Wales.

'I chose to return to York, Your Grace,' Owen managed to say.

'Indeed. And that is the end of it, eh?'

Owen disliked the pleasant tone in Thoresby's voice the gleam in his eyes. He would use the secre someday, Owen was sure of it.

'I should demand some public penance for you brutal attack on a man of the Church,' Thoresby note as he began to fuss with the documents on the tabl beside him.

Ah, now he strikes. Owen was almost relieved.

'But I cannot bring myself to add to your family grief. You may go.'

Owen sat for a moment, uncertain what to say. He be damned if he was going to thank the archbishop, bu with the knowledge of his treason in the man's hand he would be a fool to cross him.

Thoresby glanced up with a chilly smile. 'You a free to go, Archer. Go in peace.'

Still braced for attack, Owen rose with stiff digni

and bowed to the archbishop, who had already lowered his eyes. 'Your Grace,' he murmured, and withdrew.

As he crossed the archbishop's hall, eager to put distance between himself and the archbishop, he noticed Brother Michaelo standing just beyond the doorway to the porch. Changing direction, Owen escaped through the kitchen. Maeve bid him good-day, humming as she bent back to her work, all trace of Poins's sojourn already erased from her realm. It seemed to Owen a kind of sacrilege that the man's terrible suffering left no scar on the room.

But not all was as before. The Fitzbaldrics had found a house not so large nor so well situated as the bishop's, but they had decided not to spend all their time in York. Their house outside Hull beckoned and they intended to go there for a long retreat after settling into the new townhouse. Magda's herbs had improved May's sight, but could not restore it completely. Nor could she promise that it would not fail again. Adeline Fitzbaldric decided that May might best be employed as the housekeeper in the country house, instructing the servants beneath her in maintaining the house in her mistress's absence.

But they would not need to find work for Poins. On the evening of the day on which Wykeham and Lady Pagnell made their peace, Poins had asked Magda if someone might help him into the garden.

'It has drizzled all the day,' Magda said, 'and thou wilt find the ground cold on thy feet.' He could not yet wear shoes for the open sores from blisters.

'Cold is what I want,' Poins said. 'And to look up at the stars.'

Seeing the yearning in the fading eyes, Magda sent for Bolton. Between the two of them, Poins hobbled out into the kitchen yard. His breath was ragged and he shook with the effort and the pain, but Poins lifted his head to the sky and stared long at the stars, the treetops, the night garden. Then he declared it enough, he was ready for his bed.

It was no surprise to Magda when during the night his tortured breath quieted, then ceased. She thought it a kindness that May would be taken away from York soon. There were too many sad memories for her here.

On the evening after Wykeham departed Lucie and Owen retired early. The weather had turned sharply cold and they had warmed their stomachs with spiced wine as they mulled over the events of the past week. Lucie was glad that Thoresby had not burdened Owen with a penance that might encourage him to brood about his beating of Guy. Although she knew it a sin, which itself would earn a penance from her confessor, she could not help but be grimly satisfied that Owen had beaten Cisotta's murderer.

'And to think that he knew her.'

'Aye. And knew she could identify him. But when had they met before? Why will he not say?'

'I have wondered whether Cisotta would have died had she been a stranger to him.'

They fell silent, listening to the shutters rattling, branch skittering along the roof.

Owen noticed Lucie biting her lip. 'What is it?'

'I have yet to apologize to Emma for lying about the gloves.'

He laughed to hear it, her worry so wonderfully ordinary.

'I feel such a liar,' she protested.

'I doubt Emma would care, my love. Her household is at peace and you helped make it so.'

'It was only a partial lie. I do have a pair of my mother's gloves in my trunk, delicate work, for hands smaller than mine. I should love to have a pair like them.'

'Would you? Is Emma's love of finery having an influence on you?'

'All has been so bleak of late I should welcome some lovely things round me. It is the end of the season for the garden.'

Owen turned to her. 'You deserve fine clothes. You still make men trip on their tongues and say foolish things when you smile on them. And you a mother of two.'

'Four, my love. Let us never forget Martin and the child we have just lost.'

Owen crossed himself and she saw in his face the fear that she would draw away from him now, as she had done so many nights since their loss.

'But let us return to your compliment.' She touched his beard, his cheek. 'You want something.'

'Aye,' he murmured into her hair as he gently pulled her towards him. 'I want you back.'

Lucie arched her body and pressed herself against him, from shoulders to toes, and felt a stirring that had long been dormant.

In the early hours of the morning Owen woke to find Lucie's side of the bed empty. He turned up the lamp beside the bed. She stood at the window wrapped in one of her cloaks. He went to her.

'You would not go out?'

'No, no.' She turned from him, but he had already seen her tears.

'You fell asleep content, I thought.'

'I did. But I woke frightened. God has lifted the

357

darkness, He has lifted my heart from despair. But for a day, a week?'

Owen gathered her to him and held her, whispering his love. It was all he knew to do.

EPILOGUE

What had been a golden autumn had shifted into days and nights of gusty winds and drizzle that felt like needles on the face after sunset. Thoresby had the servants keep the braziers in his chamber and parlour alight from early morning until he retired. At his age he dreaded the shock of cold bedding. But he was free of Wykeham at last and tomorrow he would ride to Bishopthorpe, casting off all the cares his sojourn in York had brought. One of his last tasks was to spend a few hours in communion with his old friend, Sir Ranulf. It was noon on a market day and the minster nave was peopled with country folk gawking up at the soaring transepts as they prayed. He kept well in the shadows as he skirted the worshippers and slipped into the Pagnell chapel. But the murmur of prayer disappointed him. He had hoped to be alone here. While he hesitated, considering a later visitation, the figure kneeling before the tomb moved, the veiled head turned. It was Emma Ferriby, dressed in a plain white wimple, dark veil and gown. Her ivory rosary beads were her only ornament. She bowed her head to him, then returned to her prayers.

Thoresby knelt beside her and fell to ruminating on Sir Ranulf's departure, trying to see again the expressions that had moved across the old knight's face during the ceremony that had blessed him on his way, wishing he might understand in those memories what had gone wrong, and whether his friend had been prepared to suffer and die for his king. He remembered pride, humour and an abiding peace that affected everyone that day, cheering even Lady Pagnell and Emma. He prayed that his friend had been able to call up that peace in his last days, that he had felt it a good death, an honourable passing, and that he looked down from heaven now and smiled to see the cross-legged knight he had become in death.

Fighting tears, Thoresby rose to leave Emma in peace. But she rose also, genuflected, crossed herself with her beads and was following him out when she paused, touched the altar cloth, traced the outline of a crusader knight on the end.

'I want to thank you for making the reconciliation possible between Mother and Bishop William,' Emma said. 'She is at last able to mourn Father.'

'I am glad of it. And, I confess, grateful to have the bishop gone from York.' He held out an arm for her. She slipped her hand through it.

Out on the minster steps they paused.

'Then it is true you are headed for Bishopthorpe?' Emma asked.

'Tomorrow, God willing.'

They stood for a moment on the steps of the minster, a swirling mist beading her veil.

'What is to become of your mother's steward?' Thoresby enquired.

'Mother has no more need of him, nor would she

have him if she did. But to my amazement my brother Stephen is considering engaging him, weighing Matthew's knowledge of the estate against his poor judgement.'

'I do not wonder at your amazement. Pray God Stephen does not regret his decision.'

They lapsed again into a companionable silence.

Then Thoresby asked, 'How is your intractable son?'

Emma turned to him with a smile and he saw pride in her eyes. 'John's wounds are healing well. He speaks as if his grandfather has at last succeeded in teaching him the lesson he had so often tried to teach him in life. Foolhardiness is not the same as courage. To chase after trouble is not the way of a knight.'

So the lad felt as Thoresby did, that Sir Ranulf's influence yet lived on in those he had touched in life.

'And you, my child? Is it enough that Wykeham brought your father's heart to rest in York?'

'The dreams have ceased and I feel Father's presence in the chapel. It is enough for me.'

AUTHOR'S NOTE

History is fluid. With each passing moment our perception of the past changes in subtle ways Yet in order to create a cohesive world fo Owen Archer I've needed to establish parameters choose among theories and then adhere to them a much as I can.

A case in point is the demolition of St Mary-ad Valvas. Records indicate that the church wa demolished circa 1362 to provide space for Yor Minster's lady chapel. The Royal Commission o Monuments is firm on this. Yet in a will of 1376 cabinet is left to the church, which has inspire speculation that the church had been moved rath than demolished. I have chosen to use the Roy Commission's date. Excavations in 1967 partiall exposed the foundations, and it appeared that St Mar ad-Valvas had been a small parish church, little mo than a chapel. So I think it unlikely that it would ha been made the object of a salvage relocation.

Opinions also vary about Archbishop Thoresby's u of his York palace – I have frequently moved h household to York in the Owen Archer mysteries. I have previously remained rather vague about the layout of the palace, but the present book required that I establish a floor plan. And so it may seem to some to have grown, now sporting two halls, a porch, and an attached kitchen in the middle of two wings. I have Charles Robb to thank for the plan based on archeological evidence, the topography of the area, and the discussion of bishops' houses in Michael Thompson, *Medieval Bishops' Houses in England and Wales* (Ashgate, 1998).

Among the actual historic figures who people the Owen Archer novels are two enigmatic statesmen who seemed locked in combat all their public lives, John of Gaunt, Duke of Lancaster, and William of Wykeham, Bishop of Winchester. A career could be built on a study of either men, so contradictory do the sources seem. Lancaster is remembered as the ruthlessly ambitious second son of Edward III, determined to control his nephew Richard II in the early days of his rule, to control Parliament, and to set himself up as King of Castile and León. But there are other aspects to him that suggest a warmer character. It is believed that he was devoted to his first wife, the beautiful heiress Blanche of Lancaster, and he recognized the children he fathered with his long-term mistress Catherine Swynford even before he married her (his third wife). His open relationship with her while wed to Constance of Castile was a great scandal and harmed his political ambitions. Paradoxically, his support of the religious reformer John Wycliff was purported to have been inspired by religious devotion. It is these complexities that keep scholars engaged in studying him.

William of Wykeham is remembered as an advocate of education for those who would enter Holy Orders, founding a school for boys in Winchester and a college at Oxford, as well as having been the talented architect of Edward III's extensive renovation and expansion of Windsor Castle (although Tout's opinion is that he was not technically gifted but merely a good administrator – see reference below). Conversely, his terms as Lord Chancellor of England were riddled with administrative irregularities, particularly financial ones (his enemies claimed that he had complete control of England's finances from 1361-70 and had abused his power in appropriating sums from the treasury for his own use). Rumours abounded that he was illiterate and ill-equipped for the high offices he held in Church and State.

Gaunt seems to have been more hated than loved by his contemporaries, Wykeham more loved (or admired) than hated. This polarity in itself makes rich material for fictional characters.

The conflict between the pair came to a head in 137 in the Good Parliament, when Lancaster succeeded in stripping Wykeham of his titles and much of his income. It seemed such a personal vendetta that, as noted in the Dictionary of National Biography:

Popular prejudice sought for more hidden reasons. Hence we have the scandalous story given by the St Albans chronicler and other of his contemporaries of the doubtful birth of John of Gaunt. It was said that the queen [Phillippa of Hainault], when brought to bed at Ghent, was delivered of a female child, which she accidentally overlay, and that, fearing the king's anger, she substituted for it the son of a Flemish woman. On her deathbed the queen had confessed the secret to the Bishop of Winchester, with the injunction that, should the time ever come when there might be a prospect of John of Gaunt succeeding to the crown, the truth should be made known. It was the publication of this secret which had engendered in Lancaster his deadly hatred of Wykeham. That such a story could be fabricated and find acceptance is a sufficient indication of the extreme unpopularity of the duke, and of the widespread suspicion of his designs in regard to the succession.

The hostility between the two men became a public spectacle with the Earl of Pembroke's condemnation of Wykeham to parliament, which was instrumental in his loss of the office of Lord Chancellor in 1371. And I suspect that the increasing influence of parliament at this time facilitated the spread of gossip about those in power. For further reading about these two see Anthony Goodman, *John of Gaunt: the Exercise of Princely Power in Fourteenth-Century Europe* (Longman, 1992); George Herbert Moberly, *Life of William of Wykeham: Sometime Bishop of Winchester, and Lord High Chancellor of England* (Warren and Son, 1887); W. M. Ormrod, *The Reign of Edward III* (Tempus, 2000); and T. F. Tout, *Chapters in the Administrative History of Medieval England*, vol. III (Manchester University Press, 1928; rpt 1967).

In the 14th century the cross-legged knight was a popular motif on tombs, particularly on those of men who had fought in the Crusades. Although the connection of crusaders with the motif is not universally held, few would argue against it as a device for a man who died in the faith.

So many prominent people were buried with their bodies in one tomb, their hearts in another, Robert the Bruce being perhaps the most famous, that it might be surprising to learn that the Church officially disapproved of the practice. I won't go into the unpleasant details of how the bodies were processed, but it was a practical means by which the remains of a person dying on foreign soil could be transported home for burial. It became a symbol of status for families and churches, and a political instrument – a statement that one was important enough to have multiple burials, that a church possessed a part of a certain renowned figure, that an establishment was considered worthy of such a memorial. On 27 September 1299 Pope Boniface VIII issued a bull stating that the disembowelment and division of the bodies of nobles and statesmen was an abomination and those who continued such practices would be excommunicate. He reissued the bull the following year. But the practice had become so well established that the bull was circumvented. For a fascinating analysis see Elizabeth A. R. Brown, "Death and the Human Body in the Later Middle Ages: the Legislation of Boniface VIII on the Division of the Corpse," in *Viator* 12 (1981): 221-270. A more general study of burial practices can be found in *The Resurrection of the Body in Western Christianity, 200-1336*, Caroline Walker Bynum (Columbia University Press, 1995), and regarding childhood baptism and burial see Kathryn Ann Taglia's paper "The Cultural Construction of Childhood: Baptism, Communion and Confirmation" in *Women, Marriage, and Family in Medieval Christendom*, ed. C. M. Rousseau and J. Rosenthal (Western Michigan University, 1998).

For those puzzled by the difference between a tanner and tawyer, the former worked with larger hides usually those of cattle, and used oak bark in processing them, whereas a tawyer worked with the smaller and less durable hides of other animals such as rabbits and goats, and used alum and oil to process them. For further information see John Cherry, "Leather," in *English Medieval Industries*, John Blair and Nigel Ramsay, eds. (Hambledon Press, 1991) pp. 295-318; and Heather Swanson, *Medieval Artisans* (Basil Blackwell, 1989).

And for several of the medical treatments in this book see Faye Marie Getz, ed., *Healing and Society in Medieval England: A Middle English Translation of the Pharmaceutical Writings of Gilbertus Anglicus* (University of Wisconsin Press, 1991). For a general discussion of charms see Richard Kieckhefer, *Magic in the Middle Ages* (Cambridge University Press, 1989).

If you enjoyed The Cross-Legged Knight, *you'll love the other Owen Archer mysteries available in Arrow books*

THE APOTHECARY ROSE

It is the year of our Lord 1363. And in the cathedral city of York people are dying in mysterious circumstances. But there seems to be a common thread – the herbal remedies dispensed by Nicholas Wilton, Master Apothecary. The first victim is an anonymous pilgrim. But when a highborn nobleman dies after taking the same potion the authorities decide to act.

Dispatched to York in disguise to unravel the mystery, Owen Archer, former Captain of Archers, apprentices himself to the Apothecary. But it is from Wilton's beautiful, spirited wife Lucie that he must learn the arcane secrets of the trade. Slowly but surely Owen begins to uncover the truth. And when the deaths continue he realises to his horror he must count Lucie among the suspects.

'Enthralling and evocative … Candace Robb
recreates medieval York with ease'
Yorkshire Evening Press

THE LADY CHAPEL

High summer in the year of our Lord 1365, and Owen Archer finds himself once again called upon by Archbishop Thoresby to exercise his skills as a detective. While York celebrates the feast of Corpus Christi, a man is murdered in the shadow of the Minster, his right hand severed. All the evidence points to a wool merchant last seen quarrelling with the dead man.

But a complex web of rivalries surrounds the wool traders, and Owen is unsure where to turn first. His only witness is a young boy, his only suspect a mysterious hooded woman – and neither can be found. With Thoresby preoccupied at Windsor with the King, Owen is under intense pressure to solve the case, but he soon finds himself ensnared in a plot devised by very powerful masters …

'A gripping whodunit full of colour and atmosphere…a definite tip for tomorrow' *Time Out*

THE NUN'S TALE

When a young nun dies of a fever in the town of Beverley in the summer of 1365, she is buried quickly for fear of the plague. But one year later, a woman appears, talking of relic-trading and miracles. She claims to be the dead nun resurrected. Murder follows swiftly in her wake, and the worried Archbishop of York asks Owen Archer to investigate.

Travelling to Leeds and Scarborough to unearth clues, Owen finds only a trail of corpses, until a meeting with Geoffrey Chaucer, spy for King Edward, links the nun with mercenary soldiers and the powerful Percy family. Meanwhile, in York, the apothecary Lucie Wilton has won the mysterious woman's confidence. But the troubled secrets that start to emerge will endanger them all …

'Gripping and believable…you can almost smell the streets of 14th century York, as you delve deeper into an engrossing plot' *Prima*

CANDACE ROBB TITLES
AVAILABLE IN ARROW

☐ The Apothecary Rose	Candace Robb	£ 5.99
☐ The Lady Chapel	Candace Robb	£ 5.99
☐ The Nun's Tale	Candace Robb	£ 5.99
☐ The King's Bishop	Candace Robb	£ 5.99
☐ The Riddle of St Leonard's	Candace Robb	£ 5.99
☐ A Spy for the Redeemer	Candace Robb	£ 5.99
☐ A Trust Betrayed	Candace Robb	£ 5.99

ALL ARROW BOOKS ARE AVAILABLE THROUGH MAIL ORDER OR FROM YOUR LOCAL BOOKSHOP.

PAYMENT MAY BE MADE USING ACCESS, VISA, MASTER-CARD, DINERS CLUB, SWITCH AND AMEX, OR CHEQUE, EUROCHEQUE AND POSTAL ORDER (STERLING ONLY).

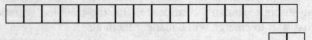

EXPIRY DATE .... SWITCH ISSUE NO. ☐☐

SIGNATURE ....

PLEASE ALLOW £2.50 FOR POST AND PACKING FOR THE FIRST BOOK AND £1.00 PER BOOK THEREAFTER.

ORDER TOTAL: £................................ (INCLUDING P&P)

ALL ORDERS TO:
ARROW BOOKS, BOOKS BY POST, TBS LIMITED, THE BOOK SERVICE, COLCHESTER ROAD, FRATING GREEN, COLCHESTER, ESSEX, CO7 7 DW, UK.

TELEPHONE: (01206) 256 000
FAX: (01206) 255 914

NAME ....

ADDRESS...

....

Please allow 28 days for delivery. Please tick box if you do not wish to receive any additional information. ☐
Prices and availability subject to change without notice.